T0062079

WHAT WAS BEFORE

THE
SEAGULL
LIBRARY OF
GERMAN
LITERATURE

WHAT WAS BEFORE

MARTIN MOSEBACH

TRANSLATED BY KÁRI DRISCOLL

LONDON NEW YORK CALCUTTA

**GOETHE
INSTITUT**

This publication has been supported by a grant from
the Goethe-Institut India

Seagull Books, 2019

First published as *Was davor geschah* by Martin Mosebach
© Carl Hanser Verlag, Munich, 2010

First published in English translation by Seagull Books, 2014
English translation © Kári Driscoll, 2014

ISBN 978 0 8574 2 718 2

British Library Cataloguing-in-Publication Data
A catalogue record for this book is available from the British Library

Typeset by Seagull Books, Calcutta, India
Printed and bound by WordsWorth India, New Delhi, India

WHAT WAS BEFORE

1

MUSICAL INTRODUCTION

'What was it like?'

'What was what like?'

'Before you met me.'

'Well, I had been living on my own in Frankfurt for a little under a year . . .'

'What was it like when you lived on your own in Frankfurt?'

'Oh, it was nothing special, it was just sort of . . .'

It didn't take me long to find a flat simply because I wasn't too picky. In fact, I went with the first one they showed me. I decided to take it on the spot even though it was actually too expensive. It was the light in the room facing the street that sold me. Not a particularly beautiful street, mind you. Buildings from just before the First World War; extraordinary to think that they had already started building those cheap buildings by then—the paper-thin walls, the meagre dimensions—though the great thunderbolt that was to usher in the desolation of our cities had yet to arrive. Even so, the new age was already in the air and the developers and architects who could smell it made their profit-maximizing decisions accordingly. But the light in the main room wasn't anything they had planned. That was the work of a towering chestnut on the other side of the street, as tall as the three-storey buildings, which, compelled by the weight of its sea of leaves, arched its way over the street towards my flat, so close that you could almost reach out from the narrow balcony of my room and grab its light green, fanned-out leaves. The tree was like a gigantic sponge that sucked in the liquid sunlight only to release it again upon the gentle touch of the summer breeze, now dyed a pale green like the water in an old glass. The whole window was filled with this undulating ocean of leaves, broad and round at the bottom, coming together sharply at the stem, attached at a single point. Its silent movement was like the breathing of a body at rest. A seemingly solid and impenetrable body which, in reality, consisted of nothing but air and the delicate membranes of the leaves.

'It's really quite dark in here,' said the landlord after he had let me into the flat. No, it wasn't dark exactly but, rather, twilit, like in a shaded arbour dotted with flecks of sunlight. As evening approached—with not a glimpse of the reddening sky visible—for a precious half hour the green grew deeper, the fresh grassiness taking on a richer emerald hue that preserved enough of the heavy light even after the rest of the room had sunk completely into the darkness of the night. This light was no longer radiant but, rather, became corporeal, trapped in the tree's crown, the way pieces of glass in early church windows glow in the sunlight without illuminating the chapel. On my first evening in the flat, I sat on a chair in the middle of the room and watched the window like a cinema screen. I was sure I had never been in a more beautiful room.

The street was slightly curved, a remnant of the country path that had wound its way through the fields before this entire neighbourhood was designed and built. It was clear not only from the tree's height that it was older than the surrounding buildings but also from the low garden wall that swerved respectfully round its trunk. This small sign of appreciation for its beauty showed that the planners had not seen themselves as demiurges whose prerogative it was to create worlds as if nothing had existed before them. The tree had been allowed to stretch from the vanished rural past into this urban present and now that the present was if not exactly old then at least showing signs of age, the tree was still there, full of life, both ancient and youthful, home to a thousand little creatures beneath its verdant canopy. And to one creature in particular, as I would discover the following evening.

As soon as I heard the first short phrase, I knew that this was no blackbird or titmouse. This voice did not belong to any of the usual songbirds one finds fluttering around the city. There were surprisingly few sparrows but lots of well-nourished pigeons, crows and magpies—these larger birds probably partly responsible for the disappearance of the smaller ones. But this whistling sound was quite different from the chirping that usually comes out of the body of a bird. It made me prick up my ears, just like the audience at the opera when they hear the soprano singing the first notes behind the scenes, muffled and far away, yet everyone knows—there she is; it's about to begin. But what was about to begin outside my window, behind the cascade of leaves, captivated me at least as powerfully as the song of any opera diva does her admirer. After all, he knows what to expect and merely hopes she will sing as beautifully as on her best recording, which he knows by heart. I, on the other hand, was completely unprepared or, rather, I had only an idea inherited from literature, a fantasy cultivated by lyric poetry which bore about as much relation to reality as does the phoenix—but that was enough, for it did, indeed, herald something extraordinary. And so I knew, while the twilight gradually spread from the rear wall through the rest of the room and the leaves outside continued to glow with their own reserves of light—this was a nightingale.

An alto, I thought, as you would say of a singer. And, in fact, this singing was incomparable to the sound produced by any musical instrument made of silver or wood even though the sound was clear, unalloyed and without blemish in a way that one associates with a mechanism or machine. But there is a reason certain singers have been compared to the nightingale, as I now realized. A particular highly artificial and ornate singing technique popular in the nineteenth century but now completely vanished from the opera stage—a technique perhaps last mastered by Amelita Galli-Curci—was without a doubt inspired by the nightingale's song. Notes that you cannot imagine could be produced by human lips, tongues, teeth, gums and vocal cords but which, rather, seem to inhabit the human body like smooth shafts which from time to time seem to issue forth, borne on the singer's breath like a shoal of silver fish, while the singer herself can only stand back, enraptured and immobile, as this sonic marvel unfolds. Only now did the word throat begin fully to reveal itself to me. The nightingale was all throat and from this gorgeous cavity, there came an effervescent lamentation, a cooing, a whirling jubilation, expressed in audacious runs, becoming trills and cadenzas before ending in a rich vibrato that seemed to emanate from within a fire-gilded pendulum. The name which accurately captured the nightingale's song was the French *Rossignol*—the rolled *r* from its throat, the delicious depth of the alto and the phrase's lilting ascent into the heavens—all of it contained in those three syllables.

And it truly was astonishing—the bodies of singers who could sing like this grew heavy and amorphous, by no means in aesthetic contradiction to their voices for it took great strength to produce, and the weightlessness of the sound was also the product of their physical power. The only thing I knew about the nightingale was that it was a small, brownish bird, like one of those now rare sparrows but more slender, a little more elongated, more youthful and refined. I presumed I would not see it no matter how persistently I stared into that sea of green. There it sat, like a solitary choirboy beneath the dome of St Peter's, transforming, for lack of a body sufficiently weighty to carry the sound, the entire tree into its resonance chamber. And the power of its voice was commensurate with the giant space.

The street was submerged in the kind of profound stillness that can only occur at certain moments arising unexpectedly in city streets, as if depopulated by some great catastrophe. Had this stillness supervened only to allow the nightingale's power to unfold unhindered? Its song was a demonstration of that power. At first I admired the full, golden depth of the notes but there then followed a short rest, a chance to draw breath before an even more forceful volley. An effortless, lusty, triumphant note had now crept into the song and it seemed to me as though it were trying to dazzle its audience with its endurance and ever-increasing exuberance. The song became a statement of invincibility. This was no siren song. The nightingale had no need of anyone else. There was neither art nor a desperate need for attention in its song. It sang the way a star shines in the cosmic, empty night. Whether it was happy or unhappy—such categories did not apply to the nightingale—its desire was sated, it had no need of hope, it was impossible to imagine a single moment in its life that would point beyond its present state of being.

Poets had prepared me for the nightingale, Hafez and Keats, but now that I was finally hearing the nightingale for the first time and realizing what a wealth of sound lay behind that name which until then had been nothing more than a signal-word to induce a certain poetic atmosphere, I suddenly felt that it was highly precarious to try to trap the nightingale in an ornate poetic cage. Never again would I forget what a nightingale truly was—not a spice, not a perfume, not a symbol but a force of nature, the mere mention of which was enough to throw any poem out of balance. The unsteady lyrical boat would surely capsize the moment the bodiless nightingale came aboard—the true, insuperable masterpiece, that is, a living creature one with its art, and that, pulsating and proud, put any other artwork to shame.

Did it ever stop singing? I don't remember the end of its song. I was so enthralled that I fell asleep—for once a not altogether uncommon case of rapture rather than boredom giving way to sleep while the singer continued to surpass herself and the previous triumphs became the foundation for even greater victories.

I had to leave town for a couple of days and, returning on the evening of the third day, I was met by a peculiar sanctity and cleanliness quite different from the atmosphere I remembered.

Even in the fading light of the evening, the street appeared tidy to the point of barrenness, its perspective lines seemed to have been drawn with a ruler. Then after a seemingly endless moment's confusion I realized —the tree was gone; its massive shadow no longer blanketed the street. Had there ever been a tree at all? The little garden wall still curved round the spot where it had once stood. But all it now encircled was a stump, cleanly severed with a chainsaw. Its edges were bright yellow but the core of the stump resembled loose tobacco. It seemed that the trunk had been completely rotten on the inside. Had the tree toppled, it would certainly have torn my balcony down with it.

2

THE MYSTERIOUS TENANT

As I said, the little flat I had moved into was in a quiet area that was actually a little out of my price range. The street was lined with a mixture of pre-war and more recent apartment buildings. There was a sterile silence hanging over it. There were no bars or supermarkets near by. In fact, there was no real reason you would want to move here. It wasn't even close to the nearest underground station. This seems to be the rule for German cities—vast swathes of deadness, a sort of urban insulation for the more lively areas whose inhabitants seem to have agreed to remain as invisible as possible.

Across the street there must have been a locksmith's that had recently relocated, leaving only the sign—a giant safety key framed in red neon—which still went on every night. This glowing red key had now become a mere decoration, its message now ambiguous—perhaps a warning never to leave your keys on the stove? The leaves of the enormous chestnut had almost entirely obscured the glowing key but ever since it had been cut down some of the key's red light penetrated my room, a faint, vaguely theatrical light that filled the empty space. I enjoyed falling asleep to it and whenever I awoke in the middle of the night, I felt as if I were in an old-fashioned darkroom.

It was a large building but most of the flats were secondary residences and I never saw most of the tenants. There were days when the feeling of abandonment was palpable even though I never left my rooms. Sensing the emptiness all around me, it was as if I were the weekend caretaker of an office building. But I liked it that way. Of the few things I have learnt, one is to appreciate those weeks and months of quiet you experience upon moving to a new city where you don't know anyone. Alone with your thoughts, hardly speaking, perhaps even a little down in the dumps—once you realize that this is a recurring event in your life, you can extract a certain density from it, in which you can practically hear time dripping away. I hadn't even unpacked my books, I just lay there on the bed in the encroaching darkness and watched the shadows that, from time to time, traversed the red glow of the key, that cool fire outside. The soundlessness of the building then grew into a gentle rushing sound like inside a seashell and that sound carried with it the occasional voice or the distant roar of a motorcycle or the short, sharp squeal of brakes, like corks floating by on a fast-flowing stream. Little details acquired a certain weight and gave me pause. Things I would never have noticed before now became a mystery, like the trace of a dream image that lingers after waking. Following leads, collecting evidence of secret goings-on and imagining my way into hidden states detectable on the surface of reality only as tiny tremors, was my carefree and of course quite aimless pastime.

When I opened the door into the hallway, I could hear a squeak, like someone playing with a rubber toy, emanating from behind the ornate frosted glass of the tall double-wing door of the adjacent flat. At first there was no name on the door but then, suddenly, one day it was equipped with a seemingly ancient brass sign—the excited squeaking next door belonged to one 'Baron Slavina'. A name which, I surmised, bore some relation to the Austro-Hungarian Empire, a provenance to which the large hunting trophy hanging in his otherwise unadorned foyer also attested. I had seen the tips of the antlers for a split second through the crack in the heavy door just before it was shut and triple-bolted.

Then one evening there were two empty red wine bottles on the floor outside the door. Even from afar they looked cheap, their labels attesting to a spurious vintage—wine of the sort you buy at the petrol station in the middle of the night. This building that I had moved into was what estate agents refer to as 'well-kept' but it would also have been apt to call it ruthlessly impersonal. You can be sure that the other flats in the building did not have empty wine bottles outside the front door. And these two fruits of some imaginary chateau stayed there for days until on Saturday evening they were finally gone. Had I not been mildly drunk on my solitude I would never even have noticed those bottles under the old-fashioned brass sign saying Baron Slavina. I am very untidy myself and I would usually be the last person to care whether there are empty red wine bottles outside other people's front door but, at that time, everything seemed to me like a still life inviting contemplation.

A few days later, I met on the stairs an old lady with long, unwashed, grey hair. She was very frail and hunched over and was wearing a sand-coloured cashmere jumper and trousers and gave me a shy, almost meek, look as though I might at any moment demand to see her papers. She was accompanied by a delicate little dachshund on a leash, a miniature, in fact, with great big doe eyes and quick little movements but just as timid as its mistress. An expensive dog, I thought, a rare breed, which seemed to glide up the comparatively steep steps with supple, snake-like movements. That day, there was a ruptured green plastic duck outside the baron's door, a scuttled bath toy. Was there a child in that huge flat? Was the squeaking produced by a three-year-old, the dog or the duck? I pondered these questions for a while, I even tried to imagine the old woman squeaking but it was no use—in her case a quiet whimper seemed more appropriate. Later, on a couple of occasions, I saw a red-haired, English-looking gentleman in a pinstripe business suit leaving the flat, shutting the door with an especially heavy thud, the sound revealing just how thickly reinforced the door was. When he saw me, the man seemed bothered by my presence, turned his head away and did not greet me. Outside the door, there were now several ill-smelling rubbish bags containing, among other things, pizza boxes with some half-eaten crusts inside. The stairwell was filled with the smell of these oil-and-spice-soaked cardboard boxes. Just at that moment, with that cold pizza cloud still hanging in the stairwell, the elderly lady on the second floor, who was hardly ever there, decided to return from her holiday. She made quite a fuss but despite her anxious attempts at ringing the doorbell and calling them on the telephone, there was no reaction from within the flat. Finally she got her cleaning lady to take the rubbish bags out. Had the red-haired Englishman in fact been Baron Slavina after all? I abandoned this theory after I heard him speaking English to the postman. How relieved I was that that buttermilk face did indeed belong to the English-speaking world!

The stairwell was now occasionally filled with chords played on the piano. Someone in Slavina's flat was making repeated attempts at mastering a mazurka by Liszt. These attempts were marked by the ambition not to deceive oneself but to truly master that difficult passage with that one dissonant chord instead of blithely passing over it as a dilettante would—I tried to match this determination to the physical appearance of the red-haired Englishman who averted his eyes whenever he met me—must not this aloofness go hand in hand with the solitary heroism of the artist? Down in the entry, there was a wheelchair marked with a Singapore Airlines label that said 'Mrs Tamara Kakabadze, c/o Slavina'. In my letterbox I found a note saying that a parcel for me had been delivered to Slavina, along with a telephone number. I called my neighbour several times, whose wide corridor was filled with the runs on the piano, but there was no answer. Not until the following evening did someone pick up. A female voice, young, distracted, said in English, 'Hello?'—the question sounded dreamy, as though the woman were sitting in a cave deep underground, tentatively testing the echo. I barely had time to ask about my parcel. 'It's outside,' she interrupted in a distant sing-song that rhymed with 'request denied.' No this was certainly no Englishwoman, she was from further afield— East Asia perhaps, whence the wheelchair had also recently flown in? I immediately lunged for the door but it was too late. Out in the hall, my parcel of books was already leaning against the wall, as if by magic, and the lock of the neighbouring door clicked shut—not violently, the way the man slammed it, but ever so softly. I imagined that the woman on the telephone had spent the afternoon in bed, probably with the curtains drawn and now that dusk was falling, she had decided to take a bath. There was no way this voice belonged to the plump Filipino woman, with the pockmarked cheeks and the velvet Alice band, I had seen emerging from the flat on Saturday mornings, laden with rubbish bags and an enormous jangly bunch of keys with which she meticulously locked the door like a castle gate. She never responded to my greetings, and instead merely gave me a disconcertingly stern look. Her caginess was in keeping with her profession—a housekeeper is supposed to be discreet. I of course was waiting for the woman with the gentle, melodic voice and naturally felt cheated and let down—all sorts of different people emerged from this flat but not she whom, I was foolishly and implausibly certain, I would be able to recognize in person purely on the basis of the sound of her voice. Was the older, dark-skinned Indian or Afghan sportsman with the drooping white moustache and the leathery lips her father? I found myself constructing a family round Baron Slavina—the old lady with the little dachshund was his mother-in-law, the Afghan was his father-in-law, the red-haired Englishman his brother-in-law from his first marriage. But even I wasn't convinced by this hypothetical family tree and it vanished from my imagination as quickly as it had come. What was the relationship between the two denim-clad young men and the soft-spoken woman? I saw them only from behind, each carrying a plastic bag with what sounded like bottles in them. A bare-chested boy opened the door for them and I never saw them again. Had the four empty champagne bottles outside the door the following day been drunk in their company? At first nothing but squeaking and the sound of the piano had come from that flat but then that too stopped and now the only sign of life from the Slavina residence was a large water stain spreading across the wall of the stairwell. Presumably his bathroom was on the other side—or was this water actually coming from upstairs?

One morning, the landlord was standing there with a workman shaking his head at the sight of the stain. He'd told Mr Slavina himself not to use the sauna. It had never been properly waterproofed, he said, despite numerous repair jobs and would have to be ripped out and until then—at that moment the Filipino woman opened the door, gave us a suspicious look, furrowed her brow and set about turning her keys in the various locks on the door. Where is Mr Slavina, the landlord asked her, to which she replied, 'Slavina no, Slavina no, no Slavina'—almost a haiku—at which she turned and went down the stairs, her facial expression never changing.

There are some mysteries which cease to engage us if they remain too obstinately irresolvable and beyond the speculative musings I indulged in before drifting off to sleep, I had no intention of going to any greater lengths to discover the nature of my neighbours' daily lives. My evenings were growing more varied. I was getting to know people in the city and starting to make plans and to go out. Titus Hopsten invited me out to his parents' house and from then on I was rarely ever at home. His sister Phoebe always had a whole entourage with her, all of whom were friendly and eager to meet a new face. One evening, there was a young Turk in a leather jacket standing outside my building. Pale-skinned and raven-haired, he thrust his nose into the cool air, as if picking up a scent, before plunging headlong into life like an eagle, completely absorbed in the business of being alive. Upstairs, the door to Slavina's flat slammed shut with its characteristic heavy thud. The young man stretched, bounded down the steps and was gone. Before him lay the future, behind him the quickly receding past.

'That's the way to live,' I thought, but I had by that point lost interest in the comings and goings in that flat. And it was months before I ever laid eyes on Baron Slavina himself.

3

THE GIRL ON THE TRAIN

Titus Hopsten's suggestion that I come out to his parents' house on Sunday afternoon—they were having 'a few people' over—wasn't really an invitation as such but then he most likely would have considered it hopelessly bourgeois to refer to requesting the presence of a near-total stranger in such terms. I imagined this young man, with his haughty good looks and slightly angular face, as harbouring a fundamental distrust of the formulaic, as if everything people said were basically impossible. The bar we were standing in was crowded with people getting off work, a heaving mass of dark suits, although some of the ties had already come off. It was an insanely hot day, of the kind not uncommon in Frankfurt, as I quickly discovered. The heat had given rise to a state of exception and everyone was really cutting loose—assuming they hadn't already succumbed to exhaustion. Titus alone seemed unaffected by the heat. He didn't sweat. It was as if his skin were made of asbestos. In fact, the hand he extended in greeting was small and light. I had met him by chance and once we'd established that we had a few acquaintances in common, I got the impression that he wanted to get away as quickly as possible. A phone call broke the spell. His consciously projected air of friendliness vanished as he turned his attention to his mobile, speaking into it in a terse and somewhat gruff tone. Then he once again gave me a warm, friendly smile whereupon his eyes again began to dart impatiently and irritably through the crowd, not as though he were looking for someone, rather, as though he weren't in a bar at all but at a reception that bored him but which he couldn't leave just then. He managed to make the invitation to Falkenstein and the exchange of phone numbers seem like a way to get rid of me, which is of course how these things usually work, as if there were some unspoken rule that you must never call a number someone's given you. And it would probably never have occurred to me to accept the invitation if it hadn't been for the fact that I had in my solitude begun to feel ever so slightly dissatisfied with my lack of company.

And so, the next day, there I was sitting on the suburban train. I was certainly curious for my colleagues were all familiar with the name Hopsten. The standard opinion, consisting of a telling mixture of morality and speculation, was that they were 'good people', a mindset of which I was not entirely free myself—although deep down, and I say this not without a modest sense of pride, I did not actually share it. I even have proof. Sitting opposite me on the train were a young woman and an older one—a girl, really, and a woman of about forty who looked thoroughly burnt out. There was no doubt that the two of them were travelling together. I thought I detected a certain affinity between the girl's artfully tangled mop of hair and the perhaps deliberately sloppily bleached yellow of the woman's. Apart from that there really was no resemblance. The older one's face was grey and her eyes were too close together. Stupid and mean-spirited, I thought to myself with some satisfaction. The younger one, by contrast, was an angelic creature, with skin that would probably blush at the merest gust of wind. Her lips, her tiny ears, her tiny nose, everything about her was perfect, childlike and yet fully formed. I allowed my eyes to wander back and forth—one was repulsive, the other, ravishing; one was slovenly, the other, fresh as the morning dew; one was worn out, the other had never known toil in her life. They were both dressed in the same way, in jeans and a white T-shirt—no, the older one's said something on it, a vitalistic slogan that clashed with her general appearance. Viva España, it said across her not inconsiderable bosom visibly held in place by a bra whereas the younger one equally visibly managed without, her pert breasts so well proportioned that Canova might have been a naturalist after all. As you can tell from my description, I indulged completely shamelessly in observing these two and, certainly, the presence of this ageing strumpet only increased my pleasure—she provided the necessary contrast to transform this fairly attractive girl into a transcendent beauty.

And how is it that I could stare with such impunity? They were both intensely preoccupied and oblivious to their surroundings. The older one was bent over her bare foot, gingerly prodding the yellowed nail of her left big toe. A small patch of red was all that was left to indicate that this protruding nail, so full of grooves and ridges that it was more like the claw of an animal, had weeks ago been painted. But now its hour was at hand, now, following this thorough examination, it was at last time to cut it. But the woman's little nail clippers were having a hard time finding purchase on this thick and overgrown toenail. Time and again she applied it, time and again this horn slipped out from under the clippers' delicate blades. The girl meanwhile had cut her finger—yes, it was wonderful, she had been peeling an apple and her red blood had dripped onto the white flesh of the apple!—but now she was clearly dissatisfied with the speed at which it was healing. Her warm, healthy, rosy skin didn't work as fast as she might have expected. She had taken the plaster off and was frowning as she examined the reddened fingertip, gently shaking her head as if telling someone off. She carefully pressed the pad of her index finger. There was no more blood. But it definitely couldn't hurt to wet the tip with saliva. With all the determination of an infant, she sucked her injured finger. A therapeutic sucking which, to her astonishment, did not, however, instantly restore her to a condition of inviolacy.

What was I doing, I asked myself with something approaching self-loathing, going to visit some rich people whom I did not know and whose emissary Titus had not exactly filled me with the promise of a warm welcome, instead of simply doing everything in my power to try to spend the weekend with this girl? After all, it was obvious that this proletarian girl—a strong word, chosen explicitly in contrast to the Hopstens—or, rather, this young girl stranded among the proletariat would engage and enchant me infinitely more than anything that might await me at the Hopstens'. No, it wasn't the hair or the clothes that united these two in my mind, it was their silent industry. I still remember how they sat there side by side like two seamstresses or two assembly workers, completely immersed in the complex tasks at hand. More than that, even, were the two of them not in fact recuperating after communally fought battles? I am sure to this day that if the girl had but glanced at me once, I would have said something to her. But was she not in truth keeping so quiet precisely in order that I might observe her at my leisure? One station before the final stop, my stop, they both got off the train at the last minute. On the platform I watched them head off in opposite directions without a word. They had absolutely nothing to do with each other.

It was a while before a taxi came along. It took me through the posh suburbs surrounding the small mediaeval town and its castle, then through open countryside, golden fields and finally a white house, ship-like with its terraces and balconies, wedged into a hollow with green waves on either side. Quite a long driveway, no name on the letterbox—this was the Hopsten house. At the entrance I was approached by the girl from the train, now wearing a skimpy summer dress that left her legs completely bare. I wasn't sure whether she had recognized me. The plaster on her finger was fresh and clean.

'*But surely she must have recognized you eventually? I must admit, I'm not much of a fan of love-at-first-sight stories. Aren't they all really just about people who have no choice or who are just gagging for it?*'

'*I'm sure you'd be right in most cases. But this really is a story of love at first sight or, rather, the prelude to one. Quite often love at first sight has a prehistory, as paradoxical as that may sound.*'

The fact that Phoebe Hopsten did not recognize me or did not want to recognize me or, with some justification, simply found our encounter on the train too insignificant to spare it a second thought did not mean that she was unfriendly. She was positively radiant but her rays were dispersed in many directions. The house and its garden were full of people, all holding wine glasses, all seemingly already quite merry in the heat. On the train, I had seen her completely lost in thought, in self-imposed isolation that forbade all contact, but now, as I watched her dancing through the crowd of people, giving each and every one of them her undivided attention for a split second, she had become even more unapproachable. I sized up the young men, most of them closer to her age than to mine, wondering which of them had a claim to her, but every time I thought I had singled one out, she had already moved on to the next, placing her plastered hand on the back of his neck or enfolding him in a fleeting embrace. I was still puzzled by my false impression of her on the train. I had truly believed that she had something to do with that awful, toenail woman and, as I now realized, I had formed a fully coherent mental image of her milieu—and what an exhilarating image it had been and how it had stimulated my imagination. I fancied myself as having discovered her, as a man who had discovered a pearl in the pigsty. And I now found it difficult to divorce myself from that image. Phoebe was a golden tessera that could form part of several different mosaics, this was what I was telling myself now—that no, I had not been mistaken, that she had no definitive social position but, rather, fit equally plausibly into any number of radically different settings. After all, did she really go with her parents? To be sure, they were highly respectable people but with her there was something else, something less respectable, which I was certain I could detect. And I had plenty of time to look. I was like a fish swimming through this beautiful pond, allowing myself to be drawn into a conversation every now and then. First with a highly amusing and somewhat plump Arab, Joseph Salam by name, who likewise knew no one, and then I even had the pleasure of speaking to the guest of honour, former minister Schmidt-Flex—yes, *the*

Schmidt-Flex, looking just as important with his white mane as he always did in the papers, accompanied by his taciturn wife, his melancholy son and his lovely daughter-in-law. A man like that is never alone.

4

POOLSIDE *OBJETS D'ART*

The Sunday afternoon was proceeding to the Hopstens' satisfaction. Particularly in their social preferences, the members of that family were of one mind—there had to be lots of people, a casual coming and going, only some of whom had to have been invited. When the weather was fine you could just turn up at the Hopstens' and you were even welcome to bring friends, so long as they were to Rosemarie's taste. She had no compunction about making her approval or disapproval of these plus-ones perfectly clear. This was always referred to as Rosemarie's 'refreshing frankness' even when she was direct to the point of being rude. Like pilgrims at a Hindu temple pond, the guests gathered round the swimming pool, a rather shallow affair, built in the twenties, which she had got tiled in black—Helga Stolzier's favourite colour—although Rosemarie now firmly believed that she had always considered turquoise or sky blue swimming pools ugly. Diving into this pool was like diving into fine ink and it was always a bit of a surprise to see the bare skin of the guests' bodies illuminated beneath the surface of the water. Rosemarie Hopsten wore a black one-piece bathing costume which showed off her statuesque figure, reminiscent of a Maillol, with her well-defined waist and full hips. She would dive into the pool and upon resurfacing, toss the hair out of her face with a flourish. When she climbed the aluminium ladder out of the pool before the eyes of her guests who lay and chatted on deckchairs all around, the dripping fabric shimmered like a seal's coat, the water droplets sparkling all around her. It was a triumphant ascent from the watery depths. All conversation halted as everyone turned to gaze at her and the strained alacrity of the catcalls she received belied the fact that some of them were genuinely trying to contain their admiration. Rosemarie was lightly tanned—she took care never to allow her beautiful, firm skin to grow leathery—and when she had dried herself, she glistened as if covered in a fine layer of dew. Bernward Hopsten got up with his characteristic wooden stiffness. His demeanour towards his wife was exactly the same as towards a total stranger. With a patient smile he took her wet towel and handed her a glass of white wine. A perfect couple, I thought, such courtesy after so many years, and yet their temperaments were so different. Rosemarie was the only one who went into the water. It was warm but not hot and Silvi Schmidt-Flex, in her minuscule bikini, kept her girlish limbs in the sun and her eyes closed, without taking part in the conversation around her. She had pronounced the water too cold. 'You see,' said Bernward to his wife but she retorted that no swimming pool of hers would be heated in June. It was a reasonable enough policy and, in any case, you couldn't have accused the Hopstens of being stingy when it came to providing for their guests. Out of a great silver bowl jutted the necks of multiple bottles of white wine that was bright and zesty and went down like water. Phoebe had already been a couple of times to fetch more from inside. Joseph Salam had managed to snare Silvi's father-in-law in a debate about the Balkans although the elder statesman had initially seemed unapproachable and had made no attempt at disguising the ironic glances with which he had been sizing Salam up. Schmidt-Flex had an instinct for identifying and avoiding anyone who wasn't the height of political respectability or otherwise remarkable for their money and influence. It had served him well all his life and right now alarm bells were ringing. Nor did he approve of the contours of fat and musculature showing through Salam's tight-fitting polo shirt. But, it is all but impossible to escape from a low-slung deckchair. Salam was leaning over him, quaffing his wine in great gulps, subjecting Schmidt-Flex to the odour of his wine-breath and, in general, seemed very sure of himself, laughing heartily at the dry morsels served up by his unwilling interlocutor. He appeared to find humour in the old man's fundamentally unhumorous statements, which the latter found hard to refute—who has ever protested that he is really not as witty as others clearly think him to be? And so finally his reserve melted away even though the old man had not had any wine at all.

'I knew Tito well,' he was saying. Had he in fact never met the Marshal, he would have said, 'Oddly enough, our paths never crossed.' Salam nodded sagely.

'Yes, he truly understood the Balkans . . .'

'Or perhaps he hadn't understood them at all.' Schmidt-Flex was slipping into didactic mode, which marked the definitive end of his self-restraint.

'Marvellous,' Salam sighed with delight, 'really he hadn't understood them at all!' But he was careful to tone down the ensuing laughter so as not to try Schmidt-Flex's patience. The son, Hans-Jörg Schmidt-Flex, was sitting beside his mother. Neither of them made any attempt at concealing their boredom. The mother was stoically contemplating the countless hours she had spent bored out of her wits at social gatherings. This included the day when she had been so bored that she thought she might lose it completely—it must have been thirty years ago at least—when she had been certain she might literally die of boredom. She remembered too the sensation of dull indifference and empty lightness that remained after she had recovered from her moment of panic. This sensation had served her well since then and made her life bearable. The same could not be said of Hans-Jörg. He wasn't bored because he was never bored. Instead he was morosely following the conversations around him, his facial expression seeming to say, 'Dear God what stupidity, what a positively idiotic thing to say.' Perhaps he would actually have to intervene at some point, at the least opportune moment of course and in such a way that he would immediately be in the wrong.

Perhaps it is a mistake to get too close to human society, particularly if, from a certain distance at least, it presents such an enchanting spectacle. The green of the fields extending into the distance on the other side of the fence, which was all but invisible in the tall grass, the gently rolling hills—ten years ago there would have been cows grazing there—the view of Kronborg Castle keep and behind it the Main plain shrouded in a smoke-coloured haze punctured by flashes of sunlight reflected off the glass facades of the Frankfurt skyline, was like an enormous landscape painting to rival the best works of the nineteenth-century Kronberg painter's colony, in which the skies are always a little too blue and the clouds look as though made of whipped cream. And set like jewels in the middle of this emerald green velvet were these people who, from a distance, appeared so charming and carefree. As I stood there by the garden fence gazing at this group of people mirrored in the rippled surface of the black swimming pool, I thought of Goethe's mandarins, who in spring 'by ponds, on grass reclining, gaily drink, write wit and learning'. But apart from these old and elderly people, the 'grown-ups', as an eighteen-year-old friend of Phoebe's quite innocently called them, there were also seven or nine young men and women of Titus' and Phoebe's generation—I was unsure of their number because they all looked alike, or was I at thirty-five already looking back as if from old age at a generation that was utterly alien to me? They all had beautiful hair and perfect teeth, they were all slender and toned—the boys, in their striped shirts and jeans, all had Titus' handsome, slightly mousey face and the same unshakeably earnest look in the eye. To be sure, Phoebe's tangled mass of golden hair did set her apart from the other girls—not everyone was prepared to go to so much effort. They were all smoking, which none of the grown-ups were, as though wary of attracting the disapproval of Schmidt-Flex, who made no bones about taking smokers to one side in order to enlighten them on the dangers of that filthy habit. On other occasions, I have seen both Rosemarie and Joseph Salam holding cigarettes.

But what really transformed this scene into one of uncommon beauty was modern technology—the cellphones which all the young people carried with them and which, when seen from afar, created a sort of spectacle which in centuries past would have been inconceivable outside the theatre. And even there, it has not been seen for a long time, not since the dramatic arts parted ways with the classical alphabet of bodily expression. The exaggerated postures of Greek and Roman art, celebrated in the Renaissance and the baroque, the bold torsions of the body, the extended arms, the cowering, the particular way of throwing back your head in despair or shielding your head with your hands, the gestures of melancholy and grief—all these postures which reveal the scope of human emotion, transforming the silent body into an eloquent medium of expression, are now only to be seen at museums, framed in gold, they are no longer to be found in nature. Or, rather, they weren't, they were extinct until the invention of the mobile telephone. Before then people would withdraw into a cocoon when they were alone. Their expressions would become constrained until they no longer expressed anything at all. If someone addressed them, they would be forced to climb out of the dull well of solitude, back to the surface, where they would take off their masks and rejoin the living. Now I was looking at a girl sitting some distance away from the others, absent-mindedly playing with a lock of blonde hair that had fallen over her face, curled up as if she were inside a hollow tree trunk. Then she unwound the lock of hair again, freeing her hand to flail about wildly in the air. Another girl was standing by the water staring raptly at her reflection, her legs interlocked like a dancer's, her head resting on her shoulder while her hand made butterfly patterns in the air. They were both on the phone but the little device which produced such beauty and transformed the ancient dream of the living statue into a reality was barely visible. Their otherwise impassive faces were now lit up, their cheeks flushed, their eyes sparkling, their bodies filled with a new type of energy. Closer to me, a young man was pacing, taking great strides with his long legs, turning on his heels as he did so. His hands made rhetorical gestures, then he plunged them into his trouser pockets, stood on tiptoe, flung his head back, thrust his face skyward, only then to double his elongated body over as if struck by a bullet, bowing his head and crouching on his haunches—would that I had ever seen an actor deliver one of Hamlet's soliloquies with such intensity and such total control of expression! He was wearing headphones which afforded him yet greater freedom of movement as he had both arms free.

But the best was yet to come—when people were getting ready to leave, and this time it wasn't a cellphone but a digital camera that provided the occasion for the emergence of such beauty. Bernward was standing by the gate having escorted some guests out to their cars and the young Schmidt-Flexes were approaching him in their cabriolet, which they had been allowed to park at the house. Hans-Jörg was at the wheel, his mournful eyes hidden behind dark glasses. Ever one for paraphernalia and accessories, he was also wearing open-backed driving gloves. Next to him stood Silvi, whose billowing linen shirt had slipped off one shoulder to reveal the strap of her bikini top against her bronzed skin. Holding the camera in both hands, eyes focused on the viewfinder, she was like a floating angel, a victory goddess bearing a golden wreath. Bernward stood still and smiled with delight at this vision. As the car stopped beside him, Silvi announced, 'I think I got a good one of you.'

'Well, that's a bit disappointing—I thought I was going to find out more about your mysterious Baron Slavina, instead you tell me about all sorts of other women.'

'No, we haven't got to Slavina yet. But it would be a mistake to forget all about him.'

'So I take it this Slavina of yours is some sort of preserve that is only to be opened in an emergency . . .?'

5

A SINGLE WHITE FEATHER

The parlours in the Hopsten house had looked quite different when it was built. A photo album from the twenties, laid out on the table for the guests' convenience, gave an impression of what they were like then, albeit mostly by virtue of the captions rather than the faded and blurry photographs mounted on the yellowed paper. The people who had it built had clearly moved on from the gloomy Wilhelmine pomp to the no-less-pompous gloom of a boldly coloured art deco, transforming the modestly sized rooms into lavishly ornamental cabinets. What looked uniformly grey and black on the photos had once been lapis lazuli fireplaces, gilded ceilings, parchment wall covering. None of these had survived the twentieth century but Rosemarie Hopsten liked to seek inspiration in the past. Helga Stolzier had fairly shrieked with delight when she saw the album which Bernward had stumbled upon at a second-hand bookshop. It is not unthinkable that the original owners of the house would have approved of her shimmering matte-grey stucco lustro walls and the black lacquer chairs with the sulphur yellow kidskin upholstery. Back then, this much was clear from one of the photos, a Blue Period Picasso had hung in this room where there now was a large Botero depicting a South American general puffed up like a balloon, who looked as though he were torturing his adversaries with whipped cream rather than electric shocks. The abundance of little trinkets arranged on side tables, windowsills and the mantelpiece made this an ideal waiting room, while through the windows you could see the green fields stretching park-like into the distance, as if no cow had ever set hoof there.

Rosemarie had left me alone, saying that she still had some matter to attend to outside. It was not hard to discern what that was, for the scullery where the dainty black Brazilian maid with pink glasses was busy ironing was not so far away that I couldn't hear what was being said there. The lady of the house sounded annoyed but the Brazilian girl was also raising her voice. I did not have to listen very carefully to follow the exchange.

'Why did you not come yesterday?'

The Brazilian girl's German was halting. She said she'd been ill.

'Well, why didn't you ring then?'

The girl said she hadn't been able to, as she'd already told her—'Phone battery dead.'

People nowadays do not tell someone to their face that they think they're lying but for Rosemarie such consideration or caution created an emotional traffic jam—she didn't believe a single word the girl was telling her and grew increasingly furious.

'If you don't want to work here you should tell me straight out.'

But she'd told her many times that she wanted to be there (this was the maid again) but if she was ill then it just wasn't possible.

'This simply isn't on . . . what would it take to pick up the phone . . .?'

The conversation had a rondo-like quality to it, winding itself tighter with each successive turn. Just then I heard the sound of a door being shut and the voices became muffled and unintelligible. I was once more left alone with myself and the objects in this treasure chamber.

Just then someone cleared their throat. This was followed by a peculiar chuckle. Only now did I notice a large cage shaped like a Chinese pagoda. Inside it sat a white cockatoo. Its head was cocked to one side and it was looking at me, all the while making crunching and cracking sounds with its slate grey beak, suggesting that it had just helped itself to one of the seeds in the porcelain bowl on its perch.

I later discovered how the cockatoo had found its way into the house—not through any particular love of animals but because Rosemarie needed something valuable and alive to complete the design for the room, a mobile *objet d'art* that didn't need winding. For a moment, she had considered the possibility of an aquarium with exotic fish but Helga had advised her against it—no matter how tasteful, an aquarium ultimately always seems petit bourgeois. But what about a rare bird?

'Feathers are very in at the moment.' Helga had no objections to a cockatoo. And no sooner was it in the house than it proved to possess enough unpredictable *élan vital* to earn its place among the inhabitants of the house, rather than its bibelots. Rosemarie was pleased with its appearance and Bernward grew quite fond of the bird. No one even objected to the faintly sweet, not unpleasant smell of bird droppings that now sometimes wafted through the room. As I later discovered, the friends of the family were used to seeing the cockatoo perched on Bernward's shoulder, with its stony nautilus beak, which despite its curvature could deliver quite a peck, held close to his soft, unprotected lips.

Probably the bird had been observing me for a while because its head did not move, the black button of its eye fixed on me. Could it even see anything with that button? It seemed as though it were sewn into the puffed-up mass of feathers with black silk thread, like the buttons used by upholsterers to keep the padding under the fabric in place. The white of its feathers was so immaculate that it looked artificial and it was precisely for this reason that it had been purchased in the first place, to be a living *objet d'art*, which indeed it was, to a far greater extent than Rosemarie could ever have imagined. The downy feathers round its chest and shoulders looked like an ermine stole but now as it spread its wings—dove's wings, angel's wings—it revealed magnificently strong pinions, each so perfect it looked as though it had been painted on but not perfect enough for its liking. It couldn't withdraw behind a screen to perform its toilette (a lacquer screen in black and gold would have been appropriate) but the fastidiousness with which it preened its perfect, firm, gossamer plumage betokened shamelessness, even vanity or perhaps contempt. It was an artist in his studio showing a wide-eyed and uncomprehending visitor a painting that looks finished only then to begin working on it in earnest. The rounded beak with its significant overbite was the bird's most important tool, although I failed to understand how it could find true purchase on anything with such rounded pliers. But the bird was used to the awkward apparatus from an early age and handled it masterfully. Mercilessly it rifled through its plumage. Whenever its head drew near to its inky black legs, it was as though it were checking the time on its watch. Its head had no anatomically predetermined position— it could be everywhere. In Japanese erotic woodcuts (again I thought of Japan, even though cockatoos are of course from South America), the lovers, always fully dressed in their billowing kimonos, are always so artfully intertwined that you have to look hard in order to discern their heads and their hands, their feet and their genitals among the frenzy of fabric. It's like an optical illusion, and the same was true here—the bird shook itself up with wild abandon, disassembling itself completely. It lost its burnished form and now looked as though it had been strangled by a cat, albeit bloodlessly—the pure white sheen of its plumage remained impeccable. And then in the blink of an eye, each and every feather was back in its right place. For a moment it sat motionless, as if allowing time to savour this freshly wrought sculpture, the return of this fuzzy ball of feathers to its true, definitive form. And then, as if someone had pulled on a string, its bright yellow crest which until then had been snugly tucked away behind its head rose, an incandescent Mohican, shining like the sun. Thus adorned in regalia, it tilted its head back and emitted a shriek—a circular saw striking concrete, sparks flying, screeching till the blade breaks.

I was convinced that the door would fly open and someone would come rushing in, thinking I was molesting the cockatoo, but nothing happened. From the distance, the strains of the rondo still drifted into the parlour. They were used to these shrieks. In this house, they were like a different kind of silence, a sign that nothing else was happening. I approached the cage. The cockatoo hopped back along its perch a little. No, its eye was not a button at all. It wasn't dull but, rather, glistened like a drop of tar in the snow. I imagined that everything this eye saw must become stuck to it like tiny fruit flies. After this eruption of noise, the cockatoo made an elegant gesture. A single white feather came loose from its plumage and sailed gently down to the seed-strewn floor of the cage. It landed close enough to the bars for me to extract it with ease. I kept it in my wallet for a while until, one day, it flew away.

I was seized by an insane notion—that this whole shimmering, grey parlour in all its stucco lustro elegance, surrounded by these emerald green fields, this yellow kidskin, the carved ivory, the freshly polished silver, the puffed-up general—that all this was, in truth, a shrine to this cockatoo. It was round this bird that all of this had been assembled and erected. It was the daemon of the house. Rosemarie and Bernward, of course Phoebe and Titus as well, were subordinate or attendant to it, like a priesthood devoted to an idol. Perched in terrible and sublime solitude in the inner sanctum of its cage, at the heart of the house, again and again, it would dissolve into chaos only to reclaim its form once more, oscillating forever between amorphous blob and inviolate bird statue. And now and then a clarion blast of its fearful voice to tell us that the hour was at hand—an ineluctable reminder of the saw blade spinning eternally over all of our heads.

Rosemarie entered the room. Invigorated by the argument, she seemed youthful and energetic. Something had come up and Phoebe sent her regrets. I was grateful for this blunt rejection—clearly she did not wish to fob me off with false excuses.

Rosemarie, however, invited me to stay. We had tea and, not
without a certain poetic irony, she showed me the various pieces
of her collection.

6

BERNWARD AND ROSEMARIE

Had I ever met a more perfect couple than Rosemarie and Bernward Hopsten? A more calm and unswerving way of belonging, an equanimous loyalty to each other, a certainty of never having to give up anything of your own and, at the same time, of never having to keep anything important from the other? And never a more public display of affection than Bernward perhaps casually putting his arm round Rosemarie's shoulder, pressing her against himself for the briefest of moments before immediately releasing her, the two of them gliding apart as effortlessly as when they had danced the jive in their student days. One summer afternoon, four of us were sitting round the swimming pool just as Bernward returned home from a trip to Chicago—not in the least bit dishevelled, he must have shaved at the airport and, in general, it was part of his overall dryness, his aridity you might even say, that he did not easily appear hot and sweaty. His spruceness was bulletproof. It was impossible to imagine him rushed and out of breath, with him everything happened at a measured pace and with the precision of a veteran snooker player. Rosemarie went up to him at the edge of the pool as if she were onstage, allowing her audience to share in the return and welcome of her spouse—when she went to embrace him, he pulled back with an ironic smile and said, 'Don't get too close, I haven't showered yet,' and she returned the smile, replete with understanding and intimacy. It didn't feel affected in the least. It was as though they had never settled into the daily routine of married life but instead still preserved the care and delicacy of the first days of their courtship. One thing I noticed immediately about this family, which outwardly was so careful to present itself as a closed corporation—Titus and Phoebe still living at home for the most part, the children's friends mingling with the parents' at all social gatherings—was the distance the parents kept from their children. In a funny way, it was almost as if they had teamed up against them. The youthful seriousness of those beautiful and elegant creatures stood in comic opposition to their playful, lively parents who, each in their own way, would gently poke fun at the callow sternness and striving of their offspring in front of others. There was no enclosed family atmosphere at the Hopsten house. The generations lived discreetly side by side. It was a pleasure to behold and there were plenty of opportunities to do so. I quickly discovered that it was impossible to get close to Phoebe, independent and reserved towards her parents as she was, except in the company of them and her brother. The two children had clearly taken it upon themselves to uphold the dignity of their parental home. They looked chagrined whenever Rosemarie occasionally slipped into her Rhenish dialect. It was a clash of two fundamentally irreconcilable visions of the family—self-confidence supported by a large, provincial fortune and a new cosmopolitanism that regarded roots as something to be severed with a sharp blade. You could hear where Bernward was from when he spoke too, if his first name hadn't already given it away. He was from the Münsterland where he grew up on a large farm that his elder brother now ran. Quite a handsome estate, which, with Bernward's unreserved approval, had not been divided up between them. Having grown up in such proximity to large sums of money, he considered all financial matters from an abstract and axiomatic standpoint without ever questioning how any concrete issue might be to his own advantage—in which accounts his family's steadily accumulating wealth was deposited and how much of it would remain with him. None of that concerned him. An ideal manager of his wife's assets, in other words. I must confess that I did once steal a glance at the Hopsten portfolio at the bank after I had got to know Titus and, afterwards, I did begin to see the family in a different light—or, to quote a phrase Rosemarie liked to use in conversations revolving round other people's money, 'Of course, that's not really important *but it adds.*'

In his sharp-nosed handsomeness, Titus always seemed slightly exasperated by his father's laissez-faire attitude, as though he were in possession of some vital information in the face of which the latter's equanimity must appear utterly unjustifiable. His dark eyes were quick to adopt a penetrating glare. He often followed these conversations with some agitation, jiggling his knees until finally his inner turmoil was transformed into an aloofness bordering on the impolite. Thus, when addressed, he would make no attempt at hiding the fact that he had been miles away and that he would have preferred to have remained there. Without their children, the Hopstens were an impressive couple. It was then that Rosemarie's not insignificant beauty truly came to the fore, her matriarchal gravity in the rich abundance of a Maillol model. Her exquisite, beautiful clothes contributed to the effect. Never the height of fashion but, rather, a personal style developed for her alone—it was with the clothes that Helga Stolzier's influence had begun. What Helga was to her, she was to her husband, albeit not quite as audacious as her inventive sartorial role model. The things she bought him were expensive, tending towards an idealized English style without really being English—I'm convinced Titus rolled his eyes whenever he saw his father wearing a scarf that was the same pattern as the lining of his raincoat, preferably with a rain hat to match. Bernward did not put up the least bit of resistance in these matters. He wore the red and yellow cashmere jumpers she laid out for him with a feeling of gratitude for being so well looked after. He listened to his son's comments of stark disapproval—never to be supported with specific reasons—with the forbearing smile of paternal pride that even in cases of conflict recognizes with a sense of satisfaction how one's offspring have grown.

And were the children, after all, not astonishingly beautiful? Their skin, their thick, shiny hair, their bright eyes, their dazzling white teeth, their health and physique were all of such high quality as had simply not existed in Bernward and Rosemarie's generation. It was obvious that neither of these two children could ever have appeared in any of those photographs of the bombed-out and displaced, the refugees and prisoners of the last century. It had always seemed to me that the way those people looked corresponded to their tragic fate—their pale features bore the portentous mark of future disasters even in photographs taken in peacetime. Phoebe and Titus would, in all likelihood, never be displaced so long as they lived. I was certain simply by looking at them that their plans (did they even already have plans?) would never be trampled under the feet of evil forces. When you were endowed as they were, the power of collective doom simply ricochetted off you. The children had inherited Rosemarie's big, darkly radiant eyes, that was obvious, but set in those clean, appealing faces they seemed completely different, cooler and tamer, and I was never sure whether they really saw everything with those eyes—was the world around them not far too insignificant to be apprehended with their gaze and allowed to enter fully into consciousness? Where was Bernward's part in these faces? His head was as square as a loaf of pumpernickel and this was only accentuated by his hairstyle which looked stuck on like a toupee. His face was framed by this slab of hair and his square jaw but his features were quite delicate, as if drawn with a fine pencil, and his smile—a contemplative, fundamentally intimate smile—hardly ever left his narrow, colourless lips. Probably even in his sleep, he kept smiling to himself. Rosemarie would not have been able to confirm this for the past several years, however. She liked to read in bed at night which meant that she slept later into the mornings whereas Bernward had to get up quite early to be in the Frankfurt office. As a member of this family, it went without saying that he simply had to be the first person there. His rural Westphalian sense of duty told him so. His father had never allowed an inspector to strip him of the privilege of overseeing the harvest personally—'It's different when the workers can see you,' was one of the paternal maxims that Bernward had carried over into his career as an asset manager in the city. Given this division of labour, separate bedrooms were the most obvious solution and, oddly, ever since Rosemarie had been sleeping alone, her nocturnal reading had stopped almost completely. For the most part, she slept the whole night through and often got up to make Bernward his coffee before he left for work. She was surprised at this development and quite innocently shared this surprise with her friend and confidante Helga who listened in silence with a characteristically mild and inscrutable expression on her face.

The shifting formations people adopt over the course of prolonged social gatherings would be an intriguing problem for a physicist. There are always various clusters with different degrees of gravitational pull, smaller competing groups form as well, but there are also guests who are able to withstand any force of social gravity and instead float freely and independently or else jealously secure the attention of a small group or even a single person. Whenever Schmidt-Flex wasn't certain that he had everyone's attention, he was quite capable of turning to a complete novice, a blank slate, and taking advantage of his vast experience to acquaint his interlocutor with the state of things from his incomparably superior vantage point. No doubt, it had been clear to him from the moment we were introduced that I was just such a nobody since my name meant nothing to him and his reservoir of names was inexhaustible, and his age only added to this resource, which grew and grew, never diminishing. With his noble, aquiline profile and the thick hair crowning his head in magnificent waves of silver, he was the natural king of all he surveyed, albeit the younger generations mostly did not remember his moderately successful term in office. The height of his influence as union spokesman also lay some distance in the past but, on the occasion of his sixtieth birthday, a trade journal had written that if the Federal Republic could be said to have such an institution as a senatorial class, then the first person one would think of as its possible representative would undoubtedly be minister Schmidt-Flex.

'You look like someone who has been brought along to this by someone else.' This is how he began our conversation, reclining comfortably in his deckchair which until recently had formed the epicentre of this gathering but which now formed a solitary island along with my little wrought-iron chair. The company's centre of gravity had shifted to the terrace where some hors d'oeuvres had been laid out.

'Don't worry about it,' he added matter-of-factly, 'many of the people here were brought by someone else, it's part of the house style. That's how you get to know people you wouldn't otherwise have come across, which, to be sure, can be a mixed blessing—the processes of social selection do serve their purpose after all.' He said he assumed I already knew the sort of money that was behind all of this. He didn't wait for me to respond, instead turned his magnificently coiffed head to look at the gently passing cumulus which had acquired a palpable firmness through the deepening shadows cast by the setting sun, and recounted the story of a fortune which had not only withstood the disaster of the war but actually flourished all the more because of it, yielding even more substantial fruit. When he mentioned the Silesian coal-hydrogenation plant that Rosemarie's grandfather had sold to a British company in the twenties, he spoke its name with the proper respect owed to a real powerhouse.

'And naturally,' (for Schmidt-Flex, naturally was another word for ingeniously, in the world of big finance genius was a natural phenomenon)—'naturally he didn't take the money but, rather, demanded the corresponding sum in English stocks . . .' At this he closed his eyes contentedly, imagining, I am sure, the world in flames—wrecked factories, petrol tanks engulfed in a sea of fire, black smoke, devastation—and those stocks and bonds untouched by all of it, as if they had nothing to do with real, imperilled resources. It wasn't magic and getting to the stockpile after the war had been hard work, now forgotten by all except Schmidt-Flex who had followed the restitution negotiations at the time.

'You see, our host here, Bernward Hopsten, highly respectable man, highly respectable family,' (this was a tiny Prussianism in Schmidt-Flex's otherwise dialect-free speech, a phrase from long-vanished officers' casinos that he had never set foot in)—'but in this context, he is of course merely the prince consort, not that there's anything wrong with that. And he's not really much like a prince consort. He's no beau, certainly not, and no social climber either, no, no, he doesn't need to be, rock-solid, you see . . .' His mind wandered, leafing through an imaginary photo album. 'Brilliant young men courted Rosemarie, she had enough to choose from but she also had her instinct. She made the right choice instinctively.' He emphasized the word and for the first time he looked me straight in the eye. Did this characterless young man know what instinct was? Schmidt-Flex had mastered the art of communicating urgent messages with an air of the utmost disinterest. Strictly speaking, there was something surprisingly indiscreet about such a venerable old gentleman revealing this sort of information, which, to be sure, was not libellous or risqué in any way but which, as we sat there drinking the Hopstens' wine, betrayed a certain distance from them that seemed faintly disloyal. And besides, what business was this of mine? It was plain to see that the Hopstens didn't make their living robbing stagecoaches on the highway and, quite apart from that, they had been nothing but generous and hospitable to a stranger such as me. This education I was receiving here as to the financial background of the household smacked of the nosiness of dinner guests who turn the plates over to check the manufacturer. But then it dawned on me what the purpose of this initiation into the Hopstens' affairs was. From my age, he no doubt realized that I belonged to the Hopsten children's circle and, from there, it was easy to deduce that it was Phoebe who had enticed me out here. Did he perhaps see himself as the Lord Privy Seal of Rosemarie Hopsten's money which would one day be Phoebe's money? Yes, it was plain to see—he wanted to burden me with the knowledge that the youthful, dancing, skittish Phoebe with her glorious hair and dewy, fresh lips was in fact a fragrant white-crested wave on a sea of money. I was not to forget about the money when I looked at her or spoke to her, when I danced with her or tried to make her laugh—I quickly discovered that behind her seriousness she loved to laugh. A quick, fleeting laugh, to be sure, that resided on the very surface of her consciousness where it rippled only to disappear as soon as it had come. All the Charlie Chaplins and Groucho Marxes of this world wouldn't have made her lose her composure. Schmidt-Flex had no idea that nothing he could tell me about Phoebe's economic situation would have come as any kind of surprise to me—and for this, I admired the elder statesman's sense of duty all the more. Even in his *otium* he could not permit himself even for a moment to lose sight of the interests of all the people present. It truly was second nature to him—he hadn't become who he was for nothing. It was impossible to tell whether his wife was listening to our conversation. Behind the traces of faded beauty in her well-preserved face, I thought I sensed some kind of disharmony, which I thought of as 'jagged'—as if some part of her face had broken off. And her mouth was contorted as if a sensitive tooth had come in contact with something sweet. I wondered what her instincts had told her over forty years ago when she married Schmidt-Flex and now that she had stayed at his side ever since. Did it still stir in her, that instinct? Or had it given up the ghost once it had delivered her into marriage?

'*Are you ever going to tell me how you met Helga? That's what this whole story is about, after all! Was she there too on that first day by the Hopstens' pool?*'

She was there, basically she was always there, but she hardly spared me more than a friendly smile—which, admittedly, in her case, made enough of an impression. Her face was a stage on

which even the most fleeting of sentiments made a grand appearance. And I wasn't surprised that she didn't recognize me even
though we had met once before because her attention was focused
on one person exclusively—Rosemarie Hopsten. She followed
her every move, watching her the way a coach watches a figure
skater, taking notes for later criticism. As chance would have it,
Helga's shop was in my immediate vicinity. As I wandered alone
through the summer evening streets, I usually passed by this magnificent establishment which you couldn't really call a mere shop.
And if it's the customers who make the shop, then this definitely
wasn't a shop. It was eternally deserted. Behind the always freshly
washed windows lay an interior realm of silence. Inside, everything was painted black. A black box in which even the smallest
detail was an event in itself. But there were so few of such
details—and not a price tag in sight. Clearly their purpose was
nothing so banal as to be sold—that I in my innocence actually
doubted that the space on the other side of the windows was governed by any sort of commercial intent. A pedestal displayed a
necklace of gigantic yellow beads—amber? plastic? rhinoceros
horn? fossilized butter? A tribal chieftain might once have worn
it on his broad, bare chest but here it had come into its own, as
it were, and would never again have to serve an earthly purpose—
from now on, it would simply lie here in this opulent blackness,
like in an almost completely extinguished memory. And then
Helga Stolzier's wide, pale face appeared against that crepuscular
back-drop, for all the world, like a big, beautiful fish ascending
towards the light from beneath the frozen surface of the water,
gently batting its fins, carried along by a current below the ice.
That healthy milky white face with that wide mouth painted deep
red and those fiery eyes. I could not yet see her long blonde plait,
like that of a Slavic wet nurse—I've never seen a Slavic wet nurse
but this was how I imagined them to be. And in her strong white
hands, smelling sweetly of soap, with those claw-like crimson fingernails, she was carrying an ostrich egg. It looked as though she
were holding it only with those dangerous nails, pinning the

magnificent egg delicately from all sides. She placed it next to the bulky necklace with a conviction that suggested that this placement had been chosen after a long period of deliberation. Then she raised her head, aware of me observing her, and looked at me like a wizard who has just carried out a solemn and mysterious rite. And had I not in fact just been witness to an astonishing metamorphosis? This ostrich egg that she had most likely acquired wholesale for all of about three euros now looked as if Marco Polo himself had brought it back from China to Venice through all manner of hardship and adversity.

I was mistaken in my original assessment of exactly when Helga Stolzier had finally proved herself indispensable to Rosemarie Hopsten as an arbiter of taste and beauty. At first I had thought that the high-flown names of the Hopsten children had been inspired by Helga Stolzier. Given how rigidly Bernward and Rosemarie's names were bound to their generation and background, it seemed unlikely that they would make a foray into a vague and distant antiquity, in Bernward's case especially—in fact, he had originally considered the name Hubert for his son but in Phoebe's case, he had decided to save himself the headache of coming up with a name. Wasn't it wonderful that Rosemarie made such a mental effort to break out of the established mould? If you held her daughter's name up against Bernward's faux-English tattersall, you could sense that in matters of taste, Rosemarie was a searcher who was prepared to be led by the most diverse of ideals. Helga never commented on the tattersall. She had a way of not saying anything that was mysterious and, at the same time, completely reassuring to most people. And, for the most part, she didn't try to foist any of the stuff from her boutique on Rosemarie. There were other sources from which to satisfy her friend's passion for collecting. The two of them travelled to auctions in London and Vienna whenever Helga found something enchanting in the catalogues and she also introduced the Hopstens to dealers she had known for years. One name in particular came up often and Rosemarie uttered it with especial delight and Rhenish emphasis—Pattitucci, who ran an establishment near the Rialto. When Rosemarie said 'Pattitucci' with her Rhenish intonation, it sounded like a sudden downpour, filling the Venetian alleys with water and causing the waves on the canals to splash against the quays. Pattitucci was a purveyor of fine wares—'Treasures!' Rosemarie would exclaim, looking gleefully at everyone around her, since by her standards the prices were really quite reasonable. But Helga with her connoisseur's eye would never have been able to purchase such objects to sell in her own boutique. 'She can't afford it,' said Rosemarie, not without a certain stern matter-of-factness—although they were the best of friends, some things nevertheless had to remain absolutely clear. The fact that she pronounced this diagnosis in English was meant to convey a sense of discretion. Whenever she spoke about business, it was obvious that financial savvy really was in her blood. She could have managed her fortune perfectly well without Bernward's help. She had no fear of numbers, no distaste for arithmetic, no provocative insouciance of the sort often associated with certain wealthy heiresses. When it came to smaller sums she was wont to exclaim disdainfully, 'Thirty euros? That's a lot of money!' 'Eighteen-fifty? That's a lot of money!' And who could deny it, when economics became a matter of morality? I was especially fond of hearing her tell stories of her shopping trips with Helga. The word buy, so central to these narratives, came to sound more like 'buoy' in Rosemarie's Rhenish intonation. There was an ineluctable buoyancy to these stories— all this buoying had nothing whatsoever to do with ordinary commerce, it took on resonances of something vital, the soul floating on the surface of a tranquil sea. There were no exigencies here, no prices, no questions of affordability or liquidity, simply pure bodily and spiritual well-being in the essential flow of existence. This buoying carried with it a strong but never self-righteous air of integrity, which could no doubt appear intimidating to anyone for whom buying and selling was not characterized by the same airy lightness.

'Look what we've just bought at Pattitucci's,' she said in a conspiratorial tone upon returning from her most recent trip to Venice. Out of a little velvet pouch she slid a small ivory Christ figure, late Romanesque with thick, heavy Barlachian eyelids and a perfectly smooth surface, a torso only, the arms had broken off. 'This thing is a pleasure to hold. Just feel how sensuously smooth it is!' She was truly enchanted at the sight of this statuette. Would she still have bought it if it had still had its arms, I wondered. Probably only Pattitucci knew the answer to that.

It is often the case with ladies who seek advice on purchases and interior decorating that the advisers themselves are kept in the shadows. The beauty you now behold is always the result of their own good taste. This was absolutely not true of Rosemarie's relationship to Helga. I noticed Helga in the throng of guests and recognized her immediately. She was looking enigmatically around her, deep in thought, as if she were alone in her boutique. She only ever spoke to the one person nearest to her heart, who, in this case, was Rosemarie. She never indulged in idle chitchat with anyone.

'Everything you see here, everything—it's all Helga!' said Rosemarie as she introduced us, and most likely she was not even banking on me taking 'everything' to be a hyperbole. Helga was wearing a batik kaftan, cutting a solemnly hibernal figure in the midst of all these people dressed in summer clothes and bathing costumes.

'She's an unhappy person, a genius,' Rosemarie whispered to me. 'And it all comes from inside her, she has no background. She's just obtained a rare set of Russian silver for me—but do you think she'd know what to do with it herself?' And indeed I now paid careful attention and, later, when some food was served, I had the definite impression that Helga showed some trepidation and cast furtive glances to either side as she struggled with her knife and fork. If Rosemarie hadn't said anything, I never would have noticed. And besides, Helga ate practically nothing.

'*I really don't like the way you're describing these people. What have Helga's table manners got to do with this story? She's a brave woman, she hasn't had an easy time of it and she's doing her best to make ends meet.*'

'*Forgive me, this was the mood at that first encounter. It was a glorious summer day but I couldn't get close to Phoebe, so I was wandering around on my own and had the sense that there was some subtle note of intrigue mixed in all this free-spirited hospitality. There was something uneasy in the air . . . you know what I mean—Helga with her ambiguous knowing silence, her demonic glances, with those ostrich eggs, the feathers, the seashells . . .*'

'*Good grief, Helga, demonic! She's the most harmless creature in the world. She just has to keep her eye on her finances, which indeed she does.*'

7

BR-R-R-AZIL

The nice thing about those Sundays at the Hopstens' was the way the generations intermingled. There were lots of young people and a few old people, then the ones who were Bernward and Rosemarie's age and others who were somewhere between theirs and their children's generation, like the young Schmidt-Flexes and me. I began to realize that although I was primarily interested in Phoebe, she did not monopolize my attention completely—if she had, I would no doubt quickly have begun to feel quite disheartened—but, rather, kindled my senses for everything else around me. It wasn't my eyes that were primarily attracted to Silvi Schmidt-Flex although, to be sure, there was plenty to be admired in that department but, rather, my ears. I was sitting near her and listening to the sound of her voice, which required no effort on my part since she talked constantly both to those sitting next to her and just to herself—as far as I could tell, thinking, for her, was clearly something to be done out loud. The fact that she was often impatiently or even gruffly undercut by her husband seemed not to faze or discourage her in the slightest. Probably she didn't perceive his coarseness as hurtful in any way but simply as a perfectly natural mode of expression, much like her monologue. She had tanned skin, probably without the need for regular sunbathing, a large, clear forehead and the earnest eyes of a child arranging the world in her own private way. In her hand, she held a glass of white wine from which she took small sips at regular intervals—Bernward saw to it that it never remained empty for long. But I observed all of this only from the sidelines, she didn't notice me at all. Her voice was bright yet soft and rounded and it had a peculiar cooing quality that imbued her vowels as well as her consonants with a wonderfully warm timbre. There was no trace of that flat and tuneless intonation that is so characteristic of modern German. Every syllable that issued from her lips was like a miniature explosion of rich, resonant sound. The first thing I noticed were her *r*s, which were ever so delicately rolled, like brilliant sterling-silver ball bearings in her throat. No sooner had I heard that sound than I yearned to hear it again. Happily, *r* is by no means an uncommon letter in German but suddenly any word without it seemed quite devoid of both body and soul. And to think that some baroque poet or other had actually set himself the unfathomable task of writing a long poem completely without the *r*. The result was a ghostly language of lukewarm lameness. As I later discovered, there was a curious historical reason for this *r* of hers. She was born in Brazil—my God the way she pronounced that word, Brazil, how it scintillated and how that *z* zinged, sizzling frivolously like oil in a pan, followed by the delectable smoothness of a fish's metallic scales—but her parents were German, Baltic German, more specifically, and their Baltic accent with that famous *r* had been preserved much better in their Brazilian exile than would have been possible had they lived in Germany. And this somewhat harsh *r* had mated with the Portuguese *r* in Silvi's throat, which clearly was predestined to produce beautiful sounds, allowing this letter, which when written reveals none of the vibrant life that lies dormant within it and seems like little more than a hinge linking two vowels, to realize its full potential. Just then Silvi said, 'Por-r-r-tugal'—that she had never been to Portugal? That she would never again set foot in Portugal? I don't remember. All I know is that the conversation seemed to have turned to Portugal and now lingered there insistently, so that the word blossomed into a magic incantation and a poetic refrain, like heavy purple velvet robes gliding down a nude body to lie in luxurious folds on the floor.

'Have you ever been a singer?' I asked her spontaneously when, her back turned towards me, she stopped talking for a moment to take a sip of wine. She didn't turn round and probably it didn't matter to her who had spoken but she answered warmly, as though she owed such warmth to the entire world, 'I've never been a singer. I haven't got a musical bone in my body.'

It sounded as though she were reciting the considered opinion of her Catholic-school music teachers, as if such a diagnosis weren't completely nonsensical when applied to her. If she had been initially silent for a long time today it was because she had dozed off a bit amid the ping-pong of voices going back and forth over her sun-bathed and boyishly firm tummy. The pair of large sunglasses concealing her alert, bright eyes behind a sumptuous veil of black hid her little nap as well. But now it was the sun that hid behind a cloud, a shadow passed over the company and suddenly the crowd seemed to change and progress to a different stage and Silvi covered herself with a colourful scarf, even though the heat had not subsided in the least, and took off her sunglasses. She was forever taking something off or putting something else on. To me it seemed less like hypersensitivity than a particular attentiveness to fluctuations in temperature, as if she had an almost animal connection with the weather and puffed up her feathers whenever the breeze turned cooler.

'I would help you,' she said to Phoebe who, just at that moment, came by with two new bottles of wine for the cooler, 'but I won't, and it's not that I'm too lazy, it's just that I tend to drop everything.' Again, that singular *r* of hers—what more pleasurable fate could a dew-covered wine bottle hope for than to be dropped by Silvi? Her comment drew attention to her hands which truly were much too small to be able to hold anything heavy but formed a perfect oval and each of her polished fingernails repeated the oval in miniature. Rosemarie was behind her, also reclining in a deckchair, and she spoke without raising her head.

'She's right,' she said without the faintest hint of accusation. 'I remember that blue Chinese glass bowl that Helga bought for me at auction—it had spent two hundred and fifty years at the bottom of the sea in a wrecked junk ship before being rescued by divers and brought to Germany, and then you dropped it.'

'Oh, that beautiful bowl,' cried Silvi. It wasn't a genuine cry of distress but it proved that Silvi was capable of producing unparalleled sonic beauty even without a single *r*. There was something tragic about this bowl's fate but it wasn't dispiriting, not when it had been mourned so melodiously, elegized even. In pitch darkness, she said, even in completely unfamiliar rooms, she was able to move about without bumping into things. You just had to turn the lights out and she wouldn't break a thing. A blown fuse in a strange house? Wouldn't affect her in the least. No, no, it wasn't that she could see in the dark—that was something else. But she was conscious of the location of the furniture, the doors and whatever bowls might be in the room (this last was directed behind her at Rosemarie) but unfortunately she only rarely had an opportunity to practise this ability which, she said, she'd had since childhood and had never lost. Her father had said she must have bat blood. She wondered if that was possible.

'Pshaw! You really do believe anything anyone tells you!' This gruff, sullen voice belonged to her husband, who had remained silent until then.

'Yes, I do believe everything.'

She spoke these words with complete seriousness as she sat up, as seriously as if she were professing her faith in God and the Church to the priest at her own baptism. 'I do believe.'

With his peculiarly cantankerous interjection, reminiscent of a querulous child who has been excluded from the other children's play, Hans-Jörg Schmidt-Flex had succeeded in attracting my attention, despite my best efforts until that point to deprive him of it. He repelled me in some unspecifiable way. I was reluctant even to look in his direction and so were the other guests, it seemed to me. Shoulders tensed whenever he tried to join a group. No one made an attempt to include him in the conversation but, rather, as I thought I had observed on several occasions, they would subtly twist it, probably quite unconsciously and certainly not by prior agreement, in such a way as to make it impossible for an outsider to understand what they were talking about. The others all knew him whereas I didn't and, yet, I was already comporting myself like them, at least as far as averting my eyes was concerned, for he had not yet tried to speak to me, perhaps sensing a faint antipathy. But such antipathy is unusual when directed at someone who has barely said a word. How he resembled his father—the same profile, that same shock of hair, albeit not yet grey but rather drab and colourless. The elder's imposing presence, so uniquely suited to public appearances, speeches, televized debates and to wreath-laying ceremonies, was entirely absent in his son, who was a pocket edition of him, not least when you saw his translucent, spider-like hands which of course were clammy to boot. Hans-Jörg probably could have passed for handsome, in a nineteen thirties kind of way, had he not been made of such meagre stuff. His skin was suety and unfresh. There was something stuffy and airless about the man. I knew exactly what it must have smelt like in his room during his student life—days after days and nights of revising for a test. Hadn't there been those industrious but not too bright students back then, forever surrounded by a pervasive unhealthy odour? To be fair, Schmidt-Flex senior was monarchical and presumably tremendously onerous to have as a father but his son was no crown prince and, after all, he had not achieved half as much as his father had at his age. The old man never missed an opportunity to point out that he had earned a doctorate in political science by the age of twenty-one—and just how many honorary degrees was it he had received since then? To me as an outsider one thing was soon clear—there were probably few people who regarded Hans-Jörg more critically or with greater disappointment than his father. How could it be otherwise? He had never lived up to his father's superiority but at the same time, the old man never let his unfortunate son out of his sight and insisted on a coordinated programme for these Sunday afternoons. And Hans-Jörg obeyed and submitted and allowed himself and his wife (this woman! I asked myself how he could ever have won her affection) to be towed along by his venerable elders. But he made it abundantly clear that he did so only reluctantly. He looked visibly pained at every word his father boomed to the company. He winced whenever the old man addressed him. His subservience relieved him of any obligation to maintain decorum. He seemed to grow ever more tight-lipped as the afternoon wore on. There was something threatening about him, like a gathering storm. Unfortunately there was only one person who would set him off—the one who least deserved it, his wife, whose charm and grace, which no one could deny, must delight the hearts of men and women alike. Was she aware of this threat looming over her? Silvi, I felt I knew that much about her already, was not equipped to evade a perilous strife of forces, least of all to ensure her own safety. She observed the inexorable deterioration of her husband's mood but did not appear to feel the need to do anything about it.

This time, I was holding the wine bottle, having deftly snatched it from Phoebe who was performing her duties as cup-bearer to the 'grown-ups', as even she innocently put it, with easy assiduity, without ever allowing this to interrupt her conversations with her peers. And so it was that I caught the attention of two women who up to that point had scarcely spared me a second glance—Phoebe, who looked at me in surprise and amusement and not without a hint of approval that I was independent and not someone you had to worry too much about, and Silvi, her eyes sparkling as I approached her holding the bottle. I could tell that she found the final sip of lukewarm wine in her glass faintly repellent but now it would be replenished from the source, like cool water from an Alpine spring.

'Just what the doctor ordered,' she said cheerfully, the *r*s gurgling like bubbles in champagne, and I felt that this enlivening, gratifying appreciation was directed not only at the wine but also at its bearer—me. I couldn't help but return her smile and so I grinned, I'm afraid you would have to say exultantly, staring straight into her bright, clear face and was about to lower the neck of the bottle when I felt myself, bottle and all, indelicately, even violently, pushed aside.

'No,' said Hans-Jörg, his quietly simmering rancour suddenly erupting into loud and acerbic disapproval, 'my wife can't have any more wine. No, she's had quite enough.' He said he had absolutely no desire to have to help her stagger up the stairs back in Frankfurt. This habitual drinking had got to stop. He made quite a scene. The conversation around us died down as people turned to look. Hans-Jörg had the righteously indignant look of a man whose task it was 'willy-nilly' to ensure a modicum of order, even if no one would thank him for his troubles. Someone had to do it.

To be sure, no one else shared this opinion, not even his father, who was otherwise a great believer in upbraiding others in public, his son in particular, but he placed great stock in issuing such 'abasements', as he called them, so casually that to anyone but their recipient they seemed little more than scathing. The nature of the aversion we all felt towards Hans-Jörg but which no one had been able to pinpoint now became clear—it was his unchivalrousness, his lack of gentlemanly feeling that would instinctively have prohibited him from humiliating a lady in public. It was Bernward who diffused the awkward situation with complaisant and harmless good cheer, as if he hadn't even noticed Hans-Jörg's ill-willed belligerence. He took the bottle from my hand and turned with all his easy Westphalian firmness to the younger man.

'I'm sure Silvi is relieved to know that you're looking out for her but I have the say around here.' He said it so amiably, fondly even, that not even Hans-Jörg could have interpreted it as a rebuke, and the entire atmosphere changed visibly. Probably Hans-Jörg's outburst hadn't been so bad after all—in fact, it was already almost forgotten. And Bernward filled Silvi's glass with ceremonious care, as if it were her first of the afternoon.

8

THE SECRET OF THE FOREST QUARTER

I'm just going to make a brief detour. It starts at the Hopstens' swimming pool and it will lead back there in due course, which makes it quite characteristic of those first months in Frankfurt that drew me ever closer to Rosemarie's circle. I have noticed that life seems to be divided into sections grouped according to a particular rubric. Everything that happens to you fits that rubric and you cannot escape it no matter how far away you go.

The only one who seemed completely oblivious to the dark cloud of calamity surrounding Hans-Jörg was Joseph Salam who had, indeed, also been introduced to the Hopstens by Hans-Jörg. Although on the few Sundays when I was there he was always there as well, he remained a foreign body in that circle, even though in this bourgeois Frankfurt context it could never have been entirely homogeneous. Was it just that he always wore the wrong clothes? Evidently he felt ill at ease in semi-casual weekend-wear. He looked like a prize fighter in the pink polo shirt he was wearing the first time we met, the elasticated sleeves cutting deep furrows into his beefy upper arms, and his pectorals, encased in ample layers of fat, resembled a woman's bosom. But he also seemed to prefer a snug fit in his suits. And clearly it wasn't that he had simply grown out of those Italian suits made from the sort of gossamer fabric that on a thinner man would tend to flutter in the wind. No, these were brand new and had all the little details that fashion houses use to distinguish one year's collection from the next year's—two-button jackets this year, for instance, as opposed to last year's three, which was especially unflattering in Salam's case as they tended to accentuate his round, firm belly in such a way as to make it appear as if he were carrying it in front of him on a tray. They were definitely expensive suits. He always reminded me of someone whose luggage has been lost by the airline and who has had to purchase a completely new wardrobe at the airport boutiques. If you think about it, airport boutiques with their sterile no-man's-land quality are designed specifically for people like Salam. They're akin to the restaurants in exclusive hotels, which have to cater to so many different tastes that they eschew any specificity. Salam's accent was Viennese but was he really from Vienna? Istanbul seemed a better fit, plus his name sounded Middle Eastern. Although he was freshly shaven and no doubt thoroughly moisturized and certainly wore more than enough aftershave, his cheeks were permanently tinged with a bluish sheen and his round, dark eyes with the girlishly long eyelashes (although such feminine accents served only to emphasize the virility of his appearance) observed everything around him with inquisitive alacrity. He was like Odysseus, having washed ashore on Scheria, now sitting, freshly bathed and newly clothed, by King Alkinoös' hearth, preparing to tell his life story. Except that no one seemed particularly interested in listening to him.

I admire people who never find themselves in embarrassing situations but I admire even more those who are able to resolve embarrassing situations and consign them to oblivion. In this, Bernward was not alone, Salam was very much his equal. I no longer dared to look at Silvi, as I did not care to see her reaction to the recent incident, and just then Salam turned to me. His robust, fleshy folds and opulent eyebrows gave him the look of a man who has reached a respectable age in the prime of health and now intends to remain at this level of stability for a long time.

'Hans-Jörg is a little tetchy,' he told me in a confidential tone, 'but don't underestimate him as a businessman.' He said he was extremely pleased with his close collaboration with Hans-Jörg and that it really had nothing to do with his illustrious name—was I completely off the mark in taking this statement to mean that this 'collaboration', as Salam called this business plan in which he hoped to ensnare Hans-Jörg, was in fact entirely dependent on that name? This is how I pictured it—Schmidt-Flex had kept his son on a short leash and occupied him with purposive and rudimentary tasks for far too long for his son to realistically be able to embark on a career of his own. Of course, Hans-Jörg was complicit in this arrangement as well. And so, it had probably even been his father's idea that he should perhaps try and do something on his own for a change. And the old man must have felt a minor surge of triumph at the fact that Hans-Jörg then turned up with Salam as his business partner. At any rate he was ready to intervene if and when the need arose. I could see how he shot regular glances in Salam's direction from afar.

'You see, he's got the verve and I've got the experience,' said Salam. Credibility, integrity—all old-fashioned concepts that could not be plotted on the newfangled charts that the economists loved so much and which were dying out as a result—these, he told me, were the basic principles of his approach. But it's not that he was some moralizing windbag, oh no he loved a good joke.

'Speaking of credibility . . .' just recently, he informed me, he had observed a street vendor in Athens selling glass-cutters. The things cut through glass as effortlessly as through a block of cheese—'This chap was going on and on about how safe these glass-cutters were but both his hands were covered in plasters.' A monument to futility, that fellow. Salam's imposing frame was seized by a powerful but soundless bout of laughter and I too had drunk enough to find this plainly self-contradictory figure who by now was probably peddling completely new and different contraptions—cut-throat electric shavers? exploding coffee machines?—singularly amusing.

'And it's the same on any scale, that's the law of correspondences,' said Salam once he had recovered sufficiently. He said his next step would be to go with Hans-Jörg to Cairo. He felt completely at home in Cairo and with his guidance, he had no doubt, Hans-Jörg too would feel at home there in no time. The way he said it sounded almost paternal, affectionate even. Certainly there weren't many people who spoke of Hans-Jörg that way. Or was this optimistic cordiality perhaps, in truth, primarily for Schmidt-Flex senior's benefit? Did it not have something of that professional calm exuded by the teachers at special schools for problem children to reassure the parents that they'd 'take good care' of this one? Nonetheless, I must admit that I actually quite liked Salam. He was a man of the world, surrounded by an aura of freedom and adventure, which in my mind I associated with some mythical Levant of old. His experience and cosmopolitanism had not made him cynical and he joyfully played whatever hand the circumstances dealt him. Everything he said revealed an underlying cheerful, philanthropic spirit, a philosophical and democratic attitude towards his fellow men with no trace of the political. Moreover, for Salam, the equality and fraternity of his fellows preceded any specific political circumstance and was not something that must first be established. Indeed, it throve best among people who were least concerned with abstract notions and political programmes and instead lived only according to their instincts, secure in the knowledge that this was how all the others lived as well. Presumably this was also why he did not seem to be aware of the predefined role he still had to play here by the swimming pool. In the final analysis, there were no predefined roles one had to play. When one arrived in new surroundings, one might not immediately have the right key that would fit the lock—but there was never a doubt in his mind that he would find the right key eventually.

The lady of the house ignored him, that was her prerogative—but one day he would get her attention.

Now take your mind far away from the black shimmering water of the Hopstens' swimming pool amid those emerald fields— that water always looked heavier than normal water to me, a substance far denser and more precious. We're off to the Austrian

Waldviertel, or Forest Quarter, a godforsaken backwater north of the quick-flowing, perennially swelling Danube. Black swimming pools are unheard of here, as are the loose clusters of urbanites that might gather round them. For all the Hopstens' laissez-faire, it was impossible to imagine the woman whom I had come here to visit as a guest at their house. In fact, it was impossible to imagine her in anyone's house but her own and she would have been the first to refuse categorically to set foot in one. An elderly lady, an acquaintance of my parents', who lived on her own in a little cabin in the woods on the outskirts of a village—'a nun who follows her own rhythm,' as my mother put it. 'Well, I don't know if I'd call her a nun,' my father interjected. They did not think of Marguerite Simserl fondly. She'd contact them only in a state of utmost distress but was resolutely unwilling to accept any form of advice. 'Nine hours I lay helpless in the forest before that farmer found me,'—this was the sort of news with which she routinely worried her friends but if someone quite reasonably suggested that she give up that little cabin and move to the city, where she also had a flat, she would hear none of it. It was as if she had an almost preternatural gift for confounding any attempt others made to stop worrying about her well-being. From what my mother told me, it seemed the web this Marguerite had spun on all sides was actually more solid and ineluctable than if she had lived in Linz or Vienna in the immediate vicinity of these people. And the number of individuals who were caught up in this web, having urgently and repeatedly to deal with this misfortune, was not insignificant.

'Since you're going to Vienna for a couple of days anyway, you could pay a visit to Marguerite,' said my mother over the telephone. There was even a legitimate reason—the old lady had said something about leaving her old cabin to me along with eight hectares of forest, in optimum condition thanks to her own tireless, back-breaking industry. Apparently she only enlisted a man's help to deal with snow damage. I just had to go there once to look at the property. I did not savour the prospect at all. How does one imagine such a visit? Burdened by the promise of a size-able inheritance, I was now supposed to turn up, weighing and measuring, and declare what I thought of her generous offer. What a terrible basis for a first meeting. My mother had absolutely no time for my misgivings. And so, I agreed to get off the train at Passau at noon that Sunday, thence to proceed to Marguerite Simserl's neck of the woods. Someone would be there to pick me up, she informed me. Sitting on the train on the way back from Vienna, I grew increasingly uneasy. If someone wants to leave something to someone else in their will, they should go ahead and do it, I thought to myself, instead of announcing it ahead of time. The grateful beneficiary will for ever remember the reading of the will as a happy moment. Instead, all hopes of an easy relationship to the decedent must be nipped in the bud by the guilty conscience of the beneficiary thus acquainted with his future inheritance—was it not inevitable that one would begin, if not exactly to wish for their death, then at least invol-untarily to wonder whether the slightest sniffle and cough might not mark their imminent departure for that undiscovered coun-try? And for this, I was sacrificing an afternoon in Phoebe's garden!

The glorious heat of those late summer days showed no sign of abating. The emerald meadows had begun to grow tired, not yellow exactly, the rainbow-shimmering clouds of water from the many sprinklers saw to that, but still a duller, less phosphorescent green. And then something surprising happened—I actually got Phoebe on the telephone, by accident, of course. If I had asked for her, the very question would have chased her away, at least that was how it was beginning to seem to me. But when I told her that I would not be coming to their house that Sunday (an announcement intended primarily for her parents, I merely held out the most tentative of hopes that the news might interest her as well) I heard such disappointment in her voice that I would have preferred to have cancelled this whole Vienna adventure outright. It was as if she perceived my trip as an act of profound infidelity. This bothered me, obviously. But there had also been a shift in my attitude towards my new-found Frankfurt existence, possibly brought about by an attendant warming of my mood. The landscape in which the city was embedded, those gently rolling highlands, steep but never craggy, which hemmed in the broad river valley, and the highlands that resumed in the distance on the other side of the river, that lush, fertile space with its wines and strawberries, chestnuts and apples, must once have been a place of joy and festivity. The city with its church spires and fortification towers embraced the river, which was just the right size—not so wide as to split the city in two and yet significant enough a presence to create the unequivocal experience of living in a city on a river. This area had always been densely populated. The entire course of the river was studded by ancient villages, on the hillsides stood castles as a reminder of the political fragmentation of this prosperous valley. There had been a veritable throng of political entities here, jostling like trout in an overpopulated fishpond. The Free Imperial City shared a few square kilometres with sundry duchies, landgraviates, principalities, dioceses, counties, right down to the Free Imperial Village of Soden, and this fragmentation had engendered a spirit of freedom—I was reminded of something Salam had said while telling me about his enterprises in the Middle East—freedom, he had said, was all well and good, and he congratulated any country that guaranteed its citizens' freedom but the most important thing was that the state keep its reach short, then the rest would take care of itself. What surprised me the most was that I now suddenly felt the presence and influence of all these historical reminiscences, which had been so thoroughly obliterated by motorway junctions, airports and the urban sprawl blanketing the plain and the hillsides. Seen from the edge of the Hopstens' swimming pool, this metropolis, bathed in sunlight, spread out at the foot of the Taunus Mountains, seemed to be filled up with the promise of all the energies it contained. It did not seem formless, rather, tightly conglomerate, despite its expanse. To be sure, it had no doubt all been much more beautiful once but hardly as highly charged as it was now. No, my infatuation with Phoebe Hopsten alone cannot have been the sole cause of such an intoxicated view of Frankfurt. At most it produced in me a state of heightened interest and stimulated my vanity, which fuelled that tiny flame. Rather, it had to do with the prospect of my brief sojourn in the godforsaken cabin I stood to inherit. It suddenly dawned on me that I found absolutely nothing appealing about such backwoods obscurity and that I was imagining this trip as a journey to the Underworld, even though the Waldviertel with its apple and pear trees heavy with fruit was no doubt just as resplendent in the late summer as the sultry Main valley, to which I had now grown accustomed.

Marguerite Simserl was an organizer. Despite her reclusion or perhaps precisely because of it, she knew how to govern. And it was not just some taxi driver who picked me up at the station but, rather, a serious and slightly pained-looking man with dyed-brown hair, as thin as a tailor in a fairy tale, who, with a look of wounded obedience, handed me his business card in lieu of salutation—a Hofrat no less, now retired of course. It was simply a matter of course for him to pick me up, he mumbled, staring at the ground. For Frau Doktor, he was always ready to do anything, he said. It sounded as though he regarded his position as the general dogsbody as both unremarkable and unchangeable and he had long since given up any resistance. My expectations could not possibly have been more fully met. The landscape we drove through was green and dense, a density made even richer and more succulent by the proximity of a murky stream. The apple trees were studded with so many red apples that the branches could barely support them. In the front yard of the farmhouse where the Hofrat lived with his sister, there was literally a monument to apple trees—a venerable, gigantic tree propped up by beams on all sides. It looked like the scaffolding round Noah's Ark. The supporting beams did not make the tree appear to be suffering under its own weight, pulled down by its own might but, rather, it seemed to be in the midst of preparations for some mysterious motility, as if this tree would soon cautiously pull itself free from the ground, shaking with violent forces, uprooting itself with a terrible groan, leaving a cloud of dust and soil behind as it lurched forth towards the horizon. 'A miraculous tree,' I said to the Hofrat, who glanced at it morosely and muttered something about what 'terribly hard work' it was to keep up.

Yes, this is how it was—the stream and the crisp succulence of the green, the gently rolling hills, so far removed from urban sprawl and over-cultivation, so perfectly preserved, spread out in the sunlight exactly as it had been aeons ago—it was all for naught if it was inhabited by such grizzled, stuffy, morose people as this former civil servant. He lived in this farmhouse but there was no actual farming any more, that much was clear from two new-looking wooden signs with faintly anthroposophic italic lettering that pointed the way to the 'massage-therapy centre' and the 'homoeopathic remedies'. Farther away stood the recently refurbished barn, an explosion of geraniums blooming in what had been the trough.

'Well, this is how we live here. We built all this ourselves,' said the Hofrat. The deep folds round his mouth gave him the appearance of a dyspeptic chain-smoker, even though he clearly hadn't touched a cigarette in years and in such homoeopathic surroundings he probably had his digestion well under control. Here in the shadow of this sublime, breath-taking apple tree, the man had every right to speak in his deep-rooted regional dialect but something about that belated, bastardized verbal boorishness irked me now. There was a kind of triumphant provincialism in it, as if there had never been an aeroplane in the sky overhead.

'Does Frau Simserl live here?'

No, he replied, although they had invited her often enough. She could live here in perfect comfort and help was always at hand. At this, the Hofrat gestured down the length of his lean body—this not exactly impressive and not particularly robust body was 'always' at Frau Doktor's service. 'We help in whatever way we can.' The words of a man who had given his entire life away in the service of altruism, the only limits to his devotion being those posed by Mother Nature. But for this very reason there was so much, so very much to be discussed, before I made my way to Frau Simserl's.

'And Waltraud' (this was the homoeopathic sister) also had 'one or two things' to tell me. I wasn't invited into the house, but in the converted barn that now housed the 'Holistic Health Centre', he served me a glass of home-made apple juice on a white birch tray. He sat in silence opposite me as I drank. The juice was really quite good. Even if it had been less healthy it would only have tasted slightly better. What position had the Hofrat held, I wondered. A relatively senior one, I imagined, where directives were issued, inquiries were carried out and decisions were made. It was impossible to imagine this man engaged in such activities even for a moment. He seemed broken. A meek and doleful self-apologizer was all that remained once the official air had been let out of him.

'You see, if it weren't for us, Frau Doktor would have passed away long ago.' It sounded like an admission of terrible guilt. It was a tone in which he might just as easily have confessed to murdering the old lady in cold blood. He drew me an outline of his life and collaboration with his sister and Frau Doktor Simserl—'But I'll spare you the details of the large number of other people, quite unpleasant characters, many of them, who also come around here from time to time.' People buzzed round Frau Doktor like flies, he told me, and just like flies they were mostly hungry and looking for food. So in addition to their other duties, his sister and he were also frequently in charge of shooing these flies away. Lest I get the wrong impression, he assured me that he was not referring to me, the Herr Doktor, but rather to thoroughly unworthy individuals, to whom Frau Doktor was nevertheless inexplicably drawn—that is, until she was made to see them for what they really were. I did not try to prevent him from calling me Herr Doktor, although I was unsure whether to take this form of address as a mark of respect or whether it was just a habitual Austrianism or perhaps even a subtle and equally Austrian form of impudence. In any case, I was glad of anything betokening distance between myself and the Hofrat. For years now, he informed me, Frau Doktor would only eat food prepared by his sister. He gestured towards the small glass jars, individually labelled and arranged on the table in a pyramid, the better to entice potential customers. Carrot purée—baby food, essentially. 'Frau Doktor can easily warm it up and spoon it out herself. That is if I don't warm it up for her, or my sister does.' Again, he said this in a tone of profound despondency. The shadow of total ruin loomed.

'We worry, we work, we wait and see,' said the Hofrat. Every so often it would be, 'My dear Herr Hofrat, be so kind as to drive me to Linz, would you?'—and he would do that too. Fortunately his sister had other matters to attend to, namely expanding the Holistic Health Centre, which wasn't quite so easy nowadays. He too found it hard to resist the deeply satisfying assertion that 'many things aren't quite so easy nowadays.' For his part, the tasks and duties imposed on him by Frau Doktor took up almost all of his time—'and on top of all that we still have to put up with . . .' Apparently there was a steady stream of young gentlemen callers—wherever did Frau Doktor find them?—she did of course have a telephone up there—'We can't really take that away from her,' he said with the look of a champion of human rights. People had quite the wrong idea about Frau Doktor's fortune, he said—it wasn't exactly tiny but this lifestyle, ostensibly all alone out in the woods but ultimately receiving twenty-four-hour care, didn't come cheap! Especially since his sister devoted all her time and energy to building up the Holistic Health Centre, not when they had all manner of wishes and demands from Frau Doktor to contend with.

'So here we stand, always at attention.' And, truly, he did look like a starving and footsore infantryman, called up just before the army's final crushing defeat. The situation here in this solitary forest quarter was clear as day—although to say so was almost an insult to the brilliant clarity of the day itself. At any rate, it was hard to reconcile with this endless litany of minor misfortunes. Out here, off the radar of civilization, in these forlorn villages, whose barns held no hay but, instead, housed Holistic Health Centres, thoughts that enter one's mind through whatever demonic inspiration remain undisturbed and untroubled, and so they are free to proliferate and take root. Here was this old lady who lived on her own out in the woods. She had evidently severed all ties to her family long ago, if they had not fled of their own accord. She was in possession of a small fortune but had no heirs. This was the idea which had taken complete control of the Hofrat, whom in any case I imagined to be mostly a tool in the healing hands of his sister. Out here, nature taught you patience through the eternal cycle of birth, death and rebirth and it was with this patience that the two siblings, quite advanced in years themselves but kept healthy through a steady diet of organic herbs and berries, awaited the inevitable demise of the old lady, who presumably had still not made her last will and testament—no, no, the Hofrat knew this all too well, he who always accompanied her on her trips to Linz to see the notary. Luckily, without him she was completely immobile. So there was still hope but this fortune, those plots of land, those bank accounts—her little cabin in the woods was by far not the most significant part of it, even though that's all she ever spoke of, but in such poetically hyperbolic terms (her hermitage, her cell, her Earthly Paradise) that the Hofrat had to assume that whenever she spoke of her cabin she was in fact referring to a much vaster fortune—but this fortune fuelled not only the imagination of the obliging siblings but also that of the wilful anchorite herself. In her reliance on others for help, this alone gave her wings.

'I'm still thinking about moving away from here,' 'I think I really would like to see Rome once more before I die,' 'I'm not rooted to this place, you know,'—phrases such as these were like a knife twisting in the Hofrat's side. It was more than he could take after all these years, and he certainly had no time for jokes. Every day, as he approached her cabin, a jar of carrot purée in his hand, he was always prepared for the possibility that he would find it shuttered, Frau Doktor up and eloped with her latest gigolo, leaving the siblings cheated out of their harvest as if by a midsummer hailstorm.

'It is all prepared,' said the Hofrat as he opened a folder. I should just be aware, he continued, that the cabin Frau Doktor wished to bequeath to me was heavily mortgaged. The most sensible thing would definitely be to place Frau Doktor's assets in a trust. In which case, seeing as he would in any case be left with all the bother and inconvenience, he would even be willing to act as trustee—that way I wouldn't have to worry about it, and besides I wasn't really familiar with the area, plus I wasn't actually Austrian—'Or are you?'

I reassured him that I wasn't, although I could tell that he would have preferred to have seen my passport. For foreigners, he told me, it was really, really bad here—even Frau Doktor, sterling Austrian though she was, had never truly settled in. The village was full of mean-spirited, xenophobic people. Frau Doktor had admittedly also done her bit to provoke them. People here didn't like new faces, and new faces, well, that had always been Frau Doktor's speciality.

The telephone rang. The voice on the other end was so piercing that I could hear it squawking loudly out of the receiver.

'He's here,' said the Hofrat with his head bowed. If he had been wearing a hat it would have been firmly in hand. 'At once, at once, at once.'

After a relatively long drive along narrow winding roads, I finally caught sight of the cabin at the edge of the forest looking out over an endless sequence of hills fading into the distance. The only sense in which this handsome old-style hunting lodge might be considered a cabin was that it was made of wood. With its wide balcony and impressive hunting trophies it looked really quite stately. The lady of the house was waiting for us at the garden gate, lean and tanned, with a short, unruly intellectual's haircut, a spare, washed-out face. Her blue-and-white-striped blouse and modest pearl necklace identified her as a member of the rural upper class. She was irate. The Hofrat had kept her waiting. No, she was not going to invite him in. He was to wait in the car. Or drive back home and wait for the telephone call telling him to come and pick me up. But first, she had to speak to me in private. Above all, she had to show me everything—how else was I supposed to get a proper impression? Her voice was delicate and high-pitched, tremulous but still girlish. Inside this old and fragile body lived a tyrannical child. But the lady's surly manner was refreshing after the conversation I'd just been having. And there was actually quite a pleasant smell in the house, no must of ages, just the clean, dry air of an orderly woodshed. Well-worn kilim rugs in beautiful colours adorned the broad floorboards. The leather armchairs were covered in a dense craquelure. There was nothing to indicate that a woman lived here, no bric-a-brac in sight. The style of Frau Doktor Simserl's house was spartan-cosy—clerical, you might even call it. She lightly ran her hands along the walls and furniture as she passed them but this uncertainty quickly dissipated and perhaps it was really just a form of coquetry, as if to indicate to me that I was not too late. As I took these first steps into the cabin, the house, following her in the conventional manner of a reserved stranger, neither of us could have suspected what was in store for us and what would come to define that afternoon in such an unforgettable way.

We had hardly exchanged the first few words—as soon as the Hofrat was out of her sight, Frau Simserl grew much friendlier and even apologized for the somewhat harsh welcome, but that man simply didn't do as he was asked. He was supposed to have taken me directly from the station up to her house—when I noticed a photograph on top of the dresser, with a candle on either side like on an altar, and in front of it a dog rose in a tiny Japanese vase. The photograph was of a young man, not yet encased in the generous rolls of fat I knew but unmistakeably with the same softly seductive, watery eyes with the long eyelashes, the full, faintly smiling lips, the same shock of thick black hair. She noticed me looking at the photo.

'What are you looking at there?'

'I've never seen such a resemblance . . . an acquaintance of mine . . . but that simply can't be . . . a businessman from Frankfurt . . .'

'That's no businessman from Frankfurt,' she said with a sharpness that spoke pride. 'He is—or, rather, he was, he's probably dead—Lebanese, although his mother was from Vienna, she worked as a dietary chef for a large merchant family in Beirut . . . He was sent to me, the one and only. I saved his life—fate brought us together and fate split us asunder. I waited here for years for him. I'm waiting still, even though I know he'll never come.'

I knew from my parents that their friend Marguerite was prone to dramatics but that mostly had to do with a broken foot or being snowed in or else the scandalous behaviour of the villagers. I was not prepared for the discovery that underneath that burnt pile of ash there still burnt a glowing ember. She appeared to have entirely forgotten I was there and now placed her lean bronzed hand gently on the picture frame, as if she were stroking the hair of the man in the photograph.

'Joseph Salam,' she said quietly, 'isn't that just the most beautiful name?'

I still don't know what to make of the unbelievable story she went on to tell me, forgetting all about the tea she had promised to make. I never even had a sip of water in her house, nor did I sit down, there was no time for such things. Marguerite Simserl was suddenly rejuvenated. No more of the tentative, gingerly steps. As she spoke, she paced and compelled me to follow her to see for myself the sites of these thrilling events. Down there was where she had found him, lying on the bank of the millrace, almost completely hidden by the osiers. Back then, thirty years ago, she only used to come out here at the weekends and in the summer. It was a complete coincidence that she found him. 'No, of course it wasn't a coincidence! Fate delivered his naked body into my arms.' Not stark naked, by the way, he was still wearing underwear, but he had been knocked unconscious and his head was bleeding heavily. Just a flesh wound, thank goodness.

The words naked and flesh, issuing from this head of hers, emaciated from years of subsisting on a diet of carrots, seemed to change her. The sound of those words enlivened her and suddenly I could tell what a vigorous, athletic figure she must once have been—not particularly feminine, more of a skiing companion, good-looking in a modest, boyish way.

It was his business partners who had done this to him, beaten him half to death and thrown him out of their car. I imagined Salam's robust, muscular rotundity—he could definitely take a beating, he was built like a punchbag really, but that time he'd clearly been blindsided. That night these men had come back and set fire to the old cowshed. The flames threatened to jump to the house but she'd stood on the roof with the garden hose. Salam was still in no fit state to be of any help—over there was where the cowshed had been, she'd never had it rebuilt, 'Or will you want to keep a cow?' This was a question that showed that in spirit she was still attending to the business at hand. She never fully drifted off into the great story of her life. Joseph had stayed for three weeks—'I never say three weeks, I always say for the summer.' That was the summer of her life. The villagers lost all respect for her. They refused to serve her at the village shop—which had long since gone under, as punishment, and she had not mourned its passing. But even such unpleasantries were precious if they reminded her of Salam. Because she had heard only little from Salam himself after he left. A couple of telephone calls, a postcard from Damascus. 'He was importing used cars into Iran, that was what he was doing. I was the one who helped him to get back on his feet. I mean, they had taken everything from him.' They had taken everything—this phrase held the key to her complete devotion. Joseph Salam may have been a player but when he played, he staked his life. Taking everything—giving everything—these too were the coordinates of her existence. 'He is the reason I ended up moving out here full-time. I couldn't bear the thought of him coming back here to find the door locked.'

'Did you tell her about Salam's life in Frankfurt?'

'Yes, but I knew right away that it was a mistake. She listened reluctantly with her eyes squeezed shut, as if she were protecting herself from being lied to. I don't think she wished him ill but this was about her—Salam's leading a trivially successful existence in Frankfurt meant that her own life had been stolen.'

'And do you believe this Iran story?'

'Why not? Everyone starts small, although in Salam's case that isn't actually even true. There's a lot to suggest that he started big and then lost it all. Slavina told me recently that Salam's been rich twice over.'

'I can't for a minute imagine your Marguerite with Salam— he's much too vulgar, surely . . .'

'Perhaps it was the vulgarity that appealed to her? Besides, he also has his cultivated side. You should see him when he eats—how daintily he cuts his food into little bites. It's a wonder he can stay so plump.'

'So what's the story on the cabin? When are we going to go there?'

'Probably never, I'm afraid. No doubt because I recognized Salam in that photograph. She must have forgotten all about making a will after that.'

9

BRANDING

Joseph Salam was working. As ever, he was impeccably dressed, wearing freshly polished shoes and one of his slightly too tight flimsy airport suits. It was a cool day but he had made himself comfortable at one of the wooden tables at the local beer garden, an elegant leather portfolio for his correspondence lay open before him and his black telephone, his memory, his archive, his library, lay in the soft cushioned palm of his hand. Out here it was harder for someone at a neighbouring table to listen in, plus you could smoke—Egyptian cigarettes naturally, Salam's favourite. He wasn't addicted but the occasional cigarette was refreshing, like a dewy fresh apple in a Taunus meadow in autumn. Such a simile only made sense now that he had become a regular guest at the Hopstens'. Before then it had been a long time since apples in meadows had played any role in his life. Salam was extremely agitated. He gave a silent nod to the waiter bringing him his beer and then resumed listening animatedly to the long-winded explanations of the voice on the other end of the line.

'Certainly,' he said at last, he understood completely but it didn't change the fact that everything had been agreed upon and all that was needed was a signature. 'I don't understand—in one week you can sign but not today? What's one week going to change?' He spoke these words sternly but then he was evidently presented with an argument that changed his attitude. Oh no, there was no hurry, there was never any hurry. 'Give it time or they'll whinge and whine, that's what I always say—yes very droll . . .' He had just made this little motto up on the spot—whinge was a favourite word of Rosemarie's. His voice involuntarily took on a faintly Rhenish intonation and with it came the jovial generosity of the Cologne accent. Once this lengthy conversation was at an end, the exaggerated tenseness drained from his face. He took off his mask, as it were, folding it away with the same equanimity as he did the piece of paper he had just used as an aide-memoire for the telephone conversation. His mind returned to a state of calm as he carefully considered his next move.

It was autumn but the tall maple casting its shadow on his table was still in full leaf and only occasionally would one of those large leaves sail slowly to the ground. Joseph Salam sat among the gently falling leaves with an autumnal serenity. He looked like a man who has fought many battles and has now found peace and to whom the gradual fading of nature is not a source of melancholy but, rather, an invitation to contemplate his own maturity. As he looked around the garden, his gaze was not searching and appraising, as was generally his wont, always ready to pick up whatever signals life sent him. How rare to see such absorption. And what strange impressions it gave.

Salam's contemplation was interrupted. Before his eyes there suddenly arose a large black T, a T composed of thick, black beams. It took a moment for him to realize that this T had not appeared before his mind's eye but that it existed in the physical world, that it really and truly was there in front of him. Directly in his line of vision, a young woman had sat down at a table with her back to him, with bad posture, her back bent, leaning on her elbows—causing her low-rise jeans to slide even further down and her black jumper to ride up exposing a round of white flesh, and in the centre of this white opening was the black T—the broad waistband of a thong, joined in the middle by the string that serves the dual purpose of covering and accentuating the gap between the buttocks. The woman was pale bordering on doughy and the occasional flashes of her profile did not look particularly promising. Even her dyed-blonde hair with the black roots looked unwashed. But that T, that T on her backside, now that was promising—it promised teasing, touching, titillation, tumbling and tempestuousness. In all likelihood, those black-framed buttocks were fresher than this chain-smoking faux-blonde's cheeks, those glutes were used to being exposed to fresh air. The young woman was accompanied by an older one, to whom she was speaking in gentle tones, although her tenderness went entirely unacknowledged. The older woman went on ranting and cursing to herself, whingeing in fact—and there it was again, Rosemarie's word. Undoubtedly she was the girl's aunt—why was there no doubt? Was it because of the black T at the end? She ordered a piece of plum tart—pasty meets pastry. What did she smell like? He recalled a butcher's daughter he'd known when he first came to Vienna as a twenty-year-old. When he was around her, it was as if he could always smell freshly made sausage. From such synaesthetically charged reminiscences he glided seamlessly into a daydream, a film, in which everything that was in the air was already unfolding.

Salam imagined pulling the thong down over those white globes, stretching the elastic waistband and snapping it back against them, as often as he liked. Laying the girl out on a bed covered in a slippery, cold nylon quilt. Why the nylon quilt? Oh no, that had to be there. He was thinking of one specific, garish quilt in a hotel in Sofia, smelling strongly of moth powder. Sliding around naked on that bed had been an unforgettable experience. Oh the rooms of his sexual conquests, he could see each quite distinctly, steeped in the thick smell of lovemaking that permeated them after a couple of hours. He had just bought an expensive belt at the airport with an exquisite buckle, decorated with the designer's monogram—his brand. What would it be like to brand the blonde with this mark, like a cow? And at that he was already envisaging himself, belt in hand, whizzing it through the air—she giggles fatuously, her pendulous breasts are enormous and as she lies there they reach up to her ample neck. He is about to put an end to this silliness. It has to be rubbed out so that erotic seriousness may be restored. With all his might, he strikes her heavy thighs. She is too surprised to cry out. She puts her hands with those ragged fingernails over her mouth and looks at him fearfully but the metallic monogram has left a blood-red mark, a heavy drop runs redly down her skin—that nylon quilt, it's already a mess, even though they're only just getting started.

In fairness to Salam, it's important to say that he took absolutely no pleasure in actual physical cruelty. Not even with girlfriends who liked that sort of thing had he been able to bring himself to hurt them. So he was genuinely startled by the power of his fantasy, his Technicolor daydream there amid the falling leaves, overwhelmed even. It really got under his skin. His face, which mere moments before had been grinning lasciviously, turned white as a sheet.

He sat there in complete silence. The girl turned round and sized him up intently. Had she sensed what had just been brewing behind her back? So she did have instinct. Salam paid the bill and sauntered unhurriedly over to the two women. He leant over the younger one and placed a business card with his mobile number on the table in front of her. As he did so, he ran the back of his index finger over the soft skin above the T. That certainly shut the yammering aunt up. Joseph Salam straightened himself and said in parting to the dumbstruck young woman, 'I should very much like to make your acquaintance.'

INVOLUNTARY EXCURSIONS INTO OTHER WORLDS

As a couple, the young Schmidt-Flexes had probably never spent as much time in other people's company as they had since that summer when Schmidt-Flex senior decreed that they would be frequenting the Hopstens and subsequently annexed himself and his entourage into their usual open-house circle. Now there was even talk of a joint holiday in Sicily. Schmidt-Flex was also desirous of an opportunity to play the host. Silvi had no trouble mingling in a crowd even though I suspect she was also perfectly content to be on her own. She spoke so freely that it seemed likely she also talked to herself even when there was no one else there. But for Hans-Jörg, these large gatherings were quite plainly a source of discomfort. He was mostly taciturn and eyed those assembled warily. Isn't there something mysterious about people whom no one likes? Whose mere appearance seems to inspire unanimous and unspoken agreement among everyone else to exclude them from the group if at all possible? Do such invisible yet nevertheless acutely perceptible stigmata truly exist as can bar a person from the company of his peers? What purpose would the existence of such a stigma serve? The fact that Hans-Jörg did everything in his power to justify that stigma, assuming there was such a thing, is another matter. But I will insist on the stated sequence—long before he said anything inappropriate or behaved in an embarrassing manner, the others had already banded against him.

And that included me, of course. Even just his penchant for paraphernalia of all sorts! Immediately apparent here in this company was above all the monstrously large watch with all manner of knobs and dials, circling his narrow, rufous-downed wrist, as if to measure cardiac murmurs. He was constantly conscious of the watch's presence and consulted it frequently, playing with the various dials and then announcing with toe-curling pedantry, barging in on someone's conversation, that moonrise would be at seven fifty-eight tonight. In addition to his sports shirt, he also always wore a small bag slung round his hips. He never took it off—what manner of sensitive and important items might it contain? Was he worried that one of the guests might try to steal his driving licence? But for me the worst was his way of walking, which was so unnatural, an affectation so blatant that as an onlooker you simply had to hide your head in vicarious shame. At some point, this leptosome must have recognized the ideal of athleticism in the form of a poolside lifeguard, the sort who wears shorts all summer and whose skin has turned the colour of gingerbread. That broad-shouldered gait, swaying from side to side, where you had to imagine the buttocks tightly clenched, that leisurely stride, dripping with authority in the midst of the cacophony of shrieks and splashes in and around the pool—this was the walk that Hans-Jörg had perfected. The strap of his bum bag circled his waist, the official chronometer measured his steps and as he went to put down his wine glass, he walked as if he were just returning from uprooting trees with his bare hands.

What did Silvi say to all of this? Surely she must have noticed how tense her husband was? Her father had taken an instant dislike to him when he first came to their ramshackle bungalow outside São Paulo, having been brought along by a friend of hers who worked for the German consulate and always had one or two Germans in tow. But her father had been such an unpredictable man. It was very difficult to figure out what he really wanted. You might say that his entire project of emigrating after the collapse of the Reich had resulted in failure. They led a wretched existence in Brazil. Things could hardly have been worse if they had stayed in Germany. On the other hand, the life that was possible within the four walls of that bungalow seemed to suit her father down to the ground. So much so that she couldn't imagine him anywhere other than in his rocking chair on the veranda or playing chess with that old friend of his, the little carafe of schnapps within arm's reach. Her brothers had barely come of age before they all went off on their own. Silvi didn't even have an address for two of them. Their father's bungalow had no adhesive power. Before long, the world of childhood had dissipated and she was left alone with her father, feeding his chickens and sensing that he was just waiting for her to take her leave as well. Not that he ever encouraged her to leave. He was not one to try to grab hold of the spokes of the wheel of fate. But he knew it was coming and was reconciled to it and perhaps even looked forward to being alone at some point, before long even. He loved her, she was sure of that, but that had nothing to do with the difficulty he had living with other people. As her mother had discovered early on.

'Flex isn't a bad family, might even be quite important,' her father had muttered quietly once Hans-Jörg had left. 'Didn't I once meet the son of a General Flex? Didn't they have quite a nice little estate down in Baden somewhere?' These questions were never answered and later on they weren't even asked.

'I find Germans so strange—so very strange—with Germans I never know where I stand,' said Silvi gaily, as if this strangeness were for her a source of endless pleasure. 'My friend from Brazil was just visiting and do you know what she said? She said German men are impossible to figure out. You go to a bar or a club full of young men, you stand around for a bit, and they come up to you and try to start a conversation, usually with some cheesy line but no cheesier than in any other country. And then you make it clear to them that you'd like to be left alone, give them the cold shoulder, pay no attention. And then the most amazing thing happens—they stop. They stop right away! Whoever has heard of such a thing?'

Silvi's soft but firm belly rippled with laughter. The incomprehensible was there to make life more entertaining. Was that the formula for her relationship with Hans-Jörg as well?

Smell quite often plays a much more important role in the genesis of attraction and repulsion than do attributes that are not tied to such sensuous signals. Propriety is an odourless quality and Hans-Jörg possessed it in abundance—this has to be said especially when considering this man whom no one liked. Everything his father did to put himself in a positive light, every form of calculated appearance and self-stylization, was completely foreign to Hans-Jörg. The constant attention to one's own advantage, the deception and flattery, the envy and cupidity—they were all by nature unknown to him. But it took me a fairly long time to notice their absence because he was also entirely devoid of the charm with which his wife was so super-abundantly endowed. I'm now fairly sure that Silvi discovered this side of her husband, possibly very early on, and it was on the basis of this discovery that she had decided to follow him to Germany. She was a creature of instinct, even though it must be said that her instinct had led her astray in this case. As it happened, Hans-Jörg inadvertently provided an explanation for his sullen, brooding, taciturn attitude, at once aloof and mistrustful, and, as always, he did so with complete disregard for the spasms of discomfort and embarrassment to which it subjected his audience.

He had been suffering from haemorrhoids for some time, you see, and had finally gone to see a doctor. Would you believe that a grown man might see fit to hold forth in polite company on the subject of such afflictions—which in one form or another are part of every life but about which for that very reason one is entitled to keep quiet, for how else is one to wrest a halfway dignified existence from the impertinences of nature—instead of exercising his God-given right to keep them to himself? To be fair, he had merely picked up on the keyword 'operation' uttered by someone else in a rather innocuous context, namely Phoebe's appendix, which only conjured up the image of the girl's lovely midriff.

'My doctor would operate in such cases as well,' said Hans-Jörg, 'but only if there's no alternative. Otherwise, he's strictly against operations.' He looked around severely, as though he were reporting on an unpleasant government measure to which every man, woman and child was now required 'strictly' to adhere and with which he, for one, was going to comply. He had had to overcome great personal reluctance in order to show the doctor the location of his discomfort, which he himself had naturally only been able to observe with the aid of a mirror. His distress was alloyed with the fear of being told something that no amount of self-observation could have prepared him for—the unconquerable shame he felt at exposing himself in a less than favourable way and the profound sense that all of this ultimately served him right. The last time he had had to drop his trousers and bend over was during his physical for military service, and that part of his examination had seemed to contain in a nutshell his future as a conscripted soldier. It seemed only too appropriate for the doctor to don a latex finger-stall—was he not in fact an untouchable, someone who could only be palpated with the very tips of the fingers? If he were to die during this examination, if this were to be the final episode to sum up his entire life, would death not have caught up with him at precisely the right moment? His scarcely suppressed anxiety and the not so much painful as vaguely menacing pressure of the examination—were these impressions not in fact the sum of everything that life had given him and that he had made of his life? Hans-Jörg was always a little sweaty, the noble brow that he got from his father forever covered in a greasy sheen, but now he looked as though he'd just been dragged out of the water.

'This can't be how he told it, surely?'

'No, this is how I imagine it. I'm basing this partly on what I learnt about him later on. You've got to anticipate a little if you want to tell a story.'

'But you're not anticipating, you're just making stuff up.'

'I wouldn't call it making stuff up. Do you know that version of patience where you deal a row of thirteen cards face-up, above

*that a row face-down and above that another row face-up? There
was a time when I played this type of patience so often that I developed an almost infallible sense of what the downturned cards were
going to be. And just like this game of patience, every story in life
is composed of upturned and downturned cards and you can figure
out by yourself which cards were face-down—but in the end all
that matters is that the game comes out.'*

'Just imagine if a historian did that . . .'

*'I'm afraid historians indeed do that—but we can stop if this
is getting too wild for you.'*

*'On the contrary. Now just tell me precisely, word for word
what was said between the doctor and Hans-Jörg.'*

The doctor was an experienced fellow, not just any old
doctor. As you can imagine, whenever he fell ill, Hans-Jörg
consulted the family physician. This proctologist had been the
head physician at a large hospital and now had a small practice
exclusively for private patients. Alopecia had exposed a pointy
skull. He was hunched over, hunchbacked almost, and looked
like a wise old dwarf, like someone you could trust, in other
words. Hans-Jörg could relax in these hands, which indeed he
did just as soon as the delicate portion of the examination was
over. There was nothing dramatic down there—this is how the
doctor broached the subject with his patient once they were
safely back in the sparse opulence of his consultation room. On
the wall there were two steel engravings of challenging operations at the Salpêtrière during Charcot's time, put there to
invoke something medical or other. Terrifying pictures they
were, in that restrained, old-fashioned black and white. Who
would want to dwell on the image of patients strapped to the
operating table having their stomachs cut open without anaesthetic? Was this the source of the doctor's reservations concerning operations?

'Many of my colleagues would operate in your case but I'm
against that,' he said in the gentle tones of superior reason. For

acute discomfort he prescribed an ointment but Hans-Jörg himself could also do much to speed up his own recovery. His sphincter, the doctor informed him, was weak. He would have to get into the habit of exercising his sphincter.

'Contract, release, contract, release,' always for a couple of minutes at a time and as often as he could over the course of the day. There were so many moments of calm in the day of even the busiest of businessmen! In the car, reading the paper, waiting for a phone call—a hundred opportunities every day to perform some quiet exercises. 'You see,' the doctor seemed to be demonstrating the work-out, fully clothed, sitting calmly behind his desk, perhaps seizing up for a moment like a wax statue—was this a sign that his sphincter was currently contracted?

'Now you try, please.'

Leaning back in his comfortable chair, Hans-Jörg dutifully contracted his sphincter, keeping his fearful gaze squarely on the wise old doctor whose eyes seemed to be looking all the way through his body, suit and all, passing probe-like right down to the tightly flexed muscle. The doctor looked satisfied.

'You see? From now on you'll just do that every day.'

But there was one major hindrance, Hans-Jörg now interjected, having submitted in silence to so much already. Sitting still in prolonged silent concentration had some very unpleasant, long-standing associations, about which he was probably the wrong doctor to talk to, so Hans-Jörg thought he might have to go see a different specialist. Not at all, replied the doctor. Just such cases that went beyond the boundaries of a single discipline were the very reason he had decided to step outside the machinery of the hospital in the first place—in order to be able to devote himself to the whole human being once more. Hans-Jörg should feel free to tell him what was on his mind.

Hans-Jörg said that the doctor would probably think him insane since his problems were difficult to articulate—visions, he suffered from visions, quite violently, in fact. And these visions would come to him precisely in those quiet moments of the day when he, as the doctor had aptly characterized it, was just sitting around doing nothing. They were uncontrollable, unsettling and emotionally draining and he always tried to brush them quickly aside, but if he must now try actively to seek out such idle moments which he had learnt to fear . . . well, the whole idea made him quite uncomfortable.

The doctor bent his pointy head over a piece of paper, as if preparing to take notes but really probably because professional experience had taught him that for certain patients, it was easier to speak of painful, intimate details if they didn't have to do so to his face but, rather, could imagine they were speaking to an absent party, as it were, like in the confessional.

'Undoubtedly visions of a sexual nature,' he said with masterful nonchalance and noted down, 'sexual fantasies—obsessive thoughts?'

No, said Hans-Jörg ardently, no, no, he didn't mean those sorts of involuntarily salacious images that alight on you like flies and then quickly buzz away again, and that also weren't hard to interpret —a completely different sort of images, completely obscure in their meaning but so powerful that he could not simply shoo them away, instead, they lingered before him like grave and portentous omens, completely occupying his thoughts.

'For instance, when I've just got off the phone and want to reflect on the conversation, I see a hand slowly tearing a white sheet of paper from a notebook. Or I see before me a milky dot with six aeroplanes travelling away from it in a star-formation— what does it mean?' These images were both powerful and fleeting—they terrorized his quiet moments but, later on, he could barely recall them, especially the worst ones. He got out a diary in which he had written down what he remembered of the visions on any given day. Here, 19 July: a wooden pavilion painted light blue with a door that sticks at first but then opens to reveal a woman, naked from the waist down, brushing her pubic hair with a little hairbrush.

'Well that one is of a sexual nature,' the doctor gently corrected.

'No, it's not,' said Hans-Jörg, a petulant stubbornness creeping into his voice, 'this brushing had nothing to do with me! 22 July: A concrete wall, tattered curtains right and left, light-coloured wood, a woman's face, distorted in triumph, literally crumbling away to all sides. I do not recognize her. Or here, 26 July: Light green wallpaper with black hexagons, like benzene rings, in front of a young, slit-eyed face, sweating from exertion, very pale, along with some light-coloured wood. Or yesterday: a wall, painted pink, in front of which a woman's greasy face, with colourless eyelashes, and the certain knowledge that she's a waitress.'

That's enough, thought the doctor, who was no longer taking notes but doodling benzene rings—the hexagons, quite artlessly drawn, now covering a substantial portion of the sheet. Hans-Jörg was waxing lyrical. Now that this long-suppressed phenomenon was out in the open, he felt the need to give the doctor a thorough account of his peculiar circumstance. He said these visions were accompanied by the terrifying feeling of slipping out of his own world, of being literally pulled out of it.

'We can't have that,' said the doctor, now no longer wise but strict. 'You can't just leave your world. You are doomed to remain in it, we all are. It's impossible just to slip out—do you take drugs? Are you a heavy drinker? Even a little can be too much! Cigarettes? Cigars? Maybe cigars don't agree with you—those are some hefty hits of nicotine you're taking, biochemically they're wreaking havoc inside you—in some cases, we even speak of an adrenaline high.'

Not from one cigar surely, thought Hans-Jörg, his face now openly defiant. It was perfectly clear to him, he said, that these images could not be coming from inside him. He was utterly incapable of producing images of any sort. It was a demonstrable fact, well established since his days at boarding school, that he was unimaginative to the point of obtuseness. He was unable to conjure a mental image of anything whatsoever. If in some work of literature or other, for instance, there was a description of a face, no matter how detailed, he could not envisage anything at all. If it said 'receding forehead', 'stocky build', 'fleshy chin' or the like, he imagined absolutely nothing. Which is why he wanted to voice his suspicion —what did the doctor think of the following possibility: Was it not conceivable that these visions were coming from outside?

'From outside?' The doctor raised his eyebrows—of course, they came from outside! Hans-Jörg must have seen the corresponding images somewhere and immediately forgotten them because of their apparent meaninglessness but these fragmentary impressions lingered in some remote part of his consciousness— perhaps because they were associated with something more important which had been more successfully repressed and now occasionally drifted to the surface, like drops of fat in the soup of memory, as it were—something like that was how Hans-Jörg should imagine it.

But Hans-Jörg wanted to imagine it differently, did in fact imagine something quite different and said so to the doctor— no, from outside in a different sense. That the spirit occasionally leaves the body and enters a different set of circumstances somewhere else, perhaps further away, leading another life in another context, and, upon its return, is sprinkled with memories at random, the way someone might return home with drops of water clinging to his raincoat.

'I'm a doctor,' the doctor said solemnly. Hans-Jörg had just insisted on his utter lack of imagination—in his professional opinion, however, he had just provided glowing proof of a wildly overactive imagination, fantasy even. Hans-Jörg was used to strict admonishments and stern 'abasements' from an early age and was likewise used to receiving them in silence and looking sullen while secretly remaining steadfast in his convictions. This mixture of submissiveness and intransigence had always kept his father busy—victories over Hans-Jörg seemed easily won at first but it inevitably turned out that nothing had been gained. The doctor wrote a prescription for St John's wort in addition to the ointment and sent the patient on his way with the words, 'Practise, practise, practise—even when it's hard.'

Poor old Schmidt-Flex, he thought, once the patient had left the genteel quiet of the consultation room.

But the following Sunday, the last before his trip to Egypt with Joseph Salam, when, by the edge of the Hopstens' swimming pool, Bernward cordially, amicably even, asked him why he was looking so serious, what possessed Hans-Jörg to reply at the top of his voice for all to hear that he was just exercising his sphincter? The people seated all around looked at him with astonishment, before deciding he must be joking, even though they had not come to expect jokes from him. But he couldn't just leave it at that. He had to explain to everyone in great detail that he was on doctor's orders to exercise his sphincter regularly, just as he was doing now, to strengthen the muscles in his anus. You see, each contraction pushes the excess blood out of the vessels down there. Silvi was wearing her oversized sunglasses and appeared completely unperturbed, as if the sound of her husband's words were as natural as the rustling of the leaves or the splashing of the water. Fortunately just then there was a commotion in the young people's camp—two boys had grabbed hold of a reluctant girl and thrown her in a high arc into the water, whereupon they had both dived in after her. The swimming pool foamed and ran over. The 'grown-ups', as Phoebe so touchingly referred to them, gratefully welcomed the distraction. Rosemarie leant over towards Bernward and whispered, 'Poor Silvi.' Hans-Jörg ran his fingers through his colourless hair, which was now standing straight up like a cockscomb. He did in fact resemble a peevish and irascible cock that has just crowed loudly and is annoyed by the silence greeting this performance.

11

ON THE EVE OF GREAT THINGS

'Have you ever even been to Egypt?'

'No, never, but I'm not going to let that get in the way of the story. There's nothing for it, I've got to make a detour to Egypt.'

'An evasive manoeuvre, presumably.'

'On the contrary. I'm convinced that that trip to Egypt was pivotal. When Hans-Jörg Schmidt-Flex was with Joseph Salam in Egypt, the entire affair ramped up—to a whole different level . . .'

In the Grand Hotel on 26 July Street there was a large bar. The television was on. A group of tourists had settled in, dressed in khaki outfits with many-pocketed jackets in the middle of the city, as if the busy avenue outside were filled not with the blaring of klaxons but Tartarin de Tarascon's lions. Grand Hotel's heyday was long past, as both its name and address testified. This whole lively downtown area was in steady decline, the new age with its high-rises had long since moved across the Nile. But it was no predilection for the aesthetic pleasures of urban decay that had led Joseph Salam and the small delegation surrounding Hans-Jörg Schmidt-Flex to this place but, rather, Hans-Jörg's parsimony—even though Salam had tried to convince him that parsimony is not a path to success in the Middle East and that, at times, one also had to know how to impress one's future business partners. For his part, he had long since stopped caring where he put up and backed down as soon as he saw how uncomfortable Hans-Jörg was with the idea of having to make a show of opulence in Cairo for people who were still far from being a secure prospect. Winning over some Egyptians was infinitely less important to him than assuaging Hans-Jörg's perennial misgivings. And the latter had inherited certain ironclad maxims from his father who held thrift to be a sign of moral and social superiority. One of the old man's favourite anecdotes concerned his own father, a genuine Prussian Privy Counsellor and Excellency, who had forced the express to Berlin to stop for him at a provincial station where, before the terrified eyes of the stationmaster, he proceeded to board a third-class carriage. That was just how it was done in those days—or was that really just a myth? Salam was getting caught up in the thrill of the chase. The following morning, Hans-Jörg, his solicitor and a certain Dr Steinbrech, who represented the software company for whom Hans-Jörg was a consultant, were meeting with the Egyptian businesspeople. They were Salam's old acquaintances from a series of business ventures that had all been built upon sand or else run into it—this near to the desert no doubt such expressions were appropriate. But had the failures that tied him to these people— more closely than successes could have—not also been the result of the riskiness of his propositions? It was a long time since he had come to them backed by such solid safeguards. And that was precisely why this time there simply had to be a profitable outcome. But for that he would really have to stay focused. Sitting here on his own in this bar, letting his eyes wander, lost in thought but still awake to his surroundings—that was just the right thing to do at a moment such as this. That evening he was going to have to bring Hans-Jörg around again in any case and the sort of sustained volubility which that required was a real drain on his resources, a haemorrhaging of physical energy which did produce results, to be sure, but which left behind a gaping void. All the more reason to sit and recharge quietly in what was for him an ever stimulating environment—a hotel bar.

The khaki brigade of hale and hearty study-trippers were now taking their leave and in the spot where they had sat appeared a young couple whose appearance was far better suited to this somewhat dilapidated bar. A lady wearing a long, gold-spangled dress and a stocky gentleman in a tuxedo. The waiter brought them two bottles of beer, the same brand as his—a local brew that he'd ordered despite knowing how insipid it was, because he wanted to get into the Egyptian mode, which meant not deviating from their tastes. The television was reporting the opening of a Moroccan hospital, the silent images accompanying the voice of Umm Kulthum singing in the background. She had been dead for many years but was still celebrated as vigorously as when she had been alive—that's loyalty, Salam thought to himself and took comfort in that thought. Egypt had not changed so much in thirty years that his experiences were no longer worth something—they were like gold he had hidden in his mattress, retaining their value in spite of the inflation of the present. On the television screen, he now saw a heavily armoured American car pull up, dignitaries and generals forming a guard of honour. A man rushed over and literally tore open the car door, an exaggerated gesture designed to prepare the way for this extraordinary royal appearance. The king of Morocco was short and thickset, positively fat irrespective of any potential underlying musculature. His suit was perfectly tailored but still a tight fit, so that if the king were to flex his chest and shoulder muscles it would crease. Because of his short stature, the monarch had had to think of a way to appear sufficiently regal. He moved stiffly with straight shoulders like a prizefighter, turning only at the hips to greet the adoring crowd outside the ring. The king had a short, bull neck and a short military haircut. His sunglasses were his regalia—he alone possessed the right to conceal his eyes. Now Mohammed IV was making a brief review, accompanied by generals in gala uniform with sabres unsheathed. The officers who had been permitted to kiss the royal hand rushed forward, bending the knee in obeisance and to grasp the proffered appendage, all of this happening at lightning speed—less a gesture of reverence than of quivering servility. The ceremony proceeded like clockwork. Salam remembered photographs of the monarch sans sunglasses, a soft, round, boyish face, pampered and amiable. Salam had also bought himself a new suit for the trip and it too clung tightly to his podgy frame. He took pleasure in his reflection. Even if you had short legs it was still quite possible to give the impression of power and might. All that mattered was how you made your appearance and how well you prepared your audience. He would have to make do without the sunglasses, however. He knew how effective his eyes, framed by those long lashes, were in suggesting trust and guilelessness and inviting others to drop their guard.

The couple opposite drew his attention away from the television. The woman appeared unhappy and perhaps a little inebriated. Salam liked what he saw. No longer young but still youthful, dirty blonde and of a ruddy brown complexion, by no means slender although the contours of her body were largely hidden by her golden chitonesque dress, but her small hands, which she ran habitually through her hair, were decidedly plump, with shiny rings adorning the short, stubby fingers. To Salam, it suddenly seemed that it was above all those little rings that made her hands look less than clean. Her companion had broad shoulders and his dress shirt was probably not exactly fresh. An animal, a real brute, Salam thought to himself and could not suppress a satisfied smile. What might have brought the two to this part of town? Well, what indeed . . . Salam had been round that particular block a few times himself—the woman wouldn't have got in if she had been on her own, surely? But the fact that she was on the verge of tears didn't really fit into the picture. He made an effort to stop staring in their direction. Intermittently he turned his attention back to the television, which was now showing another official visit from a different Arab leader. His attention was only diverted for a moment—but when he glanced back over to the couple's table, they were no longer a couple. The virile bruiser was gone. The woman had calmed down and was staring off into space, not dejectedly or blankly but, rather, as if she were mulling over something very carefully. The large pores on her cheeks were discernible despite the heavy layer of pink make-up she had used to fill them in, like spackled-up nail holes in a wall. Was he actually sitting close enough to be able to see such things or were they mere flights of fancy? In any case, they were to Salam's taste. He found himself imagining what it would be like to nibble at those cheeks. Just then the woman's coarse, masculine companion returned. Strange—he seemed completely transformed. It was as if in his trip to the toilet he had also relieved himself of everything dangerous or threatening. Suddenly this bruiser was nothing but a puny little wimp—Salam barely even recognized him. He appeared literally to have shrunk—what could it be that had given Salam the impression of such power to begin with? He came to the conclusion that it was a mistake to think of the human body in terms of its measurable dimensions as if they referred to stable facts. People existed in different states of aggregation, like water—they could turn cold and hard, expanding somewhat in the process, they could turn to liquid and resist all attempts to grasp them or they could vaporize when their mental temperature rose to an uncomfortable level. This too had to be kept in mind at all times—not just who or what someone was but in what state of aggregation they were at any given time. And in what state of aggregation was Hans-Jörg? Was he petrified and brittle? Pliable? Warm and moist? He had got to find out right away. But first things first.

He beckoned the waiter over and, as he approached, wondered whether the fleshy-handed woman might like some champagne. No, not champagne. He cultivated an aesthetic of moderation when making new acquaintances—never do more than strictly necessary to attain your goal, that was his motto. He opted for beer. The couple looked up in surprise as the bottles he had ordered were placed on their table. He raised his glass in the direction of their table and the two returned the gesture. The woman had cast off her sorrows and shot him a gentle and winsome smile—Salam was genuinely captivated by that smile. He placed his hand over his heart, which was actually beating faster. Where was Hans-Jörg right now? The question quickly drifted through his head one more time. Tomorrow was important—absolutely no two ways about it. Nevertheless, he remained seated when the couple got up with their newly replenished glasses and slowly walked over to his table.

12

INTO THE UNKNOWN

Hans-Jörg lay on the bed in his sixth-floor hotel room listening to the chorus of car horns rising from the wide avenue below. A muted, powerful music, as if a never-ending procession of horns were marching through a roar of wind and waves. But it wasn't really bothersome, not compared to the constant loud hum of the air conditioner. They've given me the engine room, thought Hans-Jörg, I won't sleep a wink. His bedroom at home was wonderfully silent, the air gently warmed by Silvi's childlike breathing. When, in deep sleep, she pushed the covers aside because she was too hot, the scent of her pure body would waft over towards him. She perspired as sweetly as an infant. He thought about her cleanliness, which still attracted him like something new, something he had never experienced in anyone else but which now at the same time seemed like a barrier, like an implicit indictment of the stale, animal fustiness that emanated from him when he awoke beside her in the mornings. It suddenly seemed disconcerting that she had apparently never felt disgusted by him. Did it really not require any effort for her to kiss him on the mouth when he'd just woken up? Even after many years of marriage, she had the ability to transform herself again and again into a virginal young woman, not in the sense of prudishness or frigidity but in terms of a perpetually astonishing shamelessness, unashamedness, rather, of the sort that only innocence can produce. But as exciting as such childlike freshness and such inexhaustible innocence had been to Hans-Jörg in the first months of their marriage, perhaps even the first year, all in all—it now seemed like a barrier between them. As if a glorious iceberg rising out of a leaden, crashing sea, her purity, the physical manifestation of her spiritual immaculacy, rose up before him. What had once been a perpetually rejuvenating joy, this turning back of time, daily, hourly, eternally returning to that initial moment, now became an insurmountable hindrance to his affection. Unexpectedly he allowed himself to wonder whether she still loved him. There was no reproach or bitterness in his doubt, at least not towards her. Was Silvi not bound eventually to reach the same conclusion as everyone else he knew and realize that he was simply unloveable?

The thick smell emanating from his mattress bore no relation to human bodies but to faded spices and the stench of old perfume. For an extra fifty dollars he could have been lying in an appealing American bed but that would be fifty dollars he had not yet earned. Joseph Salam's acquiescence in the choice of hotel, his failure to put up even the slightest resistance to this awful Grand Hotel, annoyed him now. Would it not have been better if he had had to curse and fight for staying at the cheaper hotel? Would there not have been some advantage to having won a battle at this early stage of their collaboration? Salam's immediate capitulation to his peevish parsimony felt like the sort of indulgent pity one shows obstinate old men and irascible mental patients. Certainly Hans-Jörg was well aware that Salam knew how unpopular he was—after all, he'd seen him in a large crowd at the Hopstens' a couple of times, and even a newcomer like him must have noticed what was going on.

Everyone takes an instant dislike to me, Hans-Jörg thought, and that really should be my trump card. I am fundamentally exempt from any obligation to come across as genial and not to spoil the pleasant atmosphere, because it's absolutely impossible for me not to. I could use this to my advantage against Salam. This was a strange idea. Salam had a gently instructive way of speaking to him, like the tutor to a young prince who was being groomed to enter society. Surely there was no room for power plays here? Even just the way he, the Egypt expert, had warned him against going out in the street alone, was a little humiliating. The crowds on Talaat Harb Square were supposed to be full of pickpockets but the same was true of Rome or Madrid. The streets were filled with unimaginable number of people, pushing their way through the brightly lit night—either word of the pickpocket threat had not reached the Cairenes or they were simply all pickpockets. And he was not to speak to anyone or allow anyone to speak to him—prostitution was a dangerous proposition here, Salam warned, even the most frivolous of liaisons could have dire consequences. That almost sounded like a threat, not to mention baldly impertinent. What gave someone like Salam the right to assume that visiting a brothel was a standard part of any business trip for Hans-Jörg? If anything, it said more about his own opinions on such matters. Never had Hans-Jörg felt the slightest inclination to seek the services of a prostitute. He was convinced they would be able to tell from a mile off that he did not belong in their world. Certainly such relations did not depend on sympathy or even attraction but it wasn't as if just anyone could go down there and wave some money around—no, no, he was sure it wasn't that simple. Had he not now fallen out of his own marriage, or rather slipped out if it? No doubt because Silvi was osmotically connected to all the women in the world, which meant that what every woman knew about him had now evidently reached her as well. For a moment he considered calling Silvi at home and putting their relationship to the test of the great distance between them—he would hold the receiver up to the window so that the sound of the Cairene car horns would travel all the way to her little ear in the west end of Frankfurt. At that moment it would seem to her as if he were floating on a huge empty ocean. It would open up a completely new perspective for her, with no room for antipathy and secret repulsion. He remembered that it was only eight o'clock in Frankfurt, no, not a good time to call—eight o'clock was still a time for wakefulness and conversation. This steady flow of horns and sirens only penetrated the semi-somnolent consciousness. It had to be dark. If he wanted her to hear it as he did, she would have to be resting her pretty head on her pillow and, feather light though she was, feeling the weight of her body. He was struck by how little he was perturbed by the certainty that Silvi no longer loved him. It was completely inconceivable for him that there might be anyone else after her and he was completely convinced that she felt the same way. He could not detect any signs of dissatisfaction in her. He saw her complete and utter lack of interest in other men. He remembered her indifference towards filmstars, whereas other women would openly praise their physical attributes in company, often enough producing yawning chasms of discomfort when, in the presence of their husbands, they would describe scarcely veiled fantasies in excruciating detail. He thought of the wild connoisseurship with which Rosemarie Hopsten had once praised a ballet dancer's firm little derrière during a dinner—like two clenched fists that Russian's buttocks had been and she had held up her two fists, adorned with gleaming rings, to illustrate, practically inviting her listeners to feel for themselves. None of this was imaginable with Silvi. He was utterly convinced that she did not compare his body to that of other men. Suddenly he felt very close to her, as if some of the heady air of eternity that she had breathed in her youth had wafted over to him. Suffused in that air, solitude was no longer a source of pain. A limbic peaceful lovelessness flowed through him—at least for as long as he did not think about it too carefully.

The hum of the air conditioner was suddenly unbearable. It was like a constant ringing in his ears or the fearful drone they say deaf people hear. But switching it off meant an instantaneous onrush of heat, like the rising fever of a typhoid patient—the heat took his breath away. From the room's ceiling hung a small chandelier. One of its crystal garlands was broken. He wondered what had happened to it. The chandelier was hung too high up for someone to have tugged at it. He was seized by the desire to repair it. It would have been a simple matter of reattaching the dangling glass cord at one end with a paper clip. Did he have a paper clip?

Hans-Jörg closed his eyes in a gesture of contemplation. A paper clip, he thought. Briefcase. He imagined his briefcase—damn, the image of the open case full of clear-plastic folders gave way to unbidden images, noisome and inscrutable daydreams. What was this he saw before him—a concrete wall, with tattered curtains hanging left and right, not quite reaching the floor and probably not concealing a window of any kind—but how did he know? Never in his life had he seen such a concrete wall, let alone the woman rising up in front of it, pale-skinned, with faded henna-coloured hair, laughing in silent triumph. The laughing woman's mouth was open so wide that the rest of her face all but disappeared behind it, just visible past the edge of her upper lip—otherwise it was all tongue and palate. There was something desperate about the movement of this laughter. It was like the twitching of a large fish, the roof of whose mouth has been pierced by a fisherman's hook—an oppressive image—the tattered curtains were even more frightful than the woman, more threatening, somehow—begone! He opened his eyes. The image lingered for a moment, then faded away and vanished.

What was Salam thinking to forbid him to go into the streets alone? Only now did it dawn on Hans-Jörg just how presumptuous this admonition was. From his sixth-floor window he looked down at the stream of people, the lights, the nightlife. It was self-evident that life went on at night here, wandering about outdoors to distract oneself from the heat. In the darkness at the end of the street stood the mighty palace of justice, menacing in its Mussolinesque art deco. Is it not often the case that countries with an unstable system of justice have such fortresses where the Law is held prisoner like the Minotaur in its labyrinth? A form of architecture that conveys the message to the citizens that it's probably best to make do without recourse to the law and to settle their disputes on their own? The little park in front of the courthouse was a black island, impenetrable to the light from the neon signs and the headlights of the cars. During the day, it was filled with rural families, dark-skinned men and women dressed in long jellabas, carrying plastic bags full of documents pertaining to their long, fruitless cases, occasionally holding conferences with the distracted, hurried judges and lawyers, or perhaps just messengers who came down the steps towards them and after a moment, hailed a taxi, leaving the peasant family perched patiently on the low wall in the dust. Upon their arrival, Salam had interpreted these waiting crowds for Hans-Jörg as a counterpoint to the fast track to success upon which he had set their joint venture—if only the fellahin had had a Salam of their own, they wouldn't be idling away their lives on a traffic island, they'd be rushing up those marble steps and into those dark halls towards an inevitable happy turn in their fortunes.

Hans-Jörg was wearing a light summer suit which, after taking just a few steps outside the hotel, was already completely soaked in sweat. Before him lay Cairo, out of which unspeaking waves of people welled forth, having just performed whatever dark duties in its innards, about which it was wiser to remain silent. He gazed into the darkness of the park opposite. Under the holly oaks silhouettes of people walked to and fro. Were the fellahin families who had come here from the Nile Delta seeking justice now camping there? How different the crowd seemed when you weren't observing it from above but, rather, were right in midst of it. The joyous, even Parisian character of a never-ending urban passeggiata, the boulevard exuberance of it all when seen from above became oppressive at street level, oppressive and dark. Many of the young women wore their headscarves tightly wrapped round their temples and neck like a helmet. This was no promenade, no taking the air in the heat of the summer night. It was a raging torrent from the factory gates, tired and sullen. The noise also came exclusively from the car engines. The flow of people spoke only in a murmur, a general hush hung over the crowd. On every street corner and at the exit from the cinema stood a small cluster of soldiers in thick black wool uniforms. Their rifles had wooden butts and looked like toys. Dozy illiterates—anyone who had even a little money paid to have their son exempted from military service. Hans-Jörg had been spared military service as well, his father's connections had seen to that, without the need for anything so primitive as bribing an official like here in Egypt. Why had his father done that for him, anyway? He clearly sensed that his father actually disapproved of his wish to get out of military service. So that was no way to rise in his father's estimation. But was any day that did not present an opportunity for the old man to draw on his connections not in fact a day wasted? And no doubt the general or minister Schmidt-Flex had spoken to owed him a favour. His father was the last person to allow such debts to go unpaid—for educational reasons naturally, 'People have got to learn that nothing comes for free.' Whenever he said such things he seemed genuinely distressed at the level of immaturity in the world.

Hans-Jörg was immature himself, he was acutely aware of that as he stood there in the throng of people looking over at the murky park on the other side of the street. It was inconceivable that his father would ever have stood here at the side of the road at night, being pushed about by the crowd, staring into the darkness. There were certain fruits that never ripened but, rather, proceeded straight from light green to rotting. In Sicily, he had seen figs like that. They were inedible, at most, you could squeeze out a drop of white milk—next to them, defiant and self-satisfied, stood the other fruit, brimming with ripeness and inner life. Hans-Jörg was convinced that women could tell from a single glance whether a man was ripe or unripe and shrivelled. Even Silvi had noticed the first time she laid eyes on him but to her it hadn't mattered—a man was so fundamentally different, so insurmountably different, that individual characteristics were ultimately irrelevant. But not even these Egyptian women who surrounded him like flotsam in a surging torrent made eye contact. And it's not as if they were all mousey and grey. Some of the women were extremely elegant, with heavily made-up, doll-like faces and artfully enlarged eyes, their hair closely wrapped in diaphanous headscarves, like Gothic queens, in long thin coats that emphasized the contours of their bodies like Ludo figurines. But for these women, he was nothing but air. He felt how their gazes passed directly through him, his body not even presenting a visual obstacle.

All of which meant that he was even more struck by the soft, loose, curly hair, like sleeping snakes, of a young woman on the other side of the road, walking slowly to and fro in the shade of the holly oaks, occasionally stepping into the light before disappearing back into the gloom, only her wide ruched long skirt still illuminated. She was smoking, the little dot of light outlining her rosy mouth whenever she stepped outside the reach of the streetlight and little clouds of smoke enveloping her head when she glided back into the light. Yes, her hair wasn't black, it was light brown, caramel coloured, with light streaks that were tangled—yes, now it occurred to him, like Pheobe's artfully tangled hair—and possibly due to the deceptive chiaroscuro, her skin appeared lighter than that of the other Egyptian women round her, even though she was quite possibly an Egyptian in the old-fashioned sense of the word, a Gypsy that is, a woman who, like Hans-Jörg in his own way, was subject to a different law than the majority of the drifting crowd here on 26 July Street—what proclamations had been read, what bombs had been dropped on that memorable day in July? The question flitted through his mind, as if to distract him from what he was about to do.

Salam had shown him how to cross the street in Cairo traffic —by walking, blinkered and resolute, in a straight line into the middle of the flow of traffic, just never hesitating or stopping for even a moment. Had the young woman noticed him standing there, staring at her from the kerb opposite? Impossible—he was lost in the crowd, no individual face could stand out from the others. Besides, she was concentrating on smoking. At every drag, she would study the tip of her cigarette with both eyes, making herself almost cross-eyed. It seemed it was hard to keep the cigarette lit. The way children smoke. Hans-Jörg himself had smoked his first cigarette at the age of nine that way, before running to his father to tell on the older cousin who had given it to him. There was nothing more important to the young woman than that tiny glowing red dot. She was oblivious to the man risking his life to cross the street in front of honking cars to get to her. Even the watchful young soldiers did not budge. They had no interest in the actions of this European. It was a key aspect of Hans-Jörg's sudden foray that it was almost hyper-public, taking place in a brightly lit, swirling maelstrom of people, you might even say that he was moving from a packed, light-filled auditorium onto a stage shrouded in dark promise. Or was the street perhaps some sort of optical barrier that probing eyes merely glanced off?

The young woman, from close-up unquestionably a Gypsy, lowered her cigarette and looked at him. Hans-Jörg was taken aback but immediately told himself that he wasn't actually all that surprised at how young she was. She wasn't just young, she was a child, a child with the carriage and gait of a young woman, with an astonishing degree of self-possession that constantly seemed to contradict her age not just from a distance but also at close quarters. But her face was childlike with its high rounded forehead, the button nose, the large amber eyes and the little mouth with its soft lips. Close-up, even in the uncertain light, he could see how dirty this child was. Her neck and cheeks were grey, her hair matted. If she had cried, her tears would have carved clear channels through the dust covering her young marzipan skin. And she was short—this too only became clear once Hans-Jörg was standing next to her. He had experienced similar misjudgements before with actors who seemed to shrink in person, as though they had been specially pumped up for their appearance on stage. This little girl was just such a stage performer, possessed of a far-radiating presence. He wondered whether the dirt would be slightly salty if he were to kiss her. What a thought! Hans-Jörg had no children—Silvi couldn't have them—and now the moment had come to be relieved about that. He could still remember only too clearly how perturbed he had been at the sight of the near naked body of the still-pre-adolescent Phoebe, clad in nothing but the tiniest of bikini bottoms beneath which the contours of two fairly swelling labia could be clearly discerned, as, before the eyes of the Sunday guests, she repeatedly dived into the water and climbed back out again, only to dive back in again with what had seemed to Hans-Jörg at the time to be an idiotic automatism—strange how the fully grown Phoebe now hardly moved at all, she had changed from a fidget to an idle lounger. How unappealing that childish body had appeared to him. When she was all dressed up she looked just like a little woman but beneath her blouses there was absolutely nothing there, apart from the full lips between her legs, which he tried not to look at.

The smoking child no doubt looked exactly the same underneath her trailing ruches. What was it that drew him to her? The girl seemed to ponder something as she kept her eyes fixed on him. She was serious. The gentle sway of her hips suggested a dance, a cloud of bright dust rising up round her bare feet and the hem of her skirt. Their gazes were now locked in an unswerving bond, neither party able to turn their eyes away. Why had no one over there in the light noticed them? How long could it take before the military fellahin in their black wool uniforms came charging across the street swinging their truncheons to apprehend Hans-Jörg?

'Hotel?' the girl asked abruptly. It was as if shimmering soap bubbles were coming out of her half-open mouth. Hans-Jörg shook his head so violently and with such a fearful expression on his face that one might have thought she had asked him to savour once more the state of unburdened innocence. There was so little separating him from his doom, he could feel it distinctly, but right now he was still on the safe side.

'Hotel,' the girl said a second time but this time it wasn't a question but a cool statement of fact, an order perhaps, and at that she turned and beneath the dust-laden holly oaks walked without a backward glance slowly towards the light on the far side of the road. And she didn't need to look back for Hans-Jörg followed her as if pulled by an invisible cord, and the girl knew that. She sauntered with determination. When exhaling smoke, she would turn her head from side to side, as if taking care to ensure the equal fumigation of her surroundings. A low wall blocked her path. She leapt onto it like a tightrope walker, played at keeping her balance and then leapt back down again. That was the only time she turned round and assured herself that he was still behind her. But Hans-Jörg had long since lost the capacity to do anything but follow her. His thoughts seemed to be moving alongside him, shaking their head as they reasoned with him, but his legs were slaves to a different will. It's going to cost you, he heard someone say in his ear, maybe even a lot of money. At that he felt a pang but his pace never slowed. Where was she taking him?

By now they were back in the light. The girl weaved her way through the crowd like a fish through river rapids and he followed in the narrow spaces that opened up in her wake. They passed a large tea house. The terrace was full of men smoking their water pipes, not a single table was empty. The men were looking out into the street and saw the girl with her head held high, who shook her matted hair—what would it feel like to touch? Phoebe was always a little coy in her kisses on the cheek and he hardly even touched her. He would never dare to put his hand in her hair. What did the men puffing on their hookahs think? They were locals, they knew the lay of the land—did they also know this girl? What was he even going to do with this child if they ever arrived at a destination? What was he supposed to do with that skinny, unripe body? His body was numb, nothing moved or tingled inside him as he walked, having long since become a spectacle as tea house followed tea house, and Hans-Jörg imagined the heads of the shisha smokers turning to follow them as they passed. But there was no escape from this pursuit of the girl. He had reached the point where he was now laughing at himself—an ugly, strained sound came from his mouth, as if it had escaped his father's tightly pursed lips. At this, the girl turned round once more—looking at her dirty, pretty child's face startled him afresh, her salty cheeks which no doubt promised even saltier thighs. This is the path to disaster, he told himself, never straying far from those tresses. His smile was crooked and uneasy enough. Suddenly a comforting thought occurred to him, filling him with a sense of anticipation that momentarily conquered his fear. What if this child was leading him to that room with the concrete wall, the tattered curtains and the woman with the triumphantly gaping mouth?

'Things have got to come together at last, the two levels have got to merge into one.' He spoke these words quietly, his eyes glued to the petite buttocks in front of him swaying the girl's skirt from side to side. The girl came to a halt. She fetched a new cigarette from behind her ear and lit it with the stub of the last one. He was standing directly behind her—he could easily have placed his hands on those delicate shoulders. He could already almost feel the agile, elastic feline bones beneath her skin. Why did she not keep going? Was she awaiting his touch? Hans-Jörg looked up.

They were no longer alone in the stream of people. Before him stood three powerful, broad-shouldered men in black leather jackets. It was a silent moment. They had reached their destination. The girl had gone to fetch him, as it were, and her work was done. The concrete wall, thought Hans-Jörg. He was about to become acquainted with that concrete wall under completely different circumstances than those he had just been fantasizing about. He was aware of looking indescribably empty and inane, his mouth hanging open. He was not going to put up a fight. He was not going to explain anything. He was going to let it all happen. The second stretched to infinity. The girl looked up at him, serene and apathetic. This was a procedure with which the little creature was intimately familiar, a job like any other. Passers-by glanced impassively at the group, a little black group, in the middle of which stood Hans-Jörg, sweaty and dishevelled in his loss of inner tension. Until that moment he had been walking, albeit involuntarily, but now he would allow himself to be pushed around—the leather jackets were in the right.

And just then a firm hand pushed its way under his arm and pulled him backwards. He turned round. Joseph Salam pretended not to notice the threatening goons or the little girl and addressed him cheerfully. A taxi was waiting at the kerb. Salam gave him a push, Hans-Jörg stumbled onto the back seat and Salam slammed the door behind him. The three leathery fellows crowded round the departing taxi, they put their hands on the windows and voiced their displeasure. Hans-Jörg studied the light-coloured palms of their hands intently, pressed flat against the glass. He was still shaking on the back seat when Salam again thrust his beefy hand under his arm, squeezed his lean muscles and said jovially and by no means admonishingly, 'You don't believe me, my dear fellow—didn't I tell you to steer clear of Talaat Harb?'

Hans-Jörg gradually managed a mirthless smile. The tension began to drain from him as the taxi sped away from that terrible place. He did not turn to face Salam, he did not try to explain anything and Salam did not ask. Had this man of the world grasped the nature of the situation in which he had just found his latest business partner? Or had he not even had time to notice the details? Had the little waif not already stolen away between the leather jackets? And did Hans-Jörg really owe him an explanation? Did it not really betoken a lack of respect that he felt the need to spy on him and meddle in his affairs? What business of his was Hans-Jörg's evening walk? Yes, this was the reward for being rescued from an embarrassing situation—that old obstinacy, that old petulance, they came back as though they had never been away.

Simply going back to the hotel wasn't an option. Salam sensed the need to distract him. He often found himself repeating what he considered to be the golden rules of life—never allow someone to lose face, never let anyone know that you've found them at a dead end, never notice embarrassing missteps. Apart from the incontrovertible wisdom of this rule, it also contained an element of superstition—the hope that others would be just as gracious and tactful in their dealings with him.

Good God, Salam thought to himself three hours later when he was finally back in his bed and it was less a prayer than an expression of profound relief. He could feel it just as clearly as before—he had been in the shower, rinsing off his own and others' sweat, when he was seized by the notion that he must immediately seek out Hans-Jörg. Dripping wet, he had rushed to the telephone—Hans-Jörg was not in his room. His mobile was switched off. 'And at that moment I knew,' Salam said aloud into the darkness of the room, 'I've warned him about Talaat Harb—and that's why he's on Talaat Harb right now.' Salam rehearsed the evening's events in his mind. 'Good God,' he sighed again, and now it had become a prayer, a prayer borne on admiration and gratitude. Salam held a quiet service in honour of his intuition. At that moment, an observer could have studied how the primaeval religious belief in the genius as an external force that spoke to man might have developed. It had nothing to do with vanity when Salam once more recounted to himself what unexpected inspiration had led him to Hans-Jörg at the last possible moment. There were very, very few people who could have done what he had done—'maybe no one . . . at most a woman'. In his thoughts he went through a series of intelligent women. Intelligent yes, but ingenious? And in all this there was no trace of self-aggrandizement, no pride. On the contrary, humility. Piety, even.

13

THE POWER OF MAKE-UP

Rosemarie often woke at the same time as Bernward though they slept in separate rooms. His departure from their joint bedroom had not broken their visceral conjugal bond but then the reasons for it had been entirely pragmatic. 'He would lie awake for ages and read—even just the sound of him turning the pages would drive me crazy,' as she recently told Helga. She made sure she slept eight hours a night, not a minute more or less. If she went to bed at one o'clock her eyes would admittedly open at seven thirty, Bernward's wake-up time, but she had no difficulty closing them again.

'The skin needs sleep,' was her beautician's motto, and the phrase had made a deep impression on her. It had become a commandment that she could follow without making a conscious effort. Ever since she began thinking to herself 'the skin needs sleep' as she closed her eyes, she would drift away into a deep sleep, as if put under by a hypnotist. And it paid off. Rosemarie's skin was legendary, the envy of all her female friends. No one would have suspected she was the same age as Bernward. When she looked at photos of herself at twenty-five she would say, with the gentle hostility of objectivity, that she looked better now than she had then. And after an hour in the bathroom she'd be even more beautiful than she had been upon waking. Her eyelashes were colourless and her face was puffy and a little flattened from sleep. Each morning when she awoke it truly was like being born and having to transform the features of an infant back into the semblance of herself. Rosemarie was right—she had never been more beautiful than she was now. Even her elfin daughter paled in comparison. Her body was bursting with health. Her neck and arms looked as though they were carved out of firm white crabmeat. Her tendency to a certain avoir-dupois had the great advantage of providing ample padding for her skin, which stretched tautly across her amiable curves. Her skin had a natural pearly sheen that mustn't be suppressed by any make-up she put on. It was very delicate, artistic brushwork that she carried out in front of her vanity mirror, like the gentle glazing of a pen-and-ink drawing. Her cheeks were too broad, she found, so to them she applied dark shadows. She wanted her nose to appear a little smaller, so to its bridge she applied very light shades. It was as if she had been taught to paint skin tones by an academic painter, and it was for her a constant playful pleasure to see her eyes grow larger, to make them sparkle, to make her face look less round, to see a stern and solemn expression appear on her face, like that of an opera singer, to the point where she almost no longer recognized herself. Using a large swansdown powder puff that looked like what one might imagine a freshly hatched cygnet would (in reality, they look quite different). She applied a gentle matte finish to certain parts of her face, like biscuit porcelain. She had no particular plans for that morning, incidentally, this work on her mask was part of her daily routine. The facade was not meant to impress anyone. It served to complete her persona—this was what she looked like, this was she—regardless of whether or not anyone was around to admire her. Finally she traced the outlines of her lips in red pencil followed by a thick layer of light red pigment paste, whose nougaty flavour Rosemarie particularly enjoyed. The last touch was the perfume. She used a lot and sprayed it also on her hair and on her clothes. Perfume was also not a supplement for her but, rather, a genuinely integral part of her persona. The fragrant cloud extended her body to all sides. Wherever one smelt her, there she was. The artificial scent created an aureole round her, her presence growing in an invisible and yet physically perceptible way. A person's smell was a declaration of life, the function of being alive. That was true of the stinkers as well of course who in their emanations were even more intensely themselves.

This is how Rosemarie saw it—to exude a powerful aromatic scent was to occupy airspace, to extend beyond the physical limits of one's body and to pulsate, announcing with one's scent— All of this am I.

The time for make-up was an intensive and mentally alert and industrious time. Her hands worked on their own, screwing and unscrewing lids, finding brushes, smudgers, pencils and puffs, tissue paper and cotton wool, while her spirit roamed all the more freely as her eyes were fixed in a meditative stare at the mirror. A subtle sense of unease had come over Rosemarie. She could see the ever uncomfortable moment approaching when she would have to cull from the coterie which had for a while now been agglomerating unrestrainedly and haphazardly. This was all the more unpleasant as it primarily concerned the guest whom Hans-Jörg Schmidt-Flex had brought into the house.

'Everyone gets to be a plus-one once,' Rosemarie sternly repeated the house rules. 'But after that you're a known entity and have to wait for a renewed invitation. It's hardly surprising really,' she continued in a tone of sarcastic self-admonishment, 'that the ones you would have liked to have seen again vanish without a trace whereas the ones you really wanted to get rid of come back unbidden again and again.' Mr Salam had now made an appearance on three consecutive Sundays. On two occasions the Schmidt-Flexes hadn't even been there, junior or senior, and he no longer made any reference to them. Rosemarie had avoided him from the first, and with that radiant brusqueness of hers, a characteristic mixture of hospitality and standoffishness, she had denied him any opportunity of engaging her in conversation. But nor had he actively sought out such opportunities. Salam was a man's man, that was her assessment of him, someone who wanted to talk endlessly about politics, smoke cigars and tell dirty jokes— a salesman, after all, quick with his tongue and always ready to put his foot in any door being emphatically closed in his face. Not fat, exactly—Rosemarie remained grimly even-handed—but somewhat overweight, and if, as was his right, he absolutely insisted on being somewhat overweight, then he should buy loose-fitting clothes instead of those thin Italian suits that he seemed to be bursting out of in all directions. The way his belly, his flabby musculature, his entire lower body was stuffed into that filmy sausage casing . . . well it was positively indecent. Bernward took Salam's appearance in his stride—poor Hans-Jörg obviously couldn't pick and choose whom he worked with. In such cases her husband was always calm and amused and she found this a completely appropriate attitude. The burden of worrying about the dignity of the house rested on her shoulders alone and that was a good place for it to be.

One has to be careful, she thought as she rummaged through her brushes, bad company always drives out the good. A solitary Salam might be all right for adding a bit of colour to a Sunday afternoon. A group mustn't be too sterile, there had to be room for surprises and discoveries but with Salam it was all too likely that any discoveries would be of an unpleasant nature. Then people would say, 'And where was it we met that awful fellow? Ah yes, at the Hopstens'.' She might have to have a word with Hans-Jörg after all—something along the lines of 'Next time, I think, we'd prefer it to be just us.' Having reached this decision, she felt relief as the unease caused by Salam's presence dissipated. There was now not a whit of Salam left in her thoughts. From the sound of her steps on the stairs it was clear that her resolve was completely unburdened.

She needn't have worried about the following Sunday—lots of people turned up but Salam stayed away, almost as if he had sensed something was amiss. The young Schmidt-Flexes were out of town. That Sunday was a pure, unadulterated pleasure.

No, Salam had not the faintest inkling of these plans for his elimination. How could he? He had not spent so much as a moment thinking about Rosemarie Hopsten. His Sunday visits had been so completely focused on matters of business that he honestly could not have spared a sidelong glance for overbearing hostesses.

And so it was that on the Sunday in question he was sitting in an aeroplane from Cairo, filled with the profound serenity of well-earned success. So fully did this contentment occupy his mind that there would have been no room for any extraneous thought. Nor did he have to read in order to keep himself distracted. Simply sitting there snugly—by now he practically needed a shoehorn in order to squeeze into his seat—was enough to secure his happiness. In any case, he was always willing to adjust to the circumstances. I'm going to sit here with my seat belt fastened, I'm going to sweat, I'm going to keep quiet and wallow in satisfaction, he told himself once he was finally seated. Nothing can bother me. Hans-Jörg was sleeping a few rows behind him. He'd had quite enough to do with him for the time being but the contract with the Bangladeshis was in the bag. Life was good. First came the chase, the thorny patches, the endless manoeuvring, followed by elation as body and soul float in heavenly fulfilment. When Salam flexed his muscles—and he really did have some, even if they were sheathed in a Dionysian layer of fat—he was a tough customer. But now he was soft, a knob of butter, open to every impression, there was no watchman on duty to deny entry to arresting images.

Before him, almost within groping distance, stood the air hostess, engaged in the familiar ritual of demonstrating the use of oxygen masks and the location of the nearest emergency exit. A tall, athletic woman with a magnificent, expressive body underneath her tight-fitting uniform, a woman with self-confidence and poise beyond what was required of her profession, her smile triumphant, her eyes coolly radiant. As she stood there free and fully upright before the passengers, pointing out the emergency exits, it was really her body that was on show. The inane demonstration assumed a dancerly quality. She spread her arms out wide. The manicured fingertips hung prayer-like in the air. Salam was inadvertently seized by the overwhelming need to see her armpits, which right then were hidden behind the white starched fabric of her blouse. But he was not even granted the time to express this desire with so much as a wink of his eye. She was surrounded by a crystalline aura that deflected all gazes. Salam knew them well, these crystal-armoured ladies. More than once they had awoken his hunter's instinct, luring it tantalizingly back out of its deep digestive slumber. But here he was robbed of all his faculties. Her body swaying from side to side, she strode down the aisle on long legs, as if simply walking were the source of indescribable pleasure. All around her sat the seat-belted audience, she alone free to move—and oh how she relished every movement. When she leant over the passengers it was as if she were bending down to address a group of children. But there was nothing maternal about her, at most a faintly perceptible trace of pity which Salam, who was flaring his nostrils in an effort to catch a hint of her scent, took as a personal insult. He was in an a priori inferior position, unmanned from the beginning. Just then she was leaning over another passenger who—and this was some consolation—would have just as little chance of keeping hold of her as Salam did. How old was this girl? Hardly a girl— ageless with seemingly indestructible make-up, that big wonderfully red mouth.

'She's a pro.' Salam usually only used this word to describe prostitutes but in this case, it was a statement of awe. Could a plane with her on it possibly crash? Was she not in her self-assurance ultimately the embodiment of flight safety? A woman like her did not board a plane without being sure of its safety but even an unstable aircraft would profit from her strength. Like now, for example —they had only just got off the ground and they were told to keep their seat belts fastened because of impending turbulence. Salam, in particular, was in for a turbulent ride, as the air hostess sat down on a little jump seat facing him a short distance away. She smiled as though there were nothing she enjoyed more than buckling up in anticipation of turbulence, and the straps were very tight, like braces, pressing firmly against the heaving breasts beneath her blouse. She kept her knees together, placed her hands on her thighs and sat bolt upright. The same pose in which Salam had just seen the Egyptian pharaohs sitting for all eternity at the museum, when he had been keeping an eye on Hans-Jörg—even though Cairo certainly had more interesting things to offer than a bunch of old, dead stones. Yes, like a pharaoh, like a queen in her tomb, the air hostess sat. Salam imagined that it was precisely those tight straps and the buckles that closed with that satisfying click that had heightened her sense of inner satisfaction, her feeling of triumph. Salam could feel her looking right through him. Two aquamarine sabres cutting him into pieces. Even when strapped down she was triumphant and her big mouth didn't move when the aeroplane gave a jolt and a disagreeable sound behind Salam indicated that someone had just been sick. The red of her lips, he now felt certain, would survive even a wild night. She was completely indestructible. The rest of the flight was uneventful, the air hostess was busy in the rows behind Salam but he felt a tingling in the back of his neck whenever she approached from behind. This state of perpetual tension didn't agree with him, man of action that he was. If he had got an opportunity to speak to her and she had unequivocally rejected him, his temperament would probably have withstood it quite easily but not this defencelessness, this infantilization, this ethereality. And so it was that a knot of ill disposition grew within him and his enraptured elation turned to a sort of mental hiccup, a tedious stimulation and finally a foul mood. That night, when he awoke in the pitch darkness, the image of that tall, strong woman with the glowing red mouth hung before his eyes. And then it was her mouth alone, the full lips covered in thick, beet red lipstick with little shiny dots.

'Rosemarie Hopsten,' Joseph Salam said into the silence of the night. And just then it was as if celestial hands had reached out for the strings dangling from the knot in his heart and gently pulled at them—and behold, the knot came undone.

14

THE EYE OF THE COCKATOO

Slavina later filled me in on the most important details about Salam. He knew him quite well. At some point, it seems, they'd worked together, if you want to call making phone calls, holding interviews in hotel lobbies and jetting from place to place work. 'Lui sa vivere,' said Slavina who also often spoke Italian, learnt from his mother, which, he said, did not mean 'he knows how to order wine'—that too, but that was a given, and if not, then it was no big deal—no, it had one very specific meaning: 'He knows the price of things.' What a house, a woman, a favour costs. Salam had a nose for money, the same way certain mountain guides can smell snow, even though it famously has no smell at all. Which is why, when one is nevertheless buried in an avalanche, it does not seem like a sudden, unexpected catastrophe but more like a murder in the family.

'I'm not saying Salam was rich,' said Slavina, 'but then what does rich really mean? There's rich and there's rich. I mean he didn't have a lot of money'—he was always careful to specify the proportions in which he was speaking—'but it's true that he landed some pretty big catches once or twice, although later, his luck ran out again. He's a gambler but he knows what's what.' In particular, he had an eye for people. Slavina recounted a small, as he put it, but typical incident. He and Salam had been waiting for the train to take them to the airport. The train was late and they were idly pacing the platform. Salam pointed to a young man wearing a very elegant dark brown coat. 'You see how he keeps looking down at himself, how he's admiring himself in that coat? Look, there he goes again! He's wearing that coat for the first time. Who knows where he got hold of it.' When the conductor came round on the train, the young man with the coat didn't have a ticket. 'I'd love to work with him,' Salam had said pensively as the young man was escorted off the train, 'he looks intelligent. With a bit of guidance he could really be someone someday.'

In his business affairs, he always supplemented the instinctual with careful deliberation—instinct's often ambiguous messages demand to be read and interpreted—but the way he conducted his romantic affairs was a different story. He himself would no doubt have flatly rejected the characterization that he was 'conducting' anything at all in this regard—there was no planning and care- ful execution involved. To him loving was like breathing, or even sleeping. Without question, Salam did not see himself as a seducer, if by that one meant those inveterate ladies' men who cunningly encircle their prey, trying to inspire their fantasies before moving in for the kill. Some men associate love with the hunt and think of it in terms of conquest and hence see their own roles as either martial or predatory but this was a view that Salam did not share. A large portion of the difficulties that many people experience with their lovers, the eternal problem of asynchronous desire, was completely incomprehensible to Salam and he could only have shaken his head at the rich body of literature that fed on that source. But then he didn't read. He wrote his own books every evening on the subject of his daily struggle in life, which then fluttered away into oblivion whenever he drifted off to sleep. If he had been forced to formulate a theory of love, it might have gone something like this—his desire was aroused when a woman capable of quenching it entered his field of vision—the fact that such desire arose in the first place was proof that the woman in question was ready for anything. After all, such attractions were a reciprocal affair. He could rely on this experience, perhaps also because his appetite only stirred when the woman in question was within his reach. A troubadour and worshipper of unattainable beauty he most certainly was not.

And so, the morning after his return from Egypt he turned his attention with sober determination to purely pragmatic measures. He knew he did not have much time. The extended Schmidt-Flex household's holiday in Sicily was just round the corner and who knew what might happen on such a trip. And it was not like he could put his life on hold just because the Hopstens wouldn't be hosting a pool party for a month. And in any case, he had declared war on the word postpone—a ludicrous word with no basis in reality—as if you could simply move a course of action around like a piece of furniture. If you did something on a different day then it would itself be something different, which is why 'postponing' something was in reality nothing other than 'foregoing' or 'abandoning' it, which was fundamentally out of the question. And so, on that morning, a short friendly telephone conversation with Bernward revealed that he was hard at work in his office and would be staying there all day and, in between amusing Egyptian anecdotes, epigrams almost, Salam also discovered that Titus was in Paris with a friend and that Phoebe was doing an internship, more specifically helping out in Helga Stolzier's boutique (today's task was to polish the silver). Then he called a taxi—time was of the essence. At ten o'clock he rang the Hopstens' doorbell. He was empty-handed, not being a believer in bouquets of roses or boxes of chocolates, but, above all, careful always to have his hands free.

The maid let him in. An unfamiliar face—the Brazilian had quit. Did Rosemarie know who it was? She called from her bedroom upstairs that she would be right down—'I'm not beautiful yet.' It had been a late night and she had taken the judicious decision to sleep in. Salam called back, 'You're never more beautiful than when you're not yet beautiful.' No answer. Had Rosemarie recognized his voice? Had she understood what he had said despite the slight distortion of the echo? From outside came the sound of a car engine. The maid was going to the supermarket.

Did Salam notice her departure? Did he welcome it? Did it play to his advantage? Was it part of his plan, even? If at that moment the most doggedly persistent psychoanalyst, able to see through any and all superficial motivations, had turned his implacable gaze upon Salam and submitted him to rigorous questioning, I am convinced he would have been astounded by the man's total innocence. On the entire drive out to Falkenstein, contentedly watching the changing landscape outside the window, not a single thought had entered Salam's head. But it wasn't obtuseness—in such moments he lived completely and utterly in the present. He had no plan because there was no past in which it could have been made and no future in which it could have been carried out. What exactly he thought he was doing was a question he would have been completely unable to answer. And of course he had not come up with any pretext for calling on Rosemarie unannounced on a weekday morning. No 'I left something at your house' or 'I was just in the neighbourhood,' none of that. And the possibility that he might have to beat an elegant retreat in the event that the encounter hit a dead end—that had certainly not been spared so much as a single thought.

Behind him there was a bright snap like the sound of two small polished granite balls colliding. He turned round. The snow-white cockatoo was leaning over and using its stony beak to crack open a tough seed held in place with one of its talons. With its head at that particular angle, the cockatoo's black eye was trained exactly on Salam. Work, for the cockatoo, did not mean paying less attention to the goings-on in the room.

Rosemarie completed her great facial masterpiece at leisure. On the surface, this was an indication of her nonchalance concerning an unexpected, unannounced guest. But was it not also the case that her timeless dedication to her brushes and pots and lotions was a source of confidence? As long as she was busy with that, nothing could affect her. Not then and not afterwards. She was donning her armour. Yes, that beautiful face which at that very moment she was manufacturing with such passion was, in truth, a helmet or a shield. She was herself vaguely aware of this and she felt strong and completely at one with herself, unassailable, as she descended the stairs, allowing her footfalls to echo freely in the hallway.

When Joseph Salam launched an attack he didn't waste time. The task at hand filled his entire body right down to the last cell with an unbearable intoxicating tension. The effect was noticeable. In his rotundity, he was truly not a handsome man but such appraisals are helpless in the face of an aura of confidence and the will to overcome. In classical times, one would have said that Aphrodite had doused her most loyal follower in the light of irresistible charm. Even that morning, while shaving he had noticed that his beard, in anticipation of the events in store that afternoon, had grown more vehemently. He'd seen it before. There was a shimmer of heat and vigour all around him. His eyes were soft and almost feminine beneath those long eyelashes, like in his younger years, his body strong and firm in a brand-new suit from the airport, a thin, delicate shell that he would have been able to tear apart with a single flex of his powerful shoulders.

Cockatoos have no auricles and so it's unclear how much they can hear of what's spoken at a distance. But there was not much by way of audible dialogue anyway. Rosemarie walked in and saw standing before her the very man whom she no longer wanted to see and whom she was determined to strike off her guest list. She must immediately have become aware of his heightened state of tension, his momentary allure. Salam could be an eloquent and entertaining storyteller but this was no time for conversation. At moments such as these his operational vocabulary was extraordinarily narrow. His words, uttered unremittingly sotto voce in an insistent Viennese-Arabic twang, swept aside any and all conventions of etiquette that obtain between a married woman and a casual visitor. It is scarcely possible to reproduce the few constantly repeated phrases in all their simplicity without straining credibility. He said he wanted to 'chanoodle', he longed to 'chanoodle' with Rosemarie. This stuck in her memory of the things he said as he held her hands firmly, as if in a velvet vice, and appeared not to notice the incredulous look of reluctance and uncertainty on her face. Rosemarie had by no means lost her head. That was the thing with the never-before-experienced, the unexpected and unfore-seeable—being completely paralysed while remaining completely alert and in possession of her senses, powerless to prevent whatever had to happen, according to Salam's will, right then and there in the parlour, not two steps away from the point of their initial encounter, from happening. Before drifting off to sleep, Bernward had once read her something of the sort out loud—how a squirrel, drawn as if by magic into the mouth of a snake, sitting beside the nest with its young, will be compelled to move, step by step, reluctantly, wailing and fighting with itself, towards the snake's gaping maw. Except that she didn't make a sound. She shook her head, that provocatively made-up head, but mainly at herself for allowing something to happen that she didn't want to happen but to which she acquiesced out of pure curiosity. Three weeks previously she had watched Salam fillet a large sea bass that had been placed on the table in all its splendour. Evidently he had been keen to make himself useful and perhaps to impress the others with his maître-d'hôtel skills. And now she felt like just such a plump, slippery fish being carved up by his experienced hands, in routine fashion, prepara-tory to being eaten. She watched him, astonished and entranced. He knew exactly what he wanted. His full attention was devoted to her body without the least regard for her pleasure—this was exclusively about him but his egoism did not repulse her. She felt totally stripped of all rights and entitlements because she had kept her head whereas Salam was now obeying an entirely dif-ferent law and was completely unable to register her whispered entreaties of 'please, please'. Actually she was wrong about that. As they lay side by side, exhausted and half undressed on the carpet, Salam suddenly turned to her, wiped away some of the make-up smeared round her eyes—her face, she assumed, was now thoroughly ravaged, her impression of being devoured had not been entirely unfounded—and admonished her, 'Never say please when we're making love, I don't want to hear that again. When you make love you've got to give orders.'

And are we to imagine all of this taking place in the presence of the cockatoo? In a certain sense, that beautiful bird must have been in league with Salam. If, in that tumultuous opening phase of the encounter, which was primarily aimed at inducing a state of aboulia in the victim, it had seen fit to give one of its vociferous shrieks, the spell would have been broken. The cockatoo in fact may well have been the most serious threat to Salam's plan of attack. Instead, it had limited itself to looking on with its round tar-drop eyes in which the entire room was reflected as in a tiny convex mirror. When it blinked it was like the shutter of a camera opening and closing. In any case, the image of its mistress rolling around on the carpet with Salam was now stored in the cockatoo's brain. What did such a creature think when it saw something of that sort? This was a question that Rosemarie asked herself that evening when Bernward got the cockatoo to perch on his shoulder, its beak held up to his ear.

'It seems to me that the cards you've been playing with here were mostly face-down. Basically they were all face-down, unless you're the one who's in cahoots with the cockatoo.'

'I've got my rationale, lots of small observations, but two substantial ones in particular—Rosemarie continued to speak ill of Salam. For example, whenever he wasn't there, she would refer to him as "the Balkans". Whenever he approached, she would lower her voice and whisper, "Careful, the Balkans are coming." Whenever he did something that she considered inappropriate— not getting up when Frau Schmidt-Flex entered the room, for instance—she would make snide remarks about his mother, "You can take the cook's son out of the kitchen . . ." and so on. But he was always there, even though the lady of the house scarcely said a single word to him. And if he was ever late, she was agitated, until *her ironic standoffish expression revealed that he had at last made an appearance.'*

'*That's the one thing—the other is much less interesting.'*

Very early one morning, around six o'clock, I had taken Phoebe to a party where, as usual, she immediately forgot all about me—'I much prefer it that way,' she said later, 'that way we each have something different to tell the other about the evening.' Crestfallen, I was on my way back home and passed by the apartment building that Salam had recently moved into. The door opened and out came Rosemarie, with no make-up and all but unrecognizable, quite youthful, somewhat puffy-faced, her blonde eyelashes giving her eyes a vaguely porcine appearance. I don't think she noticed me. And above all, I think the key to the whole affair lay in her unrecognizability. Rosemarie's un-made-up face was paradoxically not her real face. Rosemarie without make-up was not really Rosemarie and so, it was not hypocritical of her to push Salam as far away from her as possible and to afford him no official place but, rather, a care-fully hidden place in her life. She was ravished by his touch and it was a ravishment that she did not enjoy but against which she was utterly defenceless, just like an indigenous tribe defeated by unfamiliar weapons they didn't know and for which they were unprepared. I imagine she must have been incredibly relieved to go away with Bernward and the Schmidt-Flexes. That was a form of absolution. It wiped the recent past clean. At least until they had arrived in Sicily and her nervous agitation returned.

15

STRUGGLE, VICTORY AND RESOLUTION

For over thirty years, Villa Prisca overlooking the sea near Syracuse had been rented by the Schmidt-Flexes for the month of September or, sometimes, May, if Schmidt-Flex senior had speaking engagements in September. The house was the work of a famous archaeologist who, a hundred years ago, had discovered a potsherd with a verse of Sappho inscribed upon it and had bought the plot of land and subsequently established the house and garden. The house itself wasn't actually all that old but it looked ancient, a great white cube, its rendering, covered in moss and dark cracks, having long since become assimilated to the natural surroundings, girded by holly oaks and sheltered by a tall stone pine. The garden was dry and flowerless. Each step crunched upon the carpet of pine needles. Enormous earthenware urns stood atop weathered columnar capitals. It was a classical, extremely dignified residence for the elder statesman and there were some nice photographs of him, bronzed by the Sicilian sun, silver hair shining, posing in his white linen suit next to a towering agave flower or one of those antique urns. In any case, he looked a lot more distinguished than the long-dead archaeologist who had been small and round, with watery puppy-dog eyes like Caruso—his silver-framed photograph was displayed on the grand piano. Schmidt-Flex had known him personally. He too had been caught in the continent-spanning web of contacts continuously maintained and expanded by Hans-Jörg's father. The property now belonged to a community of heirs and had become something of an *auberge espagnole*—no one felt responsible, the house had an ever-changing occupancy and the housekeeper, who was born there, let her duties slide. At the same time, nothing was subjected to the whims of fashion or to changing tastes. The cold and stiff solemnity of those rooms was simply slipping unceremoniously into a state of neglect. In the outbuilding, a small guest house, there was hardly anything to be neglected, given how sparsely the rooms were furnished, in keeping with that Southern asceticism that does not shy away from outright discomfort. This was where Hans-Jörg and Silvi would be staying. In the Schmidt-Flex family, there was a duty to accompany the parents every September, the old man always needed people round him, especially if other guests had been invited. It was simply practical to have 'the children' (as he called them) there on such occasions as well. And had the old man not retained that tone of voice in dealing with his son, which early on he had found best suited to controlling the child? If ever he wanted to force Hans-Jörg to do something unpleasant, he would declare lovingly how he always had his son's best interests in mind and thus the latter's relegation to the outbuilding— which was undeniably degrading for, really, you could only ask very young people to stay there—had been justified by the consideration that, as his father, he had the feeling that his son really ought to be able to be alone with his wife without fear of interruption or other nuisances, which of course would have been most easily achieved had he not summoned him to Sicily in the first place. And for the sake of that priceless conjugal intimacy, they had even travelled to Villa Prisca a week before the arrival of the whole company—this time, the Hopstens would be coming as well—for, as the old Schmidt-Flexes knew, otherwise, the housekeeper, having lost her sense of initiative along with her master, would not have made up the rooms by the time they arrived. And it could easily take up to two days to get everything in order. Above all, Rosina never remembered to change the mattresses for old Dr Schmidt-Flex. The squeaky, creaking old box springs were so uncomfortable.

They had just arrived. Hans-Jörg still remembered the outbuilding from his student days but Silvi was looking in wonderment around the dingy room with its narrow iron beds and the old marble commode. Rosina had thought to pick a rose and a wisteria blossom and place them in a vase on the nightstand—such gestures of hospitality were still in place, at least.

Silvi opened the shutters. Warm air rushed in. The white curtains fluttered. Outside stood the main building with its tall windows closed with dark green shutters, as forbidding as a fortress. Silvi lay down on her bed. The springs in her mattress squeaked as did the taps in the en suite bathroom before producing a jet of rust-coloured water. Hans-Jörg was chagrined and cursed quietly under his breath, 'The standards in this country!' Meanwhile, Silvi lay motionless watching the flies buzzing around the light in the ceiling.

She was lost in thought. Hans-Jörg's agitated toing and froing while unpacking the suitcases and putting their contents away, his foul mood after banging his head against the low frame of the bathroom door—none of this prevented her from immersing herself completely in her contemplations. At that moment, she was busy pondering the question that had suddenly occurred to her as she entered the outbuilding—was it actually beautiful in Sicily? Was she seeing everything correctly, the way the wise and learned did when they praised Sicily? 'I'm so jealous,' some of her friends had said when she told them she was going to Sicily with Hans-Jörg. Were these people truly jealous of her? Did they know what they were talking about? These were not merely rhetorical questions. She genuinely did not know the answers. But this uncertainty was profoundly distressing to her. Other people issued judgements on a specific basis—they praised or criticized things according to a particular standard and they must know what that was. What did people really mean when they said something was 'beautiful'?

'Come and look,' she cried, having arrived at this expansive question, interrupting herself, 'At first there were four flies, now there are at least ten.'

It was a sultry day. Why do flies always seem to proliferate on such oppressively humid days? This was not a question Silvi was asking herself—to her the connection was self-evident, sweating and flies went together because they were both annoyances. Besides, flies seemed to like sweat. Maybe it was the salt that attracted them, reminding them of other sources of nourishment. The air appeared to have invisible walls, insurmountable barriers, for the flies would always abruptly halt their audacious flight and change direction. They followed a precise geometry, drawing trapezoids and hexagons round the light. One fly was drawing triangles but Silvi might have been wrong about that, since it's far from easy to keep one's eyes locked on a particular fly—wham, and your gaze has jumped from one to another. The flies were like engineers who have lost their pencils and thus have to keep re-measuring a room because they can't write their measurements down. Now one fly was sitting on Hans-Jörg's high, somewhat domed, forehead, another was heading for his nose. He waved his hands around irritably but there was no hope of catching the flies. They were quick and saw from a mile away every clumsy human movement coming, perhaps due to the tiny rush of air brought on by the mere flexing of one's muscles in anticipation of the blow. But it was as if the flies wanted to show him just what they thought of his evasive measures. There really were more of them now. Did the humid air actually spawn flies after all, thick and heavy and material as it was, carrying fly semen and fly eggs along with it?

'It's because the window's open,' Silvi remarked calmly. She remained motionless as though the flies had not yet discovered her. Hans-Jörg was enraged. Had they really travelled all the way to Sicily just to suffocate in the heat of an enclosed space? Silvi hadn't actually asked him to close the window but she knew this about him—he always mistook an observation for an attack. He stormed out and returned a while later with Rosina. Flies, he fumed, flies everywhere. Rosina could explain. The gardener kept goats and rabbits right behind the house.

'We're living in a goatshed,' said Hans-Jörg bitterly. His father's *façon de parler* about the couple's peace and quiet now seemed a deliberate provocation. He wasn't going to stand for it. After all, it was perfectly clear that having him stay in the guest house was another of his father's 'abasements'.

Rosina, wearing a blue-and-white-striped smock over her rotund figure, the very picture of a cook—if only she would do some cooking, but it had been arranged that she would do that only once the guests at the main house had arrived—cocked her thick-haired head to the side. She said she might have some spray in the main house. At this, Hans-Jörg turned to her in earnest and haughty condescension. A spray was absolutely out of the question. Would she have them sleep in clouds of noxious gas? Not only were they relegated to the goatshed, now they were to be poisoned to boot. Rosina shrugged her shoulders. No doubt, she had not understood everything he had said in his somewhat patchy Italian. Besides, it was time for her to go home. Her husband was waiting for his dinner.

But Hans-Jörg's fury and distemper had now given way to an urgent need for action. An immediate solution had to be found to the fly problem. Still holding forth, he walked Rosina to her small car that was parked some distance from the house. Silvi watched the ceiling, watched the flies at their restless geometry, breathed in the warm air and sank into a deep sleep.

She awoke to find a grey-haired man in a vest, his arms and chest covered in a thick, steel grey pelt, standing on a wobbly chair in the middle of the room. He was in the process of sticking a strip of golden yellow paper steeped in adhesive syrup to the lamp. Below him stood Hans-Jörg, observing this technical operation with a furrowed brow, not sparing his advice, 'a bit to the left' and 'right, a bit'. The chair's wickerwork was old and desiccated. It would probably have grudgingly supported Silvi's weight but not the heavy gardener's. With a crash the seat of the chair gave way, the gardener clinging, as a last resort, to the flypaper before crashing down through the chair which, for a moment, held him upright at the knee before both man and chair, tangled in flypaper, collapsed on the floor. But this was a mere ritardando. The gardener had escaped with a fright. The yellow strip was still in place, gleaming in the sunlight. The man left but not before advising them to shut the window. The mild aroma of artificial honey hung in the air.

Hans-Jörg was overcome by a novel sentiment. Abruptly the black bile that had consumed him since his arrival at the outbuilding gave way to the urge to hunt. A moment before, each individual fly had been further cause for outrage, now there could only be too few. Even when one of them alighted on him, he refrained from brushing it off too vehemently, as if he were trying to lull the flies into a false sense of security. And what's this? Now he had even closed the window. Then he lay next to Silvi on the bed and stared at the glistening lock of amber still swinging. He did not have to wait long.

There—the first fly flew at full tilt just past the syrupy strip, barely grazing it with one wing, but that was enough. It was stuck by that one wing, no matter how desperately and vigorously it struggled. The second fly banged its back against the glue, it too struggling but in vain. It could not break free. The third alighted confidently with all six of its legs. Once it discovered that it was trapped, it whirled its wings like propellers. You could almost hear it. Hans-Jörg was enjoying the show. Soon, the syrupy garland was covered in squirming, dithering creatures. The force of the flies' death throes caused the strip to swing gently.

'That's not nice,' said Silvi, as if in a dream. 'Oh yes it is, it's very nice,' Hans-Jörg replied, not in the least annoyed at the contradiction but with inspired fervour. 'Imagine a witch with strips of flypaper covered in living flies for garters—one of Shakespeare's weird sisters.' He was certainly well read, his papa had seen to that at least.

'Oh, now this really is too much for me.' Silvi got up and left the room. She returned with Rosina's spray can, having intrepidly searched the innumerable pantries and storerooms connected to the orphaned kitchen in the main building until she found the first rat trap—the insecticide couldn't be far away. Flies, ants and cockroaches each had their own special spray— the variety spoke volumes. It was remarkable that Hans-Jörg did not protest when she began spraying the room. He slid lamely off the bed, as if all the *Schadenfreude* had left him exhausted, drained and confused. He looked at her in bewilderment but as soon as the first wisp of poison reached his nose, he was gone. He waited in front of the house until Silvi had used up the entire can, breathing in the toxic fumes without a second thought. It had no effect on her—Hans-Jörg was sure it was all a question of the right attitude, whether poison like that was harmful or not. And there was something so down to earth about Silvi that the poison ended up neutralizing itself.

They went for a walk, first in the direction of the garden gate, far away from the house, but when they saw the cars racing past on the narrow road outside, they quickly lost their desire to leave the garden. In the orange grove below the villa, they forgot all about the traffic on the road. In the dark, leathery foliage, the oranges shone in their hard-skinned perfection, as if they were the trees' ancient jewellery, dating back to the time of the cracked urns. The ground, however, was covered in rotting oranges, abuzz with bees. Silvi's beautiful round forehead was covered in sweat but it looked appe-tizing on her, as if only adding to her freshness. Her eyes and lips gleamed, her gaze as shiny as polished stone. Hans-Jörg felt sticky and unclean. When she put her hand on his shoulder to steady herself on a low step, he recoiled because his shirt was completely soaked. Did it really not disgust her? Was she so secure in her cleanly nature that she thought her sweet smell would rub off on him? She picked an orange. As she reached into the leaves and loosed the golden orb from the branch with a gentle twist, it presented almost too lovely a picture. She dug her tiny opalescent thumbnail into the rind and quickly peeled the orange but as she began to divide it up, a straw-like, desiccated interior came into view. They strolled back to the outbuilding in silence. When she opened the door, she stopped short—what an inconceivable number of flies had been living in that room! There were dead flies everywhere, a vanquished, massacred army. Hans-Jörg took a step past Silvi into the room. The bursting chitin armour crunched beneath the soles of his shoes, the sound filling him with secret satisfaction, like the enjoyment he had felt as a boy stepping on snowberries and hearing them pop.

'Now I know what we'll do,' Silvi said, as if speaking to herself. She still had no answer to the many questions she had asked herself but something else had become clear to her. 'We'll move into the main house right away or else we'll go to a hotel.' Rosina and the gardener were nowhere to be found. They spent a long time carrying their many bags and belongings over the gravel and up to another bedroom and filling the naphthalene-smelling drawers of the large dressers there. The wardrobe was so tall that the hangers had long wooden handles attached to them—toy swords they were. A fly buzzed through the room but it quickly found its way back into the open air.

16

LITTLE CAUSES—AND EFFECTS

All the chairs and sofas in the great parlour were still draped with dust covers and it did not occur to Silvi to remove the sheets since she did not, out of principle, as it were (if she had principles at all), ever change any aspect of her surroundings from the way in which she had found it. And in her presence, Hans-Jörg forewent his ideas about things. He observed her and contemplated her but he only seldom shared with her the results of his cogitations, insofar as there were any. They were like two people who have been brought together by chance in a deserted house and who were now trying to make themselves provisionally comfortable there. For Silvi, this was the most appropriate way to live—she did not expect to feel at home anywhere, not now that she had left her father's decrepit bungalow, the 'fur farm', as his friends used to call it, even though no mink had ever been raised there. How effortlessly the bulldozers had flattened that house, it had been like watching a blackboard being erased. There may have been a certain amount of self-interest involved in old Schmidt-Flex's decision to send his son and daughter-in-law to Sicily ahead of everyone else but he actually couldn't have done them more of a favour—this uninhabited and somewhat inhospitable house with its evergreen (which in practice meant everdead) garden, this petrified world, blackened by the remorseless sun, gave one the sense that one had been there for a long time and that one would never leave. On the terrace under those high arcades in the shade, surrounded by the leaves that looked even darker against the overcast slate-grey sky, the two of them could talk, lying side by side on the wicker recliners, without looking at each other, sharing a bottle of wine and gradually coming out of their shells. Silvi had made another foray into the large kitchen wing which was hidden behind the scenes and ideally went unnoticed by visitors, for although Rosina kept up a certain degree of order in the living quarters and dusted regularly, she allowed the kitchens to languish in an uncharitable state. The cupboards with the glasses were sticky, the dented pots and pans looked as though they had been set aside for the next flea market. Atop the large refrigerator stood a picture of Saint Agatha, carrying her breasts on a platter before her, like Rosina serving her desserts, the candle in front of the picture burnt almost all the way down. But inside the fridge, there was a large clouded demijohn of local white wine which she took out onto the terrace. It was quickly depleted. The wine was fresh with a hint of resin and went down like water. Before long each had drunk several glasses, the large bottle was half empty and the condensation had long evaporated. Silvi was never bored, she didn't have to read and when she was alone with Hans-Jörg, she also didn't talk in order to pass the time. Time wasn't there to be passed, it was supposed to spread out like a warm ocean inviting you to go for a swim. They sat there in silence but it wasn't an awkward silence, it was a habitual silence, one that's not so easy to snap out of.

He rose and walked slowly in the direction of the outbuilding, she could still hear his footsteps on the gravel when he was well out of sight. She knew what he was looking for over there—the little box of Havana cigars he had bought at the airport. They had forgotten them when moving into the new room or, rather, not really forgotten—Silvi had noticed the box lying on the bedside table as she left the room but thought no more of it. But the fact that she now immediately knew that Hans-Jörg had gone to fetch his cigars showed that a certain undeniable bond had developed between them. He walked with a slight stoop, even though he wasn't tall by any means, and yet, he always looked as if he were ducking his head to go through a low door. His bad posture had something obstinate about it—others might have good posture, his father foremost among them, ramrod straight with his head thrown slightly back—but he didn't care. He did not belong in a world that valued good posture. Was he handsome? This was a question that Silvi asked herself for the first time there on the quietly creaking wicker recliner. When they were introduced back in São Paulo, her half-German friend Ingrid had mentioned it so self-evidently and appreciatively—Hans-Jörg was really handsome, she'd said, 'rather dashing' (Ingrid's father was from Vienna and many miles from home, such old-fashioned expressions lived on). Ingrid and everyone else seemed to know exactly what it meant to be handsome. Something other than beautiful, certainly. Men weren't beautiful but handsome. Hans-Jörg wasn't beautiful, that went without saying, since beauty involves a certain radiance, a triumphant victoriousness of which there was no trace in Hans-Jörg. Not that she missed it but she was unsure what being 'handsome' entailed, that everyone seemed to refer to it with such unhesitating certainty. In the past few days, he'd got some colour, imbuing the suety pallor of his forehead with a hint of freshness. That was an improvement, although Silvi felt an undefined aversion to imagining him tanned—it would have seemed like a disguise. Better he stay the way he was. But what she was supposed to think of his appearance was no greater a mystery to her than what he might think of her. Was he happy with her? Were his at times galling criticisms, his grumbling and saturninity, just the expression of sporadic mood swings or was there more behind them? What did Hans-Jörg want his wife to be like? Was she supposed to be like his mother or like Rosemarie Hopsten? If so, he was significantly wide of the mark with her. What was marriage anyway? She had observed it in other people—Rosemarie and Bernward Hopsten, for instance, that rock-solid institution of a married couple—but the notion that what she had with Hans-Jörg was a marriage was nothing but a word to her. She just couldn't see it, her own marriage— it was invisible to her. There seemed to be an assumption that being married somehow had something to do with having children. She shuddered at the thought of being suddenly saddled with a little speechless creature and being responsible for its well-being, she who was so clearly incapable of defining even her well-being. But it would have been quite unlike her to take a stand against having children, just as she very seldom took a stand against any unpleasantries she was asked to endure. Her firm decision to move into the main building was quite uncharacteristic of her. Hans-Jörg was in perfect health, as he had informed her with accusatory pride. Once he had undergone certain tests, she too had allowed the gynaecologist to examine her and had overcome her reluctance to answer his questions, and she found it at least as onerous to inform Hans-Jörg of the equally positive results of her examination—no, it wasn't her fault either that they had no children. It was incomprehensible why they had to go to such lengths to dig around in this state of affairs. If suddenly they had had a baby, she would have made a genuine effort to adjust to this new circumstance but having to talk about it and to deliver reports to her parents-in-law, that was pure torture. Was Hans-Jörg within his rights to expect this of her? Were there rules for these things? It was sad that her father was so far away, even though she knew that by now you couldn't even discuss chess problems with him. His mere physical presence would have reminded her of the years of vegetative well-being she had spent with him in that little bungalow. Back then everything you thought and did was self-evident, you didn't need a reason, let alone a justification for it. She didn't understand how he could not have warned her against allowing herself to fall into the hands of an outsider, someone who had different blood in his veins than she did.

When Hans-Jörg returned with his box of cigars, she was lost in these questions. If he had said something to her, she would not have been in a position to respond. There truly were spaces inside the self. One could take a stroll through one's thoughts that transported one spatially away from the present so that it took as long to return to it as if one had to walk a hundred yards.

In keeping with his predilection for paraphernalia, Hans-Jörg always carried specialized instruments for his cigars. And he now proceeded to lay out on the balustrade not only a special cigar lighter but also a special guillotine cutter and a small golden cigar drill that popped out of its metal casing with a twist. He had even found an ashtray. Silvi watched as he removed a cigar from the box. It suddenly seemed that he was very small, as if she were looking at him through the wrong end of a telescope. How serious and workmanlike was his approach to that cigar! It was clearly infinitely important to him. Handling and preparing it properly was of the utmost significance. He was now in a place in which she had never set foot, a place where he ruled with an expertise that afforded him profound satisfaction. The hobbyist. The smoke from the first juicy puffs created a tent round him, a tent which had proved its utility, not least in the presence of his father who was too much a man of the world to prohibit cigar smoking in his presence but who, in his role as duty-bound mentor to his son, never missed an opportunity to mutter the words lip cancer, tongue cancer, throat cancer under his breath. Shrouded in smoke, Hans-Jörg grew a little. He experienced a sense of independence, to which his careful preparations were a significant contributing factor. There are certain skills that set a man apart from his peers. He sucked the thick end of the cigar intensively. His lips puckered up and enveloped the round brown shaft. It was hard work, you had to keep at it. At first there was not much smoke but gradually the cigar began to draw admirably despite a certain wetness. Copious warm clouds of smoke poured forth from Hans-Jörg's mouth. From her recliner, Silvi watched as he tried to blow smoke rings without much success and as he literally consumed the cigar, practically devoured it. He was utterly engrossed in this activity.

I'm glad he's got his cigars, thought Silvi, now he's got what he needs. She drifted off. In her initially dreamless slumber, she sank to the level of her father's house, into her uneventful state of pure being in which she had presumably been happy.

When she awoke, Hans-Jörg was taking the final puffs on his cigar. It was gurgling, bitter, dark brown tobacco juice running out of the stump—that's how fresh it had been. In this regard, Hans-Jörg differed from most connoisseurs who typically stopped smoking when there was still a quarter or so left of the cigar. With Hans-Jörg, thrift trumped connoisseurship—he was less bothered by the mounting bitterness than by the thought of letting the valuable remains go to waste. Although cigar handbooks which he consulted avidly warned cigar smokers against removing the cigar band since there was a chance that the glue was stuck to the wrapper and would damage it if removed, he always removed the band but he did so with such care, employing a small, razor-sharp blade, that he could proudly claim never to have incurred such damage. And it was with this sense of pride derived from this diligently consumed pleasure that he threw the glowing stump in a high arc over the balustrade into the impenetrably overgrown depths below.

'Did you just throw your cigar over the wall?' Silvi was still speaking as if in a dream.

'Why?'

'Isn't that dangerous?'

Hans-Jörg sat bolt upright. A hot wave of fear rushed through him. He felt as though his heart had stopped. Every newspaper story he had ever read about wildfires caused by discarded cigarette butts suddenly emerged from his memory, along with his biting scorn for people who were so careless. He leapt to his feet and looked over the balustrade. It was a long way down but you could hardly see the ground because the entire substructure supporting the terrace was covered in an impenetrable wall of thorns, a bramble thicket that over the decades had grown into a jungle. The surface was an armour of reddish-green leaves but the interior, where the light could not penetrate, was a thick and desiccated tangle of branches. He stared into that gloom, looking for a glowing red dot. In the darkness, it couldn't very well hide. Isn't that what they said—that the glow of a cigarette at night was visible for miles? Surely you could rely on experience in such matters and if not then what good was experience anyway, if it did not serve as a guide in an emergency such as this? And what if the cigar had wound up beneath the undergrowth and was now quietly smouldering away out of sight? How long did a cigar keep burning unattended?

Without a word to Silvi he rushed out of the arcade. Further along, a steep path led down to the lower level. He slid more than walked down it. At the bottom lay a neglected meadow out of which grew the towering fairy-tale brier, almost completely obscuring the house above. Evidently the gardener had given up on this part of the property. But worse, he had used the thorn bush to dispose of the dead holly oak leaves and had been doing so for years on end no doubt. The jungle of brambles rose out of dense pillows of dried leaves. If a spark should fly into the midst of all that—Hans-Jörg didn't even need to complete the thought, before his mind's eye he could already see the mountain of brambles transformed into a towering wall of fire.

He was wearing a short-sleeved polo shirt, his feet bare except for a pair of thin slippers, but he now hurled himself headlong into the thicket, allowing the thorns to scratch his forehead, arms and feet as he plunged forward through the brier. He paused to sniff the air—if there were any smoke he would have been able to smell it by now, surely? It wasn't fair. The butt was lying there somewhere as quietly as a mouse, smouldering away. But when the first flame caught, it would already be too late.

He couldn't see anything. He couldn't smell anything. But that didn't mean anything. The garden hose that the gardener used to water the geraniums in the clay vases above! He fought his way back out to the meadow. His feet, hands and face were covered in rivers of blood mixed with sweat. On the steep path he stumbled. He thought about not getting up, just lying there and waiting for the fire, perishing in the flames, then his guilt would be consumed along with him. He staggered to his feet. He looked a fright.

He found the tap. Sure enough, there was water. The hose was dripping. Where exactly had he thrown the butt? He tried to reconstruct it in his mind. The water came out in a thin jet. It was from a cistern, which must have been almost empty. He ran back and forth with the hose, making it rain into the brier— it sounded like a gentle summer shower. He threw the hose back where he'd found it and ran back down the steep hill. Everything was as dry as dust. The water could not penetrate the thicket at all. No, there was no doubt about it—the gardener was the guilty party here. That infernal Southern laxity, the indolence that bred disaster! But while there was no sign of the water, nor was there any sign of smoke, and by now the cigar had had at least a quarter of an hour to burn its way into the dry leaves.

Silvi had remained calm this whole time, impassive even. Her question had caused him to panic but she herself was unaffected. She saw him in his sorry state and the sight of him filled her with compassion. She felt the need to wipe the blood from his dripping brow, she truly wanted to, but she was unsure whether he would react with gratitude. Hans-Jörg was so wound up that it was probably wiser to leave him in peace.

'Let's go for dinner,' she said casually, as if there were no danger in the air. As he stood in the shower—the water pressure from the ancient showerhead was also only middling—he watched the blood run down his legs and disappear, diluted, down the drain. At least there was running water in the house, the sound alone must be enough to keep any advancing blaze at bay.

They had dinner at a nearby restaurant. Wasn't that a police siren? But it was gone in an instant. It must have been some other calamity. Something bad had just happened to someone else, not Hans-Jörg—he could finish his fish unhurriedly. On the way back, before they turned onto the drive, he was nevertheless convinced he would return to find a raging inferno. The blackness, the exhausted warm breath of darkness that greeted them seemed unreal. He was walking in a dream. The house was not on fire—as if it had never been in danger of catching fire, as if nothing could have been more unlikely. He performed another quick inspection of the terrace wall, re-injuring himself in the process. His cigar had been a pitiful thing, feeble, its tiny ember utterly impotent. It would have taken quite a lot for such a thoroughly smoked cigar butt to set fire to anything at all— no spark, no rosy nest, no smouldering remains, nothing was left of it. The next day his parents would arrive. If by then the fire still hadn't started, if it waited until his father was there, then it would be the old man's responsibility. This was what Hans-Jörg told himself.

17

A WASP, A DRESS

Silvi never went on a trip without forgetting something, much to Hans-Jörg's chagrin, who really didn't want to be stingy but had to overcome an innate reluctance whenever they were required to buy things they already owned. This time there was an easy solution—because Silvi and Hans-Jörg had been appointed vanguard and quartermasters, they could make requests of the rest of the company who would be arriving later. The light summer dress, more than welcome in the Sicilian heat, had already been taken out of the wardrobe. It must still be laid out somewhere in the bedroom, they said, but had by accident not been packed along with everything else. Bernward Hopsten was happy to relieve Silvi's mother-in-law of the burden of having to worry about the dress. The old couple had enough to attend to in preparation for the long journey. Bernward thought he detected a slight note of exasperated exhaustion in Frau Schmidt-Flex's voice which this long-suffering woman ordinarily did not permit herself but which an astute observer would have discovered immediately beneath her detached and affable facade. It was as if she had come to an arrangement with her fate—that she would bear the current state of affairs quietly and without objection so long as she was not obliged to shoulder any additional burden. And this particular burden could easily turn out to be the proverbial straw that broke the camel's back. But it was not necessary to cry for help in order to receive it from Bernward—he was generally only too happy to oblige. And that was true of this case in particular.

Although their frequent social interactions that summer entitled him to regard both generations of Schmidt-Flexes as friends—at least what passed as friends in those circles—and they were now even going on a joint holiday, he had never visited the younger couple's flat. He and Rosemarie had on a number of occasions been the elder Schmidt-Flexes' guests at their acutely conventional villa, abundantly decked out in mementos of a life in the public eye and official visits, and had had explained to them the photographs adorning the grand piano, depicting Schmidt-Flex in the company of two popes, three American presidents and sundry German Nobel Prize laureates. The world's dignitaries have to submit to the same ritual as cruise-ship captains who are required to pose for photographs in their white uniforms with each individual passenger. Helga Stolzier was very curious to know what it was like at the Schmidt-Flexes', and Rosemarie dismissively filled her in— heavy, upholstered furniture, Persian rugs, chandeliers, 'all terribly bourgeois'. They had even got a Riemenschneideresque *Madonna and Child*. Helga felt both relieved and disappointed by these details. It was clear that the Schmidt-Flexes would not be exerting a dangerous influence on Rosemarie but at the same time they were also unlikely to patronize Helga's boutique. 'Don't be absurd,' Rosemarie snapped, 'they're not buying anything! The only thing those two will be buying is their coffins!'

But now Bernward would be going into Silvi's flat without her being there—a strange feeling. He really did think of it only as Silvi's flat incidentally. He did not spare Hans-Jörg a single thought. Why would he? It's generally the women who are in charge of the domestic space. If you had asked Hans-Jörg how he wanted his place to look, he probably wouldn't have known what to tell you. Giving one's individuality free rein to spread out in the flat and not only to pass judgement on aesthetic choices but actually to influence the taste with which they were made and thus settling on a particular image of one's self—nothing could have been further from that man and probably this was actually a sign of superior character—not placing too much stock in one's life.

Bernward had once walked into the guestroom that had been made available to the young Schmidt-Flexes at weekends just as

136

Silvi was taking off her shirt, her head completely obscured. Bernward had immediately taken a step back but really there hadn't been much to see. By the swimming pool, the whole world had ample opportunity to study her breasts in that skimpy bikini and, yet, now as he stepped into the empty flat, it felt similarly transgressive, certainly not a neutral act. He had picked up the keys from the neighbours. They handed them over with complete nonchalance, as if there was nothing untoward about the whole affair. He turned the key in the large double-wing front door, designed to allow heavy furniture to be carried in and out with ease. It was hardly surprising that the young Schmidt-Flexes should live in such a spacious pre-war flat. Among the city's still relatively youthful business class it was more or less de rigueur. The lock was well oiled. The door swung open. Bernward stepped inside, letting the door close behind him, which it did with a satisfying thud, the panes of cut glass rattling. He was now standing in Silvi's flat, in the foyer, the light entering through the open doorway into the adjoining room.

For a while, he stood motionless. The doors opened up several possible paths. He had heard the boards of the yellow parquet creak at his first few steps. The floor resonated strongly with every step—it was like walking on the taut skin of a drum. It was as if visitors' steps were being recorded. If Bernward were to wander around out of pure curiosity, would anyone be able to tell afterwards? This last thought took him by surprise. Far be it from him to conduct inspections of other people's places. If he had been a guest at someone's house where he knew there was a Leonardo hanging in the next room, he would not have taken so much as a step in its direction unless invited to do so by his host. In the countryside, boundary stones have long been seen as divine institutions, seat of the god Terminus who does not take kindly to being ignored, and Bernward's blood was one hundred per cent farmer's blood. It was shocking how little of it had been passed on to his children. What was it that led him, after that timeless tarrying in the entry, to abandon his ironclad principles and wander through this empty flat not once but repeatedly, like a prospective buyer?

This, then, was the flat through which Silvi, as she proudly declared, would traipse at night, never having to turn on a light even in the pitch darkness, without bumping into anything. Admittedly there wasn't much for her to bump into. The rooms echoed with emptiness. Naturally there were a few things here and there—canvas-covered sofas, lamps made out of vases that Helga Stolzier would never have permitted to enter a human dwelling, on one wall even a large Wilhelminian portrait, General Ritter von Schmidt-Flex in full regalia, with a chipped ornamental plaster frame, a painting that had originally been produced for crowded interiors where it would perhaps have been displayed on an easel hung with brocade but which was now expected to fill a bare white wall. In another room, one wall was taken up by a white bookcase, meticulously organized like in a municipal library. Evidently Hans-Jörg—these were unquestionably his books—also subscribed to various series which, still sealed in cellophane, took up entire shelves at a time. But where did he read? In the armchair by the window? Bernward did not ponder this question further. Yet another room was empty except for a number of cardboard boxes which, as Bernward discovered when he lifted the lid off one of them, had not been unpacked. Silvi's things from Brazil. The labels still displayed the address of a Brazilian shipping company. It was in this room that he encountered the first sign of life—a wasp trapped in this barren expanse was buzzing tiredly up and down the windowpane. It could see the sunlight, its tiny wasp eyes must also have perceived the lush fullness of the chestnut tree just outside the window—whether it registered it as green or not was immaterial—in any case it saw in it something wholesome and beneficial. The tiny spark of life in that banded wasp's body communicated its delicate flicker to those wide, empty rooms. But he kept his distance from the trapped insect for he knew that its sting was dangerous to him. He would be lucky if it was only his arm that swelled up.

Now he was in the bedroom. There was the bed, not excessively wide, he noted immediately—the two obviously had no trouble sleeping together. In this room, he entered a different olfactory zone. Whereas the lack of fresh air in the other rooms had only mildly affected the nonspecific clean and tidy smell—a cleaning lady had been over them with non-abrasive cleaning products—in the bedroom suddenly Silvi was there. The sweet substance into which the heat and moisture of Silvi's body transformed the otherwise rather tart lemon-lavender-vanilla scent of her perfume constituted, in the not unpleasant stuffiness of the bedroom, an almost physical presence. Had there been an armchair in the room, Bernward would have sat down and breathed in the air but there was nothing but a meagre little chair for draping clothes. It's not exactly cosy here, thought Bernward. He wasn't about to sit on the bed, that was out of the question. And there was the dress. White linen. Silvi had packed a couple that were nearly identical. It was like magic. In Bernward's current state of mind, it was by no means self-evident that here, in the heart of this flat in which he was setting foot for the first time, he would actually find the item he sought in conspicuous isolation literally exhibited in order that it might be discovered. But he left the dress hanging for the moment and took another tour of the flat. How impersonal it was! The two of them lived here like in a hotel suite, which, if anything, would have been more comfortable. Really? He thought of Rosemarie and Helga and their incessant search for exceptional decorative beauty which, as far as he was concerned, was usually pretty successful. He was not immune to the thrill of the chase when they were at Pattitucci's or somewhere similar, examining his little exquisitries. But when had he ever experienced anything in his own house like what he had here—looking from one room through the half-open door into the next room and from there into the next? In the second room, a clearly defined ray shone onto the floor, all but blinding in its incorporeality. The room beyond was shrouded in darkness, even though it did have a window looking out onto the sky which filled it with blinding white. From here, there was no furniture in sight, nothing to suggest that this was home to human beings. These were rooms to stride through—no, not through exactly, because where did they lead? At the other end, you would just have to turn round again. But now Bernward began to wonder how a first-floor window could face so much open sky as to be completely filled by it. And so he took a few steps backward through the series of rooms. Lo and behold, the mystery was solved—the white of the sky was in fact a freshly whitewashed firewall, the sky only came into view when he craned his neck.

'Bernward Hopsten, the strong, silent type. It's not as if you've really described him very carefully. You're avoiding him. Could it be that you're trying to make him appear harmless?'

'Can a man really be that harmless if his mere presence immediately makes the world seem less dangerous? The feeling that we were all living on thin ice was entirely absent whenever he was in the room. But you had to look very carefully to see that the placid harmony of togetherness emanated from this one man who rarely spoke.'

18

WITH ANOTHER'S HANDS

The Sicily trip had got off to a bad start. If it had been up to Silvi, she would have preferred not to wait for her in-laws' arrival but, rather, return home before they got there, but she never expressed this wish and in any case it would in all likelihood have been impossible to grant it. Hans-Jörg had always been a mystery to her but now she was certain that he couldn't stand her and that her mere presence pained him. She was like water—clear, shimmering, crystalline water, to be sure. If you pushed her away, she would give way easily and when she was at rest she was like a mirror that reflected whatever looked into it. Surprisingly, with the arrival of the elderly Schmidt-Flexes and the two Hopstens plus daughter, the trip nevertheless turned out to be a success. Bernward glowed with paternal affection when he saw Silvi. Rosemarie was slightly subdued, not quite the energetic machine Silvi knew from Frankfurt, much less intimidating and evidently in need of rest, spending long hours of the day in the recliner. Her parents-in-law led a ceremonious life in this long-time summer residence. They were only seen at mealtimes, on the upper loggia, the table set in the old-fashioned way with voluminous, white, fringed napkins. The setting was very dignified, the food a little unimaginative. After a week, Rosina's repertoire was essentially exhausted. Presiding over his table, Schmidt-Flex was on top form but with his monologues, this time, he was actually doing his guests a favour. The conversation might otherwise have been a little halting since, although Bernward was both cheerful and convivial, his Westphalian disposition meant he was quite content not to have to say much. Rosemarie was 'rich in thought and poor in deed' as the poet says and Hans-Jörg was lost in his brown study while his mother, with her peculiarly jagged face, was marshalling all her mental energy to endure her husband's anecdotes once more. When he said, 'The Caucasus, my dear friends, I'm afraid I'm going to have to disappoint you all there,' she could instantly have continued, 'the Caucasus will never be Switzerland.' When he said, 'My dear friend Alfred Cossery recently passed away, one of the last of the old Paris Bohemians,' she could instantly have carried on, 'who was friends with Camus and Boris Vian and lived with an immersion heater in the garret of Hôtel Louisiane . . .' Why oh why did her husband care so much about that immersion heater? The immersion heater as the sceptre of ancient Parisian artist-kings. When, having arrived in Paris after all, he added, 'Incidentally, this autumn I will in all likelihood be receiving the Grand Croix of the Légion d'honneur,' his wife could easily have picked up the thread and noted that reliable evidence suggested that he had been independently nominated by three ministers—'no really, by three different ministers!' Sometimes they actually did speak the same words in unison since he was of course not about to let her finish his sentences for him. This was for her a source of minuscule respite, the way an invalid tosses and turns in an overheated bed in search of a cooler patch. But she had stayed at his side as if there were no alternative and that very day, the newspaper had published some photos of Schmidt-Flex and his wife in black tie and evening gown at the federal press gala, locked in the stiff intimacy of the foxtrot, with the caption 'Dr Schmidt-Flex Trips the Light Fantastic with the Missus' or some similarly jaunty comment, his lips clamped shut into a crooked smile—an ironic indication that a man such as he could hold his own on the dance floor as well as at the conference table. Phoebe followed every word intently. She was stripped of the entourage of her peers and didn't appear to miss them. She played the model daughter for the entire first week until she met some people her age at the beach who introduced her to the local discotheques, after which she was never to be seen in the company of her parents, but up to that point she furnished me with nightly telephone reports. Now at a distance, she had finally discovered me and insisted that I call her daily. It was fairly disastrous, to be honest—I realized that I really should have been there in that constellation, she would not have been able to elude me there. And through the safety of the telephone she even explained that it would have been quite easy for me to tag along, what a pity that she hadn't thought of it.

It was especially amusing when she told me about old Schmidt-Flex's attempts to regulate the group's wine consumption. The house had its own wine, stored in unlabelled bottles that glistened with golden dew when they were placed on the dinner table. The wine also had a hint of apricot, it was faintly acidic, which made it seem fresh and light though it was quite alcoholic. Old Schmidt-Flex drank one glass with dinner, his wife another, Hans-Jörg always kept to water. At that rate, a bottle should easily have lasted a couple of days. But not with Bernward and Rosemarie at the table. The two were used to drinking a lot and both handled it well. No one has ever seen Bernward drunk and although Rosemarie's face did, admittedly, grow redder over the course of an evening, in the dim light of the candles and the loggia's iron lantern, swaying gently in the evening breeze, it wasn't so noticeable. They would also both routinely request wine in the late morning, with lunch still an hour away. The bottles were simply too appetizing, inviting you to quaff them the way oysters inhale seawater, and even at her first sip, Rosemarie remarked, 'You could drink a lot of this stuff.'

Schmidt-Flex's pincer-mouth twitched. It was obvious that he felt the urgent need to nip this in the bud. Here, in the South, people don't drink much, he said in a didactic tone. The Mediterranean relationship to wine is one of great moderation. Even in the literature of the Middle Ages and the Rennaissance, one encounters the figure of the dipsomaniac German, a foreign presence on the Italian soil. Bernward smiled his discreet and introverted smile but Rosemarie was following the lesson with great interest, yet another foray into cultural history of the sort that were a matter of course at this table and by no means a Schmidt-Flexian 'abasement'—it was of course inconceivable that the old man might permit himself such a thing in her case. Then she awoke from her spellbound reverie and asked gaily in her Rhenish accent whether there was any more wine.

'We'd be happy to *buoy* a few bottles—we were going to do that anyway.' This, however, was more than Schmidt-Flex could allow. In fluent Italian and for all to hear, he instructed Rosina to always keep the refrigerator stocked with wine for *i signori*— the gracious host couldn't resist this little denunciation, after all. But in the bedroom, his silvered head resting upon the enormous Sicilian monogrammed pillow, he remarked to his wife that it was odd how the Hopstens, lovely as they were, nevertheless had something of the nouveau riche about them—and at this he sat up in the triumph of a discovered paradox—even though they demonstrably were nothing of the sort! What did she think?

That's what she'd said all along, she said. When, from the quarry of her silence, Frau Schmidt-Flex suddenly and unequiv-ocally brought forth such a statement, there was something undeniably touching about it, even for her husband.

'The Schmidt-Flexes don't like Silvi,' Phoebe told me on the telephone. I imagined her speaking into the warm night, encircled by bats and eyed by a gecko. 'It's obvious at any given moment but she also told Mama.' Because of Silvi, Hans-Jörg's failure was now complete. She was not the sort of woman who could pull him out of it. Hans-Jörg needed a wife who would 'make some-thing out of him'.

'What's that supposed to mean—to make something out of a man?' Phoebe asked, palpably outraged. 'Whatever is meant to come of that? Do you dream of a wife who will make some-thing out of you?'

'In that case, things must be hunky-dory between them.' But no, apparently not. Rather than being grateful to Silvi for not trying to 'make something out of him', Hans-Jörg insisted on schooling his wife in the most awkward and embarrassing ways, trying to take her wine glass away from her and preventing Papa from refilling it. 'Good God, what an idiot!'

A group of people is more than the sum of its individual parts—this law had now been proved once again. Not only did the minor disharmonies, the reservations and the veiled criticisms that each of the people assembled in the Schmidt-Flexes' country villa nurtured against all the others not spoil the unity of the group, they actually constituted the secret cement holding it together. Everyone looked forward to mealtimes, regardless of how mercilessly they had each made fun of the others before.

And, as time went on, there was plenty to talk about. The curse of general speechlessness ebbed away. One morning, Schmidt-Flex had ordered a large taxi to take the entire company to Catania. With him, everything was organized round targeted sightseeing. Aimlessly wandering through the streets of this dilapidated and impoverished city which had once been a gleaming provincial jewel in the Kingdom of Sicily was out of the question. The city or, rather, its most important streets, palazzi and churches had been rebuilt in black tuff and white marble after they were damaged in an earthquake. The broad boulevards were designed to allow the inhabitants to flee their crumbling homes in the never unlikely event of another volcanic eruption with all the fiery consequences that followed in its wake. Everything had been created with its future destruction in mind. Unlike in other cities, the grand architecture was not built for the ages but, rather, erected as the precious frame for yet another doomsday scenario. The black palazzi were prepared for sombre mourning, the white marble of the windowsills and doorframes looked like bones embedded in the black facade. The Hopstens took everyone to lunch at a restaurant which Schmidt-Flex deemed 'overpriced'—not bad by any means but the quality of its fare was simply not properly commensurate with the cost. But Rosemarie was glad to have something other than Rosina's chicken and rice for once.

She felt like eating something. The pressure on her stomach and the tension in her jaw which had accompanied her ever since she'd got up that morning were gone. She had done something to liberate herself, something that would have been impossible the day before. Thoughts of Salam had become such a burden for her that she was scarcely capable of following the most innocuous of conversations. There was no joy in these thoughts but nor was there remorse—they contained no plans, no hopes or fears. It was as if even here, far away from Frankfurt, she was still subjected to his physical presence. He had taken such complete control of her that there was no escape. Bernward noticed her distractedness and listlessness, which had such a positive effect on the mechanics of the entire group, with novel emotions. Did this after all mark the appearance of something fundamentally unexpected, alien in their life together? Their early love— they had met at university—had fairly quickly given way to that loyal friendship admired by so many for its casual constancy. But wasn't it possible that this too had merely been a phase that one day would give way to weariness, indifference and curiosity about other people? And might that phase not be followed by yet another, in which they began to get on each other's nerves? Rosemarie's friends knew her to be of an energetic disposition, bordering at times on fractiousness, but he knew that she looked to him for support and often enough needed his help. It was this need that had now been interrupted. She seemed, he felt certain, suddenly less dependent on him. This feeling grew stronger at these unwontedly close quarters. The bedroom they shared was spacious enough that the monumental bronze double bed, a veritable altar to matrimony, felt modest in size by comparison and yet, it was unquestionably a room for two people who were used to the comfort and convenience of separate bedrooms and were now suddenly asked once more to share every breath with each other. He was not oblivious to the fact that Rosemarie lay awake at night—whenever he woke up briefly, she too was awake— and that she did not pass the time reading but, rather, stared silently into the darkness, apparently sufficiently preoccupied with her thoughts.

It was during their tour of the cathedral, led by Schmidt-Flex—armed with a copy of *Southern Baroque Art* by Sir Sacheverell Sitwell whom, as a young man at Cambridge, he confided, he had on several occasions visited at Renishaw (would he have dreamt of picking up a book by a contemporary author whom he did not know personally?)—that Rosemarie suddenly had a liberating thought. The group was slowly making its way towards the twilit nave (Schmidt-Flex pointed out the recurrence of black and white) when Rosemarie took a quick step to the side and knelt in an empty confessional. Darkness enveloped her. She breathed a sigh as the display on her phone lit up. And there it was—Salam's voice, soft, Viennese, Lebanese, in its melting cadence. Whose call had he been expecting? Rosemarie didn't know what to say. She muttered something inconsequential, audibly under pressure. Her most important message was that she couldn't talk for long and that later would be difficult too. Was he pleased to hear her voice so suddenly? She thought his tone betrayed something akin to joy. Certainly there was no trace of that in what he said. Their conversation sounded like the first tentative contact between prisoners in neighbouring cells, although Salam was definitely not kneeling in a confessional. But as insubstantial as the short conversation was—during which Rosemarie once cast a furtive glance outside but the group was nowhere to be seen; the ever-dependable Schmidt-Flex was reading a chapter of *Southern Baroque* out loud in his impeccable Cambridge accent, bathing luxuriously in his English, and Rosemarie could have spoken at length if only she had been able to think of something to say—even this brief exchange was a release. Just hearing Salam say that it was hot in Frankfurt, that he was working a lot, that he was awaiting her return, popped a balloon that had been growing intolerably round her. Suddenly, everything wasn't so bad any more. She would get a handle on it all somehow. She could do this. After all she had her phone. And suddenly there was room for little hesitations again—was it wise to call Salam like this? Would it not have been better to let him stew for a little? No, never again would she call him so quickly. Like a pious penitent she left the confessional with positive resolve that immediately strengthened her a little.

With lunch they had an exquisite wine. Silvi drank three glasses in quick succession and then said, 'It doesn't take long to have one glass too many but the thing is that you never know beforehand which glass that will be.' Her *r*s rolled freely as she waxed lyrical on her impressions of Catania which had little to do with Sitwell's insights into the nature of the 'Southern Baroque' but proved that Silvi wasn't blind.

'It really is a black-and-white city. Incredible, really. First, there were two Dalmatians running to and fro outside the church so quickly that the black-and-white spots almost appeared to blend, then there was that old black man with white hair selling lollipops, then a white car with black tyres drove past and then there were those white Brazilian sugar sacks full of charcoal next to the barbecue on the market square . . .'

Bernward asked incredulously when she had observed all these things, as if Silvi had said the most outlandish things, but he wasn't sitting near enough to catch her when she stumbled while trying to get up from the table.

'That's it,' said Hans-Jörg, suppressing his anger, and in the relief she felt after her rebirth in the confessional, Rosemarie agreed with him, although she didn't say so. She nurtured a deep resentment for falling and stumbling women, whom she deemed injurious to the honour of their sex. Poor, harmless Silvi was suddenly surrounded by silent antipathy, including that of her dignified parents-in-law.

That evening she had an opportunity to redeem herself. She was well rested and waited until after dinner to have her first glass of wine. It wasn't as if Schmidt-Flex never said anything that might have held the attention of his daughter-in-law. Since he spoke incessantly, the sheer volume of things he said made it quite likely that he would eventually say something that sparked Silvi's imagination, just as not everything he said to others began with the phrase, 'You really must learn . . .' (sometimes it was, 'I have learnt that . . .'). And during dinner, underneath that swaying lantern which would not have been out of place in the gateway of an ancient fortress, beset by an army of moths, he came to speak of his uncle, General von Schmidt-Flex, who had received an honorary knighthood—'Hans-Jörg and Silvi have his portrait, a mediocre work from a bad period, we always used to call it the "*mauvais-goût* period"'—and whose daughter Frieda had been feeble-minded. 'My aunt Frieda.' In a friend's autograph book, this Frieda had memorably written, 'Upon a sea-girt island / there dwelt two shepherds sly; / The one was named Malone, / the other was called Maley. With best wishes, your loyal friend Frieda Schmidt-Flex.' As his audience laughed, Schmidt-Flex continued, 'This poem undoubtedly refers to the Outer Hebrides—Malone is a Celtic name, I assume. But why am I telling you this?' Above all he was talking about the institution of non-hereditary ennoblement—an entirely sensible institution. Accomplishments were not necessarily hereditary after all. A brilliant father often had a less brilliant son—'in the case of my uncle, we would have wound up with a feeble-minded member of the aristocracy and there are more than enough of them to begin with.' He too was a sceptic concerning heredity. The power of governance should go to the best and the brightest. That, to him, was democracy from an entrepreneurial point of view. Having weighed the matter carefully, he had decided to place his fortune in a trust that would provide his son with a certain income but would not leave him in charge of the capital as a whole. Schmidt-Flex was often fond of weaving his stories into plaits—one amusing strand, one didactic strand and one unpleasant strand. Hans-Jörg looked down at his plate. His father's trust-fund plans were not new to him, he was even on board with the idea, his father had convinced him, but he could feel Rosemarie and Phoebe's pitying gazes and didn't know how to meet them. Perhaps the best way would be to tell everyone about the cigar incident? So that everyone knew just how lucky they were even to be sitting at this table, eating and drinking too much?

Silvi prevented this from happening. She was so taken with that little poem that she had not heard any of what came after. She had been possessed by the imps of nonsense—laughing to herself as if she were being tickled from inside. Nothing Silvi did ever looked ugly. Even when she was positively bursting with laughter she did not pull any unattractive faces. She never pulled any faces at all. Why had she wound up with a husband who was perennially pulled and contorted in all different ways?

'That wonderful, beautiful poem—let's make a game out of it—a really fun game!'

She gestured for Bernward to come over and whispered something to him, not very clearly at first apparently and interrupted by fits of giggling but, eventually, he understood. The loggia had a tall niche meant for a large vase or a statue but it was empty, at least until Bernward went and stood in it, placing both hands behind his back. He filled the niche comfortably but Silvi pushed in behind him and, petite as she was, disappeared completely behind him, even though Bernward was by no means broad-shouldered. And now she extended her arms out underneath his so that it appeared to the onlookers as if this full-grown man had a curiously truncated pair of arms and surprisingly delicate, oval hands, which was a comic sight in itself, but when Bernward began to recite the verses by Schmidt-Flex's feeble-minded aunt in a solemn and vaguely threatening tone, as if he were the stone guest, his little alien hands began to conduct and to move with didactic rhetoric, index fingers raised, to accompany the poem, and in the flickering shadowy light they truly had fused into a single body. It looked so convincing that the others did a double take before laughing. Bernward had to repeat the Hebridean poem several times because apart from this one he did not know a single poem off by heart—a shame really, he thought to himself, they're so easy to learn but he'd just never had occasion to do so until now. And he was only too happy to prolong this unwonted comedic performance, since the feeling of Silvi's body against his own and of having her agile, youthful arms firmly clenched beneath his own was a sensation that was welcome to linger. Rosemarie and Phoebe had never seen him entertain guests in such a way. He had even been incapable of playing Father Christmas convincingly when the children were little and ready to fall for any illusion. And now they watched as he, stony-faced, recounted the story of Malone and Maley, as if transported to the frozen North, giving an account of a gruesome battle in the style of the Icelandic sagas. Even Schmidt-Flex was smiling benignly. That was the highest degree of approval he could muster for other people's performances and he was always ready to provide suggestions for improvement. All the same, they had used a poem that he had introduced.

This miniature theatrical performance had a surprising effect on his wife, however. Her composure, which she had been painstakingly maintaining, literally burst into pieces. Her face crumbled and reassembled itself into an uncontrollable fit of laughter. Tears streamed down her face and when at last she had recovered she said with positively tragic seriousness, 'That was really funny.' A careful observer—of whom there were admittedly none, her reaction having worn down even the most polite attention of her companions to such a degree that having a conversation with her seemed pointless —would have noticed that this deep, rocking laughter had a visibly calming effect on her. The torment of excruciating boredom abated. She even came to associate this feeling of relief with Silvi and in the following days would occasionally look at her intently but by no means sternly and gently shake her head at the way even people you thought you knew inside out could still surprise you.

When the company began to withdraw for the night, it happened that Bernward and Silvi lingered outside for a while. It was as if the others wanted to give the evening's protagonists a little more time alone. They were not sitting close together but Bernward could reach Silvi's glass with the bottle held in his outstretched hand. For a while, neither of them spoke. From the direction of the henhouses they heard a sleepy cockcrow. It was late but not early enough for the chickens to be waking up. The cock must have been dreaming.

'Yes, they really do dream, chickens do,' said Silvi. 'When we still had chickens, there was always this quiet, secret clucking and rustling in the henhouse. For a time, my father believed in keeping his own chickens. It was probably to make up for the loss of the farm.' How she had loved those chickens. She could still see each and every one of them in her mind's eye—one had been as slender as a dove, another had plumage that didn't really look like feathers so much as fur, the brown fur of a rabbit, and when this hen had lain down, all bunched up, Silvi had even thought she could make out the long rabbit ears. Then there was a pale one, which was light brown and slender like a partridge, a wildfowl in essence, and an outsider. Another hen's behind was so enormous that it had dangled off the roost and she had asked herself how it managed to keep its balance. One young hen had looked like a black crow and had been cantankerous to boot. Another had a neck like a vulture, bare but for a thick layer of fluff. She had a particular fondness for the light-grey angora hen, its soft, delicately hued body traversed by gentle waves, in perpetual corporeal motion. And the cock's hackle, seemingly sewn together out of long, greasy yellow hairs. She had an aunt over there, her father's cousin, who would sometimes come over for dinner and would nervously scrape and prod her food around on her plate, always accompanied by the sound of scrabbling together—and then she'd stab it, 'just like a chicken! That intense look after having meticulously positioned the seed with one claw. Oh,' Silvi said, 'and when they grew old our cook would always butcher them in a flash, while the others looked on. I always wondered what they must have been thinking. Then we'd eat them and that was always comforting to me. Yes, that was lovely.'

She sounded a little sad. Bernward breathlessly listened to her .

While undressing later in the little dressing room, his gaze fell upon the tall mirror standing in the corner. For the first time in many years, he calmly looked at his naked body, studying his reflection in the mirror. Ordinarily, he was completely oblivious to his body. In front of Rosemarie, he moved with spousal insouciance. The passing years had not spared her entirely either but he paid no attention to the traces of age, it was more that the entire question of how one's body actually looked had become entirely irrelevant. His body was no longer in the competition and the question of how it might look to someone else wasn't even worth asking. And it's not as if he had completely let himself go, he quietly made sure of that, without resorting to any extreme measures, rigid diets or regimes. But how profoundly unlovely was this thinness which still looked fairly presentable when fully clothed! How sinewy and knotty his legs, how bony and crooked his feet—they literally looked like something from a Dürer sketch. How limply mammalian the sag of his chest, how tired and uneven, when he turned in a certain way, how wrinkled his skin, what a ghastly red his knees and elbows, how from his neck to his chin the skin hung in stringy lines like that of an old chicken—apropos of chickens, of which Silvi had spoken so movingly in her little soliloquy. Bernward was even-tempered by nature and the sight of himself in the mirror did not injure his pride. What might a man his age be expected to look like, who spent his days sitting behind a desk, even though he swam his lengths every morning? At some point, you stopped having a body that would arouse the desire of another human being, that someone would want to wrap their arms round and press against their own—right?

But as he lay there in the dark next to Rosemarie, who was actually sleeping soundly for once, sleep did not come to him. His heart. It was his heart. There was a faint cramp in there. He could feel his heart, pure and simple, and you're not supposed to be able to feel your heart. Was this cause for concern? Was he not of an age in which doctors urge caution? But really it wasn't an unpleasant pain. He felt pressure but it was a sweet pressure, especially when he answered it by pressing his hands to his heart and allowed himself, oh so quietly so as not to wake Rosemarie, to sigh.

19

BUSINESS ADVICE

Salam had never spared Helga Stolzier so much as a second glance. When they said hello, he barely even looked at her, right on the verge of being impolite. He knew precisely the sort of women who were an option for him. The others he didn't even notice. He showed an equal disregard for Phoebe's not insignificant beauty and for Silvi and so he barely even noticed them. What was there to talk about with a woman whom he could not hope to overwhelm in his usual style? Try as he might, he would not have had the first idea. It is not uncommon for well-meaning, would-be matchmaker friends to overlook these most fundamental dispositions of their unsuspecting victims. When Salam first came to the house and, as Rosemarie noticed out of the corner of her eye, immediately became embroiled in a serious conversation with Schmidt-Flex about the Balkans—which, as Bernward put it, meant that he must on some level be 'a worthy opponent'—that evening, when the house was once again empty, she said to her husband, 'Wouldn't he be something for Helga?'

'Isn't Helga a little too Germanic for him?' Bernward was amused by the image of the broad-shouldered, flaxen-haired Helga in the hands of the portly oriental gentleman with the soulful eyes. But Rosemarie followed up on her idea and the very next day, while on the phone with Helga—who was sitting in the shimmering lacquered cave that was her boutique—put Salam into play. She must surely have noticed him? The question was somewhat disingenuous. Rosemarie had the distinct impression that Helga was not interested in any man but always pretended not to notice and persisted in innocently suggesting to her friend that she should take a closer look at this or that gentleman. Irrespective of Helga's preferences, these were always men whom Rosemarie clearly held in fairly low esteem and who for one reason or another were not to be taken seriously. This much was clear to Helga, for whom Rosemarie was a chosen object of study. She spent a lot of time thinking about her friend and even at lively gatherings, she would be completely absorbed in observing her until, at the tiniest of signals, she suddenly leapt into action and offered to help. Over time, Rosemarie's little indications of disapproval would pile up. She found fault with Salam in all sorts of ways but her criticisms were always rather vague and Helga, conditioned through years of patient observation, understood that her criticisms in fact had to do with ineffable qualities—that Salam was simply 'impossible' socially, not really presentable, 'a misfit' in Rosemarie's English terminology. Helga was able to account for the fact that he was nevertheless consistently invited to these gatherings by imputing an idiosyncratic social philosophy to her genteel role model, something along the following lines—that a *societas perfecta* must comprise all types of things and people and that excellence can only reveal itself in contrast to deficient counterexamples. Any royal court worthy of the name needs its dwarfs and jesters as well.

Then when Rosemarie and Bernward went with the Schmidt-Flexes to Sicily, these attempts at matchmaking—if that was the word for Rosemarie's occasional, tentative, stealthy references to Salam—had stopped. For a while there was even talk of whether Helga couldn't come along to this Schmidt-Flex retreat which seemed to be spacious enough. Helga had the impression that Rosemarie genuinely wanted her there but then there was the difficult question of what to do with the cockatoo while they were away. Bernward was not keen on the idea of leaving that noble bird, his dear friend, in the hands of the new and not altogether reliable housemaid who had already on several occasions forgotten to fill its water bowl. And of course the cockatoo couldn't complain. It pained Bernward to think of the dumb, defenceless creature being so crassly neglected. Helga was the one who had brought the cockatoo into their house. She would take it to her boutique, where the contrast of its snow-white plumage against the black lacquer would present a phantasmagoria of all earthly cockatoos—it was basically meant to be in that boutique in the first place, although it was now impossible to imagine the Hopstens' life without it. And besides, Helga could hardly close the boutique for so long—once more Rosemarie's diagnosis that 'she can't afford it' proved accurate.

Rosemarie had long since stopped knowing what to wish for. The argument that someone would have to look after the cockatoo was unbeatable. Her uneasiness about leaving Helga alone in Frankfurt was great but unutterable and so she let things run their course.

It was Bernward who kept touching this sore spot of hers, making it impossible for her simply to forget about it for a while. It was really rather mean to have left Helga alone in Frankfurt, he said one oppressively hot late-summer evening in Sicily, the white summer curtains hanging motionless without the faintest hint of a breeze to stir them. He said he found the loneliness that emanated from Helga oppressive and that she reminded him of a Norn there in the midst of her boutique's perennial gloom.

'There's such an ominous atmosphere of waiting round her. To me, she seems like a woman who has waited so long she is gradually turning to stone.'

'Helga's not as lonely as she seems,' said Rosemarie, naked but for the sheet covering her, observing the huge shadows cast by the moths. She had some family, she thought, some niece or other. Didn't she sometimes mention an admirable niece of hers who had some kind of television job in Japan—business news or something like that . . .?

'I just hope that Salam will take her under his wing a little,' said Bernward. In the end Salam owed them that much. In fact he had wanted to ask Salam to do so before they left.

'You didn't!' Rosemarie sat up in bed, angry. That really would have been unfathomably tactless. Her thoughts were flitting about like the moths. If Helga was interested in anyone it was Silvi. She bored holes through Silvi with those Nordic blue eyes of hers. Just the other day, said Rosemarie, when she was looking after a cat for some friends—because Helga was always happy to do things like that, she positively enjoyed looking after other people's pets, it didn't bother her in the slightest—she and Silvi had gone to the boutique for tea. And the whole time they were having their tea, Helga had had that cat in her lap, stroking it demonstratively, practically massaging it—and giving Silvi significant looks all the while. But Silvi was such a sheep she didn't notice such things at all, said Rosemarie, adding that she found the newly established Silvi Appreciation Society utterly incomprehensible. Silvi was a sweet girl—*le mot juste*—but harmless as a glass of milk. And it had by no means escaped her attention that Bernward, in his avuncular way, had now also joined the society. He should of course have his fun, she didn't begrudge him that, but these platonic gestures of admiration, the harmlessness that Silvi exuded and that rubbed off on her admirers—well, to the impartial observer there was something vaguely embarrassing about it all. It was a proper little rant that issued forth from her mouth at that late hour. The wordmoths fluttered hither and thither but never where she wanted—and at the same time didn't want—them to go. In the end, she managed, somewhat violently, to steer the invective towards a conclusion that brought her back to her starting point, 'Don't you dare put such ideas in Salam's head.'

Meanwhile, Helga truly was alone with her thoughts and there was plenty to think about. Whenever she arrived at the Hopstens' poolside gatherings dressed in one of her embroidered kaftans, with her thick, platinum blonde hair, her big, luminous teeth and heavy rings on her large hands, she looked like a Crusader at the court of a sultan, learning the art of falconry, who spends his days playing chess or cleaving Turks in twain but has never worked a day in his life. And yet, Helga Stolzier was an industrious worker. Life, to her, was nothing but work and— quite rightly—she even regarded her visits to Rosemarie's as work. Inside, she felt, she had the strength and stamina of a workhorse. Her great undoing, as far as she was concerned, was the fact that her business was still too small for her to be able to delegate certain tasks. She designed clothes and gave advice on interior design but she also had to act out her house style for her clients. She had to convince these beauty-and-fashion-obsessed ladies that she too was obsessed with beauty and fashion. She had to act as though she too associated the clothes and designs and accessories she was selling with the dream of a different life, of love and passion, even though she had mostly abandoned such emotions, insofar as she had ever been capable of them. The way things stood, she had to make the costumes and sets backstage, as it were, and then go onstage, lavishly costumed, and perform an aria to sell her wares—albeit, since singing arias was not her forte, she generally opted for a resounding, enigmatic silence instead. That worked just as well. Rosemarie had absolutely no time for her concerns. Helga wasn't as young as she once was and she could sit and wait in her pitch-black emporium surrounded by that luxurious plunder till she was blue in the face for an opportunity to step out of her hand-to-mouth subsistence. You couldn't get rich selling individual items any more and although her kaftans were quite cheaply sewn somewhere in India, they weren't for every woman. Silvi was right about that, even though she had not the faintest idea about fashion, unfortunately. Jeans and cashmere polo-necks in winter, white linen shirts, no jewellery and flats in summer—to think what could be made out of a woman like her, Helga thought mournfully, but not with one of her kaftans naturally. 'They're for rich fat ladies,' said Silvi and then gave her such an affectionate hug that Helga couldn't hold it against her.

'Mass production', that was the magic word upon which Helga Stolzier was ruminating. Rosemarie had admonished her to keep well enough away from such things and Helga had the distinct impression that her friend was firmly against an expansion of her business activities. Knowing how possessive Rosemarie could be, it seemed clear to Helga that she wanted her all to herself but in this instance it was far simpler—Rosemarie was simply not convinced that Helga really had a nose for business and she had absolutely no intention of losing money because of her.

'I'd rather give her the money,' she said to herself, which was of course not to be taken literally—it put no strain on their friendship even when they haggled doggedly over even minor sums.

It was Slavina she turned to for help. She knew him from her shopkeeper circles and asked him, in his capacity as a banker, to take a quick look at the plans she had come up with for establishing her own brand, followed by opening more boutiques and, finally, a chain spanning all of Germany. It would be an exaggeration to say that he approached those drafts with excessive good will. Rosemarie had seen and merely smiled at them but unlike Rosemarie, Slavina knew that a great many skilled and gifted people are all but incapable of expressing a functioning business idea, so to him it looked considerably less hopeless.

'But no one is going to give you one cent for this,' he said, rapping his fingernails on the stack of paper. And he was the one who mentioned Salam's name—he was a man who knew how to write this kind of stuff so that she could actually get funded, said Slavina. In retrospect, this advice had probably been a minor effrontery on Slavina's part that allowed him to express what he truly thought of Helga's plans. But in any case Helga now had a reason to call Salam, by a circuitous route that neither Rosemarie nor Bernward could possibly have predicted. The city just wasn't all that big. But then such unlikely connections happen even in bigger cities and where Salam was concerned, everything was a potential connection anyway.

Precisely that which had always ruled out any interest on Helga's part in an alliance with Salam, of the sort Rosemarie kept intimating, now brought the two of them together. She truly was a saleswoman to the core and had developed a near-infallible sense for which side of the barricades—or the shop counter—any given person was on, whether they're picking up or dropping off. She knew exactly why she herself was in with the Hopstens —she wanted and needed them to buy her wares and that this undertaking was now intermingled with friendship, passion even, militated against neither the feelings of affection nor the business transactions. Friends are those with whom you can do good business, Helga probably would have said, and was it not true that every intimate relationship was ultimately founded on an exchange, and was the Latin word for exchange not *commercium*? When, during those genial afternoons at the Hopsten house, she would discreetly scan her surroundings—in truth she did nothing but scan her surroundings, pausing only when she encountered a friendly gaze at which she would allow her dark brown eyes to light up conspiratorially—among the throng of people, old and young alike, there was only one man whose sole reason for being there was unquestionably that he was selling something. At first this had made her uneasy but she quickly realized that it was not the Hopstens or, more specifically, Rosemarie on whom he was trying to foist or palm something off—Helga was invariably disdainful of her competition's attempts at salesmanship—but, rather, the Schmidt-Flexes, who were of no concern to Helga. Her weakness for Silvi notwithstanding, she had long since accepted that she simply wasn't ever going to be a viable client. The way she saw it, Salam and she were members of the same tribe and this common heritage, as it were, prevented the development of any tension between them. This in turn meant that Salam, with his steaming virility and watery boyish-girlish eyes, was neutralized, purely because their hunting grounds did not overlap, which was fortunate because, otherwise, Helga would have been a dangerous adversary. But since they were of like kind but not in direct competition, perhaps they could give each other some advice instead?

Salam was immediately forthcoming. 'You don't need a recommendation from Slavina, Helga,' he said warmly. Even on the telephone, the sonorous vibrations of his voice were quite palpable and other women besides Helga had felt it waft over them like a gentle summer breeze. 'We have dear friends in common, you and I.'

He came to visit her at the boutique. She had rolled down the shutters on the windows and in the back room, he discovered a magically illuminated little cell with a sofa all but buried under an avalanche of cushions. She laid out her plans for him in great detail, her calculations and ideas. Salam read the document through carefully, breathing audibly through his nose, his paw-like hands, covered in thick black hair, handling the pages with surprising delicacy. He wore on a pair of small glasses for reading that gave him the unexpected appearance of a religious scholar. Needless to say, Helga had prettied herself up once more after the day's work in preparation for Salam's visit. Her expensive perfume filled the air of that magical office like a holy cloud announcing the presence of exalted femininity but Salam was able to devote his undivided attention to the business plan because none of these preparations had even the slightest effect on him—if he were to spend six weeks in a tent in the desert with Helga he was convinced that he would not find her in the least bit appealing. He candidly, chummily even, gave her his best advice, said that it would hardly come as a surprise to her to learn that he didn't have much of an idea about the fashion business and also didn't know what the market for this sort of gear—sorry, these finely wrought accoutrements—was like but he said that, basically, you could sell anything so long as the price was right. This was an article of faith to which they both subscribed but, as with all credos, it was formulated in such a way as to give the exegete as much leeway for interpretation as possible and, notwithstanding the wisdom and erudition suggested by his glasses, in Helga's case, he was unable to say exactly what it meant. Helga felt very comfortable with this conversation which was conducted with complete professional objectivity. Even though it had not given her much to go on concretely, she felt that she had taken the first real step towards achieving her goal simply by virtue of the fact that the matter had been scrutinized from every angle by an intelligent interlocutor. The question of who was going to fund all of this remained entirely open. It wasn't so easy nowadays, said Salam, a diagnosis that served as further confirmation of his competence. Helga's project was something for connoisseurs and aficionados, he said with an expression of naked honesty. He didn't see a bank acting as partner, it would have to be either a large company willing to cultivate someone like Helga like an orchid or a private individual wanting to be part of something like this without being overly interested in the returns. It was all the easier for him to make such a statement since he knew that Rosemarie wouldn't dream of giving Helga a start-up loan. Helga too was reminded of this, not without a hint of bitterness, although she was too much of a businesswoman to take such things personally. After all, if she took only what Rosemarie freely gave her, she didn't do too badly either.

It was an animated evening though not one conversational word was spoken. It was only as he was leaving that Salam made a private remark.

'Oh, you've got a white cockatoo as well—or are you just looking after Bernward and Rosemarie's?'

The cockatoo had been sitting there quietly on its perch the whole time, only the occasional blink of its eyes revealing that it wasn't stuffed. Did it recognize Salam?

'I love that cockatoo,' said Helga and her voice grew dark, as it always did when she said the word love. It was too beautiful a word. The cockatoo cocked its head to one side—a gesture that in human terms might have been an expression of a certain scepticism but in this case it may simply have wanted to get a better look at whoever was approaching. Its white and yellow crest rose, as if pulled by an internal string. It gave a low rumbling sound, followed by a click.

'And he loves me.' As Bernward would have done, she raised her hand, presumably in order to scratch the back of the bird's neck.

Can an animal misunderstand something? Is misunderstanding not the prerogative of humans with their secret reservations, interpretations and their ambiguous language? Scarcely was Helga's large, powerful hand with their dark red fingernails within its reach before the cockatoo pecked at it with its stony beak—it must have hurt like hell because pearls of sweat formed on stoic Helga's upper lip from the pain. Her index finger was bleeding heavily. The blood welled up bright red and ran down like a small fountain. Salam immediately sprang into action. He grabbed Helga's wrist, ample but fragrant, and stuck her blood-red finger into his mouth and began sucking it vehemently, no doubt for anaesthetic reasons, and sure enough the pain grew noticeably less acute.

'Thank you,' said Helga, shaking slightly while Salam continued to suck her finger with single-minded determination. And there's no other way to explain it but that the taste of Helga's blood pulsing freely from the triangular wound made by the cockatoo's beak abruptly changed his entire impression of her. Suddenly Helga was no longer entirely sexless. It was quite miraculous. There, right in front of him, stood a woman who a moment ago had not been there at all and he already had her finger in his mouth.

Helga was so bewildered that at first she didn't understand why he had slipped her finger out of his mouth—to kiss her. She already had his tongue in her mouth, accompanied by the vivid taste of her own blood. But this moment of bewilderment soon passed and a veritable wrestling match ensued. Helga was as strong as any man and Salam was egged on by her strength and responded with the full force of his not insignificant weight. What he lacked in muscles he made up for in sheer mass. In a second of weakness, when Helga thought she would have to give up, she inhaled a hefty dose of his highly peculiar, though not exactly unpleasant odour, which helped her to carry on. They knocked over the cockatoo's perch. The bird flapped its wings as furiously as an entire chicken coop panicked at the sight of a goshawk. Finally Salam banged his head against the leg of a glass cabinet. That awakened him from his frenzy.

Dishevelled and bloodied—it was still just Helga's index finger, but it had now left its mark on Salam's shirt collar—they sat facing each other on the floor. Helga looked better than her coercive cavalier. Her plait was ironclad. She looked stern though not necessarily cross—after all, she had emerged the victor. Salam's bloodlust, perhaps that's the appropriate word for his temporary madness, had passed. It's probably healthier this way, he thought, getting up off the floor with some difficulty. He shot Helga an ironic smile that was actually meant for himself, 'You're right, let's not, should we not just forget this ever happened?'

But as is always the case with unfinished business, it's difficult to get out of your head. On Salam, the incident had an effect that was positively unprecedented. He began flirting with her whenever they met. He reserved a secret smile for her, tried to catch her eye and pretended that the two of them had some sort of agreement. And Helga was not unreceptive, albeit haughtily unapproachable. She was convinced that Salam was in love with her and although she had no intention of reciprocating, she was too familiar with the pangs of despised love not to grant a lover a certain amount of respect.

'There he was again finally—Baron Slavina. Are you going to open your jar of preserves?'

'We're not quite there yet. Naturally, his name came up now and again—Frankfurt is a small town. But it's strange, there is

often very little overlap between the different milieux. Nevertheless, there are always coincidences . . .'

    'You're a bit too fond of coincidences sometimes . . .'

    'Then let's just call that the subject of our story—the necessity of coincidence.'

    'Let's wait and see about that title . . .'

20

TIME HOLDS ITS BREATH

Snow never stays on the ground for long in the area around Frankfurt because the climate is so mild. The entire uninhabited Main plain seems to contain such immanent warmth that the frost only rarely has a chance to assert itself. Ever since the Hopstens had bought the house in Falkenstein, sledging had been one of the family's winter rituals. At first it was only the children but then the parents and their friends adopted the tradition for themselves. From the top of the Feldberg a steep path led down for a couple of kilometres through the woods, emerging practically on the Hopstens' doorstep. Planning these outings presented something of a logistical challenge as a sizeable group of people had to be transported up the mountain with their sledges. The cars were parked at the top and when everyone had reached the bottom a few would drive back up in another car and fetch them. Titus took charge of the organizing with his usual air of huffy seriousness. He had thought it all through ahead of time and planned it down to the smallest detail, which with twenty people was no mean feat. On the way up, we were tightly packed and whoever ended up on the back seat usually had to sit with a sledge in their lap. The whole thing was accompanied by general noisemaking. It was hard to believe that in the end everyone had somewhere to sit or, rather, could be squeezed in somewhere, and then we drove up the mountain on increasingly deserted, snow-covered roads—the higher up we went the deeper the snow—framed by snow-rounded rows of pine trees. Invitations to these outings were mostly issued from one day to the next or even that same afternoon. If, for once, it was cold enough and there was freshly fallen snow, it was an opportunity that had to be seized immediately. It was practically a commandment.

The moon wasn't full that night but it had only just begun to wane and would have shone brightly if it hadn't been obscured by a light fog. The ubiquitous layer of white had its own pale luminescence, an otherworldly light that stripped away all colours, even from the garish winter jackets, transforming them all into so many shades of grey. The top of the Feldberg was like the North Pole. The car park was icy smooth and the ominous radio tower from the thirties looked like some sort of science station, a remote shelter for some physicists working on their dangerous, top-secret projects. Out of the SUVs poured a throng of people like out of an Indian taxi. The bitterly cold wind blew in our faces. We stamped our feet and laughed and Rosemarie, theatrically wrapped in a wolf's pelt, exclaimed that she would have preferred to turn back then and there, that her nose would fall off in this cold. But, already, the bottles were being passed around, the lukewarm schnapps wetting our lips even though the cold was still far from chilling us to the bone. From the plain below, where Frankfurt lay, there came a rosy warm light from the street lamps along the Autobahn. It looked like the glare of a great conflagration. This is what Frankfurt must have looked like from afar during the nights of bombing in the war. The woods at the top of the mountain—so ugly at any other time of year, the desolate, scraggy spruces stuck in the dusty earth—was transformed into a long row of monumental sculptures, snowy cowls, snowy beards, snowy eyebrows drooping over closed eyelids, giving the trees the appearance of petrified prehistoric heroes, snowy heads from the dream of Ossian. Titus and Phoebe's friends hurled themselves, bellowing and shrieking, onto their sledges and rushed down the steep slope into the darkness. Soon, their voices vanished into the distance and the group that had huddled round the cars had dissipated. Everyone was seated in a tiny sledge, trying to follow the vanguard, and suddenly everyone was dispersed and scattered. I saw Phoebe glide away behind a fox-faced young man with flowing locks. I had seen him before, until that point he and I had shared the same fate of being relegated to the fringe of Phoebe's circle but now there he was, zooming off with her into the night. Salam was inappropriately dressed for the occasion in his Italian suit and black leather-soled shoes. He slipped constantly but landed softly and chuckled to himself every time, as though the evening's pleasure lay precisely in slipping and slummocking on the snow and it was inconceivable that he might feel the cold—he had a fire burning inside that turned his plump body into an oven, even when his weight propelled his sledge into one snow drift after another. Helga wore a fur coat that made her look like an Ostrogoth princess abducted by Kyrgyz mercenaries. She controlled her sledge like an obedient steed and glided at a steady pace through the night. Hans-Jörg had quickly given up and was pulling his sledge along behind him. While the others whizzed past him, he invariably got stuck. The snow, which for everyone else was smooth, became coarse for him. So he trudged through the night, letting Bernward and Silvi go on ahead. He could hear her childish squeals. This was the first time in her life that she had been sledging and was quite beside herself with joy that something so wonderful could exist. Then she too was gone. Each of us plunged into that shadowy realm under the luminous grey firmament. The soundlessness swallowed us up. What cries were still to be heard—evidently people felt that you couldn't start a sledge run without cries of joy and alarm—lay like acoustic crumbs upon the unmoved, unmoveable bell jar of this winter's night. By day, a hiking trail led through this dreary commercial woods with its protected plantation areas but in the ethereal snowy light it appeared transformed.

At first the track was icy and dropped off precipitously on either side and it was not easy to keep to the middle. But as soon as I reached the denser part of the woods where the sun could not melt the snow during the day, the path grew softer, slowing the sledge down. At the same time, the firs, transformed and distended by the snow, seemed to envelop the steep incline in a soft pillow of white. Here and there, the path was criss-crossed with animal tracks. Courbet hunted here once but in this light, his fiery red foxes, wounded and writhing in the wet snow, would have been little more than charcoal curs. The voices of the others fell away from the space round me. The milky grey clouds covered me like a duvet and the blankets of snow on the firs closed in on either side. The ride was smooth, like a knife through butter. It seemed to have neither a beginning nor an end—was it not possible that it might turn into an infinite Escher loop where the exits are always the entrances and vice versa? And as I rushed ever downward past that voluminously snow-clad underbrush, now stripped of any prickly thorniness, was I not leaving parts of myself behind—memories, characteristics, dreams, anxieties—the way one might lose a hat or a scarf along the way? This moving solitude in white suddenly cast the pressure that the presence of other people exerted on me into sharp relief—there in that solitary non-existence, the pressure was lifted and I could feel my ego grow and swell until it exploded into a thousand wispy shreds. In their place, there was now a stream of clear air that filled the gap completely and satisfyingly. As endless as this track felt as I glided along, unobstructed by any distraction, it couldn't have been more than two or three kilometres before the landscape changed and the track lost its abyssal steepness. Vistas opened up, establishing a connection to the landscape in which this small wood was embedded. And yet the memory remained vivid of the experience of finding myself for a short eternity freed from everything firmly and necessarily anchored to my self-image. And if any of the others, Silvi with her cries of joy, Bernward, strong-willed Rosemarie, Salam with his many irons in many little fires, had anything approaching the same experience as I had—the thought haunts me to this day—then would things perhaps not have turned out the way they did because there would have been no essential need for them to do so? Would each of them not have realized that, really, you don't have to be the person you think you have to be? That perhaps nothing is so indelibly written in that big book up there that the fatalists talk about. Wasn't that book in truth made up of so many blank pages which only begin to fill up with writing after the fact, after the events and experiences of our lives have come and gone?

The view opened up onto the black Altkönig, the Celtic stronghold. Spread out before me lay an inviolate winter world. It was not that a sheet had floated down and covered the mountainsides but, rather, that this entire landscape had come down from the sky that very night. This land, tamed and defiled during the day, recovered its wild alterity at night. Was the city of Frankfurt perhaps, in truth, surrounded by unending Siberian forests? And their solitude spread to the city itself when a bend in the track opened up a view into the distance—the further down I got, the clearer it became—the sea of lights on the plain also looked as though they were glowing in solitary abandonment, like large refineries or floodlit factories traversed only by a few nightwatchmen on their bicycles.

There were uncanny moments too. Suddenly a black figure rose before me, completely immobile, and as I came closer I saw the pink pinhole glow of a cigarette. I didn't recognize him until he was standing right in front of me—it was Bernward, Silvi having gone ahead on her own. The groups were in constant transformation, like raindrops on the window of a moving car. Some seemed to be a little stuck, others flowed purposefully, forming a thicker stream, which vanished as quickly as it had appeared. Occasionally I would glide into loud conversations. People ignored the night and behaved as though it were broad daylight or was this the song of the fearful in dark and dingy basements? The moon came out, flooding the white peaks in light. Not far from me I spied two heavily swathed people in silhouette. Were they kissing? I tried not to look any closer and quickly glided past.

Suddenly, Phoebe was beside me, all alone, no fox in sight. Our sledges clashed, she steered to the right, I to the left and ever so gently we keeled over into the pillows of snow. The cold stripped away all smells. Never had my nose been so close to her neck but the sweet-smelling cloud that usually surrounded her was frozen. Never had she been as unlovely as just then, her face grey from the cold, her nose red and running slightly.

'Oh, it's you,' she said but seemingly glad. Not disappointed in any case. Her voice was loud and at the same time stripped of all resonance as if I were hearing her through the veil of sleep. It was quite easy to slip into a long kiss, it was basically self-evident, but our warm saliva quickly turned cold round our mouths and Phoebe pulled away and said, 'If we keep this up we'll freeze together.'

And at that moment we were approached by other shadowy figures who revealed themselves to be Salam and Rosemarie. Rosemarie was poking fun at Salam's leather-soled shoes—what idiocy, to wear those shoes in the wintry woods!—and he interrupted her with a smile, 'I'm not complaining, I'm an expert in adapting to my surroundings.' You just had to develop a different technique, he said, and demonstrated by turning his feet outward in a Chaplinesque waddle. Bernward and Silvi came along a little later. They had evidently had an accident involving a head-on collision with a tree at high speed. Bernward had extended his arm in an effort to absorb the force of the crash and had sprained his wrist.

'People who get into accidents are so annoying,' said Rosemarie, who then nevertheless deftly examined her husband's wrist. Did he go to the hospital that evening? If so, then it was with as much discretion as everything else he did. Bernward Hopsten's sole ambition was to take up as little space as possible. Later, at any rate, when the great horde of woolly jumpers were drinking mulled wine at the Hopstens', he was back, with an elastic compress round his wrist, filling the guests' glasses with his left hand.

We had ridden through a no-man's-land on our sledges but no-man's-land is also governed by no-man's-time. We had moved through a great white sack as if we were still in the realm of the unborn. That night, the wintry wood had made everything appear as if it were not yet inevitable, as if any number of combinations were possible, all of which could dissolve again at any moment. In the light, each of us went back to the tracks we had been following before. Need I mention that Phoebe did not spare a single glance for me in that drunken night?

21

MAYONNAISE, THERE'S NOTHING TO IT

Silvi couldn't cook, as she herself freely admitted. She had nothing to hide in that respect. She envied no one's abilities—they were other people, incomprehensibly different in their construction, with inscrutable premises and backgrounds. If she ever felt a melancholy longing to trade places with another being at all, then at most it was the birds—just to fly around aimlessly, savouring the full height of physical space, that must be a divine pleasure for which she, light as a feather but still weighed down by a too-too-solid human body, would perhaps have been best suited. With regard to her parents-in-law, unconditional surrender was probably the most sensible attitude. Trying to compete with the perfection of Adelheid Schmidt-Flex's household was hopeless anyway. Recently, another benchmark and point of comparison had emerged in the shape of Rosemarie Hopsten, who seemed to be able to prepare her ambitious dinners with one hand tied behind her back. Both more modern and more exotic than the respectable-but-somewhat-frosty banquets at the Schmidt-Flexes', which clearly preserved the style of the ambassador's official dinners in the early post-war years. While others might never have got beyond their admiration and enjoyment, Silvi remained unimpressed. In this too she felt a kinship with the birds—she liked to peck a little, preferably at salted almonds or chocolate buttons, after which she wasn't hungry any more. In her case a word like full was much too crude to describe the sensation—for her, the minuscule desire to eat something was simply so fleeting that it vanished as quickly as it appeared. Her mother-in-law and Rosemarie Hopsten would watch her out of the corners of their eyes while she ate and both felt annoyed and resentful when they saw her pass a bowl on without taking anything for herself. They couldn't help feeling that Silvi had unreasonably high standards. But where would she possibly have developed standards? The black cook in her father's house, that ramshackle bungalow on the outskirts of São Paulo—there was a supermarket there now, the growing city having long since devoured that semi-rural suburb—had fed father and daughter on bean soup. On Sundays there was chicken, of which Silvi got the wings. It was part of her father's way of life never to compare one's living situation to anyone else's. His way of life was the right way—a sense of lack or insufficiency was simply inapplicable. After dinner, the cook brought the chessboard out onto the veranda just as one of her father's friends arrived. The two men were served rum and black coffee, the warm rain fell on the large-leaved weeds round the house and the men spoke little and softly and pushed the felt-bottomed chess pieces across the board. From inside, warm yellow light seeped out into the gloom. Life held its breath not for that one magical moment that everyone experiences now and again but for years which, depending on Silvi's state of mind, stretched out in her memory to eternal masses of time or condensed into pinheads of great pitch and moment. In that house, it would have been inconceivable to waste time and thought on something so basic and self-evident as food. In Silvi's kitchen, there was a shelf full of the cookbooks that Hans-Jörg would bring home from time to time—*Russian Fish Dishes* and *Cooking with a Wok* and *Tomatoes and Parmesan*. He would read through them looking for recipes that seemed simple to him. 'There, that ought to be easy to make,' he would say, handing the book to Silvi, who would look at the stylish photographs adorning these books as good-naturedly as she did everything that was placed in front of her. But she also knew, in a wordless way, that such books have nothing to do with real cooking. When Maria da Gloria peeled potatoes, her voluminous body filling the cramped and dingy kitchen at home, singing quietly to herself till the notes she sang made her body bubble and vibrate like a pot of boiling water— that was cooking. The air in her father's study would be filled with cigar smoke, it would get dark and added to this now would be the sound of the thick soup dishes that Silvi placed on the dinner table in the cone of the light from the lamp that lit it from above like a pool table and made the rest of the room appear even darker. In her mind's eye, the dining room still looked exactly the way she had left it even though since then the whole thing had been bulldozed off the face of the earth to which it had been only lightly tethered to begin with. And her father had not moved into the home where he no doubt continued his chess matches but, instead, still sat waiting on the veranda for Maria da Gloria, wiping her wet hands on her apron, to call him in for his bowl of soup. This was her life's undercurrent. Everything that happened above it, in all its infinite variety, was but a trivial little melody on top of that dark ostinato. Was it not always a possibility that this drone would swell and gradually swallow the skipping overtones until finally, like before, that was all there was?

Hans-Jörg did not blame her for not trying to cook something herself instead of always ordering something from the various Asian and Mediterranean places whenever they were hungry. Nor was he the sort of man who cooks—at most, he would fry an egg or a steak or two and, like Silvi, derived no great pleasure from eating. The 'culinary' prose of those colourful cookbooks spoke incessantly of banquets and feasts and the associated pleasures—he would have liked to know what went on inside those people who lean over their plates with such anticipation. Mostly he would have liked to see Silvi occupied in some way that he could understand. In front of other people, however, he would hold forth on the sorry state of his domestic situation—absolutely nothing on the table. Silvi was completely indisposed in this regard, he said. She was spoilt though she was of course by no means wealthy but she was ascetic in an overweening way, that was a more precise way of putting it, he continued, and in this she conformed to one of the fundamental dispositions of the Third World. In his view, it was this attitude of overweening asceticism which was one of the main reasons it was so damned impossible to make any progress there. Even if something was now apparently happening in Brazil, it didn't fool him—he knew what things were like there and had a wife from that country by his side.

Sometimes Silvi was there when he launched into these analyses. She would smile and look at him with something like admiration—how many opinions and ideas this one man had, it was simply too, too curious. He gave her a pained look in return, pursing his lips to one side, just like his father, but when he did it, this pursing had nothing of his father's strength and determination about it—it was an expression of distaste, as if he had something extremely bitter in his mouth.

'We'll have a dinner party,' Silvi announced one day, 'we'll invite Rosemarie and Bernward and cook something nice for them.'

Hans-Jörg was positively flabbergasted. Out of the question, he said, they weren't equipped for that in any way. Was Silvi planning on inviting them over for take-away pizza? They had been guests at Rosemarie's magnificent dinner table on many occasions now but, to Rosemarie's credit, it must be said that there was never the slightest hint that she expected to be invited to dinner in return. Rosemarie was generous in these matters and, besides, Silvi's inability and reluctance to cook had been discussed too often and in too much detail for there to be any doubt about it. So this plan of Silvi's was entirely unwarranted and unnecessary. Or was it? Was she perhaps averse to being identified with one single characteristic in this way? Did she simply no longer want to be just the wife who doesn't cook? In any case, her about-face had something to do with Helga Stolzier's recent influence. Whatever Helga said, she said emphatically. The expression 'to buttonhole someone' might have been coined to describe Helga's brand of intimacy. The way Helga touched Silvi while talking to her, the way she pulled her in close and latched onto her eyes with her own dark gaze, securing an unbreakable connection, could definitely be described as 'buttonholing' or 'button-holding', and when she finally let go of her interlocutor, it truly felt as though buttons had been released from buttonholes and a heavy cloak had fallen from one's shoulders.

'It's easy,' Helga whispered conspiratorially, 'and you've got to do it—it would be harmful for you if you didn't.' There was no need to specify exactly what harm might come to her.

'You find out what Bernward likes and if I can manage it, with your help of course, then I'll give it a try.' This idea had come suddenly to Silvi. Had she asked herself why everything had to depend on Bernward, she might have said that Bernward had 'always been nice' to her. He looked pleased when she walked into the room—didn't he? In a room full of people she would walk up to Bernward first. With him, it didn't matter what she said because, quite often, he would stand there without saying anything either but obviously content and relaxed about it, not bored or uncomfortable. But to ponder his inner workings to the extent of wondering—as she never had with regard to herself or Hans-Jörg—what he liked? That was something new.

Now Silvi was standing in her kitchen, that unused and therefore somewhat unreal space. She didn't know where the utensils were—what was a balloon whisk? Until now she would have presumed that it referred to a manner of being transported away quickly by a hot-air balloon. Helga was going to come and set the table. There was probably something pedagogical about her instructions on how Silvi should stir up some mayonnaise. Silvi was supposed to make the mayonnaise all by herself and this small feat was meant to give her the courage to tackle further culinary tasks. The cookbook lay open on the kitchen table next to a dozen eggs in a bowl. Silvi, wearing an apron—a highly unprofessional-looking thing, with classical columns printed on the front, from a London museum gift shop. However had this wound up in their flat?—looked like she was on the set of a TV cookery programme as the guest of a celebrity chef but the chef wasn't there and she had been left alone with the cookbook. She was supposed to break these beautiful, heavy brown eggs that were such a pleasure to hold, these most beautiful of all natural forms, but it was also satisfying to destroy this perfection. Holding one half of an egg in either hand, she was now supposed to pour the contents carefully back and forth to separate the glowing yolk from the white. The stringy gloop went into another bowl. A shame that she wasn't supposed to do anything with those lovely, viscous egg whites, except pour them down the sink. Silvi was overcome by a sudden urge to be thrifty—couldn't one do something with all this egg white?

Yes, said Helga on the phone, but that was too difficult right now, she'd show her the next time. To Silvi, every egg was a surprise. What might be inside? And every time it was a yolk, never a chick—how extraordinary that you could be so sure. There really were laws governing reality that, apparently, everyone got along with just fine. The bright yellow yolks crowded together at the bottom of the mixing bowl, an appetizing sight. And now she was supposed to destroy this perfection too and cause these yolks to explode with her whisk. Cooking was fun.

The next step was harder—with one hand, pour an unbroken stream of oil into the yolks, all the while beating the yellow mass with the whisk held in the other. Was it better to hold the whisk in her right hand and the bottle in her left or vice versa? She tried both but neither way seemed easy. Nonetheless, the oil flowed, the yolks were beaten—somehow even this worked out. Suddenly she remembered that Helga had said that the eggs mustn't be straight out of the fridge, this was very important. They had to be pre-warmed. She had completely forgotten because everything Helga said, even the most inconsequential details, was spoken so dramatically that Silvi had quickly stopped listening. Such specialized knowledge was part of Helga's mastery, and that couldn't be required here if she also claimed that making mayonnaise was 'the easiest thing in the world'. The cookbook didn't say anything about pre-warming the eggs and, after all, the cookbook was the ultimate authority for Silvi. In general, Helga's authority was waning now. Her friend had explained to her how quickly the extraordinary transformation of this egg-and-oil mixture would occur. Something magical would happen—the eggs and the oil mixed together into a soup would, through vigorous beating, suddenly start to thicken and become more substantial. Pretty soon, it would be hard to get the whisk through it and before she knew it the mixture would be as rigid and firm as thick cream. But Silvi kept whisking that yellow mixture like mad—the bottle of oil was now empty—and nothing was happening. This thickening was supposed to happen all of a sudden but even sudden transformations take some preparation. Silvi waited expectantly for the magical moment, her wrist hurt, she kept beating and beating but instead of thickening, the yolks got runnier and runnier. It became clear to her that this was the substance's final state. It would never turn thick and creamy, any more than if she took her whisk to a bowl of water.

At this, she broke out in a sweat. It was half past six. The guests were arriving at eight. She would be greeting them empty-handed. Just what Hans-Jörg was expecting. Nor would her parents-in-law be surprised—they would simply say nothing in that eloquent way of theirs and not look at her.

Another phone call to Helga. This time Helga was stern in her admonishments. She cross-examined her like a prosecutor. Had she pre-warmed the eggs, she demanded to know. Silvi grew defiant. The cookbook didn't say anything about pre-warming the eggs, she insisted. How did Helga know she hadn't pre-warmed the eggs? Was she secretly in league with the eggs? Why was the cookbook so treacherous as to leave out the most important detail? Silvi's mounting desperation far exceeded the botched mayonnaise that triggered it. The external world was completely inscrutable. She knew it and had always known it— she was incapable of reading the signals things sent out. She was fundamentally excluded from such knowledge and the ability to move about freely in the world. Where, she asked, had other people learnt the most important things, namely the ones that go unsaid? Her thoughts trailed off. Couldn't the eggs just as easily have done what the cookbook said and turned thick and firm out of sympathy for her and in accordance with her level of culinary knowledge? Even those lifeless eggs had to rub her nose in her own ignorance. Her eyes filled with tears.

This is how Helga found her, in a mixture of fury and despair. For Helga, her new friend's state of mind was a gift. With quiet confidence and the dignity of a priest she assumed control of the kitchen—quickly finding everything she needed. Things obeyed her commands. Not a single wooden spoon could hide. It was too late to buy new eggs but Helga had foreseen this and brought some herb butter—'We'll tell them you made it,' and, indeed, she stuck to this story emphatically during dinner, even though no one was buying it. But under Helga's supervision the roast beef had turned out splendidly. Every bit the conjured fairy godmother, she kept a knowing eye on it in the oven until it was pink and succulent.

Thus the only discordant note of the evening was Schmidt-Flex's appraisal of his son's choice of red wine.

'This wine is . . . good,' he said with the same benevolence as, after a school concert, he might have said, 'It was . . . lovely.'

'Just so you know,' he continued, addressing Hans-Jörg privately in a hushed voice, which was nevertheless perfectly audible to everyone at the table, 'the eighty-sevens are a significantly poorer vintage than the eighty-eights and eighty-nines. I understand that you don't want to be too extravagant for family meals such as this, the prices are completely absurd of course, absolutely no reason to go along with it but, in that case, I wouldn't go for second-best, rather, pick a simple, straightforward *vin de table*.' Old Schmidt-Flex always derived a special sense of satisfaction whenever he could recommend something simple and straightforward—a sense which on this occasion was amplified by the fact that he deemed this to have been a particularly successful 'abasement' of his son. Bernward hardly said a word that evening. Rosemarie and Schmidt-Flex led the conversation. But as they were leaving, when he found himself standing alone with Silvi for a moment, he said to her gently and politely, 'You look so sad, Silvi.'

'Oh dear,' Silvi smiled bashfully, 'I really didn't want anyone to notice.' Outside in the night it seemed to Bernward that she had been grateful.

22

THE KEYS TO ANOTHER WORLD

At a big cocktail party in honour of a retiring senior accountant at another firm—apart from a couple of colleagues and Titus Hopsten, I didn't know anyone—I noticed a very tall man standing on the sidelines with a disgruntled look on his face and who seemed to be looking for someone. If the person in question was in the room, this fellow stood a good chance of spotting them since he was a head taller than most of the other attendees, looking down on us, in both the literal and the figurative sense. My office-mate, who was originally from India but had been in Frankfurt for a while now, told me the names of everyone around us, which I promptly forgot, until he turned his head deliberately inconspicuously in the direction of the irascible giant and immediately looked away and said, 'And that's a certain Mr Slavina, just started working here at Sheera & Wasserstein, previously in London.'

Well, well, so this was the elusive Baron Slavina. But why did this knowledge fill me with a profound sense of satisfaction, as if I had just been initiated into the Eleusinian mysteries? I found it positively exhilarating to stand there and look at him out of the corner of my eye, knowing what he didn't know, namely, that we were neighbours and that I, or so I thought, knew a great many peculiar details about his life, which so far had not come together to form a coherent picture but which provided plenty of food for speculation. True, I had by then given up on my little obsession but finally setting eyes on the man who had left behind these traces, that was an unexpected and gratifying breakthrough in my investigation. I had no intention of making use of this knowledge in any way. My curiosity was perfectly idle and, therefore, of the highest degree of moral purity. I especially had no intention of going over to him and introducing myself as his neighbour, so I studiously avoided him lest his ever-circling gaze should fall upon me and he should later recognize me on the stairs in our building. Slavina had already changed out of his business suit into a green linen jacket, as if he were on his way to his country estate. His hair was quite long and parted in the English style. At first glance, he seemed an attractive man with well-proportioned features but his face was contorted from squinting, the corners of his thin-lipped mouth turned downward into a sneer that was completely at odds with this casual and inconsequential occasion. And yet, clearly, this was not some Kierkegaardian figure, who would have looked down upon this self-satisfied mercantile striving and seen the stigma of moral turpitude. But he was possessed by an impatient demon, an indomitable imp that so wound him up inside that he was compelled to find some form of outward release. This he found in the large bunch of keys he held in his hand. He was playing with them, sticking his finger through the ring and spinning the keys around, jangling and rattling them and never for an instant allowing them to come to rest. He carried out these key-ring exercises at around waist-height with the dextrous yet isolated movements of a conjuror. It was as if his head up there in the lofty heights was completely unaware of the perpetual motion of the keys down below. Was Slavina, standing there at the edge of the party, albeit towering above it, perhaps not a marginal figure at all? Could it be that his incessant key twirling was in fact turning the crank of the party and keeping it going? Was his peevish and even bitter expression perhaps caused by thoughts such as, 'Good, you're all drinking champagne and gin and tonic and having inane conversations, but what would you all do if I weren't here to keep this cocktail party going? If I stopped twirling my keys and just put them in my pocket? Someone's got to do it for you all, and that someone is me, even though you have no idea. A thankless task, you're welcome—Gratitude from the House of

Habsburg—haha!' Slavina's linen jacket was the inspiration for this final comment that had found its way into the interior monologue I was constructing for him. I allowed myself to drift slightly in his direction. Now he was actually speaking to one of the guests or, rather, speaking over his head while looking at the clouds billowing up magnificently on the other side of the glass facade, glowing pink in the auspicious glory of the sunset, just as they had when the city consisted of nothing but a couple of cottages and an intricate network of intersecting rivers. Then as now such beauty went largely unnoticed—even the fishers and ferrymen of early Frankfurt had not been pantheistic natural philosophers.

'I simply fail to see,' said Slavina in the tone of a gentleman who has been deeply wounded but who is too clever to let his interests out of his sight, 'I simply do not see why—why on earth should I?' Did the reply offered by the Italian-looking gentleman at Slavina's feet reach those lofty ears? Certainly, the latter's comments seemed to refer less to his views on inheritance tax—which was, I believe, the subject of their conversation—than to the fact that the tall man couldn't see why he should have to talk to the short one at all. This impression did not prove unfounded for no sooner had the short, elegant Italian turned away than the keys resumed their twirling, faster and more fiercely than before, in order to make up for the interruption. What would happen if that heavy bunch of keys suddenly slipped off his finger and went flying through the room to strike the porcelain temple of one of the few ladies present? But I had heard him speak, heard him announce, with loud indignation in a Viennese or, more specifically, Hietzing drawl, his refusal to accept something or other. His keys and his indignant refusal to be bamboozled into accepting something against his will melded to give Baron Slavina, for whose appearance I had waited so long that I had essentially given up hope, a solid and unmistakeable personality. I was dangerously close to him now if I still wanted to be able to remain incognito but I felt safe because it seemed to me that Slavina's angry and excruciatingly bored gaze was not truly directed at the partygoers, it was more of a mask. He looked preoccupied with thoughts of the utmost importance or as though he were waiting for someone, which concealed the fact that he was a stranger in these circles and could not find a way in. I myself have occasionally made use of this technique when, owing to a certain timidity, I have been unable to enter into conversation with people in an unfamiliar setting.

We were standing quite close to the tall glass wall that marked the boundary of the reception hall, spanning several floors of this high-rise, when my suspicions regarding Slavina's mental state were unexpectedly confirmed. He suddenly narrowed his eyes. His gaze became more intense. He had seen something that caught his attention and, just like that, his sullen look was wiped away. He was completely alert. It was he himself who had caught his eye, his reflection in the wall of glass, a little blurry, but his outline, stately enough, was unmistakeable. Like many tall people, he had bad posture and while standing around at this party he had let his control of his stance slip. His shoulders had slumped, his back was hollow. His trousers had slipped down slightly and over the belt hung a bit of a belly. And it was on precisely this protuberance that Slavina's eye now focused. He stood up straight, thrust his shoulders back and pulled in his stomach, which of course caused his trousers to sink still further. With a firm grip he pulled them back up to his navel and tucked his shirt in, which gave him a few minutes before his trousers slipped back down again. He never even had to let go of his keys. I imagined how he waged war on this belly that was on the advance, backed by his innards. It was no use dieting. I could see him performing calisthenics every morning, observing himself with a mixture of fear, self-loathing and self-delusion. When he flexed his muscles his stomach was as hard as a board—so where did this abhorrent bulge come from? One often has a completely different body while working out than during the rest of the day—how was that possible? Was his body deliberately deceiving him? Was it lulling its assiduous and ascetic owner into a false sense of security, only then to embarrass him in public? I could picture Slavina's lean, naked body underneath the linen jacket perfectly. I could picture his navel, a source of pain despite its insensitivity, framed by tiny wrinkles, like the expressionless eye of an Asian.

23

THE SERVICES OF AN OLD TYPEWRITER

'All right, so you've laid eyes on Slavina at last or, rather, swallowed him whole with your eyes. I hope you weren't too embarrassingly obvious about it. Finally a real situation in the midst of all this make-believe. How do you feel about that anyway? Making something up in order to excuse someone, that's understandable—but to denigrate them? Wouldn't it be more honest to admit what you don't know?'

'My fabrications are a kind of self-defence. Imagine you're looking at a magnificent mountain in the Swiss Alps when suddenly cracks begin to form and the whole thing crumbles in on itself before your very eyes—is one not justified in imagining what terrible tremors and explosions must have been going on inside that mountain which minutes before had stood so rock solid before you?'

'But where is this mountain in your story? The Taunus consists of gentle ridges and hills . . .'

It would be difficult to describe Rosemarie's trysts with Salam as overly affectionate. They retained the somewhat brutal abruptness of their initial encounter, which was how Salam preferred it but it also suited Rosemarie—it gave the affair an atmosphere of utmost urgency that left no time for deliberation. It was an imperative to be heeded, no questions asked. The hospitality at Salam's flat was sparse to say the least. In the fridge, there was a half-empty bottle of gin which Salam never touched—whoever might have left that behind?—and otherwise you could have a glass of water from the tap. Salam didn't like the incessant wine drinking as it put him out of commission too quickly and his motto was—readiness is all. The fact that Rosemarie's visits now assumed a certain regularity—mostly during the day, which did not in fact suit him—had not been part of his plan. He preferred his love affairs stormy, and lightning rarely strikes the same place twice, as they say. But nor did he have anything against the repetition at first. If she wanted to keep coming, it was fine by him. Her domestic and social obligations were such that her visits had to be carefully planned. Rosemarie was not liable to appear suddenly at your door. Thus the affair remained pleasantly manageable. And the time pressure between their frantic bouts of love- making, those exercises in amatory egoism that Rosemarie still found astonishing and to which she submitted as one would to an earthquake or other natural disasters, also prevented the pauses for conversation from becoming too protracted. Unless you were intent on planning a joint business venture with Salam, conversations with him tended to be rather limited. In matters of business, his imagination reached truly poetic levels of inspiration. To him, a concrete business relationship, indeed an entire national economy or even those sets of relations reverentially referred to as 'macroeconomic' were filled with lifeblood. Far from seeing them as abstract number games, to him it was all one great organism of which he too was part and which he understood in the same way as an experienced person feels at home in his own body and is able to tell better than any doctor what ails them and what they need. Rosemarie, as you know, was by no means naive when it came to business but she never wanted to discuss business with Salam though not, by any means, because she wanted him to put her in a more romantic frame of mind. What she did with him happened against her will—or so she told herself every time when she had left him and was sitting in her car. He had seduced her into highly irrational acts—for better or worse—but that did not have the slightest effect on her estimation of his status as a businessman. In that regard, her reason was perfectly intact and he knew it. When she lay by his side and looked at his pale, hirsute body— a creature of the forest, she thought, a faun, which was ironic, since Salam was the most urban character imaginable—she was afraid he would begin talking business but even he had some inhibitions. To him, she remained the epitome of the unattainable woman—not in terms of these fleeting bedroom exploits but in terms of her position in society which he was able to define more precisely than she could have. So their pillow talk was confined to only the least interesting of topics—the discussion of mutual acquaintances, notably the Schmidt-Flexes. He complained of his frustration at working with Hans-Jörg and Rosemarie expressed her sympathy, not without a certain secret satisfaction. She imagined working with Hans-Jörg to be a painful affair—his father had been harsh enough in his pronouncements about him. The old man was the sort of false patriarch who feels gratified by the failure of his descendants and takes pride in his tragic role of being the last of his illustrious lineage. Hans-Jörg's misplaced tenacity, his inflexibility, his inability to adapt to the Egyptian mentality had a disastrous effect on their negotiations in Cairo and continued to cause problems even after Salam brought the deal to a successful conclusion. All that was left to do was to pay one of the middlemen a small bribe, a laughable sum compared to the total value of the deal, no more than ten thousand euros, but it had to be transferred quickly, and Hans-Jörg had dug in his heels, sewn his pockets shut and got all high and mighty about not stooping to such unprofessional tactics. Would you say I was unprofessional? Salam wanted to know. It was a rhetorical question. Rosemarie, lost in her contemplation of that soft, curly-haired belly, did not have to answer. Salam chuckled at the memory. He even had to rescue Hans-Jörg from a child prostitute. Not an un-risky undertaking incidentally, but he said he had always had his suspicions about Hans-Jörg.

'Poor Silvi, that silly hen,' Rosemarie said dreamily. She asked Salam whether he thought or maybe even knew that she had found someone, an admirer, to distract her a little?

'There are two golden rules governing such questions.' Salam unveiled his arcanum of human nature. 'First, there is always more going on than you think and second, there is always less going on than you think.' Whereupon his mind returned to 'chanoodling'.

Meanwhile, the secret of Salam's expert advice to Helga remained safe and hence not a word was spoken about the intervention by the cockatoo that had so perfidiously rewarded Helga's love or about the violently inconclusive conclusion. Helga had decided that the whole thing was none of anyone else's business. She was not the vindictive type and besides she was worried, perhaps not without some justification, how Rosemarie—it was mainly her she was worried about—would react to hearing tell of the incident. She wouldn't have been the first person to be looked at suspiciously after describing an attempted rape. One often hears how the victims of such attacks have a hard time finding sympathy or even credence. And it was difficult to imagine someone of Helga's physique and general appearance as a helpless victim, which thankfully she also was not. Nevertheless, she felt distinctly that the details of the story, her invitation to Salam to join her for a cup of tea and help her to advance her business plan—a plan she knew Rosemarie did not support—would be difficult to explain. The question of whether Helga would say something did not preoccupy Salam in the slightest, incidentally. He had done as he must, she had done as she wished and that was the end of it. There really was nothing to tell—what would be the point of the story? It had been nothing but a misunderstanding and if Helga nevertheless felt the need to spill the beans to Rosemarie, she should feel free. He was used to dealing with disgruntled lovers and he knew how to handle it—literally with his own hands. He certainly had not sworn any oaths of fidelity to Rosemarie, he hadn't given her any perspective on the future at all, that lay well beyond the scope of their conversations, and he was convinced that she also didn't want to hear anything of that sort.

While he had more or less forgotten the entire incident and could barely even remember why he occasionally shot meaningful glances at the Norn-like Helga, she was very far from having forgotten anything. She had staved off his physical assault but it had planted something inside her that lived and grew and filled her up. A happy experience it most definitely was not, rather, a profoundly threatening one. Nonetheless, she had overcome it with physical force and strength of will and so the unpleasant became mixed with the deeply affirmative. To be sure, her decisive intervention had cut short a particular development—a development which had had to be cut short, there could be no doubt about that, but a stump remained and in it lay hidden what it might have become if allowed to develop organically. It was this sense of arrested development that took up more and more space in Helga's mind, to the point where it would sometimes boil over in a wave of fresh indignation—precisely as it had not done on that early evening when she had been self-control incarnate—and she would be plunged into the most outlandish musings, particularly whenever Salam had just shot her another conspiratorial look.

Then the winter came and the power of her secret refused to abate. It was clear that she was essentially pregnant with it, which meant that she would one day have to give birth, which meant she would have to tell Rosemarie everything. Having reached this conclusion, it nevertheless took her a while to find the right moment. She waited until the new year when Rosemarie came to visit her in her boutique and sat down at the same spot where Salam had sat on that fateful evening.

The two of them were engaged in sober planning. Helga had her birthday in November and now it was almost March but Rosemarie had promised to throw her a dinner party—after all it was a big birthday and that called for celebration, so now all they had to do was come up with a guest list 'of your people', as Rosemarie put it. She insisted that Helga view this dinner party also as an opportunity to promote her business. Which meant that there were other important ladies besides Rosemarie —ladies whom Rosemarie would otherwise not even wish to see at a distance but in honour of her friend's birthday she agreed to put such antipathies aside. Now that the issue of the guest list had come up, Rosemarie suddenly fell back on her old whimsy —how unimaginably long had it been since she had made such jokes, light-hearted and completely innocent—and asked Helga why she didn't want to invite Salam to the party. This gentle prod was all it took to pop the threadbare shell of Helga's restraint.

She had her reasons, she answered with dignity. She gave Rosemarie a full account, sparing no detail. And when she saw Rosemarie's stunned expression—which she took for an indication of incredulity—she even had the necessary physical evidence ready. She held up her finger, white and firm like a crayfish tail tipped with a hard, dark red fingernail, and there it was, fully healed but still clearly visible, the scar from her cockatoo wound. The beak had cut deeply, as though the bird's intent had been to tear off a good chunk of her finger. Under ordinary circumstances, it might have been difficult to maintain the sense of outrage, given the inherent comedy of the image of Salam sucking on her finger, but not now. Rosemarie was in no mood to see the humour in the situation.

'And then?'

A question of the utmost urgency—she had completely abandoned the necessary reserve. She had to know everything, had to squeeze every last detail out of Helga, regardless of how strange or unusual it might appear to her friend. But Helga did not find it strange or unusual. The aura of regal severity that surrounded her at those parties at the Hopstens' was now charged with noble fire. This was not the way to treat Helga Stolzier, she said. That sort of behaviour was not going to get you anywhere with her. Certainly not the way he had gone about it. If she didn't want something to happen, it didn't happen, simple as that. Helga's tendency to make pronouncements about what she was like at every opportunity, not least in matters of business, usually provoked a supercilious smile on

Rosemarie's part—we all need something to hold on to and the poor thing was so proud of her principles. But today she was full of praise—praise which drew its stirring fervour from a secret sense of relief.

That's exactly how it had to be, said Rosemarie, and that's exactly what she would expect from Helga, too. She would have been forced to change her entire opinion of her friend, had Helga given in and allowed a brute like that to satisfy his repulsive primal urges with her. In this way Helga was just like her, Rosemarie, who would sooner die than let that abhorrent man anywhere near her! The fact that this passionate outburst contradicted some of the things she had said to Helga about Salam in the past didn't matter now. Nor did Helga bring it up. It was as if Rosemarie had wanted to subject her to a rigorous examination and she had passed with flying colours. And in the animated pauses in their conversation, Rosemarie did not feel like a hypocrite or a traitor. What she did with Salam two or three times a week, the very fact that she had ever done anything with him, was now completely erased from her memory. No, that man was not part of her life. At that moment, it was completely self-evident that she and that woman named Rosemarie who seized every opportunity to take the lift up to the sixth floor of Salam's apartment building were two completely different people. Helga's back room became a place for Rosemarie to wallow in everything that made Joseph Salam repulsive. But Helga didn't actually find him all that bad. She felt that she had achieved the desired result in Rosemarie's indignation but that it did not adequately express everything she felt when she thought about the incident. When Rosemarie finally fell silent, she told her that she had consciously decided not to punish Salam for his actions. No, no, said Rosemarie, she too was of the opinion that punishment was completely beside the point in a case such as this. But in her car driving back to the Taunus, calmly going over these revelations in her mind, she clearly saw the full panorama of the precipice on which she had been teetering.

She had only to imagine what would have happened if Helga had acquiesced to Salam's entreaties—if you could refer to his bloodthirsty ambush in such benign terms—and was now likewise his lover. Rosemarie began to see her own role more clearly as well. She and Helga had come dangerously close to being bonded in highly ignoble kinship. And that would have put an end to her efforts at keeping Salam out of her life. Everywhere she looked she would have seen a casually chatting and firmly ensconced Joseph Salam. She tried to form a dispassionate assessment of the room that she still had to manoeuvre. Ending things with Salam immediately would be the most sensible course of action but unfortunately that wasn't possible. It didn't take much soul-searching for Rosemarie to see that. Had she been Queen Christina, she would simply have had him murdered, preferably in her presence. Murder was a possibility. Simply desisting, simply disappearing, raising the drawbridge, that was impossible. What would Salam do if he escaped from her supervision? She had the distinct sense that Helga still, or perhaps especially now, felt a certain curiosity about Salam. She in enmity with Salam, and Helga allied with him—that was a new nightmare scenario. It was clear what now had to happen, through small, painstaking steps if necessary—Salam had to be surgically removed, skilfully and permanently, from the tissue of her world.

When she arrived home, she was in such a whirligig of emotions that she had to seek refuge in focused activity. She had to do something right away, do something with her hands, perform some task, or else she would go mad.

She was alone in the house, luckily—that was her salvation or, rather, the first stage in it, the prelude to her great salvific opus. This consisted in an action with little accompanying thought beyond the initial decision. It also had an element of workmanship and it was this element to which Rosemarie now devoted herself wholeheartedly. Somewhere in the basement, there must still be her old typewriter on which she had written her master's thesis and her first newspaper articles thirty years ago. Rosemarie was not really one to fetishize 'vintage' objects and was ruthless in throwing things away, but her old typewriter, that was one thing she had kept. It took her half an hour searching through the orderly, dust-free basement, in innumerable boxes and cupboards, but that didn't bother her—after all, the goal was to find that old typewriter. And in the very last box, there it was, carefully packed away in a large plastic bag. And when she opened the lid, the beautiful, delicate thing presented itself in all its old-fashioned reliability. The ribbon was a little faded but when she typed a few words they were clearly legible. Tucked away in the lid was a sheet of paper from her student days when she used to write auction reports for the newspaper. Her interest in auctions had developed early on. The challenge of writing those articles lay in reporting on thirty different sales and finding a different word for 'bought' each time which was nevertheless always the perfect word in that context. And so, she had compiled a list of synonyms, which was what she now rediscovered—won, outbid, acquired, procured, went under the hammer, attained a value of, changed hands, disbursed, snagged, was awarded—and numerous other formulations which she read with great emotion and in remorseful memory of a more dispassionate time, but the feeling quickly passed.

Rosemarie carried the typewriter up to her little study on the first floor. She found some very thin gloves in a drawer and put them on. Her hands thus gloved, she opened a fresh packet of writing paper and inserted a sheet into the typewriter. Her gloved fingers typed a short text. She addressed an envelope likewise taken from a fresh packet. She moistened a stamp with a little water from a flower vase, which she applied with her gloved index finger.

Rosemarie took the newly opened packet of paper and the newly opened packet of envelopes, the letter she had just written and the typewriter and left the house. She got into her car and drove into the city. On the way she passed a large skip, into which she deposited the packets of paper and envelopes. Darkness fell.

In a suburb of Frankfurt that she had never visited—she had just kept on driving until she got to a place that neither she nor anyone else could have connected to her—was a pile of planks, broken furniture, a television and a mattress by the side of the road. There was not a soul in sight. She pulled over, got out of the car and added the typewriter to the pile. She felt as if she had just planted a bomb. She got back into her car which was parked some distance away and waited in the dark. After about half an hour, some people arrived and went through the pile looking for anything useable. She stared into the uncertain light of their torch. There, no question, one of them had picked up the typewriter in its little plastic suitcase. She waited until the people had made off with their booty. She got out once again and, sure enough, the typewriter was gone. Rosemarie was so relieved, elated even, that she was on the verge of forgetting the most important thing.

She had to post the letter. After quite a long search, she finally came across a postbox. She popped in the letter and stuck her hand into the slit to see if it was still reachable. Which indeed it was but then it fell all the way down. Her fingers grasped at thin air. It took her quite a long time to find her way back onto the Autobahn but this served only to reinforce her sense that she had done everything right. Back at the house, she burnt the piece of paper with the auction synonyms into the sink. There was a faint smell of burning in the foyer when Bernward came home. Did he even notice it?

This was the one possibility that Salam had failed to consider in his ruminations on whether Helga would keep quiet—that she would, indeed, spill the beans but he would be none the wiser.

24

TWO LETTERS AND A TRIP TO THE CINEMA

Hans-Jörg sat at his desk in the office. It was the headquarters of his small law firm but it also housed Flex-Realty LLC, a property-management firm that oversaw his father's real estate and Schmidt-Flex Consulting, which his father had set up as a command centre in his retirement and, as of recently, it was also home to Ramsesphone LLC, in whose interests he had recently travelled to Cairo with its CEO, Joseph Salam. In contrast to the frenzy of activities which the presence of all these various corporations might have led one to expect, the office was a quiet place. Schmidt-Flex conducted his business over the telephone or else received his business partners at home and Salam did not even have the keys yet, although the plan was for him to move into the adjacent empty room as soon as his company was up and running. Flex-Realty meanwhile employed an administrator to oversee the day-to-day management—not even old Schmidt-Flex expected Hans-Jörg to deal with burst water pipes and the like. The part-time secretary had placed the folder with the day's post on Hans-Jörg's desk. All the envelopes had been opened except for one with a typewritten address and no sender 'For the attention of Mr Hans-Jörg Schmidt-Flex, Ramsesphone LLC'—the company wasn't even listed on the letterbox yet and he had never received a letter with such an address, except for the Commercial Register. Hans-Jörg possessed an array of letter openers. It bothered him when the edges of an opened envelope were frayed. His letter openers had to be razor-sharp—an envelope was to be opened with a clean, surgical cut. Performing this cut gave him not inconsiderable satisfaction, one might even call it a feeling of pleasure if the idea of Hans-Jörg experiencing pleasure were not so preposterous.

The contents of the envelope came as a shock. An anonymous letter. 'Schmidt-Flex, you filthy paedophile, don't you read the papers? Do you still think that what you do in Egypt is of no concern to the German courts? Just imagine the uncomfortable investigation. How are you going to explain this to your father and your friends? The press will have a field day! But you're in luck—ten thousand euros is all it will take for this problem to go away. Wait by the phone tomorrow night. And keep your mouth shut. Or else things will run their course.'

Considering Rosemarie's agitated state of mind, her obsession with the procedure, the elaborate naivety of her precautions which had so completely clouded her reason, was it not remarkable just how clearly she had been thinking, just how simple and ingenious a solution she had found to the problem—irreparably souring the relationship between Hans-Jörg and Joesph Salam? In her state of helpless despair, she had been truly inspired. The care with which she had executed her plan ought therefore to be seen as a ritual designed to protect and nurture this spark of inspiration lest it go out and to enable her to carry it to just the right place where this spark could ignite a raging fire. And even if Salam were to see this letter, what genius of persuasion would provide him with an excuse that might allay Hans-Jörg's suspicions that he, in one way or another, was behind it—even if only by virtue of inadvertently spreading ugly rumours, by being a bigmouth, in other words? Even so, her patience would be tested to its limits for she had no means of discovering how the poison she had sent out would act, which organs it would attack first, how much pain it would cause, whether it would prove a lethal dose. And so, she abided in a strange mixture of pride at her ingenuity and a fearful numbness and began practising a gesture of complete innocence and surprise, in case the affair took an unexpected turn back in her direction. To have a clear goal and at the same time to know nothing about it or at least to forget about it, that was the task which she must now master in the long term but which caused significant tension in her in the here and now.

But how surprised she would have been, had she been witness to the way Hans-Jörg read her letter and his reaction to it.

Not every letter is interpreted by its recipient in the way intended by its author. Misunderstanding is one of the central chapters in the history of correspondence. There is an art to being unequivocal, and as far as her message was concerned, Rosemarie had been quite unequivocal and the fact that the letter referred to a particular evening on Talaat Harb, about which only Salam knew, and that the ten thousand euros in question was the same sum that was currently a bone of contention between them, was not lost on Hans-Jörg. But his thoughts quickly wandered away from this starting point along quite different paths, which Rosemarie could never have predicted.

In his mind's eye, he was transported back to the events of that late night in Cairo. He had scarcely got a proper look at the girl's face except when their eyes had met as he was still observing her from a distance, because after that he had followed her, the girl at his side and yet leading the way, with disconcertingly adult movements for her delicate little frame. From the way her little bottom moved underneath that long, colourful skirt, she was a full-grown woman. No German twelve-year-old would have been so fully formed. He remembered the grey traces of dirt on her cheeks, he remembered thinking that her skin would taste salty if he were to touch her with his lips, and he remembered her mass of long, matted hair with those greasy, lambent locks. The girl had been his magnet. He was compelled to follow her. Even in retrospect, it was clear to him that there had been absolutely no volition on his part. Once again, he felt how his feet had moved of their own accord, his head floating bewildered and perplexed above it all, all the time wondering what would happen when they had arrived at their destination through the illuminated night. One thought, a hope even, was still particularly present in his mind—that the mystery of those unwelcome, meaningless and inscrutable visions that beset him in every moment of repose might finally be solved. What the doctor who had examined his haemorrhoids had rejected with barely concealed incomprehension was now an absolute certainty—namely that these were short, involuntary glimpses of some other life, of some other world than the one inhabited by his conscious self. And it came back to him with perfect clarity just how certain he had been that these two worlds, these two lives, these two different places that his consciousness occupied at the same time—thinking, planning, speaking in one world, waking up for seconds at a time in another, as if from a drunken stupor—would merge once he and the girl had reached their destination. There was no doubt in his mind that she had been leading him to a room with a concrete wall and tattered curtains. He would have stood facing that wall with its sloppy pink paint job, hitherto glimpsed only in intrusive and involuntary senselessness. That the girl had also aroused him in some way he did not try to deny—this wasn't about finding excuses for himself or concocting mysterious motives for clearly ignominious desires. And he may well have felt desires of that sort—he remained astonishingly indifferent to the thought—but they weren't what truly consumed him, the thing which still seemed of such great importance. For now it was back, that singular, fleeting moment which Salam had blocked through his decisive intervention—Hans-Jörg was even-handed enough to remain grateful to his partner for this even now, despite everything— the moment when the two parallel tracks, which for so long his unhappy, tortured spirit had been forced to follow simultaneously, would finally merge into one. And so, it was no coincidence that it should be Salam who, in all likelihood, had written this letter —his rescue had averted the explosive moment or, rather, deferred it and now he had triggered it a second time, at a time when Hans-Jörg was in a much better position to seize it than he would have been in the turmoil that would no doubt have ensued that night in Egypt had Salam not interceded. For this time it was no longer a question of an image unassimilable to his own world. This time, there were no images at all. Perhaps this was even the end of the images. The oppressive images that had once plagued him were now embodied in this vulgar, inimical letter, the nastiness of which was nothing but a thin outer layer. Beneath it, the truth lay dormant, a creature never to be seen with the naked eye, hiding behind the multitude of fleeting impressions while also nourishing them and causing them to grow so colourful and imperative. This was a moment of pure happiness, if we take happiness to mean spontaneous, disinterested joy, the feeling of watching a ball that has been hurled from far away and has bounced back and forth among manifold obstacles and finally sunk into its designated hole, a hole shaped in precisely such a way as to receive this ball and no other and never to let it go till the end of time. The game is over, the goal achieved, rendering all further questions or actions superfluous.

The path that had led Hans-Jörg to this fulfilment nevertheless remained surprising. Looking back, he seemed to himself to have been a walking corpse that must also have exuded a smell of decay, judging by how intolerable he had evidently become to all those around him. Brooding had become his default state but this brooding never led to anything, rather, served only to reconfirm the completeness of his imprisonment. He saw only too clearly how futile all of his endeavours to enter the world in which the others lived had been. How he had always hoped and believed that a sufficiently large collection of paraphernalia would allow him to meet life's demands and how he had tried in vain to gain access to the sphere of the others' daily lives by means of a heavy-duty cigar cutter or a watch that could tell you when it was high tide. Now he could see how his hyperactivity was driven by a fatal impulse, like a wasp buzzing up and down against a glass wall until its strength is fully depleted. It must have been awful to witness him in that state but there was nothing to feel remorseful about—no one could have freed him, whether they loved him or hated him, although perhaps Silvi didn't really love him and his father didn't really hate him. It was probably more realistic to place the temperature of their feelings in the tepid range, at least as far as he was concerned. Certainly he had only been able to take Silvi away from that screwed-up little bungalow—a kind of wheel-less railway car fringed on all sides by a veranda; its clear simple form had later been spoilt by the addition of hideous extensions—because she felt that she couldn't stay there any longer. His father-in-law, whose antipathy he had felt from his very first visit, waxed poetic when describing his children—he referred to his eldest son, evidently doing well at university, as 'his brain'; the second eldest, a sportsman, was 'his strength'; Silvi's sister was 'his heart'; and Silvi was 'his soul'. But what he meant by this was less poetic—in short, he wanted to forget his brain, his strength, his heart and his soul, and to that purpose he needed to be left alone or, at best, to play chess with one of his silent friends. Family life had lost all significance for this man, his heart and his soul were free to disperse into the world as long as they didn't bother him any more.

Now Hans-Jörg understood him. For an instant, he felt the paradoxical urge to go and visit this hermit—for the great hermits of antiquity such visits had always been an occupational hazard; if you were really serious about being alone you couldn't very well complain about your fellow man's lack of interest. Poor Silvi! Others had thought the same thing but now it was he who embraced the sentiment with heartfelt sympathy—not remorse, for how could one honestly feel remorse for something that had happened so involuntarily? Was the last thing that bound them together not his constant desire to take her wine glass away from her? Even though it was none of his business if she got drunk and it didn't even really bother him—it was a state like any other. Thinking about his attempts at correcting Silvi led him to think about Salam, his flexible business manager who had evidently found it expedient to overcome the dead end in his negotiations about the aforementioned bribe of ten thousand euros by means of an explosive act of surprising unpleasantness. Salam too wanted to correct what was to his mind misplaced obstinacy, wanted to break his stubbornness. There was no doubt in Hans-Jörg's mind that it was Salam who had written the letter—quite unfairly, for it was definitely not Salam's style. Although, to be honest, people often try to refute allegations by grandly declaring that that's 'not their style'. True enough, but not even the greatest artist is always at the height of their style and besides a deliberate break with one's usual style can often turn out to be highly effective because it's so unexpected. And this was a lot of money—'Ten thousand euros, that's a lot of money!' as Rosemarie would have exclaimed, if it had been a matter of some inconsequential sum—and, in such cases, a person was liable to break with his usual style. But Hans-Jörg bore no ill will towards Salam. It now became clear that while the great wave of pleasure, the quiet deliverance associated with that ball rolling into its designated hole, remained peculiarly insubstantial in itself, its effect radiated out onto areas that were bursting with substance.

So now he was being blackmailed, he was being threatened, and it suddenly turned out that this was a completely impossible, a truly futile undertaking. Hans-Jörg did not feel threatened. And not because his would-be blackmailer actually had relatively little material for an embarrassing legal case. Hans-Jörg's doubts on that evening as to whether Salam had truly grasped the situation had not been entirely naive. Certainly nothing definite had happened and in the hustle and bustle of Talaat Harb it was not easy to determine who was actually walking alongside someone and who had simply been pushed up against someone else. But he had no need of such reassurances now for the fundamental reassurance or, rather, the serenity and stillness he now felt inside would have remained untroubled even in the face of incontrovertible evidence that he had put his arms round the little girl. This sudden, profound calm—a spiny mental shell had split open, exposing the polished mahogany kernel—came from the sudden realization that nothing bad could ever threaten him again as long as he lived, since the worst thing of all, life itself, had already happened. This was not a dark insight, however, rather, one that, as he sat there at his desk, positively filled him with a sense of pleasure. What might have sounded like a depressing conclusion was also accompanied by an immense increase in freedom. There was simply nothing left to be afraid of. When in the past he had been seized by a certain shamelessness, it had always been to see how other people would react. It had always seemed to him to be a sort of experiment he had to conduct in order to come to terms with the alterity of his fellow humans. But they had long ago passed judgement on him. With a pang, he thought of his father the way one thinks of a distant relative whose son has proved a great disappointment. And Salam! Salam, who was basically a genuinely nice guy and who had been so patient with him. The first person, really, to make an effort with Hans-Jörg, to entertain him, to decipher his moods or at least to dissipate them—not out of philanthropy, admittedly, but did it not take a firm bedrock of basic human kindness to be so dauntless and unflagging in dealing with another human being, even if it was ultimately in pursuit of one's interests? So what Salam was now threatening him with—from the dark side of his philanthropy—in such hurtful words, was simply laughable. Salam the gambler thought he was going all in but in fact he was betting far too low. He had inadvertently revealed that his funds were exhausted and he had nothing that could put pressure on Hans-Jörg.

But if Salam wanted to play games, it was Hans-Jörg's move. And if the point was to surprise and overwhelm your opponent, then it was now up to Hans-Jörg to be surprising and overwhelming, and so he too drafted a letter and then immediately wrote it out again in fair copy. He did this cheerfully, full of the joy flowing warmly through him and without the faintest hint of rancour towards Salam but, rather, with the exultation one feels when playing chess with a friend who has been cornered and has no more moves available to him.

'Dear Mr Salam,' he wrote, even though he and Salam had long been on more familiar terms, but it was the anonymous letter's informal tone that particularly irked him now, a real misstep on the part of its author, 'as majority shareholder in Ramsesphone LLC, I am writing to inform you that by the shareholders' resolution of . . . you have been relieved of your duties as CEO, effective immediately.' For any claims relating to services rendered, Salam was invited to contact Hans-Jörg's solicitor who would be handling the termination of the contract. The shareholders would be applying for the dissolution of Ramsesphone LLC under separate cover. Although his letter was signed, Hans-Jörg shared the anonymous letter writer's regret at not being able to see the look on the recipient's face when he read it.

What an implausible trajectory Rosemarie's missile had followed to strike her intended target far more surely than she could ever have hoped for in her wildest dreams!

Hans-Jörg was in high spirits for the rest of the day, untroubled by any thoughts worthy of the name. To be sure, there were plenty of inchoate thoughts, rudiments of ideas, swimming around but they never coalesced into words. His mood was comparable to the state of intoxication experienced by a Wagner aficionado after countless hours spent on the hard wooden seat in the heat and darkness of the festival hall, except that in Hans-Jörg's case it was not a full orchestra that made the music that carried him away but, rather, he himself in complete silence. When the secretary came back into his office shortly before lunch, she didn't notice anything different about him except perhaps a somewhat absent-minded friendliness, but since he often seemed absent-minded even when he was in a foul mood, she thought nothing of it. He even did some more work, dictated a couple of letters, but he had to insert solemn pauses every now and again in order to get back to that state of pure, silent elation, which waited patiently and returned to him at the end of each letter with undiminished force.

Arriving home, he was alone and was grateful to remain so, not because Silvi would have bothered him but because, at that moment, he had absolutely no need of company. Certainly not because he wanted to avoid any witnesses to the promised telephone call—he was looking forward to it—but in the context of the larger game in which he was now a player. What would Salam come up with? Writing and sending an anonymous letter is always the easiest part of blackmailing someone, no matter how much care and effort you may have put into it. Establishing subsequent contact with the victim without endangering oneself, that was something else entirely—had this stage not often proved fatal for even the most elaborate schemes? But we should not imagine Hans-Jörg sitting anxiously by the telephone. There were long stretches of that solitary evening during which he forgot all about the telephone. He wandered through the flat, opening and closing doors. He stood for a long time staring at the sequence of sparsely furnished rooms, as if he were trying to memorize the different lighting effects. The large foyer was brightly lit, the adjoining room was dark, the one beyond that was dimly illuminated by a single small lamp, invisible from this angle—how auspicious and promising that was. For the first time, he felt grateful for the fact that he and Silvi had not made any effort to furnish their flat in the traditional sense, even though there was enough furniture waiting for them at his parents' house. They had not moulded the flat to fit them and, so, it had remained a stage that could accommodate a multitude of different plays. There was an energy in that space with its high ceilings and black windows that he found appealing. He couldn't remember—or, rather, it no longer mattered; nothing needed to be forgotten—how they had lived there up to that moment. His silences, his querulous, obstinate tone on the one hand, Silvi's unapproachability in her self-possessed childishness or in the whims of the wine bottle on the other—it would henceforth be unthinkable for him so much as once to take the glass from her hand—this was one of the few clear thoughts that entered his head, even though there was something not quite right about her wine drinking—she was just as much a lightweight as he was, except that it gave him a headache but not her. She also wouldn't mind if he didn't join her for a glass of wine, they had no need of such mutual gestures. From now on he was a citizen of the free world, which she had perhaps been all along, and perhaps the discord that had coloured their relationship was simply due to the fact that although they had been living in the same flat, they had been living in two different worlds.

He did not eat or drink anything. There was no room for hunger or thirst inside him. But very late in the evening, when the telephone finally rang, he let it ring for quite a while, the thrill of the game instantly returning, and he couldn't help but smile as he picked up the receiver. Unfortunately it was only Rosemarie, in an oddly gregarious mood, apologizing for calling so late, asking how he was and somewhat absent-mindedly acknowledging the information that he was very well, thank you, before finally asking Bernward's whereabouts, as if she had only just remembered the reason for calling in the first place.

Hans-Jörg had actually thought that Silvi was at the cinema with both of the Hopstens—it was Rosemarie's idea, there was a rare screening of an old Italian cult classic that they simply couldn't miss—but it turned out Hans-Jörg had not been the only one to cancel that morning. Rosemarie too had stayed at home. She had wanted to spend the evening alone—perhaps so she could call Hans-Jörg with a distorted voice, by speaking through a handkerchief or by means of some other disguise? Easier said than done—it took real nerve to pull off something like that and who knew whether it would be possible to maintain the disguise perfectly throughout—and the thought of being recognized, even just the possibility, was more than she could stand. But must the letter not come as such a shock to a man such as Hans-Jörg that even an innocent phone call would suffice to gauge its impact? Surely he wouldn't be able to shrug it off? Something like that must surely shake a person to his core? On a day like today even the most casual reference to Salam was of course strictly off limits. His name could not be heard to issue from her mouth, the connection would be too easy to make. If Hans-Jörg had any idea of how agitated Rosemarie really was, he would certainly have been concerned. On the other hand, what did he and Silvi really want with this woman? Her husband was a different matter but he had absolutely no interest in Rosemarie, nor she in him.

Hans-Jörg went to bed. He did not give a second thought to Silvi's continued absence, instead was still just happy to be alone with himself and his surfeit of joy. He fell asleep instantly, the delightful calm of the day and evening passingly gently into oblivion. His dreams were filled with powerful, arresting images but only one remained in his memory when he awoke, which he even noted down in his diary, so greatly had the vision of that face impressed him.

He saw himself holding a baby in his arms, a naked little girl, no more than two years old, pitiably filthy, streaked with brown dirt and even some traces of dried blood, though not her own. There he stood, helpless—it was impossible to set the child down. He had to hold her in his arms even though she was greasy and sticky. But then suddenly Silvi was beside him and took the baby and dipped her in a little tub of water and washed her with a great big sponge that effortlessly removed all the dirt, and she dried her off with a soft towel and wrapped her in a big white bath towel and placed her on the bed—was it their double bed here in the bedroom? And now that little smiling face lay on the big white pillow and a wave of gratitude washed over Hans-Jörg and the vivid memory of that warm inundation remained when he awoke. He was grateful to Silvi. Yes, he was the man for Silvi, today he had become the man for Silvi. Can dreams lie? A poorly phrased question, whichever way you might care to look at the phenomenon of dreams, yet, it would not be long before Hans-Jörg would be utterly perplexed by the fact that this dream which had seemed so replete with inner truth had, at the very moment at which it presented itself to him in his sleep, in fact contained no truth at all, or at least whatever truth there might have been to it was not there any longer.

Through no fault of their own, Bernward and Silvi had become the only ones left to go to see the old Italian cult film, which neither of them in fact wanted to see, the whole 'cult film' thing being entirely Rosemarie's and Phoebe's department. They had not gone out of their way to find a way to be alone together. In fact the last and probably the only time they had had a private conversation had been on that night out on the loggia in Sicily. Planning and scheming wasn't really in Silvi's character, anyway, and she generally just went with the flow, even in situations that seemed to call out for decisive action, and simply accepted it when an incident caused her pain. Bernward, by contrast, must have made a conscious effort to avoid any opportunity to be alone with Silvi. He must have realized that it would take but the flimsiest of pretexts to take his relationship to Silvi irreversibly to another level. If one wanted to put it bluntly, one might say that he had fallen in love with her, which was not much of a feat by any means. If she had not grown up in the frozen isolation of her father's bungalow—a bit of a paradox given the unremitting heat there—before winding up with Hans-Jörg and his family, if she, like Phoebe, had been surrounded by a swarm of people her own age, then in view of her beauty and charm, men falling in love with her would have been the commonest thing in the world. Rosemarie had an acute sense of feminine beauty. She enjoyed the sight of Silvi's youthful body lying in a bikini by the swimming pool, even just for decorative reasons, but she also did her best to diminish the appeal of her beauty—Silvi, that silly thing, not the brightest spark, incorrigibly naive, completely uneducated, phenomenally ungifted, these were some of the expressions she kept up her sleeve to describe the young woman—'young', as Rosemarie would then sternly add, 'she's not as young as she used to be'—never directly criticizing but, rather, shaking her head in amusement. If only Silvi had made some use of all her languages at least. That was an area in which her skills far outstripped Rosemarie's, even Phoebe was no match, despite the fact that she and Titus had gone to the international school and spoke fluent English, because Silvi also spoke Portuguese, French and Spanish quite effortlessly. She would often switch between languages in a single sentence, but language is a just medium, as Rosemarie observed, not without a hint of smugness, and for each medium you also had to have something to say, if you wanted to be more than just a stewardess.

'And if only she were actually a stewardess at least!'

But then something had happened that completely changed Bernward's relationship to her and it had something to do with the very witlessness that the others had diagnosed in Silvi. Reading is a skill that everyone has to learn. Some people learn it faster, others more slowly, but, step by step, people acquire the ability to recognize the letters as sounds and gradually those sounds can be put together to form words. With Bernward, it had likewise been a question of learning how to read but not by laboriously practising a foreign alphabet—it had happened all at once. First came the realization that there was something to be read where previously there had been nothing but meaningless, material silence. And the text which, in a sudden burst of inspiration, he had begun to read was Silvi's body. In no way was Bernward a seasoned connoisseur of the female figure. He had no pretensions to erotic gourmandize — everything he had enjoyed up to that point had come to him in a state of pleasant thoughtlessness. But things were different with Silvi's body—he saw the way she moved in the deckchair, how she got up to get something to drink—white wine preferably, with ice cubes in Sicily—how she rubbed lotion onto her skin, how she put on her sunhat and took it off again, and through all of these movements her body spoke a language that was not always intelligible but always as euphonious as an indecipherable yet enchanting poem. The contours of her thighs, the firmness and simultaneous softness of her belly, the little wrinkles under her armpits, the armpits themselves, the turn of her neck—it all spoke of a wealth of ideas, full of ambiguous, intellectual and spiritual expression, or at least so it now seemed to Bernward in any case, something infinitely more intelligent and articulate than almost anything people said otherwise. What could possibly have expressed the enticing concavity, the warm pulsation of her armpits, their diaphanous skin, their focused redolence better than her armpits themselves? The generally received notion that there is such a thing as a soul or spirit that inhabits various different bodies—as well as hotel rooms of varying quality—but has nothing very much to do with the bodies it inhabits collapsed when it came to Silvi. Her body at least was identical with her spirit, there was no way of separating them. Without that body she was mute, with it, highly loquacious. The mellifluence of her voice was but the harbinger of the magnificent symphony, the never-ending madrigal spoken and sung by her skin, her lips, her shoulders and her breasts. But the plasticity, smell, weight, delicacy, tactility of the body—Silvi's body—were in any case superior to ordinary language. There was no need for abstractions to serve as crutches and prosthetics—the fundamental, the ideal, the universal found its superlative formulation in the visible. There was a seamless correspondence between the two. How blind did you have to be not to see this blatantly obvious secret, not to be drawn in by it and to yield to it completely and utterly? Well, basically, just as blind as Bernward had been until very recently. He felt privileged in this enlightenment which was actually not all that uncommon, even though it usually expressed itself somewhat differently than in the case of the well-read Bernward.

A man who has just found the spirit embodied in the woman he loves will not take offence at the suggestion that this spiritual enlightenment also has something to do with the vicissitudes of the body. He was not an old man, although the silhouette of old age was growing visible against the horizon. Let's be clear—it is impossible to impress a man who has just had an experience of this sort with moral quibbles. Bernward, the family man, happily married by any standard, even if the marriage might have cooled off slightly, it was all the more successful as an institution—consider the many interests he shared with Rosemarie: travelling, collecting and decorating, the joy of having a big house filled with lots of guests—was he really going to give all of that up, did he really think he ought to throw it all away? And what language did his physical appearance speak, leaving his tortured self-examinations to one side? Square in that Westphalian way, prosaically masculine, wooden and slightly creaky, albeit cultivated and solid—was this the body of a potential suitor, especially one who was already in a stable relationship? What about the embarrassment? Did he stop to consider the embarrassment it would cause? No, he didn't, but less because of his newfound enthusiasm than because it was a category which, bourgeois though he might otherwise have been, he had always regarded with complete indifference.

And what about Rosemarie? What future had he imagined for her? Bernward had the distinct impression that he did not need to worry about Rosemarie. Recently, there was a new looseness between them. For a while, the bond between them had been able to stretch but, recently, perhaps due to a careless overextension, it had lost some of its elasticity, and not because of him, or so Bernward told himself. No, things wouldn't be all that difficult with Rosemarie. Although these were his thoughts and although he was convinced that Silvi thought about him and felt affectionate towards him—like a daughter perhaps in a way; there were certainly mixed motives—for months, long, intolerably long months, he had held back and left things hanging, and hung they had, at first for him and then also for Silvi, palpably in mid-air, at least a hand's breadth above the ground whenever they were in the same room together. So if that was how it was going to be, when Rosemarie herself, impatiently and emphatically, as if secretly bothered by his presence, sent him off to the cinema with Silvi, the inevitable point had arrived at which the story took a different turn. Wasn't it just like Rosemarie to force a decision? He was often so hesitant. He mistrusted spontaneity. People who acted spontaneously often had an insufficiently clear sense of their limitations.

And so it was that Berward and Silvi ended up side by side in the dark of Bernward's car. From the moment Silvi got into the car there had been no mention of the film. Sometimes they looked at each other but when they spoke—Bernward in particular—they mostly looked straight ahead. Their heads were aligned like the profiles of a king and queen on an old medal. They were both highly emotional and therefore all but motionless. They were like two strings strung side by side on an instrument, patiently waiting to be played together for the first time, for they know that each is there only for the sake of other. These hours of anticipation were far too overwhelming to result in plans or even acts. Until the moment she had got into the car, Silvi had considered her situation to be utterly immutable and final. Her marriage to Hans-Jörg had felt like a house with many rooms inside which she was free to move about, not as a true confinement, in other words, for there was a courtyard and a view of a distant sky, but no windows facing the street and no door to the outside. Now that door had suddenly appeared, in a place she had passed by many times, and it wasn't locked but ajar. And nothing could have been more natural than to walk through it.

25

THE OLD GODDESSES

It was perhaps not without a small dose of malice on my part that I informed Salam one day that 'Frau Doktor Simserl sends her regards.' Indeed, I confess that I had been waiting for an opportunity to deliver this message in passing and by the by in the hopes of catching him off guard and observing his reaction. It is of course irremediably naive to try to put someone like Salam on the spot. His easy demeanour was no mere expression of a fleeting mental state but, rather, built firmly upon a stable inner foundation. Of course he didn't ask me how I came to know his friend. It was a small world, in his experience, where more or less everyone knew everyone else in one way or another. We were all connected through a network of strings, some hidden, some plainly visible. Some of the strings could be pulled, others pulled you.

'Thanks,' he said, suddenly slipping into straight Viennese, which otherwise was not as apparent in the way he spoke, where the letter *s* is always unvoiced. Linguistically he had now entered Frau Doktor Simserl's sphere, probably completely involuntarily.

'She's a lovely person'—again the *s* unvoiced, the statement issuing from a quiet reverie. 'How is she these days?'

This question came in response to my silence. It was as if he had been unsure whether to say more on the subject or whether he might not actually be interested to find out a little more about his old friend. I told him she was well, albeit a little on the fragile side, and that she was living alone up in her cabin in the woods, a somewhat weather-beaten old lady who spent a lot of time pottering around in the garden . . .

'An old lady?' He pricked up his ears at this description. She wasn't old, he insisted, ten years his senior at most, even though he had always teased her about her age. He said he used to call her *Zia*—auntie—just to wind her up but that she had never had much of a sense of humour and had taken the appellation to heart. The fact that he spoke Italian was probably the thing about him that excited her the most. She never left that cabin of hers, so when they spoke Italian, to her it had been like going on holiday. He was warming up now as he reminisced.

'It must be thirty years since I last heard from her.' These words expressed a certain tenderness towards his life's achievements—everything that had happened in those thirty years, filled to the brim with victories and defeats but, above all, with the daily, full-blooded joy of being a living, breathing man. But to hear tell of an 'old lady', he didn't care for that at all, as if by growing old Frau Doktor Simserl had failed to keep a promise to him, he who, with his thick, perennially greasy, steel grey hair, was no longer as young as he once was either. But even at the time he had known that if he left her, she would let herself go. He had not wanted to accept this idea out of respect for her but it had stuck with him all the same and he was sorry to hear that he had been right. He said that he was often right but mostly wished he weren't. He seemed to shake his head at this. He was unhappy in his role as a male Cassandra figure.

'It was intolerable by the end.' He gave me a look of total candour, as if overcome by a raptus of honesty. 'Between you and me, a lovely person but completely wrong for me.' He said he had found her urge to imbue every event with drama hard to bear. Everything had to be extraordinary and eternal and unconditional—'that for ever of hers!' Her life was one long invocation of 'for ever!' even though any mature person—which of course also included her, though she was by no means 'old'—knew that there is no such thing as for ever and ever. 'Nothing lasts for ever! Although . . .' and here he became lost in thought, his big eyes grew dark—this was no longer Salam the jovial and perky but Salam the contemplative, Salam the childish dreamer—or so, those darkened eyes seemed to say, those eyes which had burnt so deeply into Frau Doktor Simserl's soul. Was he thinking about how thirty years ago he had said goodbye to that cabin in the woods 'for ever' only to now find himself once again in its pull, revisiting that place in his mind and evidently finding things that had long been locked away?

'For ever and ever—that's bad enough in and of itself but on the other hand, what's the song they sing in Vienna, you know the one—"Take a sprinkling of love and a dash of devotion, then add some deception to finish the potion!" Well, she's a woman, you see, through and through, regardless of whether she's let herself go a little, and women . . .'—he sat up straight and looked me square in the eye. That long-lashed look of melancholy was gone. He was no longer in a confiding mood, nor was he dispensing paternal advice to a hopeful young man—he was now a prophet pronouncing a last, terrible revelation. 'Women—and not merely the flirtatious, the beautiful, the adventurous, the attractive ones, no, no, the plain ones too, the dull ones, the respectable and unapproachable ones, your old ladies as well, of course—wherever they go and whatever they do, talking on the telephone or cooking dinner, speaking into a microphone or selling sausages, the peach, the cherry, or whatever fruit you prefer, between their legs goes with them, always! A man can forget his sex for days—simply doesn't think about it—a woman, any woman! never. I can go for hours without thinking about the fact that I'm a man—indeed, I often do, just now for example—which with respect to women almost always puts us at a disadvantage.' He made a gesture with those firm, padded, black-haired hands of his, to mark the conclusion to this line of thought—If I, by playing the messenger, was hoping to orchestrate some sort of reunion between him and Frau Doktor Simserl, he was afraid that he would have to disappoint me. 'If she were to walk around the corner this instant and see me sitting here—I give you my word I would take to my heels and run.' Of course since I set such store by playing the messenger, he wasn't going to forbid me to return the greeting, 'but keep it short—no ornaments for her to get her claws into and to try to force me to respond further. You really wouldn't be doing her a favour.'

This show of determination recalled the stuffy intransigence of a post-office clerk who has just closed his counter and will not be persuaded to reopen it no matter how earnestly you implore him. I had not seen this form of profoundly Austrian-inflected subalternity in him before. Evidently this was a character trait that only Frau Doktor Simserl could bring out in him, who had devoted himself to being perpetually charming—a sign of real desperation.

You remember Frau Doktor Simserl's little cabin, 'my' hunting lodge. Well, I never set foot in it again. When I had asked her about the picture of Salam, this sudden and unexpected sign of life from her former lover, something she had long ago dismissed as impossible, had set something in motion in the life of that old anchorite. Something had come full circle. The law of probability dictating that you always run into chance acquaintances twice in the course of your life had proved true. But there was also something final in the repetition. It's really quite simple—if I had told Frau Doktor Simserl that Salam was dead or at least terminally ill, bankrupt, in jail, on the run, then that would only have confirmed her suspicions. She might have heaved a sigh, certainly not out of a sense of vindication but, rather, because such great misfortune served only to strengthen the bond uniting her and Salam. But she must have felt a sting in her heart at the thought of him running a cellphone company in Frankfurt. It was a brutally clear indication of just how superfluous she had been to his life, how pale and distant and almost dreamlike those once so stimulating events now appeared.

It was pure luck that someone answered when I rang her hunting lodge. It was one of the women who were in charge of feeding her in her isolation those jars of carrot-coloured purée of the kind you give to babies, the only thing she ever ate. I was told that Frau Doktor was in the hospital in St Pölten. She'd fallen. Since this was Marguerite Simserl we were talking about, these words assumed a vaguely threatening moral significance—the everyday meaning didn't seem as though it could apply to her. And when, on my next trip to Vienna, I stopped by at the hospital to pay her a visit, this ominous, archaic undertone was confirmed. It wasn't so much a hospital as what used to be known as a spittle—an asylum for people for whom nothing more can be done except, basically, keeping them alive—and what a life that was. An old tenement building on the outskirts of the city, no doubt formerly run by nuns. In the pistachio-coloured vestibule, there was a locked and bolted iron door and a plaster statue of St Joseph, underneath which the various vagrants who weren't allowed into the house could get a warm meal. A man with the ruddy brown face of a life spent out of doors and a great mass of thin, fur-like hair was sitting on one of the benches eating soup out of a metal porringer. Visitors only, he told me gravely, as if he also volunteered as a doorman. But that was as it should be, he said, because some of the people who came here didn't know how to behave themselves. Sombrely he shook his head. This man spoke High German, incidentally, not dialect, and had probably travelled a great distance to sit here and keep watch. You had to behave yourself properly, he said, that was the least you could ask. Screaming and shouting and spilling the soup—what was all that about? It seemed he was a firm believer in the rules of proper bourgeois decorum. He had absolutely no truck with some of those people. He preferred to keep to himself. But when he rang the doorbell here, he said, the nurses would say, look, here comes Joseph. They knew who he was. He said I was welcome to ask them about him inside, they wouldn't have a bad thing to say about him. He offered me a sip of his bottle of lemonade. I couldn't bring myself to accept this gesture of hospitality, I'm ashamed to say, this gesture designed to establish our equality, but thankfully, just at that moment, the door swung open.

'Frau Doktor Simserl—yes, she's definitely here,' said the nurse in the white uniform and the orthopaedic sandals but unfortunately she couldn't tell me where exactly she might be at that particular moment. In her room? Or maybe in the dining hall? The stairwell was filled with the smell of steamed leeks and onions.

The energy of this woman with her wide bottom and those clunky sandals that made her feet look enormous—the heedless, noisy way she stomped around, shouting at the top of her voice down the corridor while the open doors looked into rooms where a deathly silence reigned—it all went together to create the impression that the world of the young and healthy was so infinitely far removed from that of the ill and decrepit that it seemed impossible that youth and old age might both be stages in the life of a single organism, rather, that the young and the old must be two completely different species bearing only a superficial anatomical resemblance to each other. In Frau Doktor Simserl's room, there were two elderly ladies, each in her own bed with the covers pulled all the way up, their yellow waxen faces staring up at the ceiling out of which protruded a light with three cone-shaped lampshades. What kind of day is it when the high point consists in the light bulbs inside those lampshades coming on after untold hours of waiting, only then to go out again some hours later? The radio was on. Sprightly voices talked quickly and excitedly but this incessant babbling served only to deepen the silence surrounding the beds. The sea of noise crashed against invisible walls, the noise-foam dripping down them, but not a single sound reached the ears of the ladies. It was as though the silence itself had assumed human form in the shape of those two. The silence was now inviolable. The nurse called a loud 'hello!' into the room but nothing moved in response. I thought one of these two ladies must be Frau Doktor Simserl and so I tried to recognize her in one of these emaciated faces. Could she really have wasted away to such an extent in such a short time?

No, she still looked the same as I remembered her. The stroke had not robbed her of her face. I found her in the dining hall along with some of the other ladies who could still sit upright, wearing her usual blue-and-white-striped blouse, her hair lank, seated under a print of the Sistine Madonna and next to a teddy bear in a red-and-white Christmas hat. The four women each had a plastic plate of porridge on the table in front of them. The ones who weren't lost in deep contemplation of that porridge were busy stirring it and soiling their bibs in their attempts at conveying their spoons to their mouths. But they all looked up when the nurse and I entered the room, grey eyes peering at me for an instant before turning back to their porridge. Frau Doktor Simserl didn't recognize me and even grew angry or so it seemed, when the nurse spoke loudly into her ear, 'Frau Doktor, a visitor for you!' I had time to observe the four of them until they had finished their meal. The one closest to me had the appearance of someone haunted by louring visions, grown tyrannical from rage and indignation. She was clearly profoundly offended by something right before her eyes, her brows were heavily knit and her lower lip protruded scornfully. Was it the food that had provoked her ire? There were lumps of porridge here and there on her tray but the look of outrage was frozen upon her face. The woman sitting next to her had regressed to childhood in her old age, with smooth cheeks and a greasy forehead, shy and fearful like a virgin who has been defiled and is now plagued by a nagging sense of guilt for the crime committed against her, a timid spectre who seemed to flinch away even as she sat there in her wheelchair. The third was a significantly younger woman with an expressionless face, committed to absolute complaisance, probably she had never been a great intellect, now she was patience personified. Frau Doktor Simserl was completely absorbed by the task of holding her spoon—even the tiniest movement seemed to cost her infinite deliberation and, more often than not, these concerted mental efforts came up short and the spoon was lowered again as an outward sign of a basic mental miscalculation of the physical effort required to complete this movement. I had significant doubts that I would be able to penetrate into her consciousness at all. And yet, it was her presence that granted me a different perspective on these pitiable creatures—after all she had only recently entered this new state. When I had met her a few months previously she had still been the height of gregariousness. One is tempted to view this largely wordless and perhaps also largely thoughtless existence which these women now led as a form of loss—but perhaps they had simply reached a higher form of selfhood which was now beyond all further change? The nurse said something in the same loud voice to the pained one, who raised her head in surprise and irritation and gave her a look of infinite distance. Is this how God hears our prayers? Pessimistic intellectuals like to propound the theory that man must remain forever incomprehensible to himself—here, one could witness it at first hand. Here were these ladies, sitting with a teddy bear in an overheated room and being pushed back and forth, but in another millennium perhaps people would have erected a temple round them and worshipped them in their mute, bare life.

The plastic trays were cleared away. I fetched a stool and sat down next to Frau Doktor Simserl. She didn't turn to face me but, rather, kept her head turned away. I was hesitant to address her. It seemed pointless to say my name since we had not known each other long enough for it to have sunk in deep enough to be preserved. Then I leant in close and spoke slowly and clearly into her ear, 'Joseph Salam.' I would have given anything to see the look on her face but she turned her head even further away and, at the same time, bowed it. 'Joseph Salam?' She remained silent but this time it seemed an ominous silence. Then she opened her mouth and said in a changed, barbed voice, 'I never knew him.' And when, after a prolonged silence, she turned to look at me there was a cunning smile playing on her lips. I left thinking that for as long as she was alive, Joseph Salam was safe.

26

DINING-ROOM STILL LIFE

In the winter months, there was a naturally imposed break in the Hopstens' poolside afternoons but because Rosemarie couldn't imagine a Sunday without guests coming and going, she occasionally organized big brunches, albeit with fewer people than in the summer. This break also provided a welcome opportunity to make the necessary adjustments to the guest list. Anyone who had regularly frequented those gatherings for an entire summer without making a good impression could easily be discarded in the winter 'without hard feelings', as Rosemarie put it in one of her English phrases. She, truly, was a forceful and determined hostess but nurtured secret fears about potentially offending and thus incurring the wrath of uninvited evil fairies. The bright grey winter light imbued her rooms with a singular glow. Only now did the many precious items on tables and in vitrines, ivory, bronze, brocade, silver and gold, ebony and shimmering enamel, look as exquisite as they had when she and Helga first saw them at Pattitucci's in the dancing light reflected from the canal. The snow had gone as quickly as it had come. In shaded areas, here and there, a tiny trace of dirty white remained. The sledging outing had taken place at the last possible moment. A roaring fire burnt in the fireplace, manned by a tight-lipped and workmanlike Titus Hopsten. Never had the house seemed so thoroughly warm and festive as it did looking out at the brown lawns and bare trees outside.

As I looked around the room, I realized that Rosemarie really had managed to make a triumphant fresh start. Hardly any of the familiar faces were to be seen, just the inner circle, and even that seemed to have some holes in it. Hans-Jörg, for instance, had sent his apologies, not wanting to run into Salam if he could possibly help it—he didn't mention that bit although he knew that he would have to eventually, but at the moment he couldn't think of a reason to want to tell Rosemarie. It was convenient that he and Silvi were now no longer alone in their big flat. A few days earlier, Silvi had opened the front door to find a lean tabby cat sitting on the landing with a statuesque stoicism, as if carved out of obsidian. It was a mystery how it had got into the building but, in any case, it did not belong to either the upstairs or the downstairs neighbours. For a moment, the woman and the cat stared at each other in frozen anticipation but then the cat sprang back into full vital vigour. It dashed through Silvi's legs into the flat and through all the open doors with lightning speed, a breathless and delighted Silvi in hot pursuit. In Hans-Jörg's study it eluded its pursuer at the last second by squeezing in behind the bookshelf that covered one entire wall—or, rather, not by squeezing at all for its bones were so flexible that it fairly glided into that dark crevice as if it had always known that it would be perfectly safe back there behind that wall of heavy tomes. Silvi knelt on the floor—now she was the cat and the cat the mouse in its mouse hole—and made the sweetest cooing and coaxing sounds. With her bird-like strength, she couldn't budge the bookshelf so much as half an inch. That evening, Hans-Jörg came home in a distracted mood. He certainly did not want to think about stray cats, having just instructed his solicitor to see to the dissolution of his contract with Salam—a perfectly straightforward matter, since apart from the Egyptian enterprise they had no other joint ventures.

Silvi was practically on fire. Her every thought was consumed by the cat. She telephoned Helga. She advised her to leave the cat alone for the night, it had probably been through hell, the poor thing, and to set out some milk and a bit of minced beef on a plate for it, close the door and wait until morning. Silvi didn't sleep a wink that night. The following morning, it was just barely light outside, she ran barefoot into the study—the milk and the mince were untouched. And so it went for another day and night, while Hans-Jörg announced that he was going to have the bookcase moved away from the wall as he had no desire to sit and read beside a dead cat.

Now Silvi's moment of glory was at hand, confirming her general state of elated expectation—her ice age was finally over. She went and stood in the middle of the study—'It was a moment of inspiration'—and said loudly in a cold, stern voice, 'If you don't come out this instant, I will call the landlord and have him chase you out with a broomstick.'

Never in her life had she made a threat or issued a command. There came a rustling and a scratching from behind the bookcase. Slowly the cat pushed its head out followed by a paw which it gingerly placed on the shiny parquet as if treading on thin ice. Silvi didn't move. With its pink nose and the tentative play of its splayed whiskers, the cat tasted the milk. Then it drank. Silvi—another inspired move—slowly walked out of the room. She went into the bedroom and lay down on the still-unmade bed. And it wasn't long before a shadow fell on the door and with a quick, measured leap, the cat joined the woman on the bed.

Soon after this experience, which was by no means the end point but, rather, a prelude to ever greater intimacy and passionate love, Silvi would have preferred never to leave the house. But now there was a reason to go out which was almost as strong as the cat, no, equally strong as the cat—she wanted to share her happiness with Bernward. It was no accident that this cat had appeared on her doorstep and had chosen her—it was connected to her newfound state of being in which everything in her life suddenly seemed infinitely more meaningful. She was no longer indifferent to what happened to her and she herself was likewise no longer insignificant. On the contrary, it was extremely important to her that she live to experience the next day and the day after that and many, many more besides. Something had come over her, she suddenly appeared possessed of a power of attraction, a magnetism, capable of drawing other highly loveable beings to her, not just someone like Helga with her endless expectations. Fine, if Hans-Jörg wanted to stay at home, then at least the cat wouldn't be all alone. Hans-Jörg and the cat weren't on speaking terms but the little tabby could take care of herself for a couple of hours.

Salam had not taken the decision of whether to go where he was expected lightly. He was brooding over the letter from Hans-Jörg's solicitor which had taken him completely by surprise. Surely, his pushing for that little bit of money for their Egyptian middleman Mounir Bey, who truly had done a fine job, couldn't possibly have led to this—throwing it all away, shutting down all communication, burning bridges, erecting impenetrable barriers. Sure, he knew Hans-Jörg was hopelessly neurotic, unpredictable—although one of a neurotic's principal weaknesses is usually their predictability—a capricious, battered crown prince with deviant sexual tastes. And, after all, Salam had essentially been Hans-Jörg's guardian, his nurse, seeing him through rehabilitation—ought the entire mighty Schmidt-Flex family not in fact to be thanking him on their knees for the kind and tender way he had guided their son on his first steps to independence? The galling thing was that these people were not particularly inclined towards gratitude and were perhaps even of the opinion that it was Salam who stood to gain the most from his association with their illustrious name. Did he sense the father's imposing hand in this?

'Just wait till I get my hands on that milksop, I'll turn him round soon enough . . .' he drew strength from this conviction. But what if the old man was there too? Wouldn't it be wiser to keep a low profile for the time being and give Hans-Jörg the impression that all was well? He wasn't about to let him get away so easily—that was a phrase he had used many times before in his life. How exactly he was going to put it into action this time was still a little unclear.

Salam flipped a coin, as ever not in the hope of an oracle to guide his actions but simply because he found that it helped him to make decisions. Mostly, he did the opposite of whatever the coin-toss advised and he never went back to check whether that had been the right decision. Today, he had flipped the coin so often that he'd lost count—did fate want him to drive out to Falkenstein or not? The brunch was already winding down when he finally called Rosemarie. She sounded hoarse, self-conscious, as she often did when she answered the phone but this time the flurry of voices in the background made it sound as if she were standing at the railway station.

'I'll explain everything, I'm in the middle of a stupid dis-agreement with the Schmidt-Flexes, so I think it might be better if I don't see them today,' he said, thinking that he sounded unusually defensive. Hans-Jörg's letter had really got to him. Rosemarie broke out in a cold sweat. Her heart was pounding. There it was—the confirmation of her success. Oughtn't she feel satisfied? She curtly informed Salam that Hans-Jörg wasn't there. When Salam had hung up, he tried again to get a clear sense of his situation. When he pieced together all the evidence, didn't it suggest that his lucky streak had once again run out?

Phoebe had greeted me more warmly than usual—that night in the snow-covered forest seemed not to have been forgotten—but this warmth was also reminiscent of the casual way we greet old family friends, an aura of heightened unerotic harmlessness. What more did I deserve?

I must confess that my infatuation with Phoebe was now little more than a tiny, delicate flame. It had been replaced by vanity and a hunter's instinct. Given the way she was with young men, she must have been somewhat familiar with such sentiments. There were at least two new dogs sniffing around her. She ran her hand through the one's hair and put her arm round the other's waist, nestling up to him for a second. But I too was skulking and prowling through the house, never stop-ping long enough to talk to anyone and always ready to follow her the minute she went outside.

There was Frau Schmidt-Flex, as ever in the vicinity of her loudly pontificating husband, to whom Rosemarie was gradually introducing all the new guests and who was, therefore, in high spirits. And even his wife was smiling. I had never seen her smile, she truly had undergone a transformation. The deadly boredom against which she had struggled daily to avoid screaming at the top of her lungs was still there but it no longer hurt. The internal tension produced by her boredom was gone. She had come to terms with her boredom. Frau Schmidt-Flex had arrived at a realization otherwise reserved for mystics that there is only the flimsiest of membranes separating Heaven and Hell—well, maybe not Heaven, exactly, but a temperate, tranquil limbo, in any case. This membrane had burst while they were in Sicily and since then her mask-like coldness had melted. She now felt that she quite liked Silvi and although she was incapable of giving any kind of expression to this sentiment, at least her muted, hostile brooding was gone. One might go so far as to say that Silvi could never have expected her mother-in-law to be more forthcoming than right at this moment. Her father-in-law, on the other hand, remained an impregnable fortress.

At such large gatherings, the individuality of the guests seems to dissolve without anyone noticing. They become one mass, rolling this way and that, by turns boiling over or ebbing away.

As if in accordance with some law of physics, the entire company had just congregated in the large parlour, the conversation animated by the wine, but there was a palpable tendency towards dissolution. People began to stream into the foyer. Phoebe had got away from me, along with the skinny dog with the fondled quiff. My gaze wandered towards the dining room. It was completely deserted. No, not completely. Sitting opposite each other with their hands on the tablecloth were Silvi and Bernward.

They didn't notice me. They had been talking and were now sitting in serene silence. The sun was already low in the sky and a warm ray of sunlight fell into the room. On the table lay half a lemon and beside it stood a glass of red wine. The ray of light fell exactly on the glass, causing it to sparkle, and the lemon too became translucent—for an instant it was almost as though it were being lit from the inside by a tiny light bulb. Squinting against the light, I saw their heads in dark silhouette but then a milder light supervened and it now seemed that the red wine and the lemon had in fact been the catalysts of a change in atmosphere. Now the two figures were raised into the light. The backs of their hands flashed, they were both doused in refulgence. With quiet fervour they flowed over into the objects in the room, filling them with the life of the words they had just spoken. Bernward's head had lost its boxiness, his features appeared smooth and delicate, even attractive in a subtle, idiosyncratic way. Silvi was deeply serious. Her face, usually so animated, was relaxed and content in its immobility. What had these two been talking about? It didn't matter. The lemon and the wine glass had not needed to discuss weighty matters in order to catch fire.

'*I take it this scene is one of the few cards in your game of patience that was dealt face-up?*'

'*Yes, it was face-up. And another thing—this magnificent and successful brunch was the last time I was invited to the Hopstens'.*'

27

THAT'S HOW IT'S DONE

One of the purest pleasures in life is going to the local watering hole after a long day at the office and having a couple of beers. Every evening, between six and eight, you would find a throng of men in dark suits standing at the bar of a tiny place nestled among the glass-and-steel skyscrapers like a gingerbread house, a dingy bar with candles on the tables where the half-open door lets in the pale blue evening light and the occasional cold gust of wind. Stepping in, I always felt part of a great community that was completely absent at the office during the day but here, among these men who all felt in some way unburdened and had, at least partly, reverted to their youthful student-day selves, many of whom I knew only by sight, there suddenly emerged something like an *esprit de corps* or perhaps even a feeling of brotherhood. Most of them were still members of the lower ranks, in charge of keeping the big wheels turning. Almost everyone was speaking English, which is why I still quite clearly remember how out of this underlying Anglophone swamp there emerged a single crotchety voice with a distinct Viennese accent, 'I simply fail to see!' and not because Slavina had raised his voice, his vocal chords simply transmitted at a wavelength that cut effortlessly through the general hubbub. I pushed my way through the crowd, the men holding their golden orbs of beer were in such a good mood that my pushing only increased their mirth. I received heartfelt greetings from total strangers but I didn't want to attract attention, I wanted to get to Slavina, I wanted to hear every word he spoke, words which attained their value for me precisely because they were not directed at me.

He sat hunched over or, rather, folded in half, on a barstool. He was making himself small in order to speak into the ear of the man sitting next to him. He was again dressed in a linen jacket. I suspect he kept it in his car and changed jackets right after work because to him, the dark suit jacket was really a uniform, only to be worn at the office. I suspect this was a rigorism he had affected in London. His interlocutor was significantly shorter. Perched on that barstool, his feet barely reached the crossbar. Although he was already balding, he remained youthful in his curiosity, fired up and listening with baited breath. No, they couldn't have known each other from Slavina's firm Sheera & Wasserstein, as his comments quickly revealed—surely not even Slavina was that blasé. I squeezed in beside the short, attentive gentleman and looked the other way as I ordered a beer. I enjoyed being able to stand so close to Slavina and, yet, remain completely unnoticed, as though shielded by an invisibility cloak, for we had still not run into each other on the stairs and, recently, the only sign that his flat was even occupied had been the bags of rubbish outside the door—quite indiscreet rubbish, I might add, for on the side of one of the plastic bags, a flattened condom was plainly visible.

'I quite simply failed to see why I should have to pay even one cent for my move to Frankfurt,' Slavina was explaining. Frankfurt was a total shithole and he was certainly not going to be putting down any roots here. Which was why you had to be bloody careful. He said he had managed to convince them to pay him the same rent allowance as he'd got in London—in London he'd lived in a shoebox for that money (with a first-rate address, admittedly, which was the most important thing in London). The short fellow's eyes grew large—he'd never thought of that. He probably lived with his wife and child in a small suburban housing estate with a sandbox in the postage-stamp-sized garden and had no doubt felt like a pig in clover. It was exciting to be talking to such a sly dog who was never at home anywhere in the world. With this handsome allowance—Slavina left the exact amount unsaid—he was able to afford a giant flat here in Frankfurt but what did he want with a giant flat in this shithole? When, after all, it was only a matter of time? He simply failed to see what good it was but he was even less prepared to see why he should go without this allowance, on the contrary—but they were being difficult (and by 'they' I assume he meant Human Resources), they wanted to see the lease, otherwise they wouldn't pay.

Everything had worked out in Baron Slavina's favour. Without any great effort on his part, he had got out of the awkward position of perhaps having to foot the bill himself. He'd signed the lease on this far-too-spacious flat for his Frankfurt needs, and the bank paid the rent. And then came the kicker. Before he could move into his new flat, he'd had to spend two months in a desolate block of flats and during that time he had made the acquaintance of the woman next door. Nothing out of the ordinary, he reassured his young apprentice, but then what could you expect to find in a place like that? She worked in the administrative office of a major bank, very busy, took some pride in her work, separated, not divorced—the ideal constellation, in other words. He'd rung her doorbell in order to ask whether she had a corkscrew—a moronic chat-up line, really, but that's not how he'd meant it at all—'I really did need a corkscrew,' he said.

By now the young man was beside himself with amazement. Did Slavina even notice just how fully he commanded his attention? One thing had quite naturally led to another, he continued, which had been pleasant enough in its way, not exactly mind-blowing but he was happy to let it become a casual thing, with the requisite intervals—he said that, as a matter of principle, he never called the next day or even the day after that, just so they wouldn't get the wrong idea. As a general rule, it was best to give it a fortnight. And this woman was good enough 'on the whole' that, had things developed as per usual, he would happily have given the young man her telephone number—that would have been no problem whatsoever. The young man seemed to grow taller on his barstool, his cheeks, faintly blue-tinged with stubble, glowed a childish pink—yes, you could tell just by looking at him that if he had actually been given such a telephone number he would definitely have dialled it sooner rather than later. No, he wasn't that far removed from the life of aimless drifting, he too had a wild, coarse and cynical side to him. His family in their little house with the picket fence, they could have done without him for an evening or so. But there was also a sense of relief, you might call it a happy disappointment, that there would unfortunately be no exchange of phone numbers tonight.

Because, you see, things in Slavina's life had arranged them-selves perfectly and seemingly of their own accord. That expen-sive new palatial flat was now his—he had put up an old bronze sign he'd inherited from his parents and furnished it with a few big items and hung a hunting trophy in the foyer, the head of a Hungarian stag, a huge thing, completely absurd, really, to have kept it all these years. But he had in fact moved in with his neighbour in her kitschy little flat, full of ethno-trash and red fairy lights, but far be it from him to try to change anything, someone like her needed something for the heart, she got home late and got up early—such dedication!—hopelessly in love with her department head. It all suited him down to the ground. And for the big flat, about which his girlfriend knew nothing ('we keep our stuff separate') he'd set up a website, www.homesweet-home.de, where he rented it out by the day or the week. 'If I can get a fortnight's worth of subtenants, that's a whole month's rent for me,' and sometimes even more, rarely less. He had a Filipino woman who handled the keys, and people paid by credit card, with a hefty deposit. Slavina clapped his hands, 'I've got absolutely nothing to do with any of it.' He said that the building the flat was in had a perfect location and was perfectly suited to such business. It was mostly empty, hardly anyone lived there permanently. 'There are enough people who feel more comfortable staying in a flat than filling in a hotel regis-tration form, and I've got all the mod cons—flat-screen TV, high-speed Internet, a grand piano and a sauna and everything else that money can buy.'

He had been born on the side of life's winners, that was plain to see. But you couldn't really enjoy such victories unless you had someone to tell. For obvious reasons, he couldn't talk to the lady with the red fairy lights about it, I could see that—but was there really no one besides this straitlaced munchkin from the blueberry forests of Frankfurt's financial district? Was Slavina lonely? If he was, it was a self-imposed loneliness. Suddenly, I could see how he gave his diminutive confessor a scornful or even contemptuous look—it was as if he had suddenly realized just how unworthy, just how far removed from his own life experience this willing and humble yet admiring fellow really was. He had been hauling him in on a long bungee cord, but now he let go and watched as the surprised little man fell back down. He was brushing him off and the little man could tell and stared into his beer glass just to avoid meeting Slavina's gaze. Their entire acquaintance had been a mistake. Slavina stood up, his body surging upward until his head was touching the shelf of beer glasses attached to the ceiling. The distance between him and his interlocutor was now so great that there was no need to say anything in parting other than a gruff 'This is on you.' Slavina made for the exit. He leant forward as he walked, which gave him the air of a man with a definite goal in mind but also of a man to whom all goals are fundamentally immaterial.

28

A LOVE NEST

The day Bernward and Silvi had decided to be together for the first time behind closed doors started out like many before it, with bright grey-white light and an indeterminate mood. Bernward was not an experienced adulterer but he had been a businessman for too long not to be able to find a solution to any difficulty that might arise. And still, he was amazed at how easy it was to find a discreet flat with just a few strokes on the computer keyboard and he thought back to his student days and what a logistical nightmare it had often been to find a room for a romantic rendezvous. But the fact that these matters could all be handled in complete silence via a computer screen also meant that this part of the preparations felt very remote from any reality. Whether this was to be the beginning of a longer phase in which Bernward and Silvi would be leading a double life—each deceiving their spouses not just in the general sense of the term but perhaps forced to lie to them about their activities on a daily basis so that ultimately, thousands of lies great and small would come together to form one great deception, an umbrella term concealing the many individual acts of betrayal underneath— neither of them could say. Silvi least of all, she simply put her faith in Bernward, but he, who in his daily life was always so circumspect and forward-looking, was equally unsure. For the first time, he felt the imperative, the commandment even, of the present moment, pushing him to do what was necessary and literally forbidding him to think beyond that. Those long hours in the darkened car had not been spent exclusively in medallic adjacency but it was now time to take the next step. The thing they had been talking about and not talking about for so long now demanded action. All they could do was think of the next step, as if there were no future beyond it, because it was the only, the final step of their lives.

And until then it was business as usual, the tyranny of daily life looming larger than usual. Its triviality inserted itself like a folding screen between them and their liaison, for which they were grateful, each in their own way. They still had not truly strayed from their predetermined paths, their conversation in the darkened car still had the potential to descend into a dream, which was where it belonged, in its boldness and magical uneventfulness, in a way.

That morning, Silvi had an urgent matter to attend to that couldn't have waited any longer—the cat had to be vaccinated against worms. She didn't care whether an owner decided to turn up after all. She felt a responsibility towards this cat that she had never felt towards anything else in her life. Hans-Jörg had responded to her plan with a phrase he often used, 'If that's what you want to do, then that's what you've got to do.' She was used to this way he had of refusing to take any responsibility for her actions. There was something derisive about it, as if the rest of it was, 'You'll find out soon enough what good will come of it,' which is why she didn't and couldn't hear that this time the words were spoken in a completely different spirit and with a completely different intention, namely, as genuinely encouraging, expelling all doubt, full of confidence in her decision. This was the truly singular thing about Hans-Jörg's inner salvation—that it had no external symptoms, at least, not at first glance, that there was no need for major upheaval or change before its necessity became apparent, that he had simply attained a gratifying capacity for patience. Except that, unfortunately none of this registered with Silvi, apart from as an unwonted amiability, for which there was no apparent deeper reason. But then the cat was now taking up all of her attention.

For the trip to the vet's, she had procured a sealable basket into which she cunningly placed a saucerful of cat food, suspecting that it would be impossible to get the cat into the basket by force. The tabby was still quite feral and had already scratched Silvi, who lovingly inspected the red marks on her hand. A kiss could not have delighted her more than this sign of skittishness and freedom undiminished by the cat's newfound dependency. Her appointment was at midday but at a few minutes to twelve the cat was still not in the basket, although she had stuck her head in, wiggled her whiskers and examined the food. Who knew what experiences guided her actions? Perhaps just such a basket had already played a role in her life, which had taught her caution. Silvi felt a powerful pang of conscience when the cat overcame her misgivings, placed her paws in the basket and the lid closed behind her. The nefariousness of going against a creature's unmistakeable will in the name of care and better judgement became abundantly clear to her when she saw how the sealed basket trembled and shook as the prisoner inside hurled herself to and fro, becoming a single bundle of energy composed exclusively of teeth and claws, ready to leap out and wreak bloody havoc on the face of the first person to open the basket. How shy and pleading and afraid Silvi's voice sounded in the taxi as she tried ceaselessly to comfort the cat. Her plans for that afternoon were nothing but a distant shadow. She was just as wound up as the cat and desired nothing more than for this ordeal to be over and for the cat to forget and, thereby, to forgive her. But due to their tardiness these moments of remorse and worry and agonizing love wore on. Upon their arrival, the vet's assistant was unsure whether even to let them in. What would have happened if Silvi had had to come back that afternoon?

Back at the flat, the cat stayed in the basket for a long time after Silvi opened it. Perhaps she was a little ashamed of her histrionics and was hoping her decision to remain in the basket would be interpreted as an exercise in free will, before making a dignified and unhurried appearance and then padding purposefully, without dignifying Silvi with a glance, through the flat in the direction of the study. Only then did Silvi look at the clock and remember her rendezvous.

But it was no different for Bernward. At the office, he received an urgent telephone call from his daughter who needed picking up from the airport. She didn't so much ask to be picked up as suggest it by means of a lively description of her voluminous luggage, knowing full well that her father was incapable of resisting such a hint. The whole time she had been at school, he had been Phoebe's chauffeur, an indulgence he justified to himself by observing that these trips to her friends' houses and her riding classes and sundry other urgent destinations provided the only opportunity for him to have a quiet conversation with his daughter, to get her to tell him about her life and for him to offer his thoughts. Everything that would in the past have been called upbringing and which he had gone through at home at the hands of his—by no means despotic but assertive all the same—father had, or so he imagined, become a psychological impossibility for his entire generation. Without rejecting the idea of paternal authority out of hand, Bernward himself felt that he was utterly incapable of that sort of thing, and he saw something very similar in other members of his generation, regardless of whether they were hostile or affirmative with regard to tradition. He was sometimes astonished by the ease with which his children seemed to be able to deal with the situation they had been born into and with the world at large. Where had they learnt to speak in such easy, formulaic phrases? Where did they get their confidence in performing, their sober calculation when assessing the realities of social life, their cool single-mindedness in pursuing their interests? Who had brought them up this way? To whose authority, which must have been far more influential than his own, had they submitted themselves? Titus, in particular, seemed already very distant. With Phoebe, it was easier because of the instinctive paternal pride he felt at the sight of his beautiful daughter, and he was thankful to her for sharing her travel experiences with him and for the trace of vanished childishness that she still revealed in these enthusiastic descriptions. But as much as he looked forward to picking her up, his anticipation was tinged with nervousness. Her flight was delayed and then there was an additional half-hour delay. For a while, he stood there trying to decide whether to stay and wait for an indeterminate amount of time or simply to drive back into the city. What would have happened if the flight had arrived just a little later and Bernward too had been severely delayed not through any fault of his but simply due to circumstances beyond his control? And what if the flight were to arrive just in time and what if he got caught up in Phoebe's chatter on the drive back to Falkenstein, pulling him back into the powerful undertow of the familial sphere with all its little idiosyncrasies that no outsider could ever hope to understand? And what if then, without lifting a finger, he were simply to stay put in his study, not for long, just for the hour that Silvi would be standing on the corner waiting for him? That would be cowardly, pathetic but understandable given the gravity of the decision. He still had the option of simply disappearing. Severing all contact. Silvi too had this option and he knew he wouldn't hold it against her if she decided to make use of it. In the hours leading up to their entrance into communion with each other, each of them was alone and each of them had the right to make their own decision. That was the moment of freedom that each of them had been granted, a moment of freedom that in most people's lives rarely lasts longer and for many never comes at all. And even this highly limited freedom was questionable—did they both truly understand the nature of the decision they were making? Out with the Old and in with the New? But wasn't the New, by definition, that which was impossible to define or to describe, thus making it the worst possible object on which to base a decision?

It seemed like a small miracle when they were both there on time at the designated street corner. Even as Bernward turned the corner he was convinced that Silvi would not be there. The fact that she was—dressed in a white linen shirt, no handbag, as though she had just dashed out of the house—absolved him of any responsibility for what happened next.

He saw her standing there and the door behind which all his doubts, his deliberations and his freedom to choose resided swung silently shut. Silvi got into the car. Her short white shirt rode up a little as she sat, revealing her smooth, tanned, childlike thighs. Bernward was overcome by a profound feeling of gratitude.

'I almost didn't make it,' said Silvi.

'It was a close call for me as well,' he replied.

They drove through the quiet residential streets but were forced to stop at an intersection because of a swarm of roller-skaters coming towards them, men and woman in skintight Lycra, many wearing crash helmets, uniforms, it was a small military reconnaissance unit, rolling ever onwards, with great speed and concentration and singularity of purpose, following the order to proceed to the battleground at the double. But when this unit had zoomed by and Bernward wanted to keep going, an even larger contingent approached. This was the whole army, not marching in lockstep but, rather, swarming like a cloud of insects, surging inexorably forward with great undulating movements, bringing all other vehicles and even pedestrians to a standstill. The wheels on their roller-skates produced a low, unified rumble. The roller-skaters, of indistinguishable gender, looked neither right nor left, their gazes fixed on the back of the roller-skater in front of them—the entire city on either side of their path could have been on fire and they would not have spared a single glance for the flames. They just kept coming, there were no gaps in this endless stream, it merely ebbed and flowed like water, at times welling up behind an obstacle only then to overwhelm it with yet greater force and volume. This was no longer an army but a people, an invasion with unstoppable momentum and a clearly defined goal, as if they had to cover the entire continent as quickly as possible.

Bernward tried to reverse but that proved impossible, a line of cars had formed behind him in the narrow street. The ones at the back couldn't see what the impediment was and were blowing their horns impatiently. On the banks of the great river of roller-skaters, signs of restlessness began to emerge, an impotent rage that had absolutely no effect on the advancing troops. Nothing could stop them. What event could possibly measure up to the great dynamism of that silent migration? What destination could ever be equal to this flood of unwavering power?

Silvi calmly watched the horde go by. She was young. Did she know what drove these people?

'I'm just a little nervous about the key,' said Bernward but controlled himself. In profile, he looked subtly different. The squareness that was usually amplified by his haircut was gone. He seemed more rounded, softer. Perhaps it was because it had been a while since his last haircut and there were little curls on the back of his neck.

They pulled up in front of a large, turn-of-the-century apartment building. Silvi looked around. The old garden wall on the other side of the street had a little semicircular indent with a young sapling growing in it. She was struck by this, the way a space had been left for this tree that had obviously just been planted. There was a Filipino woman with a velvet Alice band and pockmarked cheeks standing in the street looking at her watch. Bernward went up and spoke to her. She handed him the key and walked away. Her face was impossible to read—was she annoyed at their lateness? The stairwell was spacious and cool, the smell of clean cellar vaults hung in the air. There was something positively churchlike about it. Bernward led the way. He opened the large double-wing doors of the second-floor flat. It was difficult to get the key out of the lock and as he tried jiggling it up and down, he banged his thumb against the wood hard enough to draw blood.

The spacious foyer was empty except for a large hunting trophy on the wall.

'I feel as if this were our own place,' said Silvi casually, not so much disconcerted as slightly amused. It was a big flat. Bernward had gone with the first one he found, although, for an illicit afternoon, a single room would have sufficed. Silvi wandered through the big empty rooms, it was almost like being at home, except that her emptiness was arranged in a more pleasant way whereas here there was a certain, unmistakeable, bacherloresque desolation. One room was full of opulent leather chairs, in another there was a mahogany rocking chair, who did you suppose was meant to sit there, rocking contemplatively back and forth? In the bedroom stood a large bed from some furniture warehouse or other, freshly made by the Filipino woman, who had turned down one corner invitingly and laid out two fresh towels at the foot. The whole place was bathed in light. Silvi's ability to navigate unfamiliar rooms in the pitch darkness would not have to be put to the test. There was a distinct smell in all the rooms, like damp seeping through the walls, the characteristic sweetness of wet plaster.

Bernward opened the bedroom window. He had brought along a chilled bottle of white wine in a plastic bag, Portuguese vinho verde, which, as she had mentioned at some point, brought back positive associations for Silvi. After hunting through the sparsely equipped kitchen, he even found a corkscrew. Bernward had been half expecting to have to push the cork into the bottle with the handle of a teaspoon. He was nervous but he also noticed that Silvi was not. She seemed alert and awake. She was where Bernward had taken her and that was fine by her. Nothing stood between them. They both knew why they were there, they just had to take the next step. But that was just the problem, not an insurmountable problem to be sure, nevertheless a problem whose solution would come as a surprise to both of them. All the eagerness and lust, the desire to take charge and to relinquish control, which the moment called for, failed to materialize for Bernward. It was quite impossible in the face of Silvi's innocence and candour and the touching way in which she trusted him. He had to leave it up to her. She had to be the one to determine how things proceeded. Did she realize this?

They drank their wine out of tumblers. Silvi smiled with gratitude when she saw that it was vinho verde. She sat down on the bed and gently kicked off her sandals. He sat next to her.

Just then the doorbell rang. They both jumped.

'It must be some mistake,' said Bernward but then the doorbell rang again and wouldn't stop. They didn't dare speak above a whisper, the door into the foyer was still open. Out in the stairwell they could hear loud noises and voices. Some men were walking up and down the stairs and shouting back and forth between floors. Something was up, something had happened—the stairwell was in uproar.

'Stay here,' Bernward whispered and put his jacket on— he'd removed that at least—and went to the door. Outside on the landing there stood a stocky man with sideburns, behind him he could see some workmen in blue overalls. Is Mr Slavina at home, the man asked in a gruff voice that seemed to indicate that he felt entirely justified in his assault on the doorbell.

'There's no one here, we're his guests,' said Bernward and tried to close the door.

'No we've got to come in right away,' said the man, adding that he had explicitly and repeatedly notified Mr Slavina in writing that he was not to use the sauna. It had not been installed correctly and had to be entirely redone. And now the flat downstairs had water running down the wall again. It simply wasn't on. He said he'd have to come in and have a look with his workmen, that the damage was already substantial.

Just then Silvi stepped out of the bedroom. The man with the muttonchops gave a start and then said politely, the blustering tone entirely gone, 'Good afternoon, Frau Schmidt-Flex, sorry to bother you like this . . .'

Silvi nodded at the man. She couldn't remember his name but she did still clearly remember giving him a bag of Christmas biscuits the previous year at a party held at the Flex-Realty offices.

29

SOLITUDES

'*Well you've taken your sweet time to reintroduce Slavina into the story. What are you trying to say? If Slavina hadn't decided to sublet his flat . . .? If the Schmidt-Flexes hadn't owned so much property that they could no longer keep track of it all . . .? If Slavina's guests hadn't tried to use the sauna . . .? If Bernward and Silvi hadn't gone to see that cult film . . .? If . . .?*'

'*If Silvi had married the boy next door back in Brazil . . . If her father had emigrated to Canada along with the rest of his family . . . If . . .*'

Phoebe was good at telling stories over the phone, and she would sometimes reveal an eye for detail that surprised me. At that summer's English derby, for instance, it was not the ladies' outlandish headgear or the men's light-grey top hats that had caught her attention but, rather, one of the jockeys 'with a big gorgeous head, brown and wild' sitting on a magnificent, over-sized horse that was idly walking in circles, and every movement of the horse's bored circular amble was repeated in the jockey. He'd been completely fused with his horse, said Phoebe, 'and when he spat onto the sandy ground from his high horse, his spit was white and thick like the foam dripping from the horse's mouth.' Later, she had seen him dismount and walk around on short little bowlegs, practically a hunchback, there was definitely something misshapen about him. It was wrong to see him separated from his horse—the horse's body was part of his own anatomy, which was moulded to fit the horse's in every way. On the horse he was a supernatural being, off it a hideous fragment.

No one in Rosemarie's circle of friends could believe that she had felt a bond between herself and Bernward similar to that between this jockey and his horse. Unlike the jockey, she had not been walking around on short little bowlegs. On the contrary, to many who were only fleetingly acquainted with the Hopstens, Bernward with his solid, bourgeois colourlessness had seemed like little more than a pleasantly unobtrusive grey backdrop for the bright splendour of his wife. For anyone trying to think of an example of bold feminine independence, Rosemarie quickly came to mind. A strong will in an ageless, fit, healthy body that turned heads whenever she emerged from the swimming pool—that was what people associated with Rosemarie.

Even Bernward saw her that way, and the stoic severity with which she had received his confession seemed to confirm this. He had admittedly been prepared for her to insist on some kind of interim solution, a temporary separation, just to keep up appearances, a conventional parallelism which, seen from outside, would not differ so greatly from the norm, and he was in two minds about the idea. On the one hand, he felt he owed it to her to acquiesce to any such wishes on her part and not to leave her stranded from one minute to the next but, on the other hand, he found the idea of any such solution completely intolerable. How would they ever be able to look each other in the eye with the impending dissolution of their marriage looming over them?

But he needn't have worried. Rosemarie did not ask a lot of questions and he was honest and direct in his answers, as he had been throughout the more than twenty-five years of their marriage. They had a way with each other and today was no different. But behind their words there was a frosty detachment and so he refrained from kissing her on the cheek as he left the room. Nor did he dare to pet the cockatoo, which had been following the conversation closely, cocking its head to the side the better to hear. To make a distinction between human and animal would have been just too despicable.

She sat there in silence. It was a long time before she moved. She listened to his footsteps receding. He went up the stairs to his bedroom, in the distance she could hear the cupboard doors opening and closing. Half an hour went by, during which she wondered a couple of times whether she should go after him. She remained seated. She didn't want to watch him fold his shirts, which, presumably, was what he was doing up there. How long can it take for a man to pack a suitcase? When Bernward went away on business, she would often help him pack. He had trouble getting all his things together and often forgot something. This time when he left she would send him anything he'd forgotten within the week.

He came back down the stairs. It sounded like he was dragging something. Evidently, he had chosen one of the larger suitcases. She heard the front door close.

Rosemarie had certainly not expected him to come back into the room but the sound of the door closing behind him struck her as an expression of unfathomable callousness. A moment before, she had still been frozen in her chair, now she was overcome by the need to do something right away. She had to arm herself. She had to master this new situation. The first thing was to lose any old baggage. One thing in particular was weighing her down and had to be taken care of immediately. She didn't permit herself even to think of the name Joseph Salam. That man did not exist. She was supposed to be seeing him that afternoon, when she would have heard more about Hans-Jörg's oddly hostile behaviour, which until a moment before she had been eager to do. Not any more. The thing with Salam had only been possible—and even then only barely—as long as he could be accorded only a limited degree of reality. Salam was only admissible into her life as a hermetically sealed cyst, not as someone whose existence actually impacted her real life. She shuddered at the thought of being Salam's mistress first and foremost, now that Bernward had left her. Not because she wanted to make sure she had the upper hand in the impending divorce settlement—such calculations were out of the question anyway because it was unthinkable for her to accord Salam even the tiniest part in the dissolution of her marriage. If only it were possible to wipe someone off the face of the earth just with a well-aimed thought!

But beyond such murderous fantasies, she did not spare Salam much thought. Her tone on the telephone—Bernward had been gone a little less than a quarter of an hour—was raw and curt. She addressed Salam in the imperative. He knew this tone, not from women but, rather, from certain business associates of his, such as the people for whom he had imported cars into Iran. He was hurt by Rosemarie's telephone call (short version: 'Get lost! And don't you dare call me again!') because he liked to remain a loyal friend to his mistresses for as long as possible. Had Helga perhaps had something to do with this? But as always, a woman's caprice must be respected, that was a *point d'honneur*.

Rosemarie was more voluble in laying out the new situation to her friend Helga, who had come over the moment she heard the alarming news. She arrived to find a woman who was calm and collected but who also made no secret of her anger and pain. Helga was made to deal with catastrophes of this sort. Her dramatic seriousness, which at other times could seem misplaced, lent her just the right countenance with which to receive Rosemarie's explanations. Bernward had obviously lost his mind.

'He wants to go live with an alcoholic who's eighteen years younger than him.'

'Well, he must know what he's doing,' said Helga. A phrase that is usually spoken uncharitably—in this case it was meant to say that the man must not have fully thought through what was in store for him now. She said she didn't mean the breach of trust. Rosemarie blurted out that it was precisely the breach of trust that had come as such a shock to her and to her entire view of the world and of her life in it. She would never have admitted that Bernward's presence was the very foundation of everything she did but in a wordless way that was exactly how she felt. But then how could she have given adequate and unequivocal expression to the two powerful feelings inside her in equal measure—that losing Bernward was to lose something vital and irreplaceable and that she wanted to hurt and vilify him?

'He's never worked for anyone other than our holding company—and he didn't do a bad job of that, or I should say I made sure he didn't do it badly—where we would be today if it hadn't been for my supervision, I don't know.' And soon he would be in his late fifties, how did he envisage his future? Who was going to hire someone like him? Sure, he had his contacts but, in the end, they were mostly her contacts, contacts she'd established though her holding company, and it wouldn't be easy to take them out of that context. On the contrary, he might have been able to discard her as his wife but the business side would be harder to resolve. He wanted to reduce it all to a pile of rubble—fine, but he should know that pile of rubble also belonged to him, a fine dowry for his drunkard bride, on which to build his newfound happiness. She said she was going to act quickly now. This house—she looked around with an expression of gleeful scorn—was to be sold immediately—'I'm going to sell it!' she gave an impassioned cry, as if all her previous talk of 'buoying' and selling had been a mere rehearsal for this moment. She said she had absolutely no intention of staying in Frankfurt to witness the birth of this new family.

'Bernward's starting at zero,' she said, 'with a zero on his arm and a zero in his bank account.'

'And you?' asked Helga, lending a dark resonance to the *ou* sound.

Rosemarie replied that in the end she could live anywhere she wanted. Maybe she'd go to New York for a while, or maybe Munich.

'It never fails,' thought Helga with astonishment, 'you keep a client for five years exactly.' She asked whether she should go make some tea. Rosemarie nodded. She seemed already to be adjusting to her new domicile.

But as Helga was busying herself in the kitchen where she had made so many pots of tea in the past, she suddenly heard a scream which didn't sound like it could have been made by a human or, at most, by someone being brutally tortured, someone who was being flayed alive. She rushed into the parlour. Rosemarie seemed to have turned to stone. Tears dripped down her cheeks which glinted in the light, that's how wet they were. Her features were distorted, the dark make-up round her eyes so smudged that she was all but unrecognizable.

Meanwhile, the cockatoo was sitting on its perch, craning its neck as if to get a better perspective on the situation. It puffed out its chest and gravely spread its wings like a heraldic eagle, moving them slowly up and down, more like the winnowing of a punkah than a flapping of wings, spreading them so wide that each of its flawless feathers seemed to be attempting to upstage all the others through sheer vainglorious ostentation. Really, such a gesture would have to be taken further—with its chest thus impressively puffed up the cockatoo ought to have launched itself into the air, borne on its magnificent wings to the hunt, to battle, to love and conquest. In Rosemarie's parlour, however, after this entrancing, defiant display, all the cockatoo could do was to deflate and revert to its previous state, fold away its luxuriant plumage until it was no bigger than a pigeon. Its pinions were now pressed tightly against its body like a wetsuit, the crest had disappeared completely, the tips had retracted and merged seamlessly with the feathers on the back of its neck.

For all its extraordinary intelligence—Bernward claimed the cockatoo could read every one of his thoughts—this beautiful bird certainly could not have imagined that it was precisely for this display that it had been bought in the first place. Helga Stolzier had, as we all know, felt that what Rosemarie's parlour needed was some kind of decorative element that moved, and that moved of its own accord. At first she had a work of art in mind, a large feather fan that opened and closed mechanically which, in the proper lighting, would have cast dramatic shadows on the stucco lustro, and Rosemarie had been on board, though the thing had apparently cost an arm and a leg. But then Helga had had a falling out with the gallery owner and come up with a new idea—a real live bird instead. Which is how the cockatoo had wound up in the house, where it was fed and looked after, where Bernward had tenderly scratched its neck, but where there were no other cockatoos to keep it company during the long hours it spent alone. But the lack of company and an audience did not, however, mean that it shirked its duties. Although it had been created in order to perform for the world, it gave its performances even when there was no world, insofar as the world can be said to consist of the eyes of humans and animals.

Perennially fluffing itself up, collapsing its feathers as gently as falling snow, extending its crest to its full astonishing glory and folding it away again, as if it had to be carefully stowed away after each performance, carefully preening its plumage, painstakingly combing through each snow-white feather, the startling way it would turn its entire coat inside out, as if its feathers were the lining of the duvet that was being shaken out of its cover to be dried in the sun, the way its magnificent blood-nourished plumage could be transformed into a seemingly lifeless ball of fluff and then reassembled into that beautiful, perfectly formed body where every feather was in its right place and together formed a shimmering, self-contained sculpture, as if the entire bird were made of porcelain —all of this had to be accomplished over and over again with all the requisite concentration and dedication to the art. And on top of that came the alimentary imperative, the cockatoo's diet consisting entirely of very small seeds that had to be punctiliously cracked in accordance with strict rules and whose nutritional value had to be stringently appraised and carefully examined before the slate grey beak, that stony nautilus, with surprising dexterity, extracted the sweet contents. Did the cockatoo realize that when

Bernward had left the room without saying goodbye, it would be the last time it ever saw its friend? Or had it seen each and every time Bernward left the room as a final farewell, since it was impossible to make predictions about the future based on some inherent cosmic order? Had the cockatoo in its wisdom perhaps abandoned all hope of finding an underlying universal order? Here it was witnessing the moment in which its future would be determined, with no way of influencing that decision short of dying. Was it considering the option of simply dropping down dead from its perch? But the two ladies also faced difficult questions.

If the entire contents of the house were to be packed into boxes, to be unpacked again who knows where and when, what was to become of the cockatoo? It couldn't very well sit around in some warehouse somewhere waiting for a new home. It escaped the fate of being given to Helga, although it heard Rosemarie make the offer—she was determined to get it out of the house as quickly as possible, not least because it was the only thing that was important to Bernward. All the various other precious things, some of which he had helped pick, were Rosemarie's, as far as he was concerned.

Helga got her own back on the cockatoo for pecking her finger that time, incidentally. She threw a blanket over its cage, plunging it into darkness. In those days of perpetual night its whiteness was turned entirely inward and did not radiate one millimetre beyond itself. But it was not in danger of falling once more into her hands. Helga had, in any case, moved on from the concept of having live birds in the living room. She was nothing if not radical in her changing tastes—no, no, no more cockatoos, that was a favour she would no longer be able to do Rosemarie. When I think about the patience of this cockatoo, its infinite discipline, thanks to which it would stay exactly the same till its dying day, I imagine that its heart must be a counterpart to its grey beak, a hard little pebble in its chest. For this patience was as far removed from the flutter of the human heart as any celestial rock.

'*And how did Hans-Jörg react to Silvi's confession?*'

'*Completely differently, although he was no less shocked. But Rosemarie's faith in the institution of marriage, particularly in her own, had practically been a religion, which may not always live up to the believers' hopes and expectations but to which they nevertheless continue to cling as the bedrock of their thought. For her, the worst possible thing had happened—she had not lost her faith but the object of that faith had disappeared, or, if we don't want to belabour the religious analogy, she was now like the bowlegged jockey, who has just found out that a global flu pandemic has wiped out all the horses in the world.*'

Hans-Jörg had never had any such faith. What exactly it meant to be married had remained a mystery to him. The possibility that he might love Silvi had only just dawned on him with glorious golden rays. And now that he wanted to devote this new-found strength to loving Silvi, he was suddenly faced with the prospect that he would not be using it for that purpose but rather to cope with her loss. When he had returned home, Silvi had stood facing him, and told him in simple, clear words, like an honest and clever child in the confessional, everything that had happened that afternoon, emphasizing also the encounter with the caretaker, just to ensure that there could be no doubt that the cat was out of the bag. Unlike at confession, however, she neither expected nor asked for forgiveness.

Nor did Hans-Jörg consider forgiving her but not because he was hurt—he listened to her breathlessly and did not hide the fact that he was profoundly unsettled by her description but he also made it very clear that this was not something that called for an apology or forgiveness. Something important had happened in Silvi's life, a short time after the same had happened in his. Everything was so new, even in their relationship, that it would take some time for him truly to understand it. They had no common language, as he now realized for the first time with a pang. But that this, which had felt like a new beginning to him and still did (this sense of beginning remained undiminished through any crisis) was in fact an ending—that was something he couldn't understand. To be sure, he had failed in a thousand different ways in his relationship with Silvi, as he now saw more clearly than ever, most clearly of all in that great night of revelations. But that night he had also arrived at the comforting certainty that these failures would not be punished, that there was no penance to impinge on this brilliant new beginning. Now this illusion had been shattered and the full reckoning for his failure as a husband was laid bare. They did not use any big words and it would in any case have been impossible for either of them to use the word love—impossible for Hans-Jörg because he didn't dare fly so high, for Silvi because it was far too abstract—what did that even mean, love? In her case, it meant that from now on she wanted to sleep in Bernward's bed and if that was how it was, then she might as well say that. Standing in the doorway, Hans-Jörg said, 'You know that you can come back any time, as if nothing had happened.'

'Yes,' Silvi replied and she believed him. He had not had a bad or even resentful thing to say about Bernward at all.

30

A HARBINGER OF THE FUTURE

Not far from Hans-Jörg and Silvi's flat, there was a small car park with an art nouveau monument, although it wasn't entirely clear exactly who was being commemorated, as the limestone was so coarse that the inscription was hard to read. Never before would it have occurred to Hans-Jörg to go and sit in the shade of this monument. It was usually occupied anyway by vagrants with beer cans engaged in discussions that would often erupt into intransigent shouting that caused the au pairs with their prams to give the monument a wide berth, even though there was no real danger since to these vagrants, any creature not belonging to their group was effectively invisible. They felt as alone in the middle of the city as they would in a quiet forest glade. But today, there was no one on the bench and, as he drew near, Hans-Jörg suddenly felt his legs growing weak. He couldn't imagine that they would carry him all the way to his building and up the stairs to the first floor. He felt like an invalid who has been bedridden for a long time and is taking his first tentative steps out of doors.

Well, there was the bench. He sat down. It was a purely physical operation, his will had absolutely nothing to do with it. And that's how it remained. Had he reached his predestined harbour? After all that had happened, this was what he was left with, but it was enough and would probably always have been enough—sitting on this bench. The sun came out from behind a heavy grey cloud and beamed a sharp, piercing ray directly at him, as if to nail him to the spot. Being pierced in this way was not particularly pleasant but he did not put up any resistance. Neither did the monument. In any case, the sun quickly hid behind another cloud. The light turned a pale grey once more but everything was still clearly visible. The shadows deepened. Hans-Jörg felt as though he were seeing for the first time what this place where he lived really looked like.

An elderly man approached. He was walking very slowly, in reality it was more of a shuffle. He even had a cane but was not really using it to lean on, rather, placing it as far ahead as he could and then shuffling towards this self-imposed goal. He was bent over and very fragile, almost transparent. The blue veins on the backs of his hands, on his neck and at his temples bulged, as if only barely covered by the skin. There was a light covering of wispy white hair on his bony skull, somewhat dishevelled. Hans-Jörg had the distinct impression that the old man had not combed it himself but, rather, had been dressed by someone else, like a schoolboy before being allowed out. But all the same, he was unchaperoned—he still felt up to the challenge of walking this familiar path alone. His suit flapped round his fleshless body. Not an inelegant suit, upon closer inspection, but probably bought decades ago. Perhaps it had been too tight for a while and had spent some years in the wardrobe, then it had fit again, and now thrift prohibited him from ordering a new suit to clothe his shrivelled body. With a belt and braces it just about fit, but you could have inserted three fingers into his shirt collar, out of which his wrinkled neck jutted hideously, covered in white stubble, the only thing about the old man's appearance that was abhorrent in its decrepitude. Astonishing that those milky eyes could still see at all! How strenuous it was for this old man to walk. His delicate pink tongue stuck out, licking those thin bloodless lips in an expression of complete concentration, as if the act of walking were like threading a needle. Hans-Jörg had ample time to observe him. He shuffled past at a snail's pace but with fierce determination. This was no walk in the park.

The old man stopped, hindered by something—the slightest irregularity in the ground was enough to bring his tentative progress to a halt. Hans-Jörg wanted to get up and offer to help the old man but he didn't. He remained seated. He couldn't have moved a muscle if he had tried.

This man, he was certain of it, had been sent to him. He was supposed to observe him and in order to ensure that he could take it all in, the man's forward momentum had been reduced to the absolute minimum. Later, Hans-Jörg could not remember there having been another change in the light. This epiphany had come to him quite undramatically. It was simply there, with all the wordless power of the plainly obvious. He was looking at himself. That old man was he—not in the sense that he compared himself to him, that he saw his fate mirrored in his own or that he regarded the old man as a metaphor for his own life—no, he meant it quite literally. He had seen into his own future and been granted a vision of himself as he would look in forty years' time. The present and the future and two versions of himself—as a forty-year-old and as an eighty-year-old—had inexplicably but irrefutably become merged. When he understood what was happening, with a certainty that precluded any question of how such a thing was possible, life suddenly surged into him. He forgot all about his apathetic torpor and stood up. He stared at the old man as if wanting to suck him in through his eyes. He could not allow anything this apparition had to tell him to escape him. Obviously there could be no communication between them. If he had said something to the old man he might very well have keeled over. The two of them were under a spell that must not be broken. But could one not tell a lot about a person's life just by looking at them?

A lot and at the same time very little, sadly. What trace does the joy and pain of the past leave on our faces? The most important message here was probably that in spite of everything he had been through, this man had grown old, very old even, perhaps even beyond the stage in which memory still plays its role as a second life. All the intolerable and painful things, the humiliations and embarrassments, the loneliness and contempt of so many people had not been enough to kill him. The arrows had been loosed, had hit their mark, had brought him to his knees but had not taken his life. Did this old man still remember what he had felt upon reading a certain anonymous letter years ago? Could he still have described the emptiness and self-reproach left behind when Silvi had gone? He was clearly not alone, this old man. There was someone who wiped the stains off his suit and laid out a shirt for him to wear—too big perhaps but at least clean. A wife? Did he have a second wife, one who had stood by him? Or just money enough to hire a decent nurse? And he had gone on living for so long, so infinitely long after his life had, to all intents and purposes, already ended. But there was one more thing Hans-Jörg would have liked to know—had the second forty years been a new life, starting with a new beginning, a second attempt, as it were, or had he had to keep carrying those old burdens along till the end, and had they still been what defined him, even as that old life gradually receded and faded away?

He stood up when the old man had reached the kerb. The step down onto the street yawned like an abyss before him. A taxi pulled up. Hans-Jörg took a step towards the old man, who suddenly grew unexpectedly adroit. He tumbled into the taxi, fairly rolled onto the back seat like a stuntman trained in the art of falling. Hans-Jörg was sure it was his own movement that had pushed the old man away, like a gust of wind in the autumn leaves.

31

A SEPARATION

Just as suddenly as it had arrived, the tabby cat vanished again. The roof was being repaired and the scaffolding that had been set up against the back wall facilitated her escape. It must have seemed like a miracle to find such a convenient set of steps where previously there had been only a gaping void. She had long since given up on the idea of escaping through the front door, after Silvi had so emphatically shooed her away from it. It was as if she found it demeaning to be shooed away like that. Whenever she heard Silvi's footsteps approaching the door, the cat would bolt for the farthest corner of the flat, as if to demonstrate her complete and utter indifference to that potential path to freedom. No doubt she was lulling Silvi into a false sense of security.

'The cat has lost all interest in life on the streets,' she told Helga over the telephone, 'I really think I would have to force her to leave the house.'

'She loves you,' said Helga in her sombre alto, 'it's love.' That word was just too much fun to say.

'Oh, I don't know.' Silvi always felt uncomfortable with that word and she refused to succumb to daydreams. The cat was far too withdrawn to be in love—or was she one of those noble savage souls who are ashamed of their love? It was always she who set the limit to their exchanges of affection. If she ever went near Silvi, which wasn't very often, it didn't mean she wanted to be touched. It was like a training regimen—whenever Silvi reached out, the cat would vanish. Silvi quickly learnt that she had to wait for the cat to rub up against her legs. Hans-Jörg was never allowed to pet the cat. He had tried once and the cat had drawn five claws across the back of his hand. He showed Silvi the bloody autograph accusingly but, deep down, he wasn't the least bit surprised. Why should the cat behave any differently towards him than the majority of the people he had anything to do with?

'The cat lives with you the way you live with me,' he'd said one evening sitting in front of the TV with Silvi, watching how she tried in vain to lure the cat over to her.

'That's not true. You never try to entice me,' she said without reproof, in peace and friendship.

Did the cat know what was in store for her when she squeezed through the crack in the window and jumped onto the scaffolding outside before running down the ladder like a circus animal performing a trick? She had put on a considerable amount of weight in the months she'd spent with Silvi. When she'd first moved in with the Schmidt-Flexes, you could feel every bone underneath that shaggy coat. Now she was round and heavy—only for a brief interval had she been truly beautiful. As soon as she stopped being so pitifully skinny, she was fat. Even Silvi had thought so.

'You're fat,' she had said as she opened a tin of tripe but the cat's expressionless face, watching the tin opener's every move, seemed to be saying, 'Well, then don't give me so much to eat. I'm afraid you're in charge of the nutrition around here, as we both know.' The cat had a large territory and since all the doors were always open, or else would be immediately opened at her petulant meowing command, all six rooms were under her constant control. She also knew what was underneath the sofas and beds or behind the long rows of books on the bookshelves. Everywhere there was the same thin smell of cleanliness, renewed by the cleaning lady three times a week. There were very few insects, sometimes a fly, seldom a spider. Silvi had witnessed the cat squash a moth that had been fluttering drunkenly around with a single swipe of her paw. The precision of that blow had been awe-inspiring. Pianists have to practice études for hours every day to train the muscles in their hands but the cat had retained all of her precision and economy of movement even after weeks of lying around, doing nothing. And there was almost literally nothing in the flat to stimulate her mind. It was a wasteland, a desert. Nothing vibrated in this flat, it was a deforested jungle. The life of a cat was conceived as a single voice in the vast orchestra of life. Predators played their part in it, as did prey, and creatures you simply ignored and those you either bit or loved, but, here, there was nothing of the sort, not counting that quietly humming white metal cupboard that Silvi opened several times a day, spilling light and cold air out onto the floor, and inside which those tins that only Silvi could open were kept. Was it not far more worrisome to be dependent on meat from such a cupboard, which was completely impervious to one's most fearsome attack, than to go hungry for days in the street or in the garden because one's hunt had been unsuccessful?

Then one day the cat was gone. Silvi did what her previous owners had failed to do—she went out and put up notices on lamp posts with a description: 'She doesn't have a name and won't let you pet her.' That ought to have been enough for anyone to recognize her, even at a distance, Silvi was certain—couldn't you tell just by looking at her that this cat didn't have a name? 'Generous reward.' Hans-Jörg considered this last promise unnecessary but he still helped put up the notices, shaking his head every time he read what she had got him to commit to.

Did the cat still remember those months in luxurious solitary confinement? Her paws had barely touched the ground at the foot of the ladder and she was an alley cat once more. Freezing cold and searing heat, hunger, thirst and myriad dangers would not compel her to seek protection in any human habitation. She was in complete harmony with her surroundings. She was made for the challenges of the streets. She existed in a state of total sympathy with all the good and bad things that might happen to her out here. She wasn't bothered by people throwing stones—she simply ducked and slunk away. And when vehicles braked suddenly it was as if she were encased in a pillow of air that forced the speeding cars to stop. There were also always people who venerated cats and lived to serve them. A little florist's in a wooden shack leaning up against the brick wall of a grand old villa (that had long since been converted into offices) served admirably as a base of operations. She slept among the flowerpots outside. They set out water for her, sometimes even milk, which she lapped up with her long pink tongue into her wide-open mouth. All that exercise did her good. She quickly lost weight, which increased her speed. And her independence from external conditions came to the fore. The careful precision and acrobatic elegance with which she cleaned her fur, lifting her back leg up behind her ear, were the same next to a rubbish bin as they had been on Silvi's sofa. But what happened at night would not have been possible in Silvi's living room. Silvi had only caught a tiny glimpse, in that game with the moth, basically just a domestic scene of the sort depicted on a Chinese scroll.

During the day, the cat roamed around, by no means aimlessly, she was conducting careful daylight reconnaissance of the territory, streaking through courtyards, car parks, gardens and driveways, with only short stretches on the roads. At the first sight of a dog, she would slip through the gaps in the nearest fence but not because she was running away. She did not even turn round to see her mortal enemy. At night, when the last rays of sunlight had been extinguished, she was overcome by a sense of restlessness, the ultimate imperative of her existence. She shot out of the cones of light from the streetlights into the soft phreatic dark. Here her tiger stripes really came into their own. In the bushes she was invisible, a member of the great grey cat race that lived according to the law of the hunt.

There were always rats near the restaurant in the Palmengarten, drawn there by the smell of cooking and the rubbish bins. There was a big one now, hobbling and scuttling out of a cardboard box, with an injured leg, clumsy as a guinea pig. Greed had made it incautious, as if it were living in paradise. But suddenly there appeared a tabby cat right in front of it, seemingly out of nowhere. The rat didn't put up a fight, it limply submitted to the flurry of paws, even though it had sharp teeth and could have frightened any human. The rat's legs were still twitching when there came a cracking sound. The expressionless mask with the enormous eyes loomed over the rat like the head of Medusa. Mortally wounded, it writhed in the dirt while its fate shone above it—a light had found its way through the darkness to the cat's eyes, filling them with a cold glow. Was this hunt not linked to hunger? Or was the cat disgusted by this limp, whimpering prey?

Bernward and Silvi had gone to dinner at that restaurant and were meandering slowly along the road. They had time. No one was waiting for them. Walking side by side with Silvi in the dark, Bernward could tell her something he hadn't wanted to say to her face in the brightly lit restaurant.

'Perhaps it's best if we go away somewhere for my birthday,' he said pensively. 'The children won't be coming.' Silvi turned and looked at him but he didn't look back. He was determined not to repeat the harsh words Titus and Phoebe had used in their text messages declining his invitation. After all, it was an attack on Silvi too.

She turned and looked straight ahead again. She wasn't curious and, besides, she quickly understood—thanks to her tendency always to expect the worst and her experience that she was often right to do so. Yes, this had to happen. With every breath we destroy at least one little spider's web. Everything that happens has consequences. Every action has unimaginably far-reaching repercussions. She had always been indifferent to Bernward's children but she had hoped that Titus and Phoebe would share her indifference. I'm nothing, thought Silvi, what could anyone have against me? There's nothing special about me at all.

On the other side of the street, a cat ran past, its eyes fixed directly on the ground in front of it. Wasn't that a tabby cat?

'Look, that's my cat,' Silvi grabbed Bernward's arm. The cat had disappeared behind a row of parked cars. It seemed to Silvi that the cat had deliberately looked the other way—just looked straight ahead like someone who didn't want to stop and say hello.

'That was her! She must be hiding underneath that car.' Bernward could feel the muscles in Silvi's arm tense up. He sensed that she was expecting him to do something. But the cat had made a decision of her own. She was going to cross the street. She would cross Silvi's path one last time and then disappear for ever. She wanted Silvi to see her independence for herself. It was important for the preservation of her freedom that she and Silvi meet as strangers one last time. The cat waited for an oncoming car—that was her favourite game. She liked to demonstrate her prowess at calculating the minimum velocity necessary. Setting off at the last possible moment, just fast enough—but not too fast—that the passing car would just lightly graze the tip of her tail, that was her pride and joy. Had the car just abruptly accelerated? There was a loud thud. Bernward took Silvi by the shoulders and turned her away.

'Don't look.' He led her towards the big, bright road. She didn't say a word, her head hung low. But the tabby cat was lying in the middle of the road with a bright red wound in her belly. The car had sped off. Her legs moved gently through the air. She was pawing her way through the void, practising a new way of walking in the minutes she had left to live.

32

WILL THE PATIENCE COME OUT?

'And what does any of this have to do with us?'

'Lots. Just be patient for a little longer. We have to go back to Helga, who was likewise facing a new set of circumstances.'

She had settled into her role as Rosemarie's closest friend, a role which had guaranteed her an undisputed place in the Hopsten universe. If you wanted to put it in an exaggerated and slightly mean-spirited way, you might say that hers was the position close to the empress, which in Oriental courts was reserved for the eunuchs who had the despot's confidence. Their friendship was, admittedly, troubled by the fact that Rosemarie was also Helga's customer. Such a relationship is always informed by a deep knowledge and understanding of the human soul on the part of the vendor that can perhaps best be compared to that of experienced confessors and spiritual leaders—they too must seek to understand people's secret needs and desires and discover their hidden motives. The customers' unpredictability, their whims and reservations, must be carefully studied and transformed into predictability. If ever a customer is persuaded to go somewhere they don't want to go, they might grow vindictive—a weakness revealed would often later be counterbalanced by arrogant certainty. The great inner concert in the customer's soul, a concert of greed, stinginess, mistrust, of the dream of a unique personality, of imperiousness, had to be harmonized and modulated into the climactic major chord indicating the decision to buy. Rosemarie, who considered herself to be 'the world's most good-natured person', also loved the idea of spreading fear and uncertainty, and had made Helga very nervous for a long time until her patient observations finally put those fears to rest. But how does such exhaustive knowledge of the other compare to love and friendship? Certain great souls, including many a mother, are able to unite love and a total lack of illusions but, in general, too much clear-sightedness only hurts a friendship. A wise person might prefer not to get to know her friends too well, thus keeping open the option of deliberately overlooking a given fault.

Helga's situation was compounded by the fact that the basis for their friendship, namely Rosemarie's patronage, was on the brink of collapse. In New York or Munich or wherever else, she would soon discover new muses who would easily trump Helga's inspiration. It was bound to happen anyway, thought Helga, since for Rosemarie it was a matter of devising a radically new lifestyle that would wow her existing audience, regardless of the fact that none of her existing audience would be there to see it.

And so a space opened up between Helga and Rosemarie, a distance that, to Helga's mind, had been caused by Rosemarie herself. To be sure, her friend had been badly mistreated. Her situation was lamentable, but did she not bear some of the responsibility for it? Could you really blame a man for one day seeking refuge from such a tyrant? 'She pays her price,' Helga would say, whenever the dissolution of the Hopstens' marriage came up in conversation, a phrase she had borrowed from Rosemarie, along with the air of cool superiority that went with it.

For Silvi, by contrast, she developed genuine sympathy untarnished by commercial interests and although Helga was disappointed that this beautiful young woman could think of nothing better than trading in her rich, young husband for an old one with an uncertain financial future, she still had a soft spot for Silvi, and she did not indulge Rosemarie's invectives and scornful comments except by ambiguously shaking her blonde, sternly coiffed head. Although she said nothing to Rosemarie, she stayed in touch with Silvi and was concerned when her friend would call her late at night, sometimes slurring so badly that only the delightful *r* remained intelligible. Helga wasn't sure whether Silvi was drinking more or whether in the past she just wouldn't have called her in such a state.

Hans-Jörg had insisted that his wife keep their flat which he continued to pay for even after he moved out and since neither Bernward nor Silvi were currently in a position to reject such a chivalrous offer, that's how things stayed, and so Helga was not at all surprised when Hans-Jörg asked for a word with her. She had actually been expecting something of the sort and agreed right away. At the Hopstens', they had never spoken so much as a word to each other. Hans-Jörg had hardly noticed Helga and she had taken part in the general antipathy against him, even though she actually didn't feel strongly either way. So now it was quite easy to get along.

The walls of their reciprocal reservations crumbled. Hans-Jörg found in Helga the only person who was still a friend to Silvi and so that was the only thing about her that counted. He was looking for someone he could talk to about Silvi and who could tell him how she was doing. With a heavy heart, he accepted her confirmation that Silvi must 'somehow'—Helga did nevertheless apply this small caveat—be happy, that she had awoken from her melancholy in any case but that she was perhaps a little too talkative, a little too eager to share, to be entirely at peace with herself. He honestly wanted nothing but for Silvi to be happy—for the first time since they'd met did he give this wish the appropriate weight. The fact that her happiness would not be with him but, rather, with Bernward whom he had always liked and respected still hurt. If only he could find a way to give Bernward some, well, brotherly advice—namely, that he keep an eye on Silvi's drinking. At the moment, there was no such way but he wanted to be ready and to remain as close as possible to Silvi so that he could seize the opportunity when it presented itself.

Helga did not place any great demands on the variety of his topics of conversation. To her, intensity was the most important thing and that could often be achieved by going over the same subject again and again, like a caveman rubbing two sticks together to make fire, until it was red-hot and finally produced a spark that ignited the nest that had been readied nearby. She would also have been prepared to count the beads of a rosary with him, listening patiently as he repeated the name Silvi over and over again, and helping him along if he should falter.

Intensity was always associated with the idea of business for Helga—that was her starting point, and that was her end point. That was her spirit's trajectory. And so, it was not long after her conversations with Hans-Jörg, held mostly in that magical back room of her boutique, had become a habit that their discussions about Silvi's fate became interlaced with Helga's business plans, which could then be described in great detail and jointly appraised. Helga had heard that Salam's grand attempt to fuse all the telecommunications outlets in Cairo into a single chain with the help of his Ramsesphone enterprise had come to nought— but did Ramsesphone still exist? Hadn't the company been dissolved? She decided not to mention the fact that Hans-Jörg was not the first expert she'd got to examine her plans. Experts usually don't like to hear that they're not the only ones who've been asked for advice and, besides, the advice of a Schmidt-Flex was of a completely different calibre—Hans-Jörg was someone who could not only give advice but also back that advice up financially, not least in view of the fact that the collapse of his Egyptian interests had apparently left behind a vacuum and Salam appeared to be completely out of the picture.

She played her hand pretty well. Hans-Jörg still felt that by helping Helga with her plans he was maintaining a connection to Silvi. He professed ignorance of the textile business but didn't he have cousins, his mother's brother's sons, who were somehow involved in a big textile-printing house? A textile printer right nearby, within her grasp—now that was something Rosemarie had kept from her. The balance sheet of their friendship seemed increasingly to be weighted against her favour.

And so it was that a meeting was set up between Helga and Schmidt-Flex senior who wanted to go over the details of the enterprise more closely before involving the extended family. He too began by declaring his ignorance of the textile business but in his case this was not an expression of humility but, rather, of superiority, designed to put Helga's little endeavour in its proper place. They had a long conversation in which he put Helga through her paces, with Helga responding in the spirit of obsequiousness, which the old man visibly appreciated. They also discussed personal matters. 'What is the correct pronunciation of your surname, by the way? People around here say "Stolzié" but that can't be right . . .'

'No, you're quite right, in Berlin people used to say "Stolzeer",' Helga replied, 'it's a Slavic name originally.'

What a travesty to pronounce it Stolzié, he continued, how contrary to the spirit of the French language, how positively vulgar. True to form, Schmidt-Flex was now in the process of delivering one of his signature 'abasements'. There was a thing or two Helga had to know. He grew stern and cold—Silvi was, in many ways, an impossible person, he said, a stain on the family but she was descended from a famous, you might even say a great house, and at the time Hans-Jörg's marriage had not seemed nearly as absurd as it now did in retrospect—'Do you understand?'

'As far as I know, Hans-Jörg doesn't want a divorce?' Helga spoke very carefully, feeling her way into the darkness of the future.

'There'll be a divorce no matter what,' said the father, 'irreconcilable differences, not least on the Hopsten side. Strange, how you can be so wrong about people. Not that I was ever wrong, you understand. I still clearly remember saying to my wife that the Hopstens seemed vaguely nouveau riche—even though of course they're anything but! The discrepancy was something of a joke, at the time.'

After that, things happened very quickly. She opened a second boutique in Düsseldorf and started a company with Hans-Jörg as CEO, practically at the same time, and then Helga was allowed to design her first solo collection for the aforementioned textile company and, suddenly, she had more work than she could handle. She needed to hire someone—her niece! Her niece had to quit her job at the Japanese TV station and move back to Germany. Too bad that the people who had always considered this niece of Helga's to be a sentimental invention weren't around to witness her arrival. They say there are people who mourn the deaths of their enemies because they will no longer be able to bear witness to their own success. In Helga's case, there weren't any enemies of course, just a past that had petered away to nothing, but it was a shame all the same.

'There's a noticeable malevolent undertone that creeps in whenever you're talking about Helga.'

'But you feel exactly the same way about her.'

'Yes, but that's different. I'm allowed to. You, on the other hand, ought to show a little more respect.'

'I promise you, Helga barely features in the little bit that's left.'

Because now it was Phoebe's turn. So far, my relationship with Phoebe had been one long decrescendo, a gradual fading away and trailing off, albeit with isolated passages in which the echoes swelled and trembled, but the general tendency was one of inexorable diminution. And yet it had begun at the very pinnacle of the emotional scale—the girl with the wounded finger had made a profound impression on me and her transformation into the youthful epicentre of the Hopsten house had both blinded and attracted me. You can tell that I'm describing myself like a moth drawn to a flame. But then Phoebe had done everything she could to extinguish that flame. Surrounded by attractive, ambitious young men, she had seemed to me like a Taunus Turandot, giving her suitors tasks, a different one for each of them, none of them easy. In contrast to the Chinese

Turandot, she spared the lives of the ones who failed, saving them for later use. I clearly saw how some grew tired of this indefinite, aimless circling but she always had a small pack of slavering bloodhounds at her heels, five or six of whom might have stood a real chance. It's quite possible or even likely that she sometimes granted a discreet foretaste of certain favours to counter flagging enthusiasm—after all, I too had had the pleasure of a clammy winter kiss bestowed upon me parenthetically, as it were. But it could no longer truly rekindle my desire, not once I saw that I would not be allowed to build on this development, and that it was, therefore, no development at all.

But after Bernward had left the house in Falkenstein and it was clear that it would be sold, it suddenly seemed as though there would be a significant development in our relationship after all. Phoebe had a nice little studio downtown, which had become her headquarters now that life in Falkenstein had grown unbearable. And it was then that she started calling me again, late at night mostly, to tell me her woes, though not in a self-pitying kind of way but, rather, with touching candour.

'It's so bad. It's as if my parents had died but they're still alive and completely changed, neither dead nor alive.'

Titus was disgusted at the thought of suddenly having to imagine his father as a man driven by erotic desires. He found it so embarrassing that he refused to see him. Phoebe said she didn't find it quite as unspeakable as her brother did but that she knew how things stood. She said that there was basically no more room for her in Bernward's life. He was completely absorbed with Silvi. She said that the two of them were so fully immersed in each other that they were now utterly incapable of any kind of normal interaction with other people and never saw anyone else. She asked me if I too thought Silvi was an alcoholic. She said the word quite matter-of-factly, without any moral judgement, more out of the need to prepare for future confrontations, and I told her that I didn't think so. I said that right now Silvi was still at a stage where she drank too much but that only

271

time would tell whether it developed into a real addiction—after all, perhaps her newfound happiness would gradually give her a more casual and relaxed relationship to wine, that in time the wine would stop being so important to her.

Yes, said Phoebe with a sort of sad understanding, she supposed so, although she wasn't at all sure whether that was what she hoped. She said she felt as though her mother had actually become even more distant than her father, that the break-up had made her hard. She said her mother was railing against her father like her mortal enemy. Everything was happening via their respective lawyers and in her impenetrable despair, no form of harassment was too petty. Phoebe was careful about passing judgement—she was trying to understand the situation. It was almost like an evil spell had been cast on the Hopstens. This family which so many guests, including me, had always seen as an unassailable fortress, with their obvious joy at public glitz and glamour, had suddenly vanished, as if it had never existed. You just had to rub your eyes and try to remember—had there not been, just a moment ago, an imposingly self-assured institution here known as the House of Hopsten, completely unshakeable in its form, inspiring admiration and envy in all those who beheld it? I felt as though with the fall of this proud house, with its sudden disappearance, my life which had been bound up with it, those months that had been defined by my visits to the Hopstens', had also become strangely unreal.

'Can you believe it, Mama sold the cockatoo on eBay!' When Phoebe had asked her why she had done that, Rosemarie had answered, 'Do you think I should have wrung its neck instead?' I looked in my wallet. The white feather was still there but I didn't tell Phoebe because I didn't want to hurt her. It was painful and distressing just to listen to her. In the darkness of her bedroom—Phoebe liked to talk on the telephone in the dark—she was able to find the confidence to say the things that caused her the most pain. The only thing she left out was the way her own position had suffered. Of course, she hadn't lost her friends but she had a different relationship to them now. She was no longer the gracious hostess, able to decide for herself how approachable or unapproachable she wanted to be. I was a little older than those young fox-faced friends of hers. Did Phoebe see in me a potential basis for a new institution to replace the old?

'I never had time to get a proper look at you—I regret that now,' she said. Her voice sounded gentle and innocent, as if she were suddenly turning back into the girl with the wounded finger living in the big city without any preconceived notions, free to follow the whims of chance.

When she invited me to come and see her flat, I was reluctant at first. I said I would definitely like to pay her a visit but I had absolutely no desire to spend an evening in the company of her circle of friends.

'I promise you there won't be anyone else here—even I don't enjoy evenings like that any more.'

I could hardly believe it. I would get to spend an evening with her alone. To think of everything that had had to happen to make this possible.

'*And how was that evening?*'

'*It never took place. But that was my fault. I was standing in front of her building and was just about to go through the iron gate when Helga Stolzier came walking down the street. Next to her was a young woman, her niece . . .*'

'*Don't you dare suggest that I asked you to join us for dinner.*'

'*Then I must have been mistaken. Why would I have thought that you would be happy if I joined you?*'

'*And you never even rang Phoebe's doorbell, you bastard. I thought I'd already told you, I don't like stories about love at first sight—they're all really just excuses for outrageously inconsiderate behaviour.*'

Mr Slepzak was tall, nesh, smoked a lot, drank a lot of beer in the evening, had a ruddy deadened complexion and a pot belly like a cushion strapped to his haggard frame. The list of sectors he had worked in went on for pages. His failures were only rarely his own fault—bad luck seemed to follow him. To hear him describe all the things that had happened to him, it was easy to see the parallels to Joseph Salam, whose business ventures had likewise consisted of a series of battles and who truly knew the meaning of defeat. And yet, in his case, it was quite different because whereas Mr Slepzak's life was set against a dismal backdrop of coarse hessian, behind Joseph Salam there was a blazing red conflagration—Slepzak's plight seemed somehow predetermined whereas Salam's misfortunes were more musical, like artful dissonances striving for resolution and thus hinting at hopeful new beginnings. And hence, it was Salam who had asked Mr Slepzak to meet him at the pizzeria and not the other way round. The fact that they had both recently filed for bankruptcy—Slepzak with his jeans emporium, Salam with his four outlet stores—did nothing to affect the hierarchy. Nor was the venture or, rather, the investment that Salam wanted to pitch to Slepzak central to his latest business plans, which extended far beyond the borders of Germany. Salam still had his sights set on the Orient. 'It's crazy,' he would often say, 'in Germany I feel Lebanese and in Egypt I feel German.' Evidently, he preferred to feel German.

As the choice of this pizzeria as the place in which to start a joint venture—the takeover of three phone shops selling prepaid cards, with cubicles for long distance calls to Africa and Asia—indicated, these two gentlemen were not out to 'turn a big wheel', as Salam put it, with a subtle hint of irony suggesting that he knew only too well what a big wheel looked like. Slepzak saw Salam's offer as a life raft. Recently divorced and flat broke, he was not looking for any big wheels, having long since given up trying to turn those anyway, but, rather, for a first step towards regaining his solvency. It was clear just by looking at them—On one side of the table was Slepzak, skinny and pot-bellied, on the other, Salam, all solidity and bulging muscles, whose short legs only made his thighs appear even more powerful. Which of these two was more likely to be the boss?

They had just ordered a double Fernet—poison to Slepzak, a blow to his swollen liver and refreshing to Salam as a draught of crystal-clear spring water. Slepzak was sitting with his back to the kitchen which was at the end of a long dark corridor. The counter with the serving window was like a little puppet theatre, although the neon-bright section of the room behind it did not reveal any puppets but, rather, parts of the kitchen staff. Slepzak had a long list of questions and concerns. He knew the telephone business and all its risks and had adopted a tone of determination, earnest caution and superior insight for the purposes of this interview. He didn't want to seem like someone who desperately wanted this job and, in truth, he didn't even really want it. He could already see how this would end. But it wasn't about what he wanted but what he needed. What would he do if he couldn't get his credit cards unblocked?

'A strange fellow,' thought Salam, his eyes resting idly on the man sitting across from him, 'how can he possibly think that he might say something I haven't already considered?' He allowed the other man to lecture him but, soon, it wasn't just his thoughts that were wandering but his eyes too. The unhealthy reddishness and the colourless, straw-like hair could no longer hold his attention. He was hot. Salam loosened his tie with a practised jiggle and unbuttoned his collar.

In the little puppet-theatre window in the back, there had at first been a constant toing and froing of different people but now there was one constant image—a woman at work. Her head was only ever visible for an instant, whenever she leant forward, but one pale arm, ample and quite bare in the heat from the brick oven, was seemingly busy kneading something on the kitchen surface. It did not belong to a young woman— despite its chubbiness, the musculature was somewhat saggy and as she kneaded the dough, a ripple would occasionally traverse her skin which was so delicate and soft that every hidden movement of the muscles underneath was conducted to the surface. Her elbow was pointy, wrinkled and reddish. Whenever she bent her arm, the wrinkles evened out, when she straightened it, the tiny crimson, wilted, satin rosette returned. That strength, thought Salam, that rhythmic gripping and kneading. She wasn't just working that dough with her hands, she was massaging it. That soft, round lump of dough, like a buttock —Salam brushed the thought aside with a frown. Slepzak took this to mean that he was annoyed and about to protest, so he redoubled his zeal but he no longer considered the venture quite so risky, 'as long as we handle it right!' That was the main thing for Slepzak—things had to be handled right.

Naturally, thought Joseph Salam. He was once again lost in contemplation of that arm. Suddenly, the arm was gone. Salam imagined the woman must have raised her arm to her forehead—a view of her armpit presented itself—to wipe the sweat from her brow with the back of her hand. Then the arm was back and continued to knead. Slepzak suddenly got a sense that Salam was no longer looking at him. He turned round and looked down the gloomy kitchen corridor—there was nothing there—he saw the arm but he didn't really see it. He was insusceptible to the arm. The one thing that was filling every cell in Salam's body so completely that the pressure made him restless and fidgety, Slepzak had already forgotten before he'd even really noticed it.

He's blind, thought Salam but he said nothing to Slepzak—there were reasons for this man's biography, after all.

276

'As there are for mine.' There was no self-satisfaction in this thought but, rather, the almost pious contentment with being in one's own skin. Now above all. The sight of that white arm penetrated deep inside Salam where it was transformed into fuel for his brain. Without taking his eyes off it, he interrupted Slepzak's jeremiad and let the words gush out over his thick lower lip. He spoke very quickly and determinedly. This conversation was now over. Slepzak had to be dismissed in no uncertain terms, with no room for misunderstanding. Clarity must not be sacrificed for the sake of expediency but expediency was called for.

'I'm going to go and pay.' With that, Salam stood up, shook Slepzak's hand and said 'goodbye'—deliberately not 'see you later'—secretly he was already done with this man. Even under the spell of the pale white arms, Salam never stopped thinking. A waitress rushed past but Salam didn't try to attract her attention. Fortunately she was busy and so there was nothing to stop him going into that dark corridor with the enticing neon brightness of the serving window at the far end. He casually opened the door into the kitchen. Salam did not approach a woman hunched over, peering through a hole in the wall. The owner of the pale arm stood before him, covered in flour and a little out of breath. She was pretty, with a faint double chin, pearls of sweat in the folds of baby fat on her neck, the glint of a necklace, small earrings graced glowing red earlobes, her hair was dishevelled. The woman seemed to Salam as though she had just emerged from the cloudscape of a soft white bed. Her smock was wide open at the top. A small pearl rolled back and forth between her breasts. He looked at her, she looked at him. They immediately struck up a hushed conversation. Stifled laughter, flirtatious taunts fluttered through the kitchen. Salam spoke Italian but she said just as freely that she wasn't from Italy and that he would never guess where she was really from. Suddenly, the barman was standing tall and broad next to Salam—her husband, perhaps? There was an air of pragmatic familiarity between the two, a kind of matrimonial resignation. Did the man realize what was going on? He too spoke light-heartedly but ushered Salam quickly out of the kitchen. There was something about his jest that said it could just as easily have turned deadly serious.

The following week, the woman Salam was living with at the time had occasion to dust off his suit jacket. 'Look at the state of you! You're all covered in flour!' He said that it wasn't flour. That he had been leaning against a whitewashed wall. Salam looked nonchalant. It was quite possible he was telling the truth.